PRAISE FOR

DEATH IN THE LAND OF ENCHANTMENT

"The flow and fusion of the mystery in *Death in the Land of Enchantment* is what drew me into this story, as well as the setting and little touches that give it true authenticity. And I love the sleuth, a woman after my own heart and wonderfully original."

—Carol Potenza, author of the New Mexico mystery novel *Hearts of the Missing* and winner of the 2017 Tony Hillerman Prize

"If you enjoy an author who is expert at humanizing their characters while pulling those same characters' strings, Holly Harrison is the one for you. Not only does she weave a complex tapestry of plot and mystery, her sense of humor shines through her knack for words. *Death in the Land of Enchantment* will take you on an enchanting journey through the sights, tastes, history, and likely inhabitants of New Mexico."

—Lisa McCoy, administrator of New Mexico Writers and director of the New Mexico Book Awards

"The exploits of Santa Fe detectives Louise Sanchez and Pascal Ruiz will again captivate readers through an intricate tapestry of intriguing stories and memorable characters. Don't miss this murder mystery."

—Linnea Hendrickson, retired New Mexico librarian

"I loved the way Louise Sanchez transforms from a self-effacing middle-aged woman, browbeaten by her mother and intimidated by her boss, to a detective who has the persistence and ingenuity to solve a complex murder case."

—Rosalie Rayburn, former journalist and author of *The Power of Rain*, winner of the National Federation of Press Women award

Death in the Land of Enchantment
by Holly Harrison
© Copyright 2025 Holly Harrison

ISBN 979-8-88824-661-0

All rights reserved. No part of this publication may be reproduced, stored in a retrieval system, or transmitted in any form or by any means—electronic, mechanical, photocopy, recording, or any other—except for brief quotations in printed reviews, without the prior written permission of the author.

This is a work of fiction. All the characters in this book are fictitious, and any resemblance to actual persons, living or dead, is purely coincidental. The names, incidents, dialogue, and opinions expressed are products of the author's imagination and are not to be construed as real.

Map and cover illustrations by Patricia DePalma Slesinski

Published by

◤köehlerbooks™

3705 Shore Drive
Virginia Beach, VA 23455
800-435-4811
www.koehlerbooks.com

Death in the Land of Enchantment

HOLLY HARRISON

VIRGINIA BEACH
CAPE CHARLES

This book is dedicated to my husband Phil
and the Land of Enchantment.

The web of our life is of a mingled yarn,
good and ill together.

—William Shakespeare,
All's Well That Ends Well

PROLOGUE

It was late when Justine pulled into the driveway still reeling from her encounter at the Twisted Pines Pub. Even with the bar's muted light, she was sure Webster noticed her sordid appearance. Not that it mattered. But it did. She still had her pride. She had no intention of pursuing a relationship with the man, but she desperately needed to feel like a person again. A woman.

After three glasses of bourbon, she knew she had no business behind the wheel of a car.

She should have called an Uber, but she didn't. And now she was home, in her driveway, safe. As she made her way around the car, her knees wobbled and her head felt like it was stuffed with cotton. She grabbed hold of the passenger door and gave it a yank. Harry didn't even flinch. He sat stock-still, frozen in place, his eyes fixed on the windshield. She nudged his shoulder a little harder than she intended. He didn't budge. Irritation pulsated through her body, but she knew she didn't have the strength to drag him out of the car.

She steadied herself, leaned in closer, and murmured, "We're home." When Harry was mad, he would glare at her, his eyes daggers. Once he gave her shoulder a hard push that sent her off balance and into the wall. Tonight he didn't glower, didn't stare, didn't push. He sulked— things hadn't gone his way. Sulking was much worse than mad. He turned inward and closed himself off. She knew the reason. It was Webster and the money. Harry was usually easygoing and compliant, with a sunny disposition, but when he sulked, the sun vanished and he became obstinate.

She couldn't leave him in the driveway in the middle of the night. She had only wanted a few hours out of the house—a distraction, a break—but the evening had turned out disastrous. *Good God*, she thought. What was Webster Madison, the gorgeous attorney from the online dating site, doing at the Twisted Pines? It wasn't the type of place a man like him would frequent, and certainly not somewhere you would entertain clients. And now Webster had her phone number, her real phone number. What was she to do if he called? After the Monopoly money exchange, Webster probably had her down as a wacko, which wouldn't be far off. Not for the first time in her life, she wished she had listened to her sister. Don't get personally involved.

Justine was dog-tired, the bourbon lay heavy in her stomach. She thought she might be sick. She needed Harry out of the car, into the house, and into bed. All her usual tricks were for naught. Ice cream, bubbles, TV, sleeping in his clothes. Nothing worked. Harry sulked as he stared out the windshield. He had willingly given Webster the money, but now he wanted it back. After all, a gift from Harry was only a loan. *So give it back.*

Harry had once been a mover and shaker: never still, always busy, a financial wizard, successful in anything he set his mind to. But that was before. She was out of options.

Justine squeezed her eyes tight. She would have to drive to Webster's house and ask for the money back. She imagined how embarrassing it would be on a scale of one to ten—*an eleven*. She prayed Webster still had the two bills, hadn't crumpled them in a ball and tossed them away as he left the bar. Webster would need to hand Harry the money. There was no fooling Harry. She couldn't take money from the Monopoly game and say Webster had sent it back, special delivery. Harry might have dementia, but he wasn't stupid.

She pulled out her phone and looked again at Webster's text

message, sent after he left the bar. *Is this really your number?* Although the message was typed without embellishments or emojis, the words dripped with sarcasm. Webster was hurt—he had a right to be. Mistrust was not a good way to begin a relationship, but she hadn't planned on starting one, had she? She had replied with a thumbs-up emoji—at least it wasn't a heart. Now Webster had her number for the cell phone she couldn't burn, the number she couldn't change, the number all her family, friends, doctors, and dentists had.

Justine slid behind the wheel and clenched her teeth so hard she worried a tooth would break.

CHAPTER 1

Louise Sanchez headed down the hall of her condo to her darkroom. Her phone rang and she squeezed her eyes shut, praying it wasn't the police station. She fumbled in her pocket for her phone, glanced at the screen, and exhaled a sigh of relief. "*Bueno mamá, que pasá?*" Louise smiled, imagining her mother rolling her eyes.

"We need you to join us for Sunday brunch at the Tesuque Village Market." Her mother cleared her throat. "We have news."

Louise stifled a groan. She hoped her parents hadn't found another eligible bachelor who was "perfect for her." But she hated to disappoint them any more than she already had. "Okay, sure, sounds good." Her heart sank as she glanced down the hall toward the darkroom. Maybe there would be time later. "See you in an hour."

Before leaving the condo, Louise checked her camera bag, making sure there were a few rolls of film. Just in case. Even the thought of huevos rancheros couldn't console her. She had longed to spend her one day off in the darkroom. She still hadn't developed the film she shot a few weeks ago out at Kasha-Katuwe Tent Rocks National Monument. The monument, only forty miles southwest of Santa Fe, was famous for the scenic, cone-shaped constructions formed from volcanic eruptions six or seven million years ago. Louise found the rock formations—composed of pumice, ash, and tuff deposits—perfect for black and white photos. She had steeled herself for the Canyon Trail, bypassing the easier Cave Loop Trail. Since she wasn't very athletic, it had been an arduous hike, and there was a one-way trek into a narrow "slot" canyon. On the upward climb, she had struggled with her camera equipment while suppressing surges of claustrophobia that made her heart race. But once she reached the top of the mesa, she was rewarded with magnificent views of the New Mexico mountains—Sangre de Cristo, Jemez, and Sandia—along with vistas of the Rio Grande Valley.

As she left her condo, the disappointment settled further over Louise. She was desperate for a few hours of solitude in her darkroom. The Santa Fe police captain had asked her to fill in for detective Ruiz, who was on administrative leave. She had combed through the mess in the detective's office, reviewing the stolen costume file, the case responsible for Ruiz's absence. It was a doozy, complicated by the involvement of the San Felipe Tribal Police and the FBI. What had begun as a simple burglary on the Santa Fe Opera grounds had spiraled out of control and resulted in a fiasco. A Jesus Christ costume, from a previous Christmas performance, had been stolen. Later it was found on a man tied to a cross in an abandoned pueblo. Louise thought the case would make a terrific grade B movie, but as she read on, it sounded more like a royal soap opera.

Louise headed toward Tesuque, a small village north of Santa Fe where she had grown up. A twinge of nostalgia settled over her as she rolled down the car window, letting in the morning breeze. The wind whipped through her hair, hinting at another windy afternoon. It was spring in New Mexico. A week ago the road had been glutted with pilgrims making their annual trek to the Santuario de Chimayo to pay penance and commemorate Jesus's crucifixion. But with Easter over and the pilgrims back home, the road was empty.

Louise drove past the Shidoni Gallery and Sculpture Garden, which featured one of the largest collections of contemporary sculpture in the Southwest. During high school, she had been a docent at the foundry, leading visitors on tours of the bronze-pouring process. Louise had considered becoming a sculptor, but her heart lay in photography.

Tesuque had remained a quiet village despite the influx of people from both coasts. The Village Market café hadn't been updated in years, but people went there for the food, not the decor. Louise scanned the café's dirt parking lot. It was packed, but she was able to squeeze into a spot near the back beside a mud-splattered pickup truck with mammoth wheels that reached almost to her car window.

Her parents sat at a table near the back, sipping coffee while they perused the menu. As she approached, they both jumped up and kissed her on each cheek. She was relieved they were alone, no suitor in the waiting. "What's the big news?" Louise asked, pulling out a chair.

Her mother glanced at her father, smoothed her paper place mat, and took another sip of coffee. "You never met your Aunt Simone, your Uncle Joseph's first wife, the one before Julia." Her mother spat out Julia's name as if it had a bad taste. "Simone died in childbirth, but her baby survived. Your cousin, a girl named Lisa."

Louise hardly knew her uncle, much less anything about her Aunt Simone. She couldn't remember her family talking about her dead aunt or the daughter who had survived. Her father and his brother, Joseph, were never close. Louise sensed bad blood between them, but her family never talked about unpleasant things. She controlled herself not to pick up the menu. The smell of roasted chilis and warm corn tortillas made her weak. She willed the server to come take their order, but as usual the place was crowded and understaffed. Louise nodded, feigning interest while her mother continued with the "news."

"Your Uncle Joseph passed."

"Passed?"

Her mother raised her eyes and exhaled. "Died."

"Died? When?"

"Two weeks ago." Her mother pursed her lips tight and glanced again at her father, who remained silent, stone-faced.

"Two weeks ago. Nobody bothered to tell me?"

"We were not informed right away."

"Is this the news?" Louise was incensed that a member of her family, even one estranged, had died and nobody bothered to tell her. What kind of family did that?

"Well . . . yes." Her mother ran her hands again over the paper place mat, smoothing the wrinkles. "Uncle's death is related, but there is more."

Louise wished her mother would get on with the story, and as usual couldn't control her sarcasm. "Oh, please tell?"

Her mother began to answer just as the server approached to take their orders. Louise was thankful the woman had brought her a cup of coffee and plate of bizcochitos. Louise dunked a cookie in her coffee, aware that her mother disapproved of not only dunking but eating dessert first. But her mother, preoccupied with the news, said nothing.

"The rest of the news has to do with your uncle's will, the ranch, your cousin Lisa . . ."

"The ranch in Mora?"

"Yes. In Mora." Her mother made the name of the town sound flat. She was Anglo and never had managed to get her tongue to roll her Rs.

Louise remembered a few visits to the ranch when she was small and her grandparents were still alive. But after they passed, the family rarely visited. She wished her mother would get to the point, cut to the chase. "So the news is about Lisa?"

Her mother started to bob her head up and down like one of those little bobblehead dolls as the server reappeared, setting down their orders. Louise was starving but knew her mother would insist on saying grace and maybe, God forbid, making the sign of the cross before anyone could pick up their fork. She hoped they wouldn't have to hold hands.

Her mother said grace under her breath, crossed herself, and took a bite before continuing. "Your uncle and Julia, Joseph's second wife, never had children. They divorced years ago. Lisa is Joseph's only child."

"I have no memory of Lisa. Did we ever see her? Where is she?"

"Lisa was three when Uncle married Julia. That woman wouldn't have any part of the child. She put her foot down, insisted Joseph send her away. Simone's mother lived in Tucson, took the child in, and raised her. I don't think your uncle ever made much of an attempt to see her until Julia left. By then it was too late. Lisa wouldn't have anything to do with him. Can you blame her?"

"We never saw her either," Louise said reproachfully.

"She lived in Arizona."

"It's not the moon."

"Lisa's mother wouldn't have anything to do with us. We were guilty by association."

"How do you know all this?"

"Your father." Her mother turned and scowled at the man who hadn't said one word since Louise arrived. "He is the executor of Joseph's estate. Uncle left the ranch to Lisa. But when your father contacted her, she made it clear she had no intention of ever living in Mora. She refuses to even set foot in New Mexico. Your father needs to probate Joseph's will. He offered Lisa help in selling the ranch." Her mother began to say something but picked up her fork and took a bite of eggs.

Louise always found it annoying when her mother delved out information piecemeal. She wished she would spit it out. She turned her attention to the meal, plucking a warm tortilla from the plastic basket and slathering it with butter. Again, she thought the act would incite her mother, but there was no comment.

Her father, silent and morose, had clearly had enough. He took the last bite of his carne adovada and announced, "Louise, we need you to go to the ranch with us this afternoon. We need help collecting any family heirlooms or personal items that belonged to my parents, your grandparents. Then I can get on with it, put the ranch on the market."

Her mother's mouth dropped open, then she pressed her lips together in a pout. Once again, her husband had filched her thunder.

CHAPTER 2

Detective Pascal Ruiz tried not to think about his upcoming trial as he untangled himself from the sheets. He checked his phone. There was one voicemail—his father. Pascal reckoned the old man needed some kind of help, and he suspected it had to do with his dilapidated pickup truck.

Pascal pulled on his clothes before listening to his father's message. Just as he thought, his father needed help, but he didn't say what kind. Pascal went to the kitchen hoping to find his girlfriend, Gillian, but instead found a note: *Gone for a run down by the canal.* Pascal sighed. He had corrected Gillian several times; it wasn't a canal, it was a ditch. The Mother Ditch, La Acequia Madre. Gillian knew nothing about New Mexico's ditches and irrigation, coming from the East Coast where water was abundant. He jotted down a quick message that he needed to help his father and would call her later. Then he crossed out the word canal and wrote *DITCH* in capital letters.

As he drove north toward Española, he thought about his father. The man had always been a glass-half-empty guy while his mother was the glass half full. In high school when he had decided to go to France to attend the Sorbonne—he had wanted to become a writer— his father warned him he was chasing rainbows. His mother had said, "Go. See what you can find." Maybe his father had been right. Paris, it turned out, wasn't the place he had imagined. It was another expensive city, overflowing with tourists and disgruntled residents. He had wanted to sip absinthe with writers like Hemingway and Fitzgerald. But those days, the days of hanging out in jazz joints with musicians or drinking café au lait in bistros with up-and-coming artists, were over.

After his mother died, his father sold the Santa Fe house where Pascal had grown up, finding the memories too painful. He bought a small adobe south of Española near the river. The house wasn't much to look at, but the valley was Southwest picturesque.

Pascal made his way slowly down the dirt drive, trying to avoid the worst potholes. He climbed out of his car, taking a minute to gaze across the field at the native grasses that swayed in the morning breeze. Clumps of chamisa, with its feltlike matted hairs and narrow, threadlike grayish-green leaves, were abundant. The native plants were not yet in bloom but would soon light up the landscape with yellow clusters all the way down to where the cottonwood trees marched along the banks of the Rio Grande.

Pascal gave three whacks on the front door before pushing it open.

"It's about time," his father snapped. The old man heaved himself out of the tattered easy chair, which, like his pickup, needed an upgrade.

"I have a life you know," Pascal said.

"Oh?" His father chuckled unkindly. "Heard you were on leave."

His father always could bait him, but Pascal decided not to react. "What do you need help with?"

"A friend's gone missing," his father said.

Pascal groaned. The last time someone asked him to look for a missing person, it had sent his career in a tailspin. His father didn't have many friends. He used to drink coffee at Dunkin' with some of the other teachers from the community college, but that had petered out once he retired. "A friend?"

"Yeah. Lady friend."

"A lady friend?"

His father pinched his lips together and snapped. "Yes."

Pascal smiled and shook his head. He didn't want to irritate his father. He could see the worry in the man's eyes and felt sorry for him. His mother's death had about finished him off.

"I want to hire you."

"Hire me?"

"Mary mother of Jesus, boy. Stop repeating everything I say. You're a detective, aren't you?"

"Not at the moment."

"You got to earn a living, I got some money saved. Might as well give it to you now instead of waiting until I kick the bucket."

"What's this about?"

His father motioned for Pascal to follow him into the kitchen. He set out two navy mugs on the Formica table and filled them with coffee. "I was camping out at Ghost Ranch last fall, ran into your Aunt Margaret. Hadn't seen her since her husband retired a year ago and they bought that gas-guzzling RV. I guess they got tired of driving around the country and sleeping in a tin can. They took a caretaking job out at the ranch. Marcus does repairs and Margaret works in reception and the gift shop." His father took a sip of his coffee and sighed. "Margaret was my favorite sister. When we were growing up, she could talk me into anything." His father chuckled. "To make a long story short, she started in on me, about me living alone down by the river feeling sorry for myself. She never cut me any slack. That woman," he looked up at the ceiling and let out a breath, "signed me up for a retreat at the ranch."

Pascal tried his best to keep a straight face. He couldn't picture his father participating in a retreat, but he nodded.

All the bluster seemed to dissipate from his father as he stared into his coffee cup. "A body, mind, and spirit retreat, supposed to help bring your essential parts together in harmony or some kind of bullshit."

Pascal couldn't stifle his laughter.

"I deserve that, but it wasn't as silly as it sounds."

"Sorry."

"Your mother used to make me do yoga. Have you ever stuck your butt in the air doing downward dog? It's humbling."

Pascal shook his head.

"Anyway, part of the workshop was working with clay."

"Clay?"

"Yeah, it's supposed to be therapeutic." His father took a sip of coffee and didn't meet Pascal's eyes. "We made our own clay. Dug it from La Bajada Hill. It's red, not like the gray clay you and your mother used to bring back from that abandoned pueblo. We cured it with vinegar, made pinch pots, polished them while we got in touch with our feelings."

Pascal couldn't imagine his father making a pinch pot, much less burnishing it or getting in touch with his feelings. "You made a pinch pot?"

"Yeah. We dug a pit, covered it with horse shit, and fired the pots." His father walked over to the bookcase, took down a small black pot, and held it out to Pascal.

"You must have really got in touch with your feelings by the look of the shine on this." Pascal handed the tiny pot back to his father. "It's . . . sweet."

His father grimaced and put the pot back on the shelf. "There was this lady in the class. We weren't supposed to talk while making our pots, but we sat together at lunch. She seemed real sad, in need of a friend. Turned out she's a widower too. She's the one missing."

"Okay."

"She lives in Abiquiu. Rents one of those new houses up the hill from the highway right before you get to the inn. Has a hot tub on the roof." His father smiled for the first time.

"What's she doing in Abiquiu? Not much going on out there."

His father shrugged. "Guess she likes the solitude. She's a potter."

"You're kidding." Pascal couldn't believe the only two female relationships his father ever had were with women who worked with clay.

"That's part of the reason she was taking the retreat. She wanted to learn how the Native Americans fired pottery before kilns. There's a studio next to her house."

Pascal pushed away thoughts of his mother. "Does this potter have a name?"

"Katrin Simpson."

"Okay."

"After the retreat everyone exchanged numbers. I didn't think I'd ever hear from her, but she called a week later. We started seeing each other. At first it was coffee every couple of weeks. A few times we met for dinner. I took her to Chimayo to get some of the healing dirt from the chapel. She wanted to mix it with the clay, make a pinch pot," his father sighed, "and then . . ."

"You hooked up," Pascal interrupted.

His father grimaced while his face took on color. "We became intimate."

"Maybe I should get some of that healing dirt. Spice up my love life."

"Very funny. We started seeing each other a couple times a week. Then last week I called to invite her to dinner. There was no answer. I've been calling and leaving messages every day. I was going to drive out to her house but . . ." His father stared down at his empty coffee cup.

"Let me guess. Your truck wouldn't start." Pascal regretted his tone when he saw how downtrodden his father looked.

"Will you take me to her house? I'm worried something happened to her. Maybe she fell, hurt herself."

Pascal detected some moisture around his father's eyes. Since his mother's death, the only emotion he had seen out of his father was anger. "Okay, okay. Simmer down. Let's not get carried away. Usually there's a simple explanation when someone goes missing."

"Yeah, like that boy you found out at Tonque Pueblo?"

Pascal decided to let that remark slide. "I suppose you know the way to her house?"

His father nodded.

Pascal continued. "If it's okay with you, I'd like to ask Gillian along. She's got the hots for Georgia O'Keeffe. I haven't had a chance to take her to Abiquiu yet. I sort of owe her a decent outing after the fiasco out to Tonque."

"Don't get me wrong, son, I like Gillian. Even if she's from the East Coast." He paused, seemingly hesitant about the request. "Oh, what the hell? Might not hurt to have a woman's perspective."

Pascal raised his eyebrows. "A woman's perspective?"

His father poured another cup of coffee. As they waited for Gillian, Pascal tried to make small talk but saw his father wasn't interested. They sipped their coffee in silence.

Gillian's Volvo spit clouds of dust as she made her way down the dirt drive. The station wagon was low to the ground and Pascal worried about the undercarriage. As she pulled up next to his father's pickup truck, Pascal let out a groan like a bull elephant. Birdie, the Scottish terrier from hell, was hanging out the passenger window. Even from inside the house, they could hear the dog barking. He hoped Gillian would be able to keep hold of the dog out at Abiquiu. The last thing he wanted to do was chase the mutt all over Rio Arriba County.

Pascal asked his father to ride shotgun and told Gillian to keep the dog in the back. As they headed into Española, Pascal slowed to a crawl. The town was noted for its speed traps, and a ticket was the last thing he needed with his pending trial. As usual the local drivers were erratic, creeping along then bursting into speed, weaving in and out of lanes. Once they crossed the river, the traffic thinned out and Pascal relaxed.

His father stared out the window in silence for a few miles before asking, "What's your going rate?"

"I think this case is pro bono. You're family," Pascal said, trying to lighten the mood.

"I don't need charity, I need help, and I've always found you get what you pay for. Don't you agree, Gillian?"

Before Gillian could respond, Pascal declared, "A hundred dollars a day, plus expenses."

His father's mouth dropped open, but he said nothing as he turned back toward the window.

Gillian tried to change the subject. "Did you know that the village of Abiquiu was built on the ruins of a prehistoric Tewa pueblo dating back to the thirteenth to sixteenth centuries? The town had a turbulent history, but today, as I'm sure you know, it's better known for Georgia O'Keeffe."

Pascal and his father both rolled their eyes. They weren't big O'Keefe fans.

"I visited her museum in town. I'm super excited to see where she lived, her home, get a feel for the landscape that inspired her painting." Gillian rattled on. "Do you know why Georgia bought her house in Abiquiu?"

Pascal looked at Gillian in the rearview mirror and raised his eyebrows. "The ambience?"

Gillian ignored his sarcasm. "She bought the property for its lush garden served by the local irrigation system, your beloved *acequia*." Gillian leaned forward and dramatically added, "The Mother Ditch." Then she fell back and giggled, causing Birdie to break into a series of yaps.

Obviously Gillian had seen the note with his scribbled message about the ditch. Pascal deserved the giggles but not the dog. He gritted his teeth as Birdie jumped around the back seat, lunging at the closed window.

As they neared the village, Pascal's father sat up straighter and gave directions. They turned off the highway onto a one-lane dirt road that wound north. The road, rutted and steep, made it slow going. Halfway up they passed a small ranch on the east side with a few outbuildings and an empty corral—otherwise the area was uninhabited. Before the road took a downward descent, his father motioned to turn into a driveway, which wasn't much more than a dirt path covered in weeds. Pascal mumbled curses under his breath as ruts dug into the undercarriage and bushes scraped both sides of his car. As they mounted the hill, a house came into view. It was tucked into a depression hidden from the road. The construction was new and uninteresting, but Pascal imagined a nighttime soak with a lady friend in the roof hot tub would make it a five-star venue.

Pascal warned Gillian to keep hold of the dog as she exited the backseat of the car. He watched her take in the vivid red-rock outcroppings that provided a backdrop for sprigs of yarrow and yuca. He had to admit the landscape was scenic and probably inspired O'Keefe to make it her home.

The house had an empty look. Pascal glanced at the studio south of the house and even from a distance noticed the building's secured door, video surveillance camera, and barred windows. He had a bad feeling about the place. It brought back memories of the film company warehouse, something he would like to forget. He hoped he didn't have to blow the door down. The security was overkill for a potter's studio. Unless this Katrin Simpson was a famous ceramist, there wasn't much need for anything more than a typical lock on the door. He trailed after his father, who had already made his way to the house and was ringing the doorbell over and over. Then he started pounding on it.

Pascal was surprised when his father pulled out a key and unlocked the door. Cool air rushed out. The heat must have been turned off. Though it was spring, the temperature still got down to the thirties at night. As his father called out, his greeting ricocheted through the emptiness. The house had an open plan, a large living room, dining room, kitchen area, and two bedrooms situated at opposite ends of the house. Gillian turned to check out the spare bedroom while Pascal and his father went into the master, where the blinds were drawn and the bed stripped bare. The only other piece of furniture in the room was a rustically carved armoire. Pascal's father walked over, hesitated, then pulled open the doors. It was empty.

Every last personal item had been removed. There was nothing to indicate that anyone had lived there recently.

"What's missing?" Pascal asked, even though the answer was evident.

"Everything. Paintings, books, clothes." His father looked dumbfounded.

Gillian came into the bedroom. She pressed her lips together and shrugged. "Nothing."

"Let's check out the studio." Pascal knew that unless his father had a key and knew the security code, they weren't getting inside. "You got a key?"

His father's shoulders sagged as he shook his head.

"Let's take a look."

Pascal took the lead out the back door and down a crushed stone path. He glanced at the security camera above the studio door and exchanged looks with Gillian. Then he made his way to the side of the building, staying clear of the camera. Gillian followed, tugging Birdie along. Pascal peered through one of the barred windows and waited for his eyes to adjust to the low light. The studio was equipped with a potter's wheel and two professional-looking kilns along the back wall. Two long narrow tables were set against both walls, bare except for a large pot, which was buff colored and decorated with black geometric shapes that emphasized the negative spaces, typical of Santo Domingo Pueblo pottery. Under the tables and across the floor were rows of sealed cardboard boxes. As Pascal moved to the next window, Gillian went to the other side of the studio and peered in the window.

Pascal noticed two pieces of black pottery were tucked in the back corner on a bottom shelf. Even in the muted light, he thought they were either Maria Martinez's infamous black ware pottery, or excellent copies. He wondered what they were doing in the studio. And what was in all those boxes? Pascal turned to his father and nodded his chin toward the window. "Have you ever been in the studio?"

His father pursed his lips and shook his head.

"Seen any of the pottery your girlfriend makes?"

"No, and she's not a girl."

Pascal raised his eyebrows.

His father looked sheepish. "A couple weeks ago I drove out to Ghost Ranch to drop off a prescription for your auntie. On my way back, I decided to swing by Katrin's house. She was struggling down the driveway carrying this huge box. The hatch was open on her car. I tried to take the box from her, but she turned away. She seemed distracted, not herself. She shoved the box in the back of the car and asked me to close the hatch. When she started back to the house, I peaked in the box."

"Yeah?"

"There was a piece of Native American pottery on top. A good size bowl. Looked old, weathered with cracks."

Pascal wondered if Katrin was making fake Native American pottery, or maybe storing stolen goods. "What else was in the box?"

His father shrugged. "Didn't look. Closed the hatch. When I went up to the house, Katrin didn't invite me in. Came out on the porch, said it wasn't a good time, went back inside. No explanation. That was the last time I saw her."

Something about the pottery niggled Pascal, but he couldn't put his finger on it. He wondered if he had any natural talent for being a detective. "What else do you know about Katrin?" he asked.

His father shrugged and stared down at his shoes. "Not much. She wasn't one of those ladies who goes on and on about themselves."

Gillian glanced at Pascal, raising her eyebrows without comment.

"Do you have any photos of her?"

His father brightened. "I do." He seemed pleased with himself as he took out his phone. "She told me she was camera shy. Hated how she looked in photos, refused to be photographed. I asked her if she believed, like the Native Americans, that photos could steal your soul. She laughed and said good luck with that." His father held out his phone.

Katrin Simpson stood by a late-model Jeep with her hand held up to her forehead, shielding the afternoon sun. She looked annoyed. It was difficult from that distance to tell how old she was—probably in her sixties. Her platinum gray hair was long and wiry, pulled back in an unruly ponytail. She had delicate features and her skin was pale, the kind that easily freckled in the New Mexico sun.

"Text it to me."

His father took the phone and stared at the screen lost in thought, drawn back into his sadness.

Gillian had wandered away from the studio, letting the dog tug her along.

"Come on, Gillian, let's go." Pascal turned to his father. "How about getting something to eat at the café?"

His father brightened. "Wouldn't mind some green chili stew."

"We can ask around if anyone has seen your friend."

The three piled into Pascal's SUV and drove in silence to the café. When they pulled up and climbed out of the car, there was a handmade sign taped to the front door: *Sorry, Emergency—Closed.*

Pascal and his father groaned simultaneously.

"Let's try Bodes," Pascal said as he squeezed his father's shoulder. "We can get something to eat, gas up, then head to Ghost Ranch. I'd like to have a chat with Auntie."

Gillian picked up the terrier, tossed the dog in the back seat, and leaped in, blocking her escape.

CHAPTER 3

Louise resigned herself as she followed her parents out of the café. How could she say no to them when they had given her everything for fifty years and rarely asked anything in return? But the last thing she wanted to do on her day off was drive to Mora. She barely remembered her grandparents or her uncle or the ranch. She tried not to sulk as she thought of her cousin Lisa, the lucky one—whether she knew it or not, she was the one who got away.

"We planned on taking the High Road to Taos," her mother said cheerfully.

Louise nodded with a closed-lip smile that came off as a grimace. She knew the route made sense, shorter miles-wise, but it would take forever the way her parents drove.

"Follow us, dear," her mother chirped.

Louise climbed in her car, plugged in her iPhone, cranked up the *O Brother, Where Art Thou?* soundtrack, and dutifully followed her parents north to Española. When they turned east off the highway, the landscape instantly changed. Leafless cottonwood trees and empty overgrown pastures with sagging barbed wire fences lined the two-lane road. They passed through several Spanish land grant villages—Chimayo, infamous for its chapel with a pit of healing dirt; Truchas, where *The Milagro Beanfield War* was filmed; and the Spanish settlement Las Trampas, founded in the 1750s. The villages and landscape made her itch to pull out her camera. As they climbed to higher elevations, one-seed junipers sprung up through the red earth and dotted the scenery. Finally the thick pine forests embraced the mountains that opened up to a lush valley. Resting at the foot of the Jicarita Peak was Peñasco—"Rocky" in the local Spanish dialect. They turned onto the road that led into Mora and wound their way around both sides of the Sangre de Cristo mountains. Views of the Pecos mountains popped up here and there. As they entered Mora a weathered sign was posted: *Santa Gertrudis de lo de Mora, population 528*.

Now there would be 527, Louise thought glumly.

This far north, at a little over seven thousand feet, the mountains looked much more majestic. The green of the trees, even this early in the spring, was dazzling in the early afternoon light. The land was noted for its scenic beauty with the eastern prairies giving rise to the rugged peaks of the mountains.

The ranch was on the north side of town. It was a small spread for Mora County, only 170 acres. Louise shut off her engine and loaded her camera, ready to capture the scenery. As she opened her car door, the pungent smell of pinon smoke permeated the air. The cattle her grandparents had raised on this patch of land were long gone. The fields were overgrown with four-foot tall elm tree shoots dotting the pasture. The land would need to be cleared and replanted if it were to be used again. This was where her father had been raised. It was so desolate, foreign. He rarely talked about his childhood or his family, and she never asked. Now that she was here, she wanted to know more.

The ranch house, typical of the area, had two stories and an attic but modest by today's standards. She followed her parents up the steps to the covered front porch. Through the front door to the right was a parlor, or what Louise imagined a parlor to be. It was evident that the room was rarely used. The few pieces of furniture, a couch and two chairs, looked as if they had never been put to use. The room was devoid of any personal items, no knickknacks or pictures, not even a candy dish.

Straight ahead of the front door were stairs leading to the second floor. Louise hoped there would be something to make their trip worthwhile. As they wandered through the house, Louise saw disappointment and sadness spread across her father's face. It made her heart ache. Where were the photographs, photo albums, or family relics? Nothing was left of his parents, his brother, his family, his childhood.

"Let's check out the attic," Louise chirped.

Her mother made a look as if to say, *Over my dead body*, but her father brightened.

He led the way to a ladder that pulled down from the ceiling and revealed an opening. "Used to hide up there from Joseph." He smiled, but it was a sad smile.

"You two go. I want to look in the kitchen. There might be some china, glassware, who knows," Louise's mother said, opening her eyes wide in anticipation.

Louise couldn't read her father's expression, but squeezed his arm. "I'll go up and check it out. You don't have to. If I find anything, I'll call down."

Her father turned away from his wife and said stoically, "I'll follow you."

Louise climbed up the ladder, which wasn't as hard as it looked but would be challenging for her father. She hoped he wouldn't lose his balance. When she reached the top, she searched for the light switch, flipped it on, and let out a groan. The entire floor was filled with boxes. Her father made his way up the ladder and pulled himself up through the opening.

"¡*Dios mío!*" he wailed, and then began to sneeze and cough in the attic's musty air. The furnace had been turned off weeks ago, but the attic was suffocating. Beads of sweat formed on Louise's brow—her spirits sank. It would take forever to go through all these boxes. She was irritated that whoever packed them and neatly taped them shut hadn't bothered to label them.

Louise scanned the room. Besides the boxes, the only other item was an old trunk wedged in the far corner. It looked like one of those on the back of a stagecoach in an old TV Western. Two well-worn leather straps were slung over the rounded top of the chest. She weaved her way through the maze of boxes. "Hey, Dad. Look at this. Do you recognize this trunk?"

Her father glanced toward the trunk with scrunched eyebrows.

"This might be your heirloom." Louise waved her arm through the air theatrically.

Her father weaved his way across the room, careful not to trip over the boxes. He looked down at the trunk and his eyes landed on the name carved in the top. *Simone.* Lisa's mother.

"Let's open it," Louise said. "If not heirlooms, maybe there's treasure inside. Maybe money, jewels."

Her father looked up at her with trepidation. She wondered if he knew or suspected what was inside the trunk. He bent down and slowly started to unbuckle each strap. The trunk's snaps were old and rusty and took all her father's strength to undo them. As each buckle released from the tongue, it made a loud clank, causing Louise to flinch.

Her father reached down to lift the lid, as her mother called out from the bottom of the ladder. "Hey, are you two doing okay up there? What did you find?"

Her father had been holding his breath and let it out in a huff. "Lots of boxes and a trunk. We'll need to get someone to move them downstairs so we can go through them. It's hot as hell up here."

"Not much in the kitchen," her mother said brightly. "I did find a lovely pitcher that I'm sure must have been your mother's."

"We'll be down shortly."

Her father turned back and lifted the lid. It opened easily and Louise wondered if someone had looked inside recently. They stared into the trunk's dark cavity. A worn and tattered hand-stitched quilt rested on the top. Her father picked up the quilt with such tenderness it made Louise suspect he had opened the trunk before and knew what lay below. He handed the quilt to her. There was nowhere to put it, so she set it on the floor. Her father took each item out of the trunk and laid them in a row. A little hat, a white shawl, a black and white fringed shawl with tassels, and a wooden candelabra with seven candlesticks and seven white candles.

"What is all this?" Louise asked.

Her father let out a long sigh. He pointed to the hat. "A yarmulke, a skullcap. It's what Orthodox Jews wear in public, like the pope's zucchetto. It symbolizes man's separation from God. Then he pointed to the two shawls. "Prayer shawls. White symbolizes purity and innocence, and the black-and-white-striped one with knotted fringes is called a tallit." Last he pointed to the candelabra. "A menorah. It's old." He pointed to the candles and raised his eyebrows. "Partially burned."

"Simone was Jewish?"

Her father nodded, then added, "Jewish blood."

"You knew?"

"My brother told me years ago." He chuckled sadly. "In the days we still confided in each other. Simone's mother sent her the trunk shortly after they were married, as a wedding present. Simone had refused to open it and had one of the ranch hands put it in the attic. Joseph forgot about it until one day he needed to store some boxes up here and decided to open it. He confronted Simone. She said it was one of her mother's sadistic jokes."

"Jesus." The Lord's name slipped out before Louise could stop herself.

Her father shot her a look.

"Sorry."

"Later Simone told Joseph that her ancestors brought the chest when they immigrated to New Mexico sometime during the Spanish colonial period. The trunk had been passed down in her family through generations. I was curious and did a little research on my own. I was able to access the Inquisition trial records through an online portal. The trial records listed names of people that refused to convert and were forced to leave the country. I couldn't verify if Simone's ancestors were among them, but I had the menorah appraised. It's from the sixteenth century, which dates it to the time of the Spanish Inquisition." He picked up the menorah and pointed to the candle at the center. "One could remove this piece, leaving three candles on each side, and convert it to a Christian cross." Her father stared at her sadly. "That little feat could save your life."

Louise couldn't find her words. It was as if someone punched her in the stomach and she had no more air. She had heard vague references to conversos and Crypto-Jews. She knew some had immigrated from Spain to the Southwest. It seemed like something from a bygone era.

Why did Simone's family keep it a secret all these years? Questions about her aunt whirled around in her head. Why had Simone hidden her heritage, denied it, tucked away her family's religious relics in the attic? The candles had been burned. *Who burned them?* she wondered. Did Simone practice her religion in secret? An involuntary shudder traveled down her spine as she thought of the horrors her aunt's ancestors must have experienced. Louise couldn't imagine what lengths the Jews had to go to in order to survive, including being forced to convert to Christianity.

She took out her camera and took photos of the items. It's what she did when she didn't know what else to do. Her father stood mute with the menorah in his grasp. "Could you hold up the quilt for me to photograph?"

He set down the menorah and picked up the quilt. He unfolded it and held it up. Even in its tattered shape the squares told a long-ago story, and tears came to Louise's eyes as she searched for their meaning. In the center was a word elaborately embroidered in red and gold thread. *ANUSIM.* Louise reached forward, pointing "Do you know what this means?"

Her father closed his eyes as he nodded. "It's ancient Hebrew for 'people who have been forced.' It was applied to Jews who were made to abandon their religion." He paused and lowered his voice. "It became the term of choice for the Crypto-Jews in the Southwest."

Louise wanted to understand. She couldn't fathom the cruelty of mankind. That was why it was hard for her to be a good Christian, a Catholic, knowing what had been done in the name of her religion, in the name of God, in the name of Jesus Christ.

Louise was well aware of the obsession many northern New Mexicans had with their Castilian Spanish heritage. Her parents had done research on an ancestry website and been delighted to find their ancestors were directly descended from Spain—not Mexico. But in light of the Crusades and the Inquisition, that wasn't anything to brag about. And poor cousin Lisa. She never knew her mother or possibly anything about her heritage, and now for a second time she had lost her father.

Louise knew the rift between her father and his brother was linked to resentment. Her uncle was forced to stay on the ranch in Mora to care for her aging grandparents while her father gallivanted off to college and became a successful attorney. Rift or no rift, she couldn't believe how callous her parents were, not telling her about Uncle's passing. Had there been a rosary, a viewing, a funeral, a wake? If so, she hadn't been invited. Even though she rarely saw her uncle, he was family—she should have had an opportunity to say goodbye.

They put the objects back in the trunk, covered them with the quilt, and latched the two belts. Louise promised she would help her father go through the boxes once they were down from the attic. But now she wanted to get out of there.

She drove away, leaving the farm and Mora behind, and thought about how an object or event could change your life. A hidden chest could change Lisa's like the college frat party had changed hers. Her whole world had shifted during spring break her junior year of college after having too much to drink at a party. Her roommate,

Beverly Longmire, had intervened, escorted her back to the dorm and tucked her safely in bed. The next morning, when Louise opened her eyes, something tickled her neck. It was Beverly's lips.

CHAPTER 4

Pascal turned off the highway onto the dirt road leading to Ghost Ranch. Over the years his father had visited the ranch, camping under the cottonwood trees and fishing in Abiquiu Dam. That's all the spiritual enlightenment he had ever needed, that is until he signed up for the healing workshop where he met his lady friend, Katrin Simpson.

Pascal noticed the shift in the light as they bumped along the road. He glanced in his rearview mirror and saw Gillian glued to the window. The towering rock walls and vivid colors had a hypnotic effect that was disorienting. Gillian had told him she had researched the ranch's long and varied history and struggled to wrap her mind around the land that 200 million years ago sat on the equator and was inhabited by dinosaurs. Pascal was glad she hadn't come across the ranch's more recent violent and turbulent past. He knew she wanted to discover Georgia O'Keeffe's love of the place.

Pascal pulled up in front of the administrative building and shut off the car.

Gillian grabbed the dog's leash, making sure she had a tight hold before opening the door. "You guys go ahead. I need to walk Birdie."

The two men got out of the car and climbed the steps. Pascal's Aunt Margaret sat behind a long counter, phone to her ear, making notes on a calendar. When she looked up, she squealed like a stuck pig, dropped the phone, rounded the desk, and grasped both men in a bear hug. Then, realizing what she'd done, ran back behind the desk and made apologies to whoever was on the phone.

"Now." Margaret looked at the two men suspiciously. "What are you two boys doing out here? Nothing to do with trouble I hope." She gave each a stern look. Margaret, always the family disciplinarian, tried to keep her younger brothers in line.

Pascal's father backed up and slid onto the bench across from the reception desk. He left Pascal to ask his questions.

"I need some information on one of your workshop participants." Pascal jutted his chin toward his father. "Dad's lady friend, Katrin Simpson, the one he met at the Mind, Body, Wellness, and Clay retreat."

"Oh"—Margaret fidgeted—"What kind of information?"

"Did you know that your brother hooked up with her after the retreat?"

Pascal's father picked up a magazine off the bench and held it up to his face.

"Oh, my little brother." She pursed her lips as she wagged her head.

"I take it participants fill out forms, provide some kind of background information."

"Well, but . . ."

Pascal knew his aunt was a by-the-book person, not apt to step over the line. The records contained personal information that was not to be shared.

"Ms. Simpson has disappeared. She might be involved in something illegal."

Margaret looked over at her brother, who continued to hold the magazine in front of his face. "Put that silly magazine down and get up here. Making your son do your talking. Good Lord, *hermanito*."

Pascal's father jumped up. "I'm worried about Katrin. We need any information you have. Can you look up what she put on her registration form?"

Margaret closed her eyes, took in a deep breath, and let it out. Pascal knew that the sigh meant they would get the information.

They followed Margaret to a small office where she retrieved the registration form and made a copy. The form only had basic contact information. Pascal noticed Katrin's address was in Denver. He wondered if she had rented the Abiquiu house after attending the workshop. Maybe after meeting his father.

"Thanks, *Tia*." Pascal gave her a hug.

"When's the trial, *mijito*?" Margaret asked in a soft voice.

"Hasn't been scheduled yet. I'll let you know."

His aunt made the sign of the cross before turning to her brother. "And you."

Pascal's dad shrugged, staring at his shoes like a naughty boy. It was a role he always played with his sister.

"My friend Gillian came along with us, wanted to see Georgia O'Keeffe country."

Margaret chuckled. "Let me guess. East Coast?"

Pascal sighed. "Okay if we take a little tour of the ranch?"

"Be my guest. Just don't—"

"Oh, we won't," he interrupted. They each gave Margaret a hug.

As they left the building, barking sounds ricocheted off the canyon's outcroppings. Pascal hoped the dog hadn't broken loose or cornered a rattler. That's all he needed. They quickly made their way down the path, and as they came around a bend, they spotted Gillian. Sure enough, Birdie had pulled loose from her leash and chased a rabbit up against a boulder. The dog and rabbit were at a standoff. Gillian crept toward the leash. The rabbit spooked, and the terrier lunged forward. The dog grabbed the rabbit, and with one violent shake of her head, broke the little bunny's neck. She dropped it on the ground, looked at Gillian, and wagged her tail. Mission accomplished.

Gilliam gasped. "No, no, no." Tears streamed down her face.

Pascal took Gillian in his arms and squeezed her tight. "It's the dog's nature, Gilly. It's what she was bred to do. In Scotland they send terriers down holes for varmints, and when the dog latches onto an animal, they pull the dog out by the tail."

Gillian continued to sob.

"One less rodent won't make a difference in the world," Pascal added.

Gillian pulled away from Pascal with a look of horror on her face. "That's a horrible thing to say. Rabbits aren't rodents."

"It's nature."

"We need to at least bury the poor bunny." Gillian sniffled.

Pascal's father piped up. "You got a shovel?"

Gillian glared at him, shook her head, but knew she was outnumbered.

Pascal's father walked over, picked up the rabbit by one of its hind legs, and flung it into the brush.

Birdie tugged at her leash, then threw her head back and let out a sorrowful howl that stopped everyone in their tracks.

"I hate New Mexico!" Gillian wailed.

CHAPTER 5

Louise arrived at the police station at half past seven. It was Monday—start of a new week, a new job, a new office. She wanted to settle in and get organized. Her cell phone chimed with the sound of church bells. When she bought a new cell phone, she hadn't been able to decide on a ringtone, but finally settled on the bells. She thought they would be pleasant, unobtrusive. But they made her feel guilty. Catholic guilt. She was a lapsed Catholic, rarely attending services except for high holidays. She answered the call to silence the bells without looking at the screen. "Sanchez."

"Don't hang up," Pascal said.

Louise stifled a groan. After twenty-nine years with the police force, she had looked forward to retirement this summer. An even thirty sounded perfect, or at least it was an even number. But her plans had been pushed back the night Harold Butler's partner came down with the flu. She had volunteered to fill in even though it meant an extra shift. The night had been unusually quiet. They finished their rounds without even issuing a traffic warning. As they made their way back to the station, they got a call. An explosion at a warehouse on the west side of town near the horse park. Louise had worked eighteen hours that day. She was beat and looked forward to going home for a long hot soak in the tub with a glass of wine. An explosion would mean complications, possibly the Feds.

When they had arrived at the warehouse, Pascal Ruiz was

already at the scene. Louise had found it strange, wondering how he got there before they did. Ruiz, as usual, had offered a feasible explanation. Claimed he happened to be across the street showing his girlfriend, Gillian Jasper, the horse park when he saw something suspicious. Though he never clarified what was suspicious, his explanation sounded plausible, and what did she care? He was the detective and would end up working the case. Maybe his presence would expedite things.

Unfortunately, it didn't turn out that way. Ruiz had crossed the line, and not for the first time in his short career. He was implicated in the explosion and put on administrative leave. His position was vacant. The department was stretched to its limits, and there were budgetary problems in the state government. The police force hadn't had to furlough anyone yet, but there was a hiring freeze in all government offices. Ruiz's partner, Matt Padilla, was still on medical leave with further complications from an appendectomy.

Several years ago, Louise had decided to stop being a patrol officer. She was tired of the monotonous driving around and handing out citations to pissed-off people. The captain had suggested she might consider becoming a detective. The Santa Fe Community College offered a criminal investigative certificate. She had enrolled and took several courses, but never finished the program. She decided that a patrol officer was a better fit. But then Louise, with almost thirty years of experience on the force and some investigative coursework under her belt, was asked to fill in until Padilla returned in a few weeks.

"What's up?" She knew she shouldn't be talking to Pascal. He was awaiting trial, and she would be expected to provide evidence for the prosecution.

"A missing person."

Louise groaned into the phone. She liked Pascal, but the man was a loose cannon. "Not another missing person?" Images of Bobby Pilot on the cross out in Tonque Pueblo popped into her head. Pascal had been assigned a simple burglary case involving a stolen Jesus costume at the Santa Fe Opera. The costume had turned up on Pilot. The pueblo was out of jurisdiction, but that didn't stop Pascal.

"Yeah, my father's lady friend, Katrin Simpson. She lives in Abiquiu, or did. Seems the little lady has up and vanished. We checked her house yesterday. It was empty. Looks like she moved out."

"Well, sometimes ladies don't want to say goodbye. Don't want to make a scene."

"Very funny," Pascal said dryly. "Sounds like you have experience."

"Your father should file a missing person's report. That is, if the woman's been missing at least three days."

"There's something else that seems a little strange."

Now Louise groaned louder into the phone. "What?"

"The woman was a potter. She had a studio next to her house. I checked it out. It was armed with a massive door, a security camera, and barred windows."

"Please don't tell me you blew the door down."

"I'm not a repeat offender. I peeked through one of the barred windows. The studio was full of sealed boxes. There was official-looking writing on the side of the boxes, but I couldn't read it through the window."

Louise groaned again—not more boxes. She wondered for a moment what "official-looking writing" looked like, but decided not to ask.

"And there were three pots on the shelf in the back. Two looked like Maria Martinez's work. It made me wonder if my dad's lady friend made the pottery or if it came from somewhere else. You haven't heard anything about missing or stolen Native American pottery?"

Louise considered hanging up and knew she should, but she liked Pascal. "A few months ago, an online gallery—can't remember the name—posted pictures of old Native American pottery for sale. They were fakes. The site was taken down right before the Feds moved in. I don't think they ever found out who hosted the site or what happened to the pottery."

"Could you ask around? I'd appreciate it. I'm curious. Also, could you check on my father's lady friend? He's worried."

Louise hesitated. She should say no, but . . . "I'll check around, let you know if I find out anything."

"We just left Ghost Ranch. My auntie works in the office and gave me Katrin Simpson's contact information. Her permanent address is in Denver. My dad has a picture of her."

Louise sighed. "Okay, send me her photo and any info you have. Things are quiet right now. I'll see what I can find out."

"Thanks, Louise. I appreciate it."

"Hey, what do you know about the Crypto-Jews?" Louise asked.

"Well, that's a non sequitur." Pascal chuckled.

"My uncle passed."

"Another non sequitur, but sorry to hear that."

"Thanks. He had a ranch in Mora. I was helping my parents get the ranch ready to put on the market. My dad and I found a trunk in the attic that belonged to my uncle's first wife. It had some Jewish religious relics in it." Louise had no idea why she was telling Pascal this.

"Cool. Yeah, I know about the Spanish Inquisition. Some Jews migrated from Spain and Portugal to the Southwest. The conversos in Spain were forced into Catholicism but were still viewed with suspicion. They suffered centuries of anti-Semitism and became scapegoats. They were blamed for a plague, accused of poisoning peoples' water, etc. King Ferdinand and Queen Isabella suspected that even trusted conversos were secretly practicing their old religion. They seized the conversos' wealth and used it to fund the Inquisition against the Muslims."

"Boy, you're a wealth of information."

"Yeah, when I came back from France, I did some research on the Spanish Inquisition for a historical novel I wanted to write. I never finished. Too depressing."

"You are a man of many talents," Louise said.

"Yeah, but it doesn't pay the rent."

Louise had to agree. Neither did photography. Santa Fe was an expensive town to live in on a policewoman's salary.

Pascal continued. "You should talk to my father. Back in the eighties he became friends with Stanley Hordes. At the time, Hordes was the New Mexico state historian. He told my dad he'd heard rumors about Hispanos lighting candles on Friday night and abstaining from eating pork. During his tenure, Hordes researched and interviewed hundreds of people. He discovered that the Jews in New Mexico were Sephardic, from Spain. Many were derived from the converso community that was forced to convert to Catholicism. The ones that continued to practice Judaism in secret were referred to as Crypto-Jews. He wrote a book about it. Can't remember the name. You should talk to my dad."

"I'll check out Hordes's book. Maybe get a copy for my cousin." Louise hesitated. "Maybe I'll give your dad a call."

"Don't forget to ask around about any stolen Native American pottery."

"Sure. Later."

CHAPTER 6

Louise had never had an interest in technology, never participated in social media, not even Instagram. She believed online images were two-dimensional, vacuous, soulless. Internet searches were the bane of her existence. But she had agreed to look into Pascal's father's missing lady friend. She googled Katrin Simpson and several images appeared, including a scantily dressed young woman and an obscure cartoon figure. There were links to Facebook, Instagram, YouTube, Twitter, and even to the TV show *The Simpsons*. There were public-record files, but in order to access them she would need to set up an account and pay a fee. She didn't want any paper trail that would lead back to Pascal. The New Mexico DMV didn't list any records for Katrin Simpson. She couldn't access Colorado's DMV without a legitimate reason, and Pascal definitely was not a legitimate reason.

Louise closed her web browser and deleted her internet history, just in case. At least she made an attempt to find out something about Katrin Simpson. She glanced at the clock. Eight forty-five. It was going to be another long, boring day. She swiveled in Pascal's desk chair, causing it to squeak. The chair was too low for her short stature, making it difficult to use the desktop computer. She had tried to adjust the chair but had set it too high; her toes could barely touch the floor. Now it was back to the low position. She hoped Pascal's partner would return soon, so she could go back to patrol duty and her old desk chair that was the perfect height.

Louise stood, rummaged through the piles of papers scattered across the desk, and picked up her cell phone. She needed to call her cousin Lisa, offer her condolences for her father's death. She dialed the number her father had given her. It immediately went to a generic voicemail message. "Hey, Lisa. We never met, but this is your cousin Louise in Santa Fe. I was sorry to hear about your father's passing. I wanted to"—Louise's desk phone rang—"I'll be in touch soon." She disconnected and picked up the desk phone receiver—the line was dead. She started to redial her cousin when the office door burst open.

Susie, the receptionist, stood in the doorway, hands on her hips, squinting menacingly across the room. "Why didn't you answer your phone . . . Detective?"

Louise blurted out, "My uncle died."

"Your Uncle Joseph? From Mora?"

"Yeah." Louise wondered how Susie knew her uncle's name, where he had lived, and that he died.

"That was two weeks ago."

"How do you know?"

"Don't you read the paper, *chica*?" Susie shook her head in dismay. Before Louise could make an excuse, Susie said, "There's been a murder . . . up on Laredo."

Violent crimes in Santa Fe were higher than the national average, and the murder rate had steadily increased over the last several years. But Louise hadn't expected to be assigned one her first week on the job, a job she wasn't prepared for.

"A murder?"

"That's what I said. Are you listening?"

"I'm listening."

"Carl Nuthers finished his shift and was on his way back to the station when he got the call. He's securing the scene. Waiting for you."

Louise tingled with trepidation, her nerves on high alert. Someone was killed. "My first case, from start to finish," she mumbled under her breath. "A simple murder. Nothing muddy or murky." Nothing convoluted like Ruiz's fiasco with the stolen Jesus costume. Susie handed Louise a torn piece of paper with the address, and she stuffed it in her coat pocket. As she left the station she started humming the old Kingston Trio song "Tom Dooley."

Susie shook her head. Louise was a good patrol officer, but no detective—and Susie knew it.

When Louise pulled into the circular driveway in front of the house, she saw the grounds were well groomed but filled with an abundance of thirsty plants, plants that had no business in the Southwest. She suppressed a whistle as she took in the house. The place must be worth several million dollars. She had to control herself not to pull her camera out of her bag and start shooting. Carl Nuthers, a patrol officer on the force, was hanging the last strip of the bright yellow plastic crime tape.

"Hey, Carl?" Louise called out.

Carl looked up and smiled. "Hey, Louise."

Louise ducked under the yellow tape. "What have we got here?"

"Looks like murder, stabbed in the heart, a big butcher knife." Carl pursed his lips together and shook his head.

"Oh dear, and not even Valentine's Day."

Carl chuckled. Louise could always lighten the mood, even when there was a man lying dead on his living room floor.

Louise checked herself. The comment was more befitting to a duty cop than a homicide detective, even if she was only filling in the position. But those comments popped out of her mouth before she realized what she was saying. "Any particulars?"

Carl took out a small notebook from the front breast pocket of his uniform. He flipped through the pages and found the information from the emergency operator. "Mrs. Navarro took the 911 call."

Louise was encouraged. Navarro, one of the best emergency operators, could squeeze every last drop of information from a caller while they waited for the police and medical assistance to arrive.

Carl looked down at his notes. "The victim is, um, *was* Webster Madison. An attorney. Worked for a private equity firm, Albatross."

Louise stifled a chuckle. Albatross was an unfortunate name for a firm that provided financial services. She hoped the company had chosen the name for the oceanic bird with ten feet wingspans and not any of the synonyms that came to mind. "Who called it in?"

"The housekeeper."

"Family?"

Carl shrugged.

Louise nodded her chin toward the front door. "Any sign of forced entry?"

"Nope. The housekeeper arrived around eight. The front door was unlocked, the alarm off. She spotted Mr. Madison sprawled on the living room floor."

"Anything else?"

"The housekeeper must not have had a cell phone."

Louise raised her eyebrows. "How did she make the call?"

"Well, when the lady called 911, Navarro told her to stay put until the police arrived. But the housekeeper had already left to find a phone."

"Where did she make the call?"

"Rail Runner Station."

Louise found that a bit odd. Why go all the way to the train station to call 911? "I'll need the particulars."

"The woman gave her name and address, no phone number. Maybe she doesn't have one."

"Who doesn't own a phone these days?"

Carl shrugged.

Already the crime was clouding up. This wasn't the first murder Louise had been involved in, but it would be the first she was responsible to solve. With Ruiz and Padilla out of the picture, she was on her own. A feeling of uncertainty settled in her stomach.

"Thanks, Carl. Before you leave I'll need the housekeeper's info."

Louise made her way up the winding cobblestone walkway and caught sight of Dr. Elena Maithe on the doorstep. The doctor's red wool coat swung open, revealing a white lab coat. The medical examiner was new to Santa Fe. Louise hadn't worked with her before.

Louise, unsure of the protocol in a murder case, nodded at the woman. She seldom watched TV but racked her brain for any mysteries she might have seen. She had read Agatha Christie's mysteries with her famous detective, Hercules Poirot. But she thought it was strange that he always gave his head a tap, referring to his little gray cells. Who did that in real life? Poirot was adept at finding clues in every hint of disorder, the smell of the carpet or disarray of a flower bed. Christie's books were riddled with unfair plot twists like identical twins or easily available, deadly chemicals.

The doctor returned Louise's nod and marched into the house, her three-inch heels clacking on the Saltillo tiles.

Louise trailed after her like a little puppy. The two women came to a halt side by side and peered down at the dead man, spread eagle on the carpet. A butcher knife, like the one Louise used to crush garlic cloves, protruded from his chest.

"Who do I have the honor?" the doctor asked, nodding her chin toward the man.

"Webster Madison." Before Louise could check herself she added, "Well, that knife looks like the culprit."

The medical examiner was silent as she crouched down next to Madison's body. Louise was thankful that the doctor hadn't raised her eyes to the ceiling, saying, *Duh!* She needed to get her little gray cells working before making a fool of herself. She thought of the board game Clue, her childhood favorite. The Where: living room; the Weapon: knife; the Who? Maybe solving a murder wasn't that difficult after all.

Dr. Maithe looked up at Louise with a benign smile. Her hazel eyes were an unusual shade of yellowish-brown with flecks of gold, green, and auburn radiating from the pupils. The same color eyes that had captured Louise's heart years ago her junior year of college. True hazel eyes were uncommon; only five percent of the population had them. They were associated with spontaneity and boldness, which fit her college friend to a tee. She wondered if the doctor possessed those qualities as well.

While Louise waited for the doctor's opinion, she studied the woman. The medical examiner was about her age, but the doctor took far better care with her appearance. Her makeup perfectly applied, hair neatly constrained in a chignon, silk scarf around her neck and small diamond studs sparkling in her ears.

"It might appear the knife is the culprit, Detective, but only a quarter of stab wounds result in death. Hmm, the knife is aimed at his heart." She opened her eyes wide with mock surprise. "Possibly a crime of passion?"

Louise ignored the medical examiner's sarcasm but was relieved not to be chastised.

"I'll need to perform an autopsy to be certain of the cause and approximate time of death." Dr. Maithe leaned forward and started prodding the man. "Rigor mortis has set in, so I don't think the body was moved after death. Not much blood though . . . strange. Still need further examination to be certain."

Louise bobbed her head up and down, at a loss for words. She felt awkward as she hovered over the body. She was grateful the doctor had shared her thoughts. Anything would help at this point. What did she know about murder? Louise searched for something to ask. "What do you think killed him?"

The doctor studied the man's chest area. "From the placement of the knife, it might have punctured his left lung, which would result in a buildup of air causing the lung to collapse— serious breathing problems." The doctor pursed her lips then looked up at Louise. "If that was the case, the air in the chest would push on the heart and other body parts. A punctured lung needs to be treated *tout suite*." The doctor snapped her fingers for emphasis. "Otherwise, as what seems to have occurred in Mr. Madison's case, a tension pneumothorax appears, resulting in death."

Louise stared at the knife. "Forensics will need to take prints from the knife."

"I would prefer to leave it in place until I get our man back to the lab. That way I can better determine the point of entry, document the incision, see what damage lies below." Dr. Maithe rocked back on her heels and held out her palms toward Louise. "Promise, I won't smudge the prints."

Louise smiled, finding the doctor charming. She stole one more look at the woman's hazel eyes. "Anything on him?"

The doctor rummaged around in Madison's pockets and found two bills, a twenty and a one, in the right front pocket of his jeans. She chuckled as she held out the money to Louise. "He wouldn't get far with this."

It was play money, maybe from a Monopoly set. She wondered what Madison was doing with play money and whether the amount was significant. Twenty-one? As she held the bills she realized too late that she should have worn gloves. Now her prints were on them. She chastised herself as she searched through her bag for a pair of gloves and struggled to pull them on her damp hands. She needed to get up to speed, stop playing around. This was murder. She took out an evidence bag, slid the money in, and sealed it.

Louise looked down at Webster Madison, trying to avoid the knife stuck in his chest. He was what most women would refer to as handsome, maybe even gorgeous. Madison looked to be in his late forties, early fifties. Around his temples a few gray stands commingled with his coal black hair, producing a distinguished look, one that would avow confidence, an advantage in the legal profession. Not a hair on his head was out of place, indicating there hadn't been a struggle. Someone he knew? Someone he had invited in? Someone he couldn't refuse? Someone who wanted him dead? Trying not to look at the knife, she focused on his blue-striped shirt that was open three buttons at the neck, revealing a pendant necklace: a golden ram with emerald eyes, the Aries zodiac symbol. She glanced at his feet. No shoes. His skin, lightly tanned and hairless; no calluses, lumps, or knots; toes that lay in a neat row with well-cared-for nails trimmed short. The doctor reached over to close Madison's eyes as Louise stole a look. They were strikingly aqua blue—Mediterranean pools of color.

Dr. Maithe slowly pushed herself away from the floor. She was stiff and had trouble getting up. Louise resisted the urge to reach out and assist. Once the doctor was upright, she smoothed down her lab coat. "I should have some preliminary results for you by late afternoon if all goes well." She looked down at Madison one last time. "What a waste."

Louise nodded. She wondered what the waste was. Did the doctor always refer to a murder as a waste, or was the comment intended specifically for Webster Madison? After all, he was handsome, successful, and in the prime of his life.

Once Louise was alone, she reached in her bag and pulled out her camera. Taking photos had always comforted her. As a teenager, her parents had indulged her interest in photography, hoping she would attend the University of New Mexico's photography program. But Louise chose Drexel University's Antoinette Westphal College of Media Arts & Design. Philadelphia wasn't New York or Los Angeles, but it would do. At the end of her junior year, everything had fallen apart. She had become involved with a woman who broke her heart and her spirit. She came home, refused to finish her degree, and surprised everyone, even herself, when she joined the Santa Fe police force.

Her pride and joy was a 1972 Olympus OM-1, the world's smallest and lightest 35mm single-lens reflex camera. She loved the darkroom experience, alone in the dark with only the glow of the red light and the smell of chemicals, waiting expectantly for the pictures to appear as if by magic. You never knew what might develop, unlike digital, which was immediate, predictable, disposable. No mystery. No surprise. No lasting images. Everything these days was instantaneous. No delayed gratification. But film was impractical for police work. She needed something quicker, less messy, and once she learned how to manipulate digital images, getting prints instantly without hours in a darkroom was easier to accept.

Louise knew that forensics would document the murder, but she wanted her own photos. She circled the body, methodically moving counterclockwise while she snapped shots. Then she moved to the doorway and took a series of photos approaching the body. She was a visual person—she needed images. Words could never provide the entire story.

Carl had dutifully outlined the body with yellow spray paint. When the paramedics lifted Madison onto the gurney, the man's essence remained. For some unfathomable reason, Louise worried about the yellow spray paint. It would be impossible to remove from the luxurious, creamy wool carpet.

Louise eyed a mid-century chair in a corner of the room and recognized the design. She had studied Frank Lloyd Wright in a college architecture course. Wright intended the chair to harmonize with humanity and the environment. Louise knew it would be uncomfortable and settled on the couch, waiting for the paramedics. As she looked around the room, she thought the inside of the house was opposite the outside. The living room was elegant, modern, spacious, but mostly empty. The style was the antithesis of a Santa Fe adobe—no vigas, latillas, or rustic straw poking its way out of white plaster. The walls, highly glazed in a neutral eggshell hue, made you want to run your hands across them. The ceiling spanned twenty feet, epitomizing the void, and enormous windows provided stunning views of the Sangre de Cristo and, in the distance, the Pecos mountains. A large abstract, expressionistic painting hung on the opposite wall. The painting looked like a Helen Frankenthaler, with its stained pigment creating veils of color bleeding into the raw canvas. Even the swaths of color couldn't erase the sense of nothingness that lingered in the room.

On the opposite wall hung another abstract painting, the counterpoint to Frankenthaler's, stark and daunting, with shades of black and gray as well as metallic streaks. It made her think of her recent fiftieth birthday—middle-aged, over the hill, lacking definition and substance.

Her parents had pleaded for a celebration. "Half a century!" Her mother had beamed as if it was an accomplishment. She didn't have any close friends, hadn't dated anyone in the last decade. Who would she invite, Carl Nuthers and his wife? Other officers? She squirmed at the thought of them in her parents' formal living room, dodging caterers holding trays of champagne and shrimp puff pastries. They would be looking for the beer keg and some hot wings.

She agreed to dinner at the Compound Restaurant. The three of them. Her mother had chatted about the upcoming opera season while downing Nantucket sea scallops and black caviar with champagne. Louise thought she had dodged the bullet as she took the last bite of beef tenderloin. But out came a cake, lavishly decorated with multicolored flowers and a little plaque that read, *Happy Fiftieth, Daughter*. The waiter shot Louise a smug, close-lipped smile before he plunged an enormous *50* candle deep among the candied flowers. It was a passive-aggressive gesture and, if she was paying the bill, he wouldn't get much of a tip. Then with more flourish than necessary, the waiter lit the candle and burst into "Happy Birthday," his beaming baritone making Louise shrink back. Mortified, she slunk down in her chair while some of the other patrons dutifully joined in. The waiter cut three enormous pieces of cake and took their coffee orders. After the champagne, wine, and rich food, Louise couldn't imagine eating a bite of the cake, but she choked down a few forkfuls, grateful the evening was almost over. She couldn't bear to disappoint her mother, but she always did.

Her parents had never approved of her life choices. They were disappointed when she had dropped out of college, and they were devastated when she joined the Santa Fe police force. It was not only a menial job, but a dangerous one. They were certain after a few months she would beg to go back to college. She had never told them about Julia—how could she?

Her promotion as a detective appeased them. A detective sounded better than a police officer. Now when their friends asked about Louise, they said she worked for the police bureau and changed the subject.

Louise glanced around Madison's living room, taking in the lack of personal items—no photos, no mementos, no knickknacks. There weren't any desks or cabinets to rummage through for clues. The house was edited down to a few well-placed pieces of furniture. It resembled a home ready for the market, staged for sale.

She made her way through the house, letting her camera capture and record the emptiness. It was no surprise that the kitchen, besides top-of-the-line stainless steel appliances, was totally empty. The pristine six-inch ebony granite countertops were bare, not even a coffee pot or toaster. The room looked as if it had never been used for food preparation. She opened the cabinets one by one: no food, no dishes, no silverware, no knives, and no butcher knife. Strange. Whoever killed Madison must have brought the knife to the house.

She left the kitchen and continued to the north side of the adobe. At the end of the hall stood a twelve-foot carved mahogany door leading to a separate wing. Louise recognized the carving, a replica of one of Masaccio's frescoes that portrayed an angel expelling Adam and Eve from the Garden of Eden. She had seen the original at the Brancacci Chapel in Florence during a high school graduation trip. The carving depicted Adam and Eve after they had eaten from the forbidden fruit and were cast out into the world to suffer the consequences of their sin. Louise remembered being fascinated with Masaccio's fresco. It uncharacteristically captured the emotion of the couple's embarrassment. She stepped back and took a photo of the carving before opening the door.

The wing was comprised of a series of three unfurnished rooms, empty, no sign of anyone living there. As she made her way back toward the door, she noticed a beam of light under a pocket door, which blended into the surrounding walls, making it almost undetectable. Louise perked up—a secret room. She slid the door open and found a library, or what had been intended to be a library, but nobody had bothered to fill it with books. She wondered whether Madison was moving in or out. Three of the walls were covered in floor-to-ceiling custom-built bookcases painted a glossy periwinkle blue. The only furniture in the room was a small ebony desk and chair against the opposite wall. She rummaged through the empty drawers, running her hand underneath each one. But unlike in the movies, nothing was taped to the drawer's bottoms. As she started to get up, her foot brushed against something under the desk: a small black trash can, empty except for a crumpled piece of paper. She pulled it out, smoothing the wrinkles on the desk. It was a grainy black and white photocopy of a woman. Louise couldn't tell the woman's age. She could be fifty or seventy. On the upper right side of the photo was printed *BABBLE, Singles Seeking Singles*. She folded the photo and put it in an evidence bag.

As Louise left the wing, she stopped again to admire the door's carving. She wondered if the subject matter was significant or if she was merely grasping at straws. The meager evidence—Monopoly money and a crumpled photocopy of an unidentified woman—was all she had to go on, except, of course, the murder weapon.

Louise made one last stop at the master bedroom, which was also minimally furnished. But other than Madison's clothes and shoes, neatly arranged in the closet, there was nothing. She made her way back to the living room. Forensics was late and still hadn't arrived. She tried not to be annoyed as she settled on the sofa. She took out her phone and searched for Madison's company, Albatross. The website featured a large photograph of an Albatross with its wings spread ready for flight. Below the bird was a brief statement that the company provided financial backing for start-ups and other endeavors. The site was as sparse as Madison's house. No employee or client list, and no mention of Webster Madison. The firm listed an office in the Opulent Building, a few blocks from the department of health on St. Francis Drive. She made note of the address and phone number. Next she googled Babble and found it was a senior online dating site. It professed it had changed, for the better, the way people date and find friends, as well as the perception of meeting online. Women were in charge. Louise approved.

The front door burst open and Johnson and Wilson from forensics entered, weighed down with equipment. "Sorry we're late," Johnson said, not offering an explanation. He looked down at the yellow spray-painted outline of Webster Madison. "I see the good doctor already swooped up the victim—took him to her lair." The two men chuckled and jabbed each other with their elbows. There was always competition between forensics and the medical examiner's office. Their roles overlapped and often there wasn't a clear distinction between their responsibilities. Both departments were charged with collecting information, formulating theories, and scrutinizing and reconciling the evidence. Often it came down to whoever got to the scene first. Today it was Dr. Maithe. "Hey, Sanchez." Johnson gave his chin a tilt toward Louise. "Congrats on your promotion."

"Thanks," Louise said.

"How about a walk-through?" Johnson took out a logbook as Wilson hung his camera around his neck. The boys were saddled up, ready to ride. "Give us a general idea about what went down. Then we'll get busy with prints and evidence."

Louise pushed herself off the sofa and joined the two men across the room. She identified the victim and gave them an overview of the crime scene—stabbed in the heart, no break-in, no struggle, no witnesses. Housekeeper called 911 around eight this morning. "Dr. Maithe should have the results of the autopsy later this afternoon. You'll need to dust the knife. It's still in the victim, who is on the way to the lab right now." Louise pulled out the two evidence bags that contained the Monopoly money and the photocopy of the woman, then handed them over. "These need to be dusted. You'll probably find my prints on the money. I need both back before I leave."

Johnson took the evidence bags, nodded, and pulled out the money. He looked at Louise, giving her a lopsided grin. "You're kidding."

Louise shrugged. "They were the only thing in the guy's pockets. Hey, are you familiar with the Babble online dating site?"

"Do I look that desperate?"

Before Louise could answer Carl Nuthers came in through the front door. He nodded at the two men and then handed Louise a folded piece of paper. "The housekeeper." He pressed his lips together and raised his eyebrows, the expression suggesting he had some opinions of his own on the matter.

"What?" Louise asked.

"Don't want to cloud your opinion."

Louise unfolded the paper and looked at the name and address. "Did you check with the train station?"

"Yeah. The attendant at the depot said a young woman came in all hysterical. Begged to use the phone. Said it was an emergency; someone had been stabbed."

Louise stuffed the paper in her purse. "I'll check with forensics and then I'm out of here. I need to talk to the station attendant, then pay a visit to the housekeeper." Louise jutted her chin toward Johnson and Wilson. "When they leave make sure everything is locked up and secure. Then see if any of the neighbors heard anything or saw anyone in the last twenty-four hours. Try and get their take on Webster Madison. I'll catch up with you back at the station."

Carl tipped an imaginary hat. Louise rolled her eyes even though she thought the gesture was sweet.

CHAPTER 7

Louise left Madison's house and headed down Paseo de Peralta toward the Santa Fe Depot. The station was the end of the line for the Rail Runner commuter train. She still couldn't imagine why the housekeeper went all the way to the train station to call 911. There were closer places to report a crime, such as the Santa Fe police station. She pulled into the parking lot next to Tomasita's Mexican Restaurant. The aroma of food drifted across the lot and made her knees weak. Her meager breakfast, a banana and coffee, had long been digested and hadn't provided much sustenance. But food would have to wait.

The depot was made up of two small rooms. One housed racks of New Mexico promotional materials, a restroom, and an information counter. A middle-aged couple sat on the one bench looking at a map. Louise peeked in the other room. A gray muzzled Labrador lay on a blanket next to a woman selling empanadas and coffee. The dog lifted his head and thumped his tail. Louise smiled at the woman, shook her head, and went over to the information counter.

An elderly man looked up from his crossword puzzle. "Can I help you?"

Louise positioned herself so the couple on the bench couldn't see her badge and lowered her voice. "Santa Fe Police Department."

The man sat up straighter as a look of alarm spread across his face. "Is it about that woman? The one who used the phone to call

911?" The man's pallor took on an even paler shade as sweat started to bead on his forehead.

Louise didn't want to make the man uncomfortable. "I need to ask you a few questions."

He leaned forward and whispered, "We aren't supposed to let anyone use the phone. It's only for emergencies. The lady was so upset, kept pleading, tears were running down her face, messing her makeup."

Louise scanned the area behind the counter. She didn't see a phone anywhere. "Where's the telephone?"

The man tilted his head toward a curtain on the south wall.

"Can I see it, please? Has anyone used it since the woman made her call this morning?"

"No. I mean"—the man stammered—"you can see the phone, but nobody has used it." He winced as he gingerly lowered himself off the stool, went over, and pulled back the curtain to reveal a tiny alcove. An old-fashioned black landline sat on a small desk.

"Nobody is allowed to touch the phone until it's dusted for prints," Louise said, using the voice she used with unruly children.

The man nodded, eyes wide.

"Why don't you take a seat? I need to make a call and then you can tell me what happened."

Louise called Johnson. They had finished with Madison's house and were packing up. She asked them to swing by the depot and dust the telephone for prints, then she walked back over to the counter and took out her notebook and a pencil. "Mr. . . . ?"

"Tucker, Thomas Tucker. I work a couple days a week at the station. Gets me out of the house; a little extra money never hurts." The man rubbed his hands together nervously.

Louise needed to put him at ease—didn't want him to keel over from a heart attack or stroke. "It must be an interesting job, meeting all kinds of people who need information?"

"Well, most people come in to get warm or cold, depending on the weather, or use the bathroom. Few ask for information—what time the train leaves or what time the train arrives."

"What time did the woman come into the depot?" Louise knew when the 911 call was placed, but it never hurt to double-check.

"Eight fifteen a.m. The southbound train had just pulled out of the station."

"Was anyone else in the depot?"

"No." He nodded toward the second room. "Mrs. Coriz comes in around nine."

"Can you tell me exactly what happened?"

"Well, let's see. I came on duty at eight, opened up, checked the restroom, made sure it was clean and supplied. When the eight fifteen train started up, the depot door swung open. It startled me. This lady rushed in all out of breath as if someone had been chasing her. She was doubled over, clutching her stomach." The attendant acted out the movement. "I asked if she was okay, but she held out her hand, you know, for me to wait. So I waited. Once she caught her breath, she asked to use the phone, said it was an emergency. I told her I couldn't let her use the phone. She became more and more upset, hysterical. I gave up and pulled out the phone for her. She dialed 911."

"Did the woman have an accent?"

"No. I could tell she was cultured."

"How's that?"

"She used proper English. No slang. A lot of people these days are lazy, no respect for the English language. I used to teach junior high language arts."

"Did you overhear any of her phone conversation?"

"I'm not one to eavesdrop, ma'am," Mr. Tucker said indignantly.

Louise thought that was too bad. She could get a transcript from the emergency operator, but it never hurts to have collaboration. "Could you describe the woman?"

"She was young, maybe twenties or early thirties. Pretty girl, cute little blond bob and freckles across her nose. You don't see many girls with freckles these days, do you?"

Louise shrugged. "How about height and weight?"

"Tall and slim, could use a few pounds on her bones."

"How was she dressed?"

He smiled broadly. "Smartly, I would say. Yes, sir. A lot of young people I see getting on and off the train dress as if they were going to mow the lawn. Shorts, tank tops, ripped jeans, sloppy outfits. They look as if they're headed to a backyard barbecue, not Santa Fe, the state capital." The man was relaxed now, no longer worried, no chance of a heart attack.

"Could you describe her outfit?"

"She wore dark blue slacks, not jeans, well pressed. A pink cashmere sweater and a navy blue trench coat. She had on these red high heels, which worried me. The cobblestones, you know, are responsible for a lot of twisted ankles."

Louise took out her camera. "Mind if I take some pictures?"

He shrugged as he slid his crossword puzzle under the counter. She snapped photos of the phone and a few around the station to kill time. As she started to go into the next room to buy an empanada, the guys from forensics came in the door.

Louise thanked the attendant for his help. She gave him her card and told him to call if he thought of anything else. But she knew witnesses seldom, if ever, called.

She climbed into the patrol car and unfolded the paper with the housekeeper's information. Camille Lautrec. Sounded French. A poor French housekeeper, maybe a refugee. There wasn't a phone number. Who didn't have a phone these days? She looked at the address and wrinkled her forehead. The Zocalo. The poor French housekeeper lived in an exclusive condominium development. Maybe she was a live-in housekeeper and pulled extra shifts cleaning other people's houses. Over the years, as a patrol officer,

Louise had traversed every inch of Santa Fe, including the area surrounding the complex. But since the Zocalo employed their own security team, she never had been inside the gates. The complex was constructed in the foothills at the base of the Sangre de Cristo mountains, north of downtown. It was a convenient location, close to the plaza and not far from the opera or the ski basin. What more could a housekeeper want?

The development was comprised of an imposing collection of buildings, sharp-edged constructions juxtaposed in shades of ocher and orange, varied in height. She looked up at the buildings framed by the vibrant sapphire sky, dotted with puffs of white clouds. Low junipers peppered the hillsides. Picture-postcard perfect. Louise wondered again how a housekeeper afforded such a place. She pulled into a visitor parking spot in front of Lautrec's building, which was slathered in brilliant ocher stucco. The lobby enveloped her in a tranquil and serene cocoon. The minimalist decor was reminiscent of Webster Madison's house.

Lautrec's condo was on the second floor. There was an elevator, but Louise decided to take the stairs—it never hurt to get a little exercise. She made her way down the hall to the apartment. As she reached out to ring the bell, the door swung open. A middle-aged woman stood in the doorway dressed in a designer suit that hugged her slim body in all the right places. A paisley silk scarf flowed around her throat, hiding any signs of age, and a classic Birkin bag hung on her crooked arm.

The woman must have been startled, but her face remained absolutely poised, revealing nothing. "Can I help you?" She had a slight French accent, though it could have been her inflection or Louise's imagination. The depot attendant had said the 911 caller was cultured, and there was no doubt this woman was educated, privileged, monied. But she didn't fit the rest of the description. Lautrec was older, her dark hair pulled in a chignon. No blond flip, and certainly no freckles across her nose.

Louise pulled out her identification. "Detective Sanchez, Santa Fe Police Department. I'm looking for Camille Lautrec."

The woman studied Louise's identification for longer than seemed necessary. Finally she met Louise's eyes, totally composed. She crinkled her perfectly shaped eyebrows and tilted her head slightly. The woman emitted confidence, a sense of entitlement.

Louise herself came from a prominent local family, but being Hispanic, she had suffered WASPish attitudes over the years. Her patience could easily outwait Lautrec. She had practiced polite forbearance since birth. "Are you Camille Lautrec?"

The woman gave her head a curt nod.

"May I come in? I need to ask you a few questions."

"What's this about"—Camille looked down at the identification badge that Louise still held open in her hand and said with a slight note of wariness—"Detective Sanchez?"

Louise wondered whether the woman was playing games, or just didn't have a clue. "It concerns Webster Madison."

"Webster Madison?"

"Yes."

"What about Mr. Madison?" Camille asked, exasperated.

"He was murdered."

At once the little color in the woman's face drained out. It was as if a bucket of water had splashed away all of her pigment. Her legs wobbled and she reached out for the doorknob, missing and crumpling to the floor. Louise was too slow to break the woman's fall. Lautrec's breath came out in gasps as she struggled to take in oxygen. Louise recognized the signs of shock, pushed her way past the woman, and fetched a glass of water from the kitchen.

When she returned Lautrec remained splayed on the floor, and her previous composure had evaporated. She took a sip of water and tucked her legs to the side, mermaid-style, ladylike. Her eyes darted around the room, searching for something to make sense of the news. Louise thought Lautrec was either an extremely good actress or she didn't know anything about Madison's death. One thing was for sure: this woman wasn't Madison's housekeeper.

Lautrec drank a few more sips of water and took in a deep breath, rounded her lips, and let it out as if cooling soup. Louise took hold of the woman's arm and easily pulled her to her feet. The woman was slim, trim, probably didn't weigh much over a hundred pounds.

Desperation clouded her eyes as she whispered, "Webster?"

Louise nodded as she led her over to the sofa. "I'm sorry, Ms. Lautrec. I need to ask you a few questions."

Camille nodded and looked away, not meeting Louise's eyes.

"Were you at Mr. Madison's house this morning?"

"This morning?" Camille gasped. "I haven't seen Webster since..." She started to sniffle and pulled out a dainty silk handkerchief, one cultured women used to dab their eyes, never to blow snot from their nose.

Louise gave the woman a moment to collect herself. She probably should ask if she was Madison's housekeeper, but as she glanced around the well-appointed room, the idea seemed ludicrous. "When was the last time you saw Mr. Madison?"

"About two weeks ago."

"Does he have a housekeeper?" Even as Louise asked the question she thought it sounded like something out of Downton Abbey.

"Housekeeper? How would I know? He probably had a service like most people."

"Do you know anyone who would want to harm Mr. Madison?"

The woman's skin paled even more. None of her original color had returned. Louise knew from experience that Madison's death was going to hit her hard as soon as the shock wore off. Louise waited, giving the woman a moment. She thought she detected fear in Camille's eyes, but the woman turned away and shook her head.

Louise noticed Lautrec's hesitation and suspected she might know more than she was letting on. "Is there someone you could call, Ms. Lautrec, to be with you?"

Camille shook her head as tears pooled around her eyes.

Money can't buy everything, Louise thought. "Do you know of any family members, friends, or acquaintances of Mr. Madison?"

"His parents died in a car accident his junior year of college. He was an only child. He recently moved to Santa Fe for work. Don't know if he has friends in town."

"Do you know anything about the company he works for, Albatross?"

"Not much. It's something to do with money." She shrugged. "Finance, investments, venture capital."

"Mr. Madison was the company's attorney?"

"I think he was under contract to help with some financial problems."

"Do you know how his work was going?"

"No." Lautrec's eyes hardened. "We didn't talk about work."

"What did you talk about?"

Camille pursed her lips. "What does anyone talk about?" For some reason the question had struck a chord, made the woman angry. Louise thought it best to let it go for now.

"How did you know Mr. Madison?"

For the first time, Camille Lautrec looked uncomfortable. She squeezed her eyes closed in an attempt to block everything out.

Louise waited. She needed to get as much information as possible from this woman. She knew if she pushed too hard, she would get nothing. "Were you a client of the Babble online dating site?"

Camille closed her eyes again, took in a deep breath, and let it out slowly. "I recently moved to Santa Fe and . . . I registered on the site."

"How does it work, you know, how do you meet people online?"

Camille looked at Louise skeptically.

Louise knew Lautrec thought she was the type who needed help finding a man, but she asked anyway. "Give me an overview."

Camille raised her eyes and sighed. Then listed the steps in a rapid monotone. "You register, create a profile, scan people, swipe left—no—or right—yes. If two people swipe right, it's a match. Contact the person, set up a meeting. Somewhere public so the person doesn't slit your throat, at least not on the first date."

"So you and Madison both swiped right?"

"Is this necessary? The man is dead."

"I'm sorry, Ms. Lautrec. I'm trying to find out who killed Mr. Madison."

"No."

Louise was confused. "Okay. Who did what?"

"Neither I nor Webster did anything online. I knew Webster from college."

Louise was surprised. "Oh?"

Camille closed her eyes. "Ohio State. We dated our junior and senior year. After graduation we went our separate ways. He to the Northwestern law school, and I had a scholarship to CalArts in Santa Clarita."

Louise couldn't help being impressed and a little envious, not with Northwestern, but with CalArts. She would have given her eyeteeth to study there. Or at least at one time in her life she would have. But that was a long time ago.

"So neither of you swiped yes on your profiles?"

"That's correct."

"Then how did you get in touch with Mr. Madison?"

Camille looked away and sighed. "After I saw his profile on Babble, I googled him, found out his address, and went to his house."

"If you recognized him, why didn't you swipe yes? What were your intentions?"

"My intentions?" Camille asked indignantly.

"Yes."

"I wanted to talk to him, not date him. Say hello."

Louise, intrigued, wondered what Camille wanted to talk to Madison about. "So you went to his house. And?"

"Jesus, are you kidding?"

"No."

"We talked about old times, college. He asked if we could meet for a drink sometime. We never had that drink. He never called." Camille squeezed her eyes shut and whispered, "He was the same old Webster."

Louise detected a bitterness in Camille. She gave the woman a few minutes before she continued with the interview. "A woman called 911 this morning and reported Madison's murder. When she arrived at his house around eight, she found him dead in the living room. She claimed to be his housekeeper."

Camille's eyes were glazing over. She seemed far away, maybe thinking about her relationship with Madison, maybe lost opportunities. Louise knew something about that.

"She gave the emergency operator your name and address."

The last bit of pigment drained from Camille's face as she stammered, "My . . . my name? I don't understand."

"The woman placed the emergency call from the Santa Fe Depot. Do you know why the woman would give your name and address?"

Camille shook her head. "No."

"Don't worry, I interviewed the attendant and you don't fit the woman's description. She was younger, probably in her twenties, blond, close to six feet tall."

Camille's pale face took on an odd shade of green, and she looked as if she was going to be sick. Louise refilled her glass of water in the kitchen. She briefly considered bringing a saucepan.

"It's strange the 911 caller gave your name."

Camille barely moved her head from one side to the other as she sank into the cushions, downcast. Louise couldn't bring herself to continue the interview.

"Is there anything I can do for you, Ms. Lautrec?"

Camille gave her head a definitive shake and tried to square her shoulders. Louise thought the woman was holding back but also knew Lautrec wasn't in any state to reveal more. She took out her card and handed it to Camille. The woman's hand trembled as she held the card up to her face.

"If you think of anything else, please give me a call. I'll see myself out." Louise rose from her chair and walked across the room, then stopped and turned. "I need to take your picture."

"Now?"

"If you don't mind."

Louise could tell the woman certainly did mind, since she reached up and tried to smooth down her hair before giving up and letting her hand fall limply to her side. Louise raised her camera and snapped the photo. Then she put her camera in the case and picked up her purse.

"How did he die?" Camille asked.

"Knife in the heart." Louise knew it was cruel and overly dramatic, but she understood it was better not to sugarcoat murder. It was a grisly business.

Camille lowered her head and Louise could hear muffled sobs as she let herself out of the condominium.

CHAPTER 8

Carl Nuthers took a cursory look around Madison's house after forensics packed up their bags and left. He considered resetting the alarm, but what was the point? Nothing to steal, only a few pieces of uncomfortable furniture and paintings that looked as if they were done by preschoolers having a bad day. People with money were a mystery to him. If he owned this house, he would put it on the market, buy a ranch up in Chama, retire, and fish the river to his heart's content. He pulled the door closed and made sure the yellow crime tape was secured firmly in place. He knew the tape wasn't going to keep anyone out, it only provided a warning that law-abiding citizens would heed.

It was almost lunchtime. He thought longingly of his sack lunch in the break room fridge —roast beef sandwich, potato salad, and a dill pickle. Last night his wife had baked chocolate chip cookies, and he was sure she put a few in his sack. But lunch would have to wait. Louise had asked him to interview the neighbors before heading back to the station.

As Carl crossed the street, he took in the water-thirsty plants with names he didn't know and shook his head in dismay. He climbed up the two steps to the Saltillo-tiled porch. A row of white rocking chairs, more fitting for a southern veranda, squeaked in the afternoon breeze. The sound made him edgy, and he scratched at his neck again. He rang the doorbell, glanced around, then held his finger on the bell for almost a minute. Nothing. He made his way to the front window. As he cupped his hands against the glass, a car pulled into the driveway, spitting gravel.

A young woman jumped out of the vehicle. "Can I help you?" She stood with hands on her hips, glaring at Carl. The girl's red hair frizzed in all directions, giving her an electrified appearance. Before Carl could open his mouth, an enormous golden retriever, who looked as if it had never missed a meal, leaped out of the car. The dog spotted Carl, bounded over, and started sniffing his crotch.

Carl, caught in the act of snooping, took a minute to collect himself while fending off the dog. "Officer Nuthers. Santa Fe Police Department."

"Police? Was there a break-in?" The young woman's demeanor changed to worry.

"No."

"Shiloh, come!" the woman shouted, but the dog ignored her, continuing to sniff Carl up and down as he flagged his enormous tail back and forth.

"Do you live here?" Carl asked.

"Shi-loh."

Carl waited for an answer.

"I'm house-sitting for the Logans."

Carl took out his notebook and held the nub of his pencil expectantly. "Name?"

"Am I in trouble?"

"No. Name?"

"Mary McCarthy."

Carl scribbled her name in his notebook. "Ms. McCarthy, can we go inside? I need to ask you a few questions. There's been a situation." Carl jerked his chin toward Madison's house.

The young woman placed her hand above her eyes to shield the sun and looked across the street. "I've been gone all day."

She turned away, grabbed her purse off the front seat of the car, and opened the back door. A small boy, not more than five or six years old, climbed out and took her hand. Like the girl, he was redheaded and freckled. Carl thought the boy looked like one of those little orphans in *Oliver*, the Charles Dickens movie.

The young woman screamed, "Shiloh!" then headed for the front door. As soon as she unlocked the door, the dog darted past her and disappeared down the hall. Carl was relieved the dog was engaged elsewhere for the moment—he felt slobbered from head to toe. Not being a dog person, he didn't find it a pleasant experience.

Mary settled in an overstuffed chair nearest the front door and clutched her purse tightly in her lap. She looked as if she had been sent to the principal's office. "Can I see some identification?"

Carl gave her a point for that and felt remiss as he handed over his identification. Mary scrutinized it, glancing from Carl's face to the document several times. The young boy hung on her shoulder, staring at Carl with saucer-shaped green eyes. Then he disentangled himself and slipped away. Finally, Carl had had enough. He leaned forward and took his ID out of Mary's hand, tucking it away.

"What time did you leave the house this morning?"

"A little after seven. That's when I'm supposed to be at work. Shiloh was giving me a hard time. He goes to doggy daycare twice a week. Hates it, wouldn't get in the car. Don't know how he knows what day it is, but he does."

"Do you know the man who lives across the street, Webster Madison?"

"No."

"Did you notice anything unusual last night or this morning before you left?"

"No."

Mary seemed to be a person of few words. And none of them were helpful.

"Did you see anyone go in or out of Mr. Madison's house in the last couple of days? Notice a strange car?"

"No."

"Or anything out of the ordinary?"

"No."

Carl sighed, wondering how detectives ever solved crimes. "Mr. Madison's housekeeper found him when she arrived for work this morning—dead."

Mary didn't react to the news but pursed her lips as she wrinkled her brow. "That's strange."

Carl took in a deep breath, trying to be patient. He found young people exasperating. "Why is it strange that the housekeeper discovered the man dead?"

"I don't think he has, uh, a housekeeper."

"I thought you didn't know Mr. Madison."

"I don't. But whoever lives in that house uses the same cleaning service as the Logans, Able Bodies. The two houses are on the same schedule. The agency sends four people to clean both houses twice weekly, Tuesday and Friday mornings. They start here at eight o'clock, finish around ten, and go across the street to clean until noon."

Now he was getting somewhere. If the woman who reported Madison's murder worked for Able Bodies, she wasn't scheduled to clean that day. So what was she doing at Madison's house? And, if the woman didn't work for the cleaning service, then who was she, and why did she say she was the housekeeper?

"Is there anything else you can tell me?"

Mary shrugged and shook her head.

"Thanks for your help." Carl handed the woman Louise Sanchez's card. "If you think of anything else, please don't hesitate to call Detective Sanchez. She's in charge of the case."

CHAPTER 9

Louise left Camille Lautrec's condo and drove back to the station. She found the lobby empty, nobody behind the counter, the room dark. Either there had been a power outage or Susie, in an attempt to mitigate another migraine, had turned off the fluorescent lights again. *That woman is definitely in the wrong job*, Louise thought. This place could be a headache with or without fluorescent lights.

Susie popped her head around the corner. "Hey, Sanchez."

"Power out again or another late night?"

Susie cocked her head. "You have no respect for those of us who have to sit under these abominable lights eight hours a day. Did you know that the UV radiation causes migraines, eye strain, dizziness—cancer."

Louise held up her palms in surrender. "Whoa. I feel for you, sister."

"Yeah, I bet, *chica*."

"Is the captain in?"

"He's in his office. I'd stand clear. The commissioner is in there with him. They've been holed up for twenty-five minutes, which is a new record. The commissioner is ranting and raving about streamlining the force." She grimaced as she slid her finger across her neck. "Trimming the fat."

"And how do you know this?"

Susie pointed a finger at her temple and shot Louise a lopsided grin.

Louise hoped Susie wasn't right. The force was already down a detective and two duty cops. She couldn't believe the commissioner wanted to cut more bodies, especially during tourist season. Crime was up, and everyone on the force was overworked, pulling second shifts.

Louise would wait, give the captain time to simmer down. On her way down the hall, she stuck her head in the break room and spotted a half-empty box of Krispy Kreme doughnuts on the counter, a note stuck to the top: *Enjoy*. "Bless whoever you are," she mumbled as she lifted a cream-filled, chocolate-covered doughnut out of the box. She wasn't the least bit guilty as she bit into it, smearing cream all over her mouth. After all, she had taken the stairs at Lautrec's condo yesterday.

As she left the break room, she spotted Carl Nuthers coming down the hall. "Hey, Carl, any luck with the neighbors?"

"Yeah, talked to a girl. She's house-sitting for the neighbors across the street, the Logans. She didn't see or hear anything, but she didn't think Madison had a housekeeper. He uses the same agency the Logans use, Able Bodies. They come twice a week but not on Mondays. They're scheduled for Tuesday and Friday. I gave her your card."

"Thanks, Carl. I'll check out Able Bodies."

Louise pushed open the door to Ruiz's old office, licking a bit of cream from her lips. Pascal's phone call on Sunday had put her on edge. Jesus, she couldn't believe he had sucked her into his problems, asking for help with his father's missing lady friend and going on about some suspicious Native American pottery. She had bigger fish to fry, a murder to solve, not to mention testifying at the upcoming trial, Pascal's trial. And when would she have time to help her father with the boxes from her uncle's ranch? She felt sorry for herself as she scanned the room. She was a squatter, invading someone else's space, even though Pascal had sanctioned it. Still, she was an intruder. She didn't have time to make any changes in the office, make it her space, at least not until after the trial. And who knew how long the captain would want her to fill in? After all, she was a patrol officer, not a detective.

She needed her workspace more usable, more productive. She stared at the perpetually slow clock above and the blank whiteboard on the north wall. She opened her MacBook Pro laptop on the desk. The police force used PCs, but Louise was a Mac person. Her laptop stored all her photos and she needed images. They told the story—in black and white and color—unlike words that could be twisted and convoluted.

She sat down at the desk. It was a mess, piled high with his paperwork that should have been processed and filed weeks ago. She didn't have time to deal with Ruiz's past, or his present. While she stuffed papers in a cardboard box, she ticked off what she had accomplished so far. There were three pieces of evidence from the crime scene—the murder weapon, some play money, and a photo of a woman. But who were the suspects? Crimes were a puzzle that needed to be solved. Questions swirled in Louise's head—who was this woman who called in the murder? Why did she identify herself as the housekeeper? Why did she give Camille Lautrec's name and address? Lautrec didn't fit the depot attendant's description of the 911 caller. Was it a sadistic joke? Maybe a jilted lover? Was the intention to incriminate Lautrec? Too many questions and no answers.

She wraked her brain trying to remember the detective courses she took at the community college while she plugged her camera into the computer. She uploaded the photos she took at the crime scene and chose ones to print. The printer whirled as it spit them out. She took the last bite of her doughnut and washed it down with a bottle of water stashed in the drawer.

She had skipped lunch—it was time she took a diet seriously—but knew when the sugar rush from the doughnut wore off, she would crash. Her mind drifted aimlessly as she stared at the empty whiteboard. She pulled out a yellow pad and made three headings: *Facts, Questions, Calls.* Under *Facts*: stabbed with a knife, no sign of a break-in or burglary. Under *Questions*: crime of passion, silence. Under *Calls*: Able Bodies the cleaning service, Babble the online dating site. She googled Babble's website and scanned the home page, quickly realizing the site was designed to protect their clients' privacy. She clicked on the contact button. There was no phone number, only a memo for inquiries. She typed a short note concerning the murder of one of the clients of the dating site. She demanded a return call ASAP.

She thought about the only other clue, the play money found on Madison. Could the money be a link? More likely a joke, but . . .

Louise dialed the Able Bodies cleaning service. The receptionist sounded bored, as if police inquiries were a daily occurrence. The woman yawned right into the receiver and then announced the boss, Aster Winters, was out to lunch. Louise left a message for Ms. Winters to return her call as soon as she could. She considered adding, "It concerns a murder," but decided it was best not to tip her hand.

The printer deposited the last photo onto the floor and quieted. Louise scooped them up, organizing them on the whiteboard. She pinned the photos of Webster Madison at the top of the board and scribbled *Victim*. Below Madison she added the series of photos from the interior of the house. In the middle, she taped the website home pages for the cleaning service and the online dating site. As she started to tape the last picture, a rap on the door startled her. She quickly stuck up the photo of Camille Lautrec before turning around. The captain stood in the doorway, a sour look on his face.

"Sir?"

"The commissioner was here. Wants Ruiz out, off the books, even before the trial. I tried to explain that's not procedure, but . . ." He took in a deep breath and let it out. "Sorry, not your problem. You have your own fish to fry. Your first week in the position and a murder dumped in your lap."

She smiled, trying not to look as overwhelmed as she felt. "Yes, a murder."

"Who was first on the scene?"

"Carl Nuthers. He was a few blocks away when he got the call. He secured the area until I arrived. When I left I asked him to canvass the neighbors, the Logan family. See if they heard or saw anything last night."

The captain made his way across the room to the whiteboard. "Nothing like throwing you from the frying pan into the fire. What do you have so far?"

Louise grabbed the pointer off her desk and joined the captain. She was glad she had posted the pictures. It lessened her anxiety and made it easy to give the captain a summary. She gave sharp taps with her pointer as she described the victim. "Webster Madison, attorney, mid-fifties, stabbed in the heart with a butcher knife. No sign of a break-in, robbery, or struggle."

"Who called it in?"

"That's the number one question. A woman called 911 a little after eight this morning from the Santa Fe Depot."

"The train depot?"

Louise nodded. "The woman burst into the depot and begged the attendant, Mr. Tucker, to use the phone. Said it was an emergency. Dialed 911, reported the murder, and gave Madison's address. The woman identified herself as the housekeeper and gave the name Camille Lautrec." Louise pointed to the picture she had taken of Lautrec.

The captain raised his eyebrows. "The housekeeper?" He stared at the photo of Lautrec, and even in her distraught state, she could read his thoughts: The woman couldn't possibly be mistaken for a housekeeper.

"Well, probably not. At least I don't think so. I interviewed her yesterday at her condo, the Zocalo."

The captain raised his eyebrows again. "Not the housekeeper."

Louise shook her head. "She doesn't fit the attendant's description of the 911 caller."

"What's Lautrec's story?"

"She recently moved here from LA. According to her online profile she's the new head of the costume department at the Santa Fe Opera."

The captain groaned. "Not the opera again. The commissioner will have a coronary."

"Lautrec admitted she knew Madison in college. She came across his profile on an online dating site, Babble. She assured me she didn't pursue him online. She found his address and stopped by his house two weeks ago to say hi. She insists that was the last time she saw him. The people who live across the street are out of town. The house sitter told Carl Nuthers that Able Bodies cleaned both the Madison and Logan residences twice a week, but not on Monday."

"So who is this woman who called in the murder?"

"I asked Lautrec about the 911 caller. She claims she had no idea who the woman was or why she used her name. The emergency operator had instructed the caller to remain at the crime scene. But it didn't matter—the woman had already left Madison's and was at the train depot. The depot attendant described the woman as young, in her twenties, well dressed, cultured. She didn't sound like a housekeeper either."

"This case sounds like a doozy. Right up Ruiz's alley. Too bad he's out of commission." The captain's body sagged. He looked worn out. "What else do you have?"

"I'm waiting for the pathologist report. Forensics is working on the prints. I left messages at Able Bodies and Babble. Neither have returned my calls."

"You're going to need some help with the case. Put Montoya on any small tasks. Have him look into the companies. He's good at desk work and knows his way around computers."

"Thanks, will do. I would appreciate the help."

The captain nodded. "Anything else?"

"When I searched the house, there was a separate wing with a library, or at least what someday might be the library. No books on the shelves yet. The only thing I found in the room was a photocopy of this woman." Louise pulled out the photo of the woman from the evidence bag and handed it to the captain. "It's grainy. Looks like a photo of a photo. Also, it has the name of the online dating site at the top of the page. The woman must be registered with the site."

The captain studied the picture.

"I don't suppose you recognize her?"

The captain shook his head. "Looks sort of familiar. Pass it around the station, see if anyone recognizes her." He handed the picture back. "This case seems a little sordid. Online dating. I don't like it." He wrinkled his nose. "Watch your back, Sanchez. Keep me updated."

She tacked the picture of the woman on the wall in the center. "Will do, sir."

"As I said, I think you need to call in the troops. Don't forget to get Montoya to help. See what he can dig up. Tell him I suggested it. He's a little gun-shy taking on projects after the Ruiz catastrophe."

"Thanks. I'll tread lightly." She smiled warmly at the captain.

He nodded. "Let me know if I can do anything." He took one more look at the bulletin board, shook his head, turned, and left the room.

Louise stared at the photos. So many pieces but no pie. She knew something was missing, but what could it be?

CHAPTER 10

Sanchez found working patrol duty alone doable, but she soon discovered working a murder case alone was far different. It was daunting, like trying to solve a crime in a vacuum. No one to bounce things off of. Detectives always worked in pairs, or at least had sidekicks: Sherlock and Watson, Poirot and Hastings, Morse and Lewis, Lynley and Havers. Even Nick Charles had his wife, Nora, not to mention their fox terrier, Asta. Maybe she should get a dog? But she wasn't a dog person. The captain's suggestion to ask Rupert Montoya to help with the case was a nice gesture, but it wasn't the same as working with a partner, someone on your wavelength, someone invested in solving the case.

Louise decided she needed help and asked Rupert to come to her office. She hoped meeting on her turf would give her an edge, establish her position. But as Rupert came into the office, he scanned the room, taking stock. His attitude screamed that she was an intruder. It put her on edge. She steeled herself, shook off the impostor feelings, and plunged ahead. "The captain suggested you might have time to cross off some tasks for the Madison murder case."

"Yeah. Sure. Whatever you need," Rupert said, looking everywhere but at Louise.

"Thanks. I'm stretched thin with this case." *And out of my league,* she thought, but didn't add it.

"What do you need?" Montoya asked curtly. He had a no-nonsense reputation around the station.

Louise wished he would lighten up. "I need you to contact Babble. It's a senior online dating site. We need to find the identity of this woman." Louise pointed to the photocopy of the mystery woman fastened on the whiteboard. She took the woman's picture down and made him a copy.

"I'll see what I can find out. Have a few things I'm working on. I'll give you an update by the end of the day."

She nodded and looked down at her desk. She could tell Rupert was a bit annoyed at being given a to-do list.

The cleaning service still hadn't returned her call. No respect for the law anymore. Maybe Rupert, being a man, would have better luck getting information from the agency. But she knew that delegating tasks sometimes took more time and effort than doing the job yourself. Delegating meant someone might not deliver—disappointment.

After Rupert left, Louise twisted her chair around and stared out the window. There wasn't much of a view, only a stucco wall of the neighboring building. She couldn't even tell what the weather was outside. She turned back to her desk and decided to put in a call to Albatross. She dialed the number and on the third ring a woman answered with a heavy British accent, sounding like Margaret Thatcher in a rush. No pretense, no preamble. "Albatross."

"Detective Sanchez, Santa Fe Police Department. I need to speak to whoever is in charge of the company."

"Mr. Roche," the woman offered flatly without explanation.

Give me a break, Louise thought. "May I speak with him?"

"Mr. Roche is out of the country."

Louise imagined the woman was gasping, out of breath from spitting out that many words. "Is there someone else I can speak with? Maybe the second in command?"

"There isn't a second."

Louise found that strange and considered asking for a third. She needed to jolt this woman into some helpful response. "It concerns Mr. Madison."

"Webster? Webster Madison?" The woman sounded perplexed.

Louise lost her patience, gritted her teeth so she didn't say things she would regret later. "Correct. Webster Madison."

"Mr. Madison is no longer employed here."

"Since when?"

"That is privileged information."

Louise started to laugh, then checked herself and said, "This is a police matter." She wanted to add "*honey*," but didn't. She was sure this woman was no honey. She was an iron fist. Impregnable. "I need to speak to someone in charge."

"What is this about?"

Louise sighed. "It concerns Webster Madison's murder." Louise heard the woman take in a sharp breath and felt a small sense of satisfaction. "I need to speak to someone in charge. Now."

"There isn't anyone."

The line went dead.

CHAPTER 11

Louise felt a familiar knot in her stomach, the place her frustrations always settled. Yesterday felt like the longest day of her life, and she had little to show for it. Rupert had promised to have the information on the dating site by the end of the day, but he had been called away. His son had broken his arm, and he'd spent all afternoon in the emergency room. When Louise caught up with him this morning, he confessed the online dating site was impenetrable. Even with all his computer expertise and previous hacking skills, he had found it impossible to track down the company's leader. The website was a maze.

Although it was only the second day of the case, Louise was frustrated. She was getting nowhere. Every clue seemed to be a dead end. She was sure the woman in the photocopy was a client of Babble—why else would the site be printed at the top of the page? The company could easily identify the woman, but there was no one to ask at Babble. The police department's facial-recognition profile hadn't come up with any matches. But that only meant the woman hadn't been arrested or didn't have a record. Louise had passed the photo around the station in hopes someone would recognize her, but she was met with shrugs and headshakes. She even texted the picture to Matt Padilla, who was back in the hospital with a secondary infection after his appendix surgery. Padilla also thought the woman looked familiar, but he couldn't place her either.

Since Rupert hadn't any luck getting in Babble's back door, Louise considered the front door. She would need someone willing to register on the site. Rupert was too young, too honest, even though she knew he'd had his day stepping over the line.

Louise, busy with the murder case, had forgotten about Pascal's call on Sunday. She hadn't thought about the missing woman or the Native American pottery. But maybe, if she found out something about either the woman or the pottery, Pascal would ask his father to sign up on Babble. The idea caused sweat to bead across her forehead and pool under her eyes. She was playing with fire, and it could turn out badly for both of them. If anyone found out they were collaborating, or even talking to each other, they would be gone yesterday.

Louise turned on her computer, and while waiting for the ancient machine to warm up, she called her mother. If anyone knew anything about missing or stolen Native American pottery, it would be her mother. She was a member of the New Mexico Museum Foundation, not to mention the current president of the board.

"Hi. Sorry I haven't called to thank you for brunch on Sunday. Yesterday I was assigned a murder case." Louise could almost hear her mother's arm making the sign of the cross.

"Oh dear. A murder?"

"I can't get into it right now, but I'll share all the gory details later."

"You were always such a thoughtful daughter," her mother said sarcastically.

"Have you heard anything about missing or stolen Native American pottery recently?"

Her mother sighed. "Don't you read the paper?"

"You mean the Santa Fe paper, *The New Mexican*?"

"Yes."

"Sometimes I read it at the station." Louise instinctively crossed her fingers.

"So I take it, even though you are a law officer, an article about the disappearance of archaeological pottery in your hometown wasn't brought to your attention? What do you do all day at that station?"

"Solve murders. But no, I never saw the article or heard about any missing pottery." Louise felt a need to defend herself and the force. "And usually we don't have time to read the paper because we're solving crimes."

"Oh?" her mother asked sarcastically. "Well the missing boxes of pottery were part of a shipment from an older, cramped location to a newer one. The archaeologists spent over a year examining and categorizing every piece of pottery to make sure each one could be moved safely to the new location. After the move, there were a number of boxes unaccounted for. A pretty high number, I think. They never arrived at the new destination, seemed to have simply disappeared."

Louise was perplexed why she hadn't heard anything about the missing pottery. "Was the pottery ever recovered?"

"I don't know. I don't think so. There were rumors that the boxes might have been mislabeled, maybe misplaced, lost, stolen. Who knows? We at the foundation were just told the case is still under investigation."

"Who's investigating the missing pottery?" Louise asked, even though she was sure it was the Feds.

"I don't know. I suspect the FBI. If you want, I'll ask around, see if there has been any resolution."

"That would be super. Thanks, Mom. I'll check out the article."

"You might want to subscribe to your local paper. Keep up with things. Be a responsible citizen."

"I'll consider it."

"Good luck with your murder." Her mother hesitated, then added, "Please be careful, sweetie."

"Love you, *Mamacita*."

Louise hung up the phone and turned toward her workstation. The ancient computer was finally up and running. She searched *The Santa Fe New Mexican* for the article on the missing pottery. Two articles popped up, one from two years ago and one three months ago. But when she clicked on the articles, she was blocked. She needed a subscription. Exasperated, she pulled out her credit card and signed up for a three-month online subscription. At least it would please her mother.

The older article described the Museum of Indian Art's collection, which represented the most complete assemblage of Indigenous New Mexico ceramics anywhere in the world. The collection provided a continuous record of sixteen hundred years of human habitation and Indigenous pottery-making in the state. The archaeological and excavated pottery collections from the Mogollon range in southwest New Mexico spanned from 400 AD to 1540 when Franciso Vásquez de Coronado led the first Spanish army into New Mexico in their unsuccessful search for the Seven Cities of Gold. The article mentioned the museum's laboratory was overcrowded, making it difficult for students and scholars to study the collection. A grant was awarded to assess and catalogue the pottery, preparing the collection for a move to a new facility, the Center for New Mexico Archaeology.

The second and more recent article, dated three months ago, was brief. It reported that thirty-nine boxes of ancient Native American pottery went missing sometime during the move from the museum to the new facility. The museum was investigating whether the boxes were mislabeled, lost, or possibly stolen.

Louise wondered if there was any connection between the missing lady friend of Pascal's father and the boxes in her pottery studio. She shook her head, realizing she was getting sidetracked and should focus on solving Madison's murder. But she needed a favor from Pascal. Reluctantly, she dialed his number.

"Ruiz."

"Hey. Emailed you two articles from *The New Mexican* you might find interesting. Thirty-nine boxes of Native American pottery disappeared during a move to a new facility. I'm sort of tied up right now with this murder case, so the ball is in your court. My mother said she thought the Feds were looking into it."

"Wow. Thanks. I appreciate it."

"Good. I need a favor."

"Name it."

"I need to identify the woman whose picture I found in Madison's trash can. Can you help me get into the Babble online dating site?"

"Why don't you put the screws to the company? Make them give the woman up."

"Both Rupert and I have tried. The site is impregnable."

"Are you sure the woman ever registered with the site?"

"Not positive, but her picture had the Babble logo at the top of the page. And Madison was a client of the dating site. Her picture was the only thing in the library, practically the only thing in the entire house. The woman has to be connected with Madison's death."

"Did you find out anything from the medical examiner?"

"Not much yet. She hasn't finished the autopsy. According to the doctor, whoever stabbed Madison would have to be strong. The knife was inserted five inches into his chest. It's strange there wasn't any sign of struggle though."

"What about forensics?"

"Still working on the prints, fibers, and toxicology. Not that I have anything or anyone to compare them to."

"I'm still looking for my dad's missing friend. He filed a missing person's report at the Española station. They weren't encouraging."

"Sorry. When I get a break, I'll see if I can find anything out about Ms. Simpson."

"Thanks, anything would help. I have to keep a low profile. Don't want to leave any footprints."

"Maybe your dad could sign up for the dating site and help me identify the woman?"

Pascal chuckled. "Right off the bat I would say no. I'll run it by him. Did you ever call and ask him about Hordes and tell him about your Jewish relics?"

"No. You're not trying to set me up with your old man, are you?" Louise asked.

"Sorry, you're out of luck. His heart lies elsewhere, Sanchez."

"This murder case—I feel like a fish out of water. I'm over my head."

"That's an oxymoron." Pascal laughed. "I still have some connections. I'll check with my guy about Albatross."

"You have a guy?"

Pascal chuckled again.

"Let me know if you hear anything from your *guy*."

"Hey, text me the picture of the mystery woman. Maybe I'll recognize her."

CHAPTER 12

Louise hung over the edge of the bed and eyed her cell phone, which had somehow fallen under the bedside table. As she bent down to pick it up, her head spun. She steadied herself on the side of the table and groaned as she looked at her screen. Three missed calls: the captain, Pascal, and forensics. How had she missed the captain's call . . . *again*? She wondered if she would be kicked off the force before clicking on his voicemail. The annoyance in his voice made her grimace. He asked her to return the call ASAP. But she checked the other voicemails and dialed Pascal on the off chance he recognized the mystery woman. If he had, she would have something to share with the captain, unruffle his feathers.

"Hey, sleeping beauty. Where have you been?" Pascal teased.

Louise couldn't muster the energy to lie. "I overslept . . ."

"Too much red wine?"

"Bingo."

Pascal laughed. "Good for you. I have to warn you, though. Take it from me, you're on a slippery slope."

"Yeah, yeah, yeah. I hear you. Talking from experience?"

"Don't you know it."

Louise was fond of Pascal. He was like a pesky little brother. It would be fun working with him, being on a team, bouncing things around. They had the same rhythm, and at times, the same disregard for protocol. They would get in so much trouble. "What's so urgent?"

"I couldn't shake the feeling that I had seen the woman from the dating site before. Had trouble sleeping last night, speaking of red wine."

Louise hated to ask God for anything—she wasn't a good Christian—but she silently prayed he had identified the woman.

"It came to me in the morning. It was two months ago, a slow time at the station, sandwiched between my two big cases, the stolen Stradivarius and the Jesus costume theft. Gillian had her heart set on attending this concert at the Lensic, but the tickets were sold out. She sulked for days. I pulled some strings and got two tickets."

Louise wondered if the strings were from a little birdie or Pascal's guy. She suppressed her impatience with the tale and asked out of politeness, "Classical concert?"

"Yeah. Highbrow stuff. Escher String Quartet and the pianist Wei Luo. Not exactly my cup of tea, but my little lady ate it up."

Louise raised her eyebrows. *Little lady? What is it with guys? They seem to be stuck in the fifties.*

"When we left the concert there was a commotion outside. A patrolman was taking a statement from a woman—the woman in the photo. Her husband, who has dementia, wandered away in the crowd after the concert. I wasn't involved in the search, but Gillian remembered the missing man's name. Harrison Pearlman."

"The financial whiz?" Louise's parents had used Pearlman at one time.

"Sanchez, you surprise me." Pascal chuckled. "Pearlman and his wife attended the concert with another couple. When they left the theater, Pearlman got separated. His wife couldn't find him so they alerted the police, who joined the search. There was no sign of Pearlman in the area, so they issued a Silver Alert."

"I take it they found him."

"Yeah, he ended up on the Rail Runner, the last train to Albuquerque that night. Tried to pay for his ticket with play money."

"Play money?" Louise's ears tingled. "Do you know how much?"

Pascal laughed. "No."

"Seriously, it's important."

"Seriously, I don't know. Anyway, a security guard on the train saw the Silver Alert and Pearlman was intercepted in Bernalillo."

"What's Pearlman's wife's name?"

"Justine."

"Justine what?" Louise felt as if she was pulling teeth.

"Pearlman? I don't know. Google it."

"Just a sec." Louise put him on speaker and googled Harrison Pearlman. Wikipedia popped up, then she opened the link and clicked the personal life tab. "It lists his wife as Justine Dupont, writer. She's written a prize-winning collection of short stories and a novel, as well as published articles in various magazines. *Atlantic Monthly* and *The New Yorker*.

"*The New Yorker*?"

Louise could feel the jealousy ooze out of Pascal. "Yeah, and she didn't take her man's name either—a liberated woman."

"It looks as if Ms. Dupont might have been involved in some extracurricular activities. Possibly murder." Pascal tittered.

"Maybe. I owe you one, bro."

"Yeah, maybe you can pull some strings at my trial."

Louise froze and her breath caught. She knew it would be in her best interest to steer clear of Pascal once he was officially charged. But if there was anything she could do, which *wouldn't* get her fired or require her to break the law, she would gladly do it. "Yeah." She forced a laugh.

"Kidding. Later, gator."

"After a while, crocodile."

Louise was elated to finally identify the mystery woman and almost danced to the kitchen. She inserted a pod into the coffee machine, checking the water level. While the coffee brewed, she dialed the station. She didn't realize she was holding her breath until Susie, the station receptionist, told her the captain was tied up in a meeting. She would let him know that Louise returned his call. Then Louise put in a call to forensics and was informed the report had been emailed to the station, but they wanted to go over a few details once she read it. She said she would get back to them later that morning.

Louise needed a shower, breakfast, and an aspirin. She didn't have time for anything but the aspirin. She grabbed a stale apple fritter from the fridge on her way out the door. The sun seemed overly bright and she dug in her bag for her sunglasses. It was one of those cloudless New Mexico days that caused you to squint and hold your hand protectively to your brow. Although it was April, there was little sign of spring yet. The past winter had been a dry one, and the mountain snow had already melted. It would provide little runoff for the summer irrigation. To make things worse, there had been little rain that spring, adding to the drought conditions. Water would be scarce. Tempers would flare.

When Louise got to the station, she retrieved the forensics report from her email. There was a rap on her door, but before she could respond, it swung open and the captain stood red-faced, agitated. Louise sucked in her breath. She had never seen him so angry. He fumed as he stomped across the room. She flinched, trying to force air into her depleted lungs. She prayed that Pascal wasn't the cause of his wrath.

"Sir?" Louise croaked.

"The commissioner . . . he put the screws to the DA. They're going to charge Ruiz. Yesterday Judge Nichols settled his current case out of court. He agreed to clear the rest of his docket until after Ruiz's trial. It will begin next week."

Louise felt as if something heavy had landed on her chest. She couldn't get enough oxygen. She knew the trial would happen eventually, but next week? She wasn't ready, didn't have time. She searched for something to say. The stacks were against Pascal, especially with the commissioner wanting him gone.

"Not that Ruiz isn't without fault in this fiasco." The captain unclenched his fists and let his hands fall to his side, his entire body sagged. "But . . . I feel responsible for his involvement."

Louise was taken aback. How could the captain be responsible? She scanned her brain, trying to think of some way to change the subject. The last thing she wanted was to be privy to something untoward that involved the captain. It would turn out badly. "Why don't you have a seat, sir?"

The captain pulled up a chair and sank down heavily. "I don't mean to involve you. You got enough on your plate." He raised his hands, palms up, and shrugged. "You're the one who brought in Ruiz. You're already involved."

"Sir, you have always made it clear that we're a team. And expected to support one another, no matter what." Louise sensed the captain wanted to unload. "What's this about?"

The captain clenched his fists again. "I asked Ruiz to look into the disappearance of my niece's boyfriend." He rubbed his hands together as if he could erase his involvement, then added almost in a whisper. "Off the record." With some effort the captain squared his shoulders and took in a deep breath and let it out slowly. "My niece was working on a TV Western out at the Diamond Tail Ranch south of Santa Fe. Her boyfriend had disappeared and she asked for my help. Ruiz agreed to look into it. Seemed happy to take a day off, get out of town. As you know Ruiz found the boyfriend on the San Felipe Reservation. Not our jurisdiction. He should have left it to the tribal police."

"But he didn't."

"No. You know all that. The boyfriend was on a cross, dressed in a Jesus costume. Ruiz suspected the costume was the one stolen from the Santa Fe Opera storage shed. The costume was his case. He became obsessed with getting it back." The captain let out a huff. "He had called that night asking for a search warrant for the film company's warehouse. It was Easter weekend and he had nothing to substantiate a warrant."

Louise shook her head, knowing where the events were going.

"So he blew up the door to the warehouse."

"He stepped over the line, sir."

"I know, but if I hadn't asked Ruiz to look for the boy, none of this would have happened."

"You didn't ask him to blow up the door to the building."

The captain chuckled and shook his head. "No, I didn't ask him to do that. Don't know what came over him."

Louise pursed her lips. She knew Pascal had a reputation for bending the rules to solve a case. But blowing up a building? That was over-the-top.

The captain shifted in his seat, the worry returned to his eyes. "You'll be asked to testify at the trial. I don't want it to turn into a witch hunt. I'm not asking you to cover up for Ruiz. Make them work for their information. Answer the questions and keep your testimony short, simple."

"Yes, sir. I understand."

"The commissioner would love to nail Ruiz to a cross, which would be ironic." The captain chuckled again. "He wants to throw him off the force, have him rot in jail. There's some bad blood between them."

Louise wondered what the source of the bad blood was, but thought best not to ask.

"I don't want the trial to interfere with your job. The murder investigation is your priority."

Louise was relieved to be back on solid ground, change the subject, focus on the murder. "I found out the identity of the woman whose picture was in the victim's trash can. Her name is Justine Dupont."

"Good. Have you interviewed her yet?"

"No. Only found out this morning." Louise prayed the captain wouldn't ask how she found out. "Forensics sent their report this morning. I'm printing it out." Louise nodded across the room toward the printer. "They want to go over a few things in the report once I've read it."

"I won't keep you." The captain took hold of the chair's arms and pushed himself up.

"Sir, have you heard anything about the Native American pottery that disappeared recently during a move to a new facility?"

The captain looked uncomfortable. "What's this about, Sanchez?"

"My mother is on the museum board. She asked me about it. The board has been kept in the dark; they haven't been told anything. I said I'd ask." Louise had a pang of guilt for stretching the truth.

"The Feds, as usual, grabbed up the case almost before the museum reported the missing boxes. Don't know how they moved in so quickly. They haven't told us anything yet, as usual. Keeping us in the dark, too. I guess the matter is still under investigation."

Louise nodded. "Thanks. I'll let my mother know."

"Keep me apprised about your progress on the murder case."

"Yes, sir." Louise sighed with relief as the captain closed the office door. After she passed along the information about the pottery to Pascal, she would still owe him a favor—but she knew she should stay clear. She headed out of the office. It was time to pay a visit to the Dupont-Pearlman residence.

CHAPTER 13

The Dupont-Pearlmans resided in an upscale neighborhood north of downtown. The houses in the area were adobe, finished with customary dark brown stucco and adhering to the Santa Fe height restrictions. But there wasn't anything typical about them. The walls shot up in various angles with massive windows that let in an abundance of light and sun, unlike traditional adobes designed to keep out the high desert heat. At least the yard, except for the tea rose bushes that bordered the front of the house, was appropriately landscaped with drought-tolerant plants.

Louise parked on the street in front of the house and made one more attempt to remove the stain from her blouse with a damp napkin. Her efforts only made it worse. She tried to tug her jacket over the stain, but the spot was smack between her heavy breasts. She would need to button the jacket all the way up to her neck, which wasn't an option.

The house had an uninhabited, empty feeling. Maybe Dupont and her husband were still asleep or not at home. The front door was painted the classic Taos blue, a color that supposedly protects households from harm. Louise thought of Pearlman, who had been a financial wizard, and knew the paint hadn't done its job. There wasn't a doorbell, only an enormous knocker, incongruously shaped like a whale. She grabbed the knocker and gave it a few sharp raps as she glanced around. The enormous front window was bare, exposed; the curtains, if there were any, were pulled back out of sight. She glanced down at the two planters with wilted pansies that sat on either side of the door. Louise wondered if the flowers were left over from winter or new spring offerings. Either way, no one had bothered to care for them. She gave the knocker three more raps and heard movement inside the house. The door opened, but not wide enough for Louise to see who was on the other side.

She pulled out her badge and held it toward the opening. "Detective Sanchez, Santa Fe Police Department. I'm looking for Justine Dupont."

The door opened a few more inches, revealing a woman, bleary-eyed, squinting in the early afternoon sun. She stared at Louise's badge as a look of confusion mixed with dread spread across her face. Her brow wrinkled. Her housecoat hung open, exposing a stained flannel nightgown with a rip at the neck, her feet bare. Louise no longer worried about the stain on her blouse.

"Are you Ms. Dupont?" Louise asked softly.

"Yes. Is this about my husband?" More lines of worry wrinkled across her forehead.

"No." Louise took in a deep breath and sighed. "Could I come in?"

"Ah . . . sorry . . . not," Justine stammered, glancing over her shoulder, "a good time."

"I need to ask you some questions."

"Questions?"

"About Webster Madison."

Justine tried not to react. It was too late. "Oh, God. We didn't mean to bother him. Harry, my husband, he needed his money back, wouldn't budge . . ." the woman rambled on as her entire body seemed to sag with exhaustion. "Harry wouldn't get out of the car, it was late, I was at my wit's end."

Louise tried to make sense of the woman's ramblings, which were becoming more and more disjointed. Her eyes darted back and forth, making Louise dizzy. "Ms. Dupont. Please, let's talk inside." Louise tilted her head toward a neighbor who was waving fervently as she made her way across the street. Justine, in a panic, ushered Louise into the foyer and slammed the door. The force of the air sent a huge mobile, hung from the vaulted ceiling, whirling around. It was reminiscent of Calder's multicolored designs. Louise wondered if it was an original.

Justine Dupont planted herself in the foyer's exit, blocking Louise's entrance into the house. The entryway was an ample size, but there was nowhere to sit. Not even a bench. An antique French farm table stacked with piles of unopened mail was pushed against the north wall. It was the second hint of dysfunction, after Dupont's appearance. Opposite the table was a floor-to-ceiling glass wall that looked out onto an enclosed patio whose central feature, the only feature, was a massive fountain with carved swans. The fountain looked forlorn, disconnected and dry.

The floor's radiant heat permeated the soles of Louise's shoes. The overheated room caused beads of sweat to gather at her hairline. Justine shoved her hands in her bathrobe and stood her ground. Louise wondered if the woman intended to keep her sequestered in the entry for the entire interview. What was Justine Dupont hiding?

"Don't you think you would be more comfortable if we sat down?" Louise said softly.

Justine glanced fleetingly around the entry, realizing there was nowhere to sit. All at once, she lost her resolve. Whatever had been holding her upright drained from her body. Justine's shoulders sagged and her neck struggled to keep her head up. Defeated, she turned and walked into the living room.

Louise followed her and muffled a gasp as she sucked in air. She clamped her mouth shut. How could someone let their house, especially one as beautifully appointed as this one, become such disarray? Maybe teenage boys left on their own, but not a grown woman, a published author. Her husband suffered from dementia, but he had been well known and respected, at least in the financial world. She hoped Pearlman's condition made him oblivious to the mess.

Justine held on to the nearest chair, a wingback, upholstered in a luxurious fabric embroidered with birds. Her lips pursed tightly as she swept her hand out in invitation for Louise to sit. Then she went over to the coffee table and with one swoop shoved the detritus off onto the plush oriental carpet. She bent down and made a half-hearted effort to make room on the sofa next to the unfolded laundry. She gave up, pulled her housecoat tight around her, sank down onto a pile of towels, and squeezed her arms protectively across her chest.

Louise wondered where Justine's husband was. Hopefully not stuck under a mountain of laundry in another room or locked in a closet. She took out her notebook and pencil, noticing the point had broken off. She rummaged in her purse for a ballpoint before meeting Justine's eyes. "What is your relationship with Webster Madison?"

Justine recoiled and gave her head a slight shake. "Relationship?"

"Yes, relationship."

"I don't have a relationship with Webster Madison."

"Do you know Mr. Madison?"

Louise watched as Justine's face lost all color.

"Know?"

"Yes, know. Is he a friend, an acquaintance, your lawyer?"

"Well, I know who he is."

Once again, Louise felt like she was pulling teeth. In the mysteries she watched on television, the interviews always went smoothly, guilty parties confessed, cases wrapped up in less than an hour. But this wasn't television. She decided to take a different approach. "Are you a client of the Babble online dating site?"

Justine didn't answer and Louise was losing her patience with this woman. "Ms. Dupont?" Louise tried to sound forceful without panicking the woman—it might not take much for her to make a run for it. Justine Dupont was definitely on the verge.

Justine looked up at Louise and started to open her mouth as Harry staggered into the room wearing pajama bottoms, nothing on top and only one sock. His hair stuck out in all directions, his face grizzled, hadn't seen a razor in days. He looked as if he climbed out of bed after a fitful night. He stared across the room at Louise, then turned to Justine.

"Harry." Justine pushed herself off the sofa. "This is Ms. . . ." She turned toward Louise in hopes she would supply her last name.

"Detective Sanchez," Louise said flatly.

Harry scratched his bare chest while Justine rummaged through the pile of laundry on the sofa and pulled out a black long-sleeve T-shirt. Harry, his arms hanging limply at his side, continued to stare at Louise. He didn't make an effort to help Justine as she struggled to get the shirt over his head. She pulled each arm through the sleeves and yanked the shirt in place. Then she took hold of Harry's arm, guided him to the couch, and pushed him down in the pile of clothes. As she bent down to put on his missing sock, Harry grabbed the remote control and turned on the TV, the sound full blast. Justine struggled for the remote and finally jerked it out of his hand, lowering the volume. Harry reached over, snatched it back, and started flipping through the channels.

"Detective," Justine implored. "As I said"—she tilted her head toward Harry—"not a good time. I need to fix my husband lunch and get him ready for a doctor's appointment this afternoon. I would be glad to answer any questions at another time. I don't have much to offer. I didn't know Mr. Madison. What is this about?"

Louise could kick herself. She had blown the interview, kaput, total disaster. That's why you bring people into the station, put them in an interrogation room and don't let them leave until you get what you want. There was no way to salvage the situation now. There would be constant interruptions. She should have told Ms. Dupont the reason she was here when she answered the door. But she hadn't.

Harry scanned through the channels, stopping on a quiet underwater scene as Louise blurted out louder than intended, "Webster Madison was found murdered Monday morning."

Justine stared at Louise, her mouth slack, and then a noise

emitted as if she had been punched in the stomach. Harry turned to another channel and found the remote's volume button, pressing it all the way. Justine bent forward, resting her hands on her face.

Louise sprung out of the chair, marched across the room, stood in front of Harry, and held out her hand. She wasn't sure he would give up the remote but if not, she wasn't about to get into a tussle. She would pull the plug. She blocked Harry's view of the TV until she got his attention. He scrunched his eyebrows, glaring at her.

"The remote, please," she demanded in her most authoritarian tone, the one she enlisted for dogs that jumped on her or sniffed her crotch.

Harry squinted menacingly and handed over the remote. She pushed the mute button. The relief was instantaneous. She stuck the remote in her pocket. She needed to get control of the situation, and she suppressed the urge to scream.

Justine lowered her hands from her face. Her eyes were glassy, but there weren't any tears. The woman looked more dazed than sad. Shock was a typical reaction to news of this sort.

"I need to ask you some questions regarding Mr. Madison, about your relationship with him."

Justine nodded.

"When was the last time you saw Mr. Madison?"

"I was with my husband at the Twisted Pines, the bar at the mall, Sunday night and saw him there."

"That was the last time?"

"Yes." Justine sighed. "Harry had given Webster some play money at the bar ... he wouldn't get out of the car ... I was desperate ... drove to his house ... nobody was home."

"We can continue the interview in the morning. Can someone look after your husband for a few hours?"

Justine gave a slight nod.

Louise took out her card. "Call me once you have made arrangements." There was no way Louise wanted to come back to this house—far too depressing. She got up to leave and turned to Justine. "We don't have to meet at the station. Maybe a café." The woman closed her eyes and made an audible sigh of relief.

Louise slid behind the wheel of her cruiser as a sense of ennui came over her. She leaned her head back against the vinyl seat and closed her eyes. Pearlman's dementia had ended his career and put his wife's life on hold. Louise couldn't imagine Justine Dupont plunging a butcher knife into Webster Madison. The woman didn't have the strength or the resolve, although she admitted going to Madison's house the night he was murdered. Louise opened her eyes and looked across the street. The neighbor, the one who had waved at them earlier, stood in front of her picture window, hands on her hips.

Louise closed her eyes again. She thought of Pascal, his trial next week, and a twinge of uneasiness prickled her spine. Was she about to traverse a similar slippery slope, in danger of hitting a mogul, wiping out, ending her career on a bad note? She had broken protocol again. But she couldn't stand the thought of dragging Dupont into the station, putting her in a cramped interrogation room, having her sit on a filthy orange plastic chair, leaving her to stare at the punched and graffitied walls and subjecting her to the lingering smell of fear. She couldn't do that to the woman.

She looked at her phone and groaned. Two missed calls, the captain and Pascal. "Damn, damn, damn," she cursed, banging her palm on the dashboard. How did she miss the captain's call again? His message was brisk, and his annoyance was evident. She knew his number one rule: Answer your phone. She was relieved he hadn't asked her to return his call. He left the telephone number for Brady Nelson, the precinct's sketch artist. Nelson would be able to draw a picture of the 911 caller from the train depot attendant's description. The 911 caller was the top suspect in the case.

She listened to Ruiz's message asking her to return his call. She was grateful for his help with the case, but she knew she should steer clear with his trial on Monday. Any time now she would be deposed and expected to testify against him.

The neighbor across the street was still glaring out her front window. Louise needed to get a move on, drive away before the woman either came out of the house and confronted her or made a report to the police. As a beat cop, Louise had followed up on neighbors' reports on suspicious activity. Nine times out of ten they turned out to be nothing. Someone waiting for her mother to finish drying her hair, or who pulled over to take a call. She drove away and resisted the urge to stick out her tongue at the neighbor.

CHAPTER 14

When the detective closed the front door, a sense of relief flowed over Justine. She pressed her eye to the peephole, which the prior owners of the house had installed in the massive oak door. It had a high-end optical glass lens with a 220-degree visual angle, offering extremely wide coverage with fishbowl distortion but only a head-to-toe view of anyone standing on the porch. It was useless to capture anything farther away.

Justine went to the living room, leaned toward the picture window, and peeked out. She sucked in her breath and flattened herself against the wall, trying to slow her heart that pounded in her chest. The detective was still parked out front. Possible scenarios whirled through her head and made her sway off balance. What was the detective waiting for? Why hadn't she driven away? Did she have car trouble? Was she calling for backup? Would she be arrested? What would happen to Harry? How did she get herself in such a predicament?

Justine moaned. It was her sister's fault. She was the one who had suggested Justine write an online dating article. She knew she shouldn't get personally involved; her sister had warned her, but she didn't listen. Her sister always said, "Life is a roller coaster—it has its ups and downs." Her life now had been reduced to an analogy, and not a good one. The roller coaster was definitely going down.

She chastised herself for not answering the detective's questions. Be done with it. Justine leaned her head against the wall and gently banged it three times in an attempt to knock some sense into her brain. Sweat trickled down her face. All she wanted to do was crumple to the floor and curl up in a fetal position. She was a prisoner in her own house, in her own life.

She tried to wipe the image of Webster Madison dead, murdered. She wanted to remember him alive, smiling with a flawless row of white teeth, perfect probably from birth, and his immaculately coiffed black hair with a touch of curl dusting his forehead. She remembered his necklace at the bar, the same one he had worn at the restaurant, the Aries zodiac symbol. The golden ram's emerald eyes glowed seductively in the bar's subdued light. It had caused her to wobble unsteadily on her stool.

The TV was muted, the room silent and vacant, as if all life had been sucked out. "Harry?" she called out frantically as she made her way through the house. She found her husband in the kitchen. He was leaning against the counter, a half-eaten bag of cookies in his hand, crumbs stuck in the stubble of his unshaven face. She took the cookies away and shot him a *bad boy* look as she roughed up his hair. His face, blank and expressionless, stared back at her, but she detected something in his eyes. Was it caution, cunning, suspicion? She couldn't tell anymore. Each day her husband became more of a mystery.

She guided Harry over to the kitchen table and made him a sandwich. "Be right back, honey."

She didn't expect a reply, but she hesitated in the doorway until he picked up his sandwich and started eating. Then she went through each room of the house, checking the latches on the windows. She should have been relieved there was no sign of entry, but she wasn't. Nothing out of place, but how would she be able to tell? The alarm system had been disarmed months ago after the fourth time Harry had set it off. The police were sympathetic, but their hands were tied. It was the law. Neighbors complained about alarms blasting for no reason. The next time it happened they would be cited and fined.

Justine felt enervated. She wanted to pull the covers over her head and sleep. The editor from *Senior Living* had called three times last week to inquire about the status of the article. His first call had been tactful, the next expectant, and finally the last confrontational. He could no longer disguise his annoyance—he had deadlines, certainly she understood the way the publishing world worked. She had missed her deadline, and the article still needed some refinement. In light of Webster's death, how could she continue? Somehow, she felt responsible.

For years writing, the actual physical act of putting words down on paper or typing on the computer, had been who she was. When her words stopped, her psyche shriveled, she was reduced to nothing. The online dating article, no Pulitzer Prize–winning piece, somehow had begun to heal her. As the keys on her laptop clicked away, forming paragraph after paragraph, a tiny piece of her came back to life. Justine's shoulders sagged, her arms hung limply at her side as she scanned her living room. *Bedlam*, *chaos*, *pandemonium* were words that popped into her head like cartoon bubbles. She wondered how her house had become so disheveled. Her life was like a river slowly rising outside the door, the banks ready to overflow and suck everything downstream.

Justine glanced at the wingback chair in the corner of the room. When Harry's mind started to deteriorate, her sister suggested reupholstering the chair. She replaced the worn and dreary Southwestern pattern with a designer fabric called "Alma Silhouette." For a while the dreamy, blurred, colorless design had lifted Justine's spirits, but recently it reminded her how everything was slipping away. Definition, focus, clarity.

She eyed the laundry basket on the couch, clothes piled high, neglected, unfolded. Harry came into the room, half his sandwich in hand, and plopped on the sofa. He nestled among the load of clothes she had pulled from the dryer that morning, searching for a clean pair of undies. He stretched forward toward the TV, shifting his head from side to side as he tried to look around the vacuum cleaner parked between him and the screen. The coffee table was amassed with unread newspapers, magazines, flyers, dirty dishes from last night's supper (or maybe the night before), empty fast-food containers, a six-pack of cola unopened, room temperature.

A sudden sadness made her knees weak as she stared down at the vintage maple wood floor, once nourished with rich oils and burnished to a high shine, now worn down to the raw and scarred, faded gray in places. Dust bunnies mounted in every corner and grew larger every day. She knew it would have to end; she would need to pull herself together, straighten up before the home health aide returned. The aide had been called away to tend to her aging mother, who had slipped and broken her hip. Justine had implored the agency not to send a replacement, insisting the adjustment to a new person would be disruptive for Harry's fragile state, even though she knew it was her who would be bothered, not Harry. The agency wasn't happy about it, but they eventually conceded.

She looked over at the dining table—rarely used, not even for holidays. Not for Thanksgiving, not for Christmas dinner. The last thing she remembered on the table was their son's Monopoly set. Her heart sank as she thought of Leo. Even before she and Harry married, they had decided not to have children. They both had careers and couldn't fathom having the time to raise and care for a child. At forty-two she found herself pregnant. They vacillated whether to keep the baby until it was too late.

Leo was an intense child and from an early age tried to engage his parents. On Leo's sixth birthday, he received a Monopoly game. It became a battleground. He would set up the game in hopes of snagging his mother's attention. The race car was his token, and he would push it around the board making car noises until Justine thought she would tear her hair out. Finally, to quiet him, she agreed to play a short game. Leo handed her the iron, which she took as an insult. She set the kitchen timer in the middle of the board and played for the allotted thirty minutes. When the timer went off, he begged for more time, but she ignored his pleas. So Leo played by himself, moving from one side of the table to the other, stockpiling money, purchasing real estate, and amassing houses and hotels. Once Leo was tucked into bed at night, Justine couldn't resist checking out the game. She didn't own any properties, her cash was low, and she often found the iron sequestered in jail.

A week before Christmas, Justine had looked in the coat closet for gloves and a scarf and spotted the Monopoly game. Tears welled in her eyes, and a terrible sound escaped from somewhere deep inside her. Leo must have finally given up and stuffed the game back in the closet. She hadn't even noticed it was gone. She pulled the box down, set it up on the dining table, and played as Leo had, moving the race car and then the iron around the board. Then Harry took notice and started taking the money, slipping the bills into his wallet. Next he took the houses and made winding trains around every available surface. Finally, she gathered up what she could find of the game and put it back under the winter scarves and gloves.

Justine made her way to the sofa, careful not to trip over the train tracks that circled the television set. That's all she needed—take a fall, break a hip, end up in the hospital. Each time she met one of Harry's needs, there came another. Her husband was good-natured and not demanding, but he needed help with everything. Her life had become one interruption after another.

Harry turned the sound back on the TV, which had stopped on an infomercial channel where a charismatic saleswoman hawked tacky jewelry sets. The woman on the screen instantly captivated Harry's attention. Her low-cut dress displayed an ample bosom that bulged out seductively. Her bleached-blond bouffant hairdo was plastered with spray, not a strand out of place, her eyelashes thick with mascara. Justine wondered how the woman kept her lids open. Harry, with all his lost memories, still had an eye for the ladies.

Justine caught her own image in the gilded starburst mirror that hung on the opposite wall and sucked in her breath. She saw a tangled mess of gray hair, no makeup, dressed in the same food-stained sweatshirt she had worn for the last three days. Nausea churned in her stomach as she made her way to the bathroom. Her reflection, close up in the medicine cabinet mirror, was crueler, revealing wrinkles around her puffy eyes and sags below her chin. How had she gotten so old, so unkempt?

As Justine came back into the living room, Harry was attempting to open one of the soda cans, his face twisted with frustration. She took in his appearance, which wasn't much better than hers. His salt-and pepper hair, past due for a cut, stuck out in unruly spirals. It curled around his ears unattractively and hung down halfway over his eyes. His shirt was already stained. They were quite a pair. Finally the pop-top sprung open and Coke spurted on Harry, soaking the unopened mail on the coffee table. She grabbed a towel out of the laundry basket and half-heartedly dabbed at the mess.

She dialed her sister. Thankfully she didn't pick up, and Justine left a message saying she needed her to watch Harry in the morning. She would drop him off at nine. She considered tacking on a lie, a meeting with the editor or a doctor's appointment she had forgotten about. She decided to provide no explanation. The less said the better.

CHAPTER 15

The next morning as Louise left her condo, her mother's voice echoed in her head. "Too many balls to keep in the air, missy. One has to drop. What you need is a Do List." It was weird how her mother pronounced *a*—short, like "ah." Every time Louise thought about her mother's Do List, she thought of Shakespeare's farce, *Much Ado About Nothing.* She loved the play and watched the film adaptation whenever she needed a laugh. Her first introduction to the Bard had been in high school, but it wasn't until college that she appreciated Shakespeare's humor, or the word "nothing" itself, which is a double entendre. An "O-thing" or "nothing" was Elizabethan slang for "vagina," derived from the pun of a woman having "nothing" between her legs. Louise chuckled, wondering if Shakespeare was aware of the pun and if its application was intentional.

She drove the short distance to the medical examiner's office and tried to expunge the thought of "O-thing" out of her head. She forced herself to consider the case, the facts, the missing links. All she had was a dead body and a young unidentified woman who reported the murder. As she rode the elevator to the fourth floor, she hoped the good doctor had discovered something useful during the examination of Webster Madison.

Dr. Elena Maithe sat in a tiny windowless office tucked in a corner at the end of the hallway. Her chair was crammed up against the back wall. The room wasn't much more than a closet, barely accommodating her desk. File folders were scattered over every available surface. Her computer monitor flickered in the dim light as the doctor leaned close to the screen, pecking at the keyboard with two fingers. Louise stood outside the doorway and observed the woman before clearing her throat. The doctor stopped typing and looked over her reading glasses that had slid down her nose, in danger of falling off. Louise resisted the urge to walk over and push them back up.

"Detective." The doctor removed her glasses and leaned back in her chair. "Have you found someone to identify the body?"

"The body?"

The doctor raised her eyebrows. "Webster Madison. Have you forgotten him already?"

Louise wasn't sure how to respond.

"We need an official identification before we can release the body. Someone, preferably a relative, needs to say yeah or nay."

"No. I haven't found anyone." Louise sensed the doctor's immediate disappointment. Again, it was evident that Louise was unprepared for this job. Of course someone needed to identify the body. Even in television mysteries, after someone died, they brought in a distraught relative or friend for identification. She hadn't considered that it was her responsibility. "As far as we know, Madison doesn't have any living relatives, but I interviewed a woman who knew him." Louise realized this was a stretch. Lautrec had dated the man in college and she hadn't seen him in years until a brief encounter a few weeks ago. "I can see if she would identify the body."

"The sooner the better."

"How's the report coming?"

"I'm about finished with the write-up. If you have the time I can go over it with you now."

"That would be great," Louise chirped, trying unsuccessfully to suppress a smile.

The doctor stood and turned sideways in order to maneuver

around her desk. "Thank God I don't have to spend much time in this shithole. They keep promising me a bigger space but . . ." She huffed.

Louise wasn't prudish, but she was taken aback at the doctor's profanity. She imagined working with the dead must mute one's filters. As she followed the doctor down the hall to the elevator, the woman's white coat swung suggestively, making Louise feel off-balance. The elevator doors closed and the two stood side by side in silence as they descended into the clammy air below. When the doors opened, an overwhelming stench of chemicals stung Louise's eyes, causing them to water. Even the cinder block walls seemed to ooze the acrid smell. The place gave Louise the creeps. She had never been in an autopsy room and tried not to think of the room's purpose, dissecting bodies. She had visited the hospital morgue a few times. It was only a cavernous walk-in refrigerator filled with bodies laid out on sheet-covered stretchers, waiting to be claimed. As the doctor punched in numbers on the keypad and pushed open the door, Louise realized she was holding her breath and let it out in a huff.

The doctor stretched out her arm in invitation. "After you, Detective."

Louise suspected the woman was enjoying herself. A live body. After all, the doctor spent most of her days with the dead, cutting them up, examining their parts and innards. She tried to erase the thought, but it made her stomach lurch and her mouth go dry. Some of her initial attraction to the doctor started to slip away, which was just as well.

In contrast to Dr. Maithe's cramped office upstairs, the autopsy room was spacious, vast. Room enough to host a dance party. The only pieces of furniture were two white tables resting on black pedestal bases. They were arranged side by side near the back of the room. A series of lockers covered one wall, and Louise did her best not to think of their contents. The other wall was taken up by several cabinets. Otherwise, the room was empty except for the gurney, the elephant in the room. It sat in the middle, draped with a white sheet.

Louise knew it covered Madison's autopsied body. Above the gurney various apparatuses, which looked similar to dental equipment for a giant, hung from the ceiling on pulleys. Louise didn't want to think about the equipment or its use either. Everything was clean, sanitized, sterile. They were in the basement, below ground. Louise noticed what looked like a window on the far wall, but upon closer inspection it was an illusion, just a mirror.

Dr. Maithe strode over to the gurney, motioning with her head for Louise to follow. She ceremoniously pulled down the sheet and Louise half expected her to blurt out, "Ta-Da!" She had to fight not to make a noise as she sucked in her breath. Thankfully Madison's cobalt blue eyes remained closed. Even with his skin losing all pigment, the man somehow kept his good looks. She wondered what he had done to be killed, stabbed in the heart and left for dead.

As if the doctor had read Louise's mind, she offered wistfully, "Yes, he is gorgeous, isn't he? Wish I could say it was a pleasure to work on him."

Louise shivered and tried to steer the doctor back to the task at hand. "What about the pathology report?"

"Oh, yes. Our man here had ingested some interesting stuff. Probably why someone was able to stab him without much of a struggle. I performed a preliminary toxicology. Needed to send it to the lab for more inclusive information."

Louise, relieved, looked away from the body, giving the doctor her full attention. "What did you find?"

"Can't be one hundred percent sure. I suspect Rohypnol. On the street it's called Roofies, Rope, Pinga. It's one of the preferred date-rape drugs."

"Date-rape?" Louise admitted that Madison was good-looking but couldn't fathom someone using drugs to have their way with him.

"It's basically a tranquilizer, similar to valium. Tasteless, colorless, easily dissolved in a drink. Sedation occurs rapidly, within thirty minutes, and has a range of effects: slurred speech, incoordination, amnesia. If mixed with alcohol it can be serious, lead to respiratory depression, aspiration, death."

"Alcohol?"

"Yeppers." The doctor made a *tsk-tsk* sound with her mouth. "Our boy reeked of bourbon and wine." The doctor looked down at Madison. "Strange."

"Strange?"

"Are you going to repeat everything I say?" the doctor said as she narrowed her eyes.

"Sorry. New at this."

Dr. Maithe pressed her lips together and seemed to consider something. "I'll point you in the right direction, make a few suggestions. It's my job. I'm on your team, Detective." The doctor winked at her.

Louise managed to mumble, "Thanks." She wondered if the doctor was flirting with her, or maybe the woman had Tourette's syndrome. Before she could stop herself, her eyes moved to the doctor's left hand. No ring.

"I'd check out Madison's liquor cabinet. Forensics took the wine glass for prints. Make sure they sent it along to the lab. You'll need to know if there was something in the wine. If not, and if there's no bourbon in the house, the man probably had a drink somewhere else that night. Good luck with that."

Louise took out her notebook and scribbled down some things to follow up on. She would add them to her Ado List later. She thought of Shakespeare and, again, the "nothing" clouded her mind. She needed to rename her list, something less suggestive.

The doctor turned her attention back to Madison. She pulled the sheet down to the man's waist, exposing his perfectly muscled chest. Wisps of dark curls sprung out between his nipples. Besides the four-inch incision on the left side of his chest, right above his heart, the man's body was flawless. His pectorals, well developed, indicated regular workouts. He looked to be in excellent physical condition except for the pallid hue of his skin that lacked any signs of life. Louise may not be attracted to men, but still it was a shame to lose such a perfect specimen of the male species.

The doctor pointed to the incision on the chest. "You were correct, Detective. Stabbed in the heart. The heart has four valves that ensure the blood only flows in one direction. The aortic valve is between the left ventricle and the aorta." The doctor pointed toward the incision again. "The knife severed his aorta. He bled to death internally. Simple, straightforward. There are no signs of a struggle or other injuries. It's unlikely he would have stood still and let someone stab him in the heart. Someone drugged him, put it in his wine, bourbon, or Coca-Cola. That amount of drug in his system either totally disarmed him, rendering him unable to put up a fight, or he passed out and then was stabbed."

"Anything else?" Louise asked.

The doctor sighed as she pulled the sheet up over Madison's face. "As I mentioned, I need someone to make an official identification. Bring the woman in tomorrow morning, around nine?" She turned to Louise. "Oh, and I'll need instructions for the body."

"The body?"

"Please. Don't start repeating everything I say." The doctor scrunched her eyebrows in irritation.

Louise stared at the doctor's perfectly shaped brows, noticing how they were almost half circles and a shade darker than her light brown hair. The doctor was a woman who made an effort. "Sorry," Louise said. She knew repeating was a bad habit, but she had never been a brilliant conversationalist. Pictures were her mode of expression. She found repeating a useful technique that provided time to process and respond, even though she was aware it annoyed most people, even herself.

Dr. Maithe walked Louise to the elevator, her lab coat brushing against Louise. As the elevator door opened, the doctor placed her hand lightly on Louise's shoulder and gave it a squeeze. The warmth of her palm radiated through Louise's body. The doctor leaned forward, her breath tickling Louise's ear. "Forensics, third floor." Louise felt a slight twinge in her abdomen and couldn't bring herself to meet the medical examiner's eyes.

CHAPTER 16

The elevator door opened on the third floor and Louise jumped out, thankful to leave the chemical fumes in the basement below. The forensic department's reception area was anything but welcoming. The room, a neutral zone without definition, was entirely beige—the carpet, the walls, the blinds. Even the chipped Formica-topped desk was beige except for its gray metal legs. The table was similar to ones found in institutions or schools in less prosperous neighborhoods. A desk sat in the middle of the room, unmanned or unwomaned. The only item on the desk was an intercom with an instructional placard. Louise didn't bother with the instructions; she pushed the button and waited.

After a moment static crinkled through the intercom, followed by an exasperated voice. "Yes?"

"Detective Sanchez."

"Yes?"

"I need to follow up on the results for the Webster Madison murder."

"Yes."

Louise willed herself not to scream. "Yes."

"Enter." A door behind the desk buzzed and Louise scrambled over. She couldn't bear to ask the woman to buzz it open again.

An elderly woman stood with her back to Louise, inserting folders into slots along the wall. The woman's gray-blue permed ringlets clung to her head like a helmet. She was clothed in the fashion certain-aged women insisted on dressing. Her tweed pleated skirt hung on her bony body below her knees. Her skirt most likely covered rolled-up hose, grandmother style. Her black pumps were scuffed and had seen better days, or better care. Louise was sure the woman was the same person who had buzzed her in, but when she turned around, she appeared startled to find someone in the room.

"Detective?"

Louise heard the irritation in the woman's voice. *Duh*, she thought, but simply replied, "Yes."

The woman walked over to the desk and flipped through a stack of files. "Hmm, Madison, Madison," she mumbled under her breath, sounding as if the name had a bad taste. Finally, she pulled out an envelope. "Ah. Here it is." A smug expression crossed her face, as though she was pleased with herself.

Louise kept herself from snatching the file out the woman's hand. "I need to talk to someone about the results."

The woman raised her eyebrows and pursed her lips.

"Forensics left me a message. They wanted to discuss something in the findings—in person."

The woman sat down at her desk, pulled her phone up close to her, and punched a button. "Detective . . ." She looked up at Louise, pursing her lips.

"Detective Sanchez."

"Detective Sanchez. She says"—the woman squinted suspiciously at Louise—"you need to discuss the Madison case . . . in person."

A look of disappointment clouded the woman's face as she set the phone back in the cradle. Louise felt a pang of pity for the woman as she rose from her chair with an air of submission.

"This way." She opened the door without meeting Louise's gaze.

Johnson, who had been at Madison's house with her that first day, stood in the doorway and beamed at the woman, giving her a wink. "Thank you, Mrs. Anderson."

After the woman left, Louise tilted her head toward the door. "Great security."

Johnson chuckled. "Got to safeguard our evidence. Mrs. Anderson has worked here for years. She's efficient and takes her job seriously, maybe a little too seriously."

Louise had a different opinion but kept it to herself. "I read the report, seemed straightforward. What did you want to discuss?"

"The wine glass. We didn't detect anything other than wine. We're sure it was a Napa Valley chardonnay, Far Niente most likely. We couldn't pinpoint the exact year, could be a 2016 or 2017. It was strange because we didn't find a bottle of chardonnay or any bottles of wine in his house."

Louise couldn't tell if Johnson was joking about the wine, but he was a strange duck. "Any liquor? Bourbon?"

"Nope."

"Great. The medical examiner says Madison was poisoned with a date-rape drug. He reeked of bourbon, so if nothing was in the wine, he must have ingested the drug somewhere else."

"Yeah, good luck with that. Maybe the killer took the glass . . . or could have been at a bar, someone's house, his office."

"Well, we can rule out his office because he didn't have one. What about prints?"

"No prints on the knife handle, but the same sets were on the door handle and the wine glass. Madison's prints are everywhere around the house. The play money had several prints: Madison's, yours. We checked your file." Johnson grinned. "The other set probably belongs to whoever gave him the money."

"Anything else?"

"That's about it for now. We've sent the glass to toxicology for confirmation. If you have any questions"—he pulled out a card and handed it to her—"here's my direct line." He winked at Louise.

Louise flashed him a smile and turned to leave. Then she remembered the missing Native American pottery. "I was wondering if you've heard anything about stolen or missing Native American pottery?"

Johnson laughed. "New case?"

"Personal."

"Always is."

"A friend's friend has gone missing."

"And what does this have to do with tea in China?"

"Might be connected."

Johnson hesitated. "A few months ago we got a call from the Museum of Indian Arts. The laboratory had shipped their entire collection of pottery to a new facility. But after the move, thirty-nine boxes were unaccounted for. The museum wasn't sure what happened. They called us, but when we arrived at the new center the Feds were all over the place. They said it was their case, we weren't needed." Johnson puffed out his lips in a pout. "Hurt my feelings."

Louise chuckled. "The Feds have a way of doing that. Thanks for the info." That confirmed the information her mother had provided, but as she left the building, she still had more questions than answers.

CHAPTER 17

Pascal gave up on sleeping. He had tossed and turned for the last couple hours, lying on one side and then the other. Even tried his back. No matter the position, it was useless. He looked over at Gillian, motionless and inert. She slept peacefully, one leg out of the covers. For a moment he worried she might have stopped breathing, and in a panic he licked his finger and held it under her nostrils. She twitched, turned over, and pulled her leg under the covers. He was relieved he hadn't woken her. Still, he was jealous she could sleep so soundly. He gave up and slipped out of bed.

The room was so bright, glowing as if it was midday. He stared out the enormous, curtainless window at the full moon illuminating the blue-black sky as it made its way west. He went to the kitchen and put on the kettle. He was groggy but edgy. He paced around the room, anxious for the pot to whistle. Gillian preferred her mother's single-serve coffee maker, proclaiming, "No fuss, no muss." But he prided himself as a French press man. Finally the kettle whistled and he poured the water in the press, stirred the grounds, and checked his watch. As he waited for the coffee to steep, he thought of Katrin Simpson, his father's missing lady friend. His aunt had given him her contact information in Denver, but the calls had all gone to voicemail. He hadn't been able to track down information on the missing pottery. The boxes in the Abiquiu studio taunted him. He couldn't afford to be caught trespassing, much less leading another break-in—it would add fuel to his trial's fire. He would get time for sure.

He paced around the house, and with each sip of coffee he realized sleep was out of the question. He needed to do something and decided to drive around, clear his head, be back home before Gillian woke. Last night, Gillian had talked about her latest idea, opening her mother's art gallery. He'd promised he would help her today, inventory the artwork, sort the paperwork, go through the books. He knew she thought it would provide a distraction while he waited for his trial, but that was the last thing he wanted to spend time doing. He wasn't interested in art or the gallery. He needed to help his father, not to mention figure out his future, think about his options, get his life together. If he didn't go to jail, he would at least lose his job, and he needed one. He didn't want to be a kept man, even by Gillian, whom he liked, maybe even started to love. He thought, not for the first time, that it might not have been a good idea moving in with her so soon after beginning a relationship.

Even as he headed toward Española, he convinced himself he was only taking a drive, clearing his head. The hum of the engine and the tires licking the highway settled him as he made his way north. He briefly considered checking on his father but kept going. When he crossed the river, he knew where he was going, and what he was going to do. He hoped it wouldn't get him in more trouble.

As he neared Abiquiu, the moon bounced off the red- and sand-colored cliffs. The sky, now almost a daytime blue, was speckled with white stars. He turned off the highway onto the dirt road that led to where Katrin Simpson had lived. As he mounted the hill, he overshot the driveway and had to back up. There was something about the place that looked different. He couldn't put his finger on it. Maybe it was the way the moonlight danced around, illuminating the clumps of dried rabbit bush and strands of buffalo grass that had forced their way through the caliche. He shook off the eerie feeling that crept up his spine, figuring it was due to lack of sleep. He carefully made his way to the back of the house. The absolute silence unnerved him. Even in a small city like Santa Fe there was always a drone of background sounds, night and day. He made his way down the path, careful not to slip on the pea gravel, taking in deep breaths of the ice cold air to slow his racing heart. He was playing with fire. Trespassing.

The studio's front door was still secured with bolts, and the video-surveillance camera blinked a red warning. He stayed clear as he made his way to the side of the building. He cupped his hands against the closest window. It was after five and the moon had started to sink toward the horizon. It wasn't much help illuminating the inside of the studio. But as his eyes adjusted to the dim light, he saw the boxes were still there, taking up most of the floor. The two Maria pots sat on the back table. He counted the boxes. Thirty-nine. Then made his way to the other window and counted again. Thirty-nine. Then he counted one more time to make sure. Thirty-nine boxes. It could be a coincidence.

As he started back to Santa Fe, he wondered what to do about the boxes. If they did contain the stolen pottery, he hoped Katrin Simpson wasn't involved. His father liked her, and he would be crushed. He couldn't involve Louise. She had her hands full with the murder case, and murder trumped everything. Every other crime, even stolen antiquities, became inconsequential—or at least put on hold—in light of murder.

He checked his watch. A quarter to six. Gillian had teased him relentlessly about wearing a watch, saying nobody wears one these days. They use their cell phones. But he loved his Gumeti pilot watch, with its automatic movement. He excused the fact that it lost a few minutes periodically and relished that you never had to wind or change a battery. It was waterproof to a thousand feet, but there wasn't much use for that in New Mexico. What he loved best was how the watch looked on his wrist. As he drove east, the last bits of moonlight illuminated the changing landscape.

As he crossed the river his phone rang. "Morning, sunshine."

"Where are you? Is everything all right?" Gillian sounded more irritated than worried.

"Couldn't sleep. Took a drive to clear my head."

"Yeah?"

"Yeah."

"You still on for the gallery today?" she asked crossly.

"Sure. Heading home."

"I'm going for a run. When I get back, I want to get started right away. I'm psyched."

"See you soon." Pascal disconnected.

The thirty-nine boxes in the studio niggled him. There were too many coincidences. A subsidiary of Albatross owned the Abiquiu property. A coincidence? Maybe. But he knew that Albatross was a shell company under investigation for money laundering. Pascal had done some research on stolen antiquities a few years ago for a novel he was working on but never finished. He discovered the ownership and provenance of art objects and antiquities bought and sold were cloaked in secrecy. Nobody, neither buyers nor sellers, wanted to be named. Certain collectors willingly paid extraordinary prices in cash for art, even if the works were suspected stolen. The situation created an ideal opportunity for criminals in need of ways to launder money. Recently, he had read an article about the archaeological advocacy organization, the Antiquities Coalition. The Coalition has strong political connections and lots of money to support their lobbying efforts. But even though they have pressured Congress for legislation to prevent private collecting in the trade, so far they have been unsuccessful.

Pascal made his way through Española and felt a slight pang of guilt as he drove past the road leading to his father's house. But he had promised Gillian he would be home soon to help with the gallery. He rationalized that his father was probably still asleep. He would check in with him later in the day.

Gillian insisted on walking to the gallery since parking in Santa

Fe was always a challenge. She skipped along the sidewalk, giddy with her new venture. The gallery sat on a side street, a few blocks from the plaza, a prime location. But the building looked a little run down. It could use a new coat of stucco and some fresh trim paint. As Gillian inserted the key in the door, an alarm buzzed loudly, making them take a step back. Gillian dug in her purse for the alarm code and punched in the numbers. Pascal sighed, exhaling the air he had been holding. Even though Gillian owned the gallery, or would if she ever finished probating her mother's will, Pascal didn't want to explain the situation to a pair of suits when they showed up. At the least, they would recognize him, have a good laugh—and spread the story around the station.

The gallery was long and narrow with high ceilings, well suited for displaying artwork. The red oak floors had seen better days, but the rich wood softened the stark white walls. Pascal gave Gillian a close-lipped smile and asked, "Where do you want to start?"

She pointed to the two doors at the far side of the room. "There's a storage room and an office off the gallery space. Let's check out the storage room first."

Pascal dutifully followed Gillian. The storage room had the musty smell of disuse mixed with turpentine and paint. There were seven paintings stacked along two walls. At the far end of the room, below a small, barred window, was an enormous flat file to store prints and photographs.

Gillian, looking officious, took out a notebook and pen. "Let's catalogue the paintings first. Each should have the size on the back but if not . . ." She smiled and held out a tape measure.

Pascal rattled off the information taped to the back of each piece of artwork: name, media, size, date, and artist. As he maneuvered the last painting out from the wall, he sucked in his breath. It was a large, sixty-two-by-eighty-four-inch abstract oil painting with vivid background colors, slashes of black, and thick, glossy brushstrokes that looked angry. He recognized the painting. It was one of

Madeline's. His face flushed hot, as he remembered their drive back to Truchas after her art opening in Taos. Madeline's old station wagon had broken down somewhere on the High Road, and they had smoked a few joints and drank a third of a bottle of Jameson. Madeline suggested they strip off their clothes, easier to stay warm skin to skin—and he had to admit, she had been right. As he held the painting, he hoped his flushed face wouldn't give him away.

Gillian raised her eyebrows with her pen, ready to record.

Pascal, still thinking about Madeline, stared at the painting.

"Pascal," Gillian said exasperated. "What's the matter?"

He maneuvered the painting around so he could read the back. *Dark Day at Sunset*, 2014, *62 x 84 inches, oil on canvas.*

Gillian raised her eyebrows. "Artist?"

"Madeline Cody."

"Your old girlfriend, the one you suspected of stealing Mischa's violin?"

He nodded. What more could he say?

"Well, that has to go. It's . . ." Gillian racked her brain to describe what she thought of the painting. "It's horrible."

Pascal nodded. He had to agree. The painting was horrible. It had been in the Taos show and was the only one that hadn't sold. Madeline had brought it home and offered it to him, but it was too big for his little adobe, and besides, it was too ugly. It scared the hell out of him. Last he knew of the painting, Madeline had stashed it in her garage in Truchas.

Gillian narrowed her eyes. "Let's check out the flat file."

Pascal inched the painting back over against the wall. He wondered what Gillian intended to do with the painting but hoped it didn't involve him. He was still trying to shake Madeline out of his head. The last time he had seen her, she had made a fool of him. He had suspected she was involved in the violin heist and had asked her to come to the station for an interview. She had shown up with her attorney, Brian Netsworthy, his high school nemesis. The interview was a disaster.

Pascal had neglected to ask if she had an alibi before bringing her in. She had a solid one, had been in Denver at her art retrospective.

The first three drawers of the flat file were empty except for a few pieces of mat board and tissue paper meant to separate artwork. The fourth drawer contained two black-and-white photographs. Gillian, careful not to touch the front of the photographs, held on to the edges as she pulled them out. She set them on top of the file. One, taken at White Sands, looked like an abstract painting. The other one depicted a large stand of young bare-leaf aspen trees, bunched together naked in winter, in front of a dark, ominous mound of a mountain. Gillian scribbled down the name of each print and edition number. She worked her eyes over to the right for the photographer's signature. "Oh, wow. I can't believe it. These are Louise's photographs."

"Louise Sanchez?"

"Yes." She beamed over at Pascal. "Aren't they beautiful? She captured the ambience of New Mexico."

"The ambience?" Pascal chuckled, thankful for the distraction. He didn't want to think about Madeline or her ghastly painting. It made his heart ache and his stomach gurgle.

Gillian looked mischievous. "I have an idea."

"Yeah?"

"I'll tell you later." She shrugged. "Need to work it out."

Pascal hated when Gillian did that, put him off. He wished she wouldn't mention something if she didn't want to talk about it right then. The irritation was irrational, and he wondered if it was because of Madeline.

"We have to tackle the office."

Pascal tried not to groan, but one slipped out and disappointment spread over Gillian's face. He needed to buck up, support her project, be her guy. He rubbed his hands together with a lopsided grin. "Let's get to it, sunshine."

The office was a mess. Papers everywhere, nothing organized, nothing filed. It reminded him of his office at the station—or what used to be his office. Pascal figured it was payback time. What goes around, comes around. They worked in silence separating the paperwork into piles. *Bills, invoices, letters, miscellaneous* until their eyes burned and their stomachs growled with hunger.

Gillian found an accordion file in one of the desk drawers and stuffed the separated piles into the sleeves. "We can work on this at home, on the couch with a glass of wine." She glanced around the office, pressed her lips together, and then sighed.

Pascal knew she was thinking of her mother, the mother who left her behind, the mother she hardly knew. "Tacos at the Plaza Taqueria, *señorita*?" he said, fluttering his eyelashes.

CHAPTER 18

The night before Louise had flipped through the TV channels in search of something entertaining, or at least mind-numbing. Finally she gave up and started reading a thriller before drifting off around midnight. She tossed and turned, suffering bad FBI dreams until her alarm blasted an old Iggy Pop punk song, "Lust for Life." She wondered how in hell the song had made its way to her playlist.

She willed the fog to clear her head as she inserted a pod of French roast into the machine and reached for a bottle of aspirin. She downed three as the machine released the last bit of steam. Louise knew coffee and aspirin was a bad combination, but . . .

She stared bleary-eyed at her Ado List sitting on the counter. She had a busy day—interviewing Justine Dupont as well as meeting the sketch artist and train attendant at the station. Maybe today she would make some headway on the case. Louise pulled out a small recorder from her bag, inserted a new tape, and checked the battery. She didn't want to rely on her memory or note-taking skills. Dupont's statement needed to be recorded, typed up, and signed. As she popped in another pod of coffee, she checked to make sure the pictures of Justine and Camille were in her briefcase. Once the artist finished with the 911 caller's sketch, she could add that as well.

The medical examiner's request for someone to identify Madison's body annoyed her. It seemed unreasonable, and there was no way she would ask Justine Dupont. The woman had her hands full with her husband's dementia. But she couldn't totally rule her out as a suspect. It depended on what Dupont had to say at the interview this morning. Camille Lautrec, the college girlfriend, would be the best candidate to identify his body. For some reason Louise felt a pang of sympathy for the woman, though, and worried she would collapse in the autopsy room. The doctor would roll her eyes in disdain.

The aspirins still hadn't taken effect, and she needed to shower and dress. She rifled through her closet for something to wear. Now that she was a detective, each day brought a new challenge. What to wear? A patrol officer wore a uniform—simple, no decisions to make. Fashion had never been her strong point and she rarely shopped for clothes. The few dresses she owned were presents from her mother. Too frilly or dressy. Inappropriate for murder and mayhem. She pulled out a pair of dark green plaid slacks and pulled them on. As she zipped them, she sucked in her stomach in fear the zipper would snag her tummy. She couldn't fasten the button, so she slipped on a thick belt. When she looked in the mirror she sighed in despair. Scottish Highland dancing came to mind. She rummaged around in her closet for a tunic top to cover her waist and any bulges below.

As she left her condo, she caught her reflection in the hall mirror. It was disheartening, but she raised her chin and squared her shoulders. She imagined her mother jabbing her between the shoulder blades, chiming, "Squeeze the lemon!" Louise had a full day ahead, a tight schedule to maintain—no time for slouching.

She glanced at her phone while waiting for the elevator: Already behind schedule. No time to stop at the station before her interview with Justine Dupont. She had arranged for them to meet at Tia Sophia's, a restaurant close to the station. She had thought it wouldn't be crowded midweek, but when she entered, it was packed and noisy. The sign next to the door said, *Seat Yourself.* Louise chose a table near the kitchen bordered by two empty tables and sat down. Justine walked in the door, and even from a distance Louise could tell the woman didn't look well. Her body sagged listlessly and the bags under her eyes were even darker and more foreboding than yesterday. Today the woman looked as if she had been rode hard and put away wet. Louise hoped nothing terrible had happened in the last twenty-four hours. She jumped up and knocked her knee on the table, swearing under her breath while waving her hand in the air like a cheerleader.

The tables in the café were set close together in order to fit as many customers as possible. Justine made her way through the maze, mumbling "sorry" and "excuse me." Once Justine sat down, she offered a good morning with so little enthusiasm Louise wondered why she bothered.

Louise was famished. She pushed a menu across the table toward Justine. "Shall we order first?"

Justine picked it up and stared vacantly at the offerings. "Ah . . . coffee."

Louise began to regret meeting at the restaurant. Her stomach growled audibly as she scanned the menu. "The eggs benedict looks good."

Justine stared at her with a blank expression.

The server set down two waters and held her pencil up expectantly, flashing a small smile.

The memory of not being able to button her pants this morning was a wake-up call. Louise looked up at the server. "Egg white omelet, whole wheat toast, coffee."

"Butter or dry?" the server asked, raising her eyebrows.

"Dry," Louise whispered.

Justine handed the menu to the server without making eye contact. "Blueberry muffin, coffee, black."

The server rolled her eyes as she left.

A slight gasp escaped Justine's lips as Louise pulled out the tape recorder and set it on the table. "I need to make sure I don't misinterpret the information you share." Then she added with a chirp, "Don't want to misconstrue."

Justine pressed her lips together, her expression making it clear she wasn't happy about the recorder. She glanced around, fiddling with the silverware.

Louise steeled herself as she clicked on the recorder. "Interview with Justine Dupont." She felt silly but added the date and time before asking her first question. "How did you meet Webster Madison?"

"Online."

"Online?"

Justine narrowed her eyes. "It was an accident."

"Accident?" Louise suppressed a laugh. "How do you *accidentally* meet someone online?"

Justine scowled. "I have a contract with *Senior Living* to write articles about online dating and manage an advice column. I was doing research, reviewing the dating site . . ." Justine sighed. "I knocked my coffee cup off my desk and when I bent down to pick it up, I accidentally swiped right on Webster Madison's profile."

Before Louise could check herself, she guffawed. The story was a little far-fetched, but after all, the woman wrote fiction. Maybe she should check out her books. "And?"

Justine looked pained but said nothing.

"So a relationship developed?" Louise offered.

"No."

Louise raised her eyebrows. "No?" She realized she was repeating again and needed to stop. It would only annoy Dupont, not to mention waste valuable time. "I guess he didn't swipe right?"

"Yes . . . he did."

Louise raised her eyebrows. "So what happened?"

"We exchanged a few texts. I needed to understand the online dating process firsthand. What it's like to search for someone on a website and then begin a relationship online."

"That was it?"

A young couple made their way to the back of the restaurant and took one of the empty tables next to them. Justine stared at the recorder with a pained expression.

Louise reached over and turned off the recorder. Maybe without being taped, Dupont would be more forthcoming. "Okay. Off the record."

Justine started to speak as the server appeared with their order. Justine picked up her coffee cup, blew on it, then took a sip. Once the server left, she let out a heavy sigh. "I agreed to meet Mr. Madison at a restaurant. It was strictly business, research for my article."

"Did Madison know that?"

Justine picked at her blueberry muffin. "No."

"And?"

"As you know, my husband suffers from dementia. I have never cheated on him—never considered it and never would. But . . ." Justine looked up at the ceiling, took in a deep breath, and exhaled. "I found Mr. Madison attractive and his interest in me, well, gratifying. He caught me at a vulnerable moment and I agreed to meet him for dinner."

"And?"

"As I said, the meeting was for work, but . . ."

Louise waited. She knew it was best to give people time to collect their thoughts.

"It was a lovely evening. Under different circumstances, in which I wasn't married, a relationship might have developed. Who knows. Madison was a generous conversationalist. He showed a real interest in my writing, which was flattering. He had read my work years ago and wanted to discuss it, especially my novel, *New Territory*. Are you familiar with it?"

Louise shook her head. She started to turn the recorder back on as Justine grabbed her hand firmly. "Is that necessary?"

Louise hesitated, then decided the woman seemed to be more forthcoming without the recorder. She took out a pencil and a notebook. She stared at Justine without blinking. "What was the book about?"

"My novel? *New Territory*?"

Louise nodded, annoyed at the correction.

"It's about . . ." Justine hesitated. "It's about love and loss, how it could either destroy you or make you stronger."

Louise thought the book was right up her alley. She would have to see if it was available at the library. "So you met Madison for dinner. Then what?"

"When we finished dinner, I begged off with an excuse about a deadline. I left the restaurant—alone—threw the phone, the one I purchased for my research, in a trash can on the sidewalk. I had no intention of seeing the man again."

"But you did?"

"Yes, two times."

"Two?"

Justine closed her eyes. Louise wondered if the woman wanted to wipe away the memory of Madison dead on his living room floor.

"The first time was about a week and a half ago. I had an appointment with my attorney, whose office is in the Opulent Building on Cordova. After the meeting I took the elevator to the lobby. When the doors opened, I saw Webster. He was standing near the front door staring at a mail drop. All of a sudden he punched the wall. It startled me. I backed into the elevator. As the doors started to close, he turned. I'm sure he saw me. He looked so angry. I went up to the third floor and waited a few minutes. When I went back to the lobby, he was gone."

"That's it?"

"I checked out the mailbox. It belonged to the financial company he worked for, Albatross. I looked at the building directory but the company didn't have an office, only a mail drop."

Louise thought the missing office fit with the absent secretary and elusive boss. Something wasn't right. "When was the second time you saw Madison?"

"Sunday night." Justine swallowed hard and took another sip of coffee. "My husband and I had gone to the Twisted Pines in the

DeVargas Center for a drink. Sometimes I like to get out of the house for a change of scenery. The bar isn't far and it wasn't likely I would run into anyone who knew us."

Louise was familiar with the Twisted Pines. She tried not to take offense at Justine's remark. She had been there a few times. It was a favorite with the officers on the force.

"My husband and I were sitting at the bar when Madison appeared out of nowhere. I was surprised to see him there. The Twisted Pines didn't seem the kind of bar he would frequent. He told me he met a client for a drink earlier. I thought that was strange—an attorney for an investment company bringing a client to the Twisted Pines? A mall bar? Also, he never mentioned seeing me at the Opulent Building."

Louise tucked away the information about the client, possibly another suspect. She took a sip of her black coffee, the acidic taste souring her empty stomach. She needed cream, heavy cream. "Go on."

"As soon as Madison joined us, my husband became agitated. Trouble with his straw, one of those paper ones that don't hurt the sea life. It had become unraveled and he couldn't make it work."

Louise glanced at her watch. It was already half past nine. She needed to wrap up the interview in the next twenty minutes and get back to the station to meet the sketch artist.

"Mr. Madison acted like he had no intention of leaving, so I introduced him to Harry—without explanation."

"Did Madison order a drink at the bar?"

"Yes, bourbon."

Louise willed her face expressionless but could feel her heart pick up a beat. "Do you know what he was drinking earlier with the client?"

"No." Justine scrunched her eyebrows. "He told the bartender he would have whatever I was drinking."

Louise, disappointed, nodded for her to continue.

"Harry has this thing about money. When our son, Leo, was young, Harry carried Monopoly money in his wallet as a joke. Anytime Leo bothered Harry—begged him to play a game or set up the train—he would pull out a few bills and tell Leo to buy himself a Coke. Harry wasn't one to play anything. It was cruel."

Louise was aghast. She was grateful for her own father.

"Now I put play money in Harry's wallet. If a person bothers him, he'll give them a few bills. Pay them off. Get rid of them. Like he did our son. They usually are taken aback but don't say anything."

Louise had to ask even though she knew the answer. "Did Harry give Madison money Sunday night?"

Justine's eyes flitted nervously. "Yes."

"How much?"

"His usual. A twenty and a one."

Louise looked down at her plate. Her egg white omelet was stone-cold. She was famished but couldn't bring herself to take even one bite of it, much less the unbuttered toast. She took a sip of her coffee that not only didn't have cream, but now had grown tepid. "Go on."

"Madison was concerned that my number had been disconnected. I didn't offer an explanation. What could I say? Anyway, I could tell he was done and I was relieved. But he must have changed his mind because before he left, he asked for my new number. My phone was on the bar in plain sight. I couldn't say I didn't have one. He typed my number into his phone and said he would be in touch."

Louise's phone vibrated on the table. She glanced at the screen and saw it was from the station. "Sorry, have to take this."

Justine shrugged her shoulders and looked away.

"Sanchez."

"The sketch artist is here," said Susie.

"Set him up in the conference room with some coffee. I'll be there shortly." Louise ended the call and turned back to Justine. "So, Madison left the bar . . ."

"Harry and I left shortly after. On the way home Harry became agitated. When I parked the car, he refused to get out. He wanted his money back, but it was late." Justine squeezed her eyes shut. "I was exhausted . . . I couldn't leave him in the car. I was out of options, so I drove to Madison's house. I knew it would be humiliating but I needed to get Harry's money back. When I pulled into Webster's driveway, the house was dark. I rang the bell anyway, even knocked on the door. I assumed he must have gone somewhere after he left the bar."

"What time was that?"

"It was close to eleven. I left and drove back home. When I pulled into the driveway, Harry leaped out of the car and peed on my rosebushes. I was furious."

Louise covered her grin with a cough. "Anything else?"

Justine shook her head.

"How did you know where Madison lived?"

Justine pressed her lips together. "After I agreed to meet him for dinner, I did some research. Being a detective, you know it's important to find out as much as possible about your sources. Writers are adept at tracking down information and people. Even though I was going to meet Madison in a public place, I was a little wary. Didn't want to get the axe in the parking lot."

Louise grinned. "Better safe than sorry."

"Madison was at least ten years younger and very attractive. His interest made me a little suspicious. I wanted to make sure he was who he said he was. I researched his company. There's something off there, but this was before I saw him at the Opulent Building. After that I knew everything wasn't what it seemed. Anyway, when I was first researching, Madison checked out—an attorney, went to the Pritzker School of Law at Northwestern, graduated first in his class. I found his address online and drove by his house one afternoon. At least he wasn't after my money." She smiled, then her sadness came back.

Louise had a lot of new information but wasn't sure where it fit in. The bourbon connection was intriguing and the play money was explained. Madison must have liked Justine, so when she disappeared, he got pissed off, crumpled up her profile page, and threw it away. Louise needed to find out who the client was, the one Madison met at the bar. Maybe she should stop by the Twisted Pines, have a chat with the bartender. But for now she better get back to the station. "I appreciate your willingness to share this information. I realize it's a delicate situation for you. Your relationship could be misconstrued."

Justine pursed her lips together and said nothing.

"Madison's murder would definitely spice up your online dating article. A cautionary tale, perhaps?" Louise said, opening her eyes wide.

CHAPTER 19

Justine exited the restaurant and immediately wished she had worn a warmer coat. The crisp air felt more like winter than spring. As she made her way along the sidewalk, the indignation of being interrogated—about the death of a man she barely knew—increased with each step. She couldn't believe the detective suggested Madison's murder would spice up her online dating article. *Over my dead body*, Justine thought.

She knew the detective was right about her meeting with Webster Madison. It could be misconstrued. But she wasn't some lonely woman looking for a man online. She had an assignment. Not to mention she was a successful writer. Her novel, *New Territory*, had been well received. She had several short stories under her belt, one of which had been short-listed for the PEN/Malamud Award. As she made her way to her car, she listed in her head all her accomplishments, including various publications; *Vanity Fair*, *Cosmo*, and her crowning glory, *The New Yorker*, had accepted an excerpt from her new novel. Of course, the novel was the one she had been working on for too many years. The one she hadn't been able to finish.

Everything had come to a halt as her husband's behavior changed. Simple, everyday tasks, like getting dressed, became difficult for him. Sometimes he was confused, sometimes withdrawn. As Harry lost his words, she did too. Day by day her ability to write slipped away word by word. It had been months since she had written anything—

not a paragraph, a sentence, or even a grocery list. Each time she sat down at her desk to work, the computer buzzed so loudly that she had to stick cotton in her ears to concentrate. Then the monitor seemed to flicker, making her dizzy, nauseous. When she stared at the keyboard, the letters danced around, rearranged, out of order. Something choked out all her intentions. She wondered if she was losing her mind. Once she became dizzy and had to crawl out of her office into the living room, where she found Harry watching a Spanish soap opera. She didn't have the strength to pull herself up onto the couch and fell into a deep, disturbing sleep, the sounds of Spanish swirling in her head.

She had been so desperate to end her writer's block that she took on the assignment, the one her sister had suggested. Now the thought of her online dating article, "Better Safe than Sorry," made her laugh. The assignment was intended to get her writing again, but instead made her a murder suspect. She supposed the detective didn't believe her story about accidentally swiping on Madison's profile, but it *was* an accident. She had to admit, once it happened the idea titillated her. Something new and different.

After swiping yes on Madison's profile, she was sure he wouldn't reciprocate. He was too young, too handsome. But if he did, she had promised herself she would decline his invitation, make up some excuse. But she hadn't.

As she drove to her sister's house to fetch Harry, she thought of the dinner with Webster at Vanessie. She had picked the location. The piano lounge was dated, no longer popular or part of the nightlife scene. Its faded status guaranteed that she would not run into anyone she knew, not that she knew many people these days. Most of their couple friends had slowly slipped away. She couldn't blame them. Besides Harry's inability to participate in conversations, he often became agitated in social situations.

She had arrived at Vanessie early in order to secure a table near the back and keep an eye on the door. Webster was late, and she was about to leave when he rushed in making profuse apologies. The waiter held the menus in hand and tried not to roll his eyes. She had been disappointed when Webster ordered a bottle of French rosé, an unusual choice for a man—she had her heart set on a Manhattan. But better to keep her wits about her. She was thankful for the lounge's muted light, which helped her avoid Webster's eyes. This was strictly business, and she needed to focus on the article. She had barely scribbled down an outline for her piece, and the due date was approaching. Her sister had agreed to stay with Harry for a few hours while she supposedly worked. She didn't dare reveal her plan to meet a man she matched with on a dating site, even if it had been an accident. Instead she had stretched the truth, saying it was an interview with someone that had online dating experience.

While she had studied the menu, she stole glances at Webster. It was obvious he was too young for her, not that a relationship was even a consideration. Still, one could fantasize. She assumed their age difference didn't bother him. His attention was flattering, and it had been a long time since anyone showed an interest in her. As she sipped the rosé, she found herself imagining it as a real date, the beginning of something new. She found Webster not only attractive but easy to talk to. His interest in her writing was flattering. He had read all her books and was especially fixated on her novel, *New Territory*. He pulled out a well-worn copy and asked sheepishly if she would sign it. She signed the book, handed it back, and attempted to steer the conversation toward his online dating experience.

Webster was honest but excessively modest. It was an unusual trait for a man, especially a man with his good looks and intelligence. He had a knack for saying little about himself while extracting a plethora of information from her before she realized it. At the end of the two allotted hours, she left with an excuse of a deadline. She gave him the phone number of the burner phone but realized she had enjoyed the evening too much. On the way to her car, she had tossed the phone in a trash can. No more Webster.

Now, she pulled into her sister's driveway and the front door swung open. Her sister buzzed around her like an angry bee, spitting out questions about where she had been, but Justine swatted them away, making excuses, lies. She needed to get away from her sister and mumbled something about Harry having an appointment that afternoon. She hated untruths even though sometimes they were necessary, especially when her sister was involved.

She fastened Harry's seat belt and backed out of the driveway, ignoring her sister, who was standing in the doorway, hands on her hips. She would need to patch things up later. But now her only thought was food. Sustenance. Her stomach rumbled and she felt lightheaded. She had only picked at her blueberry muffin. There was no way she could have eaten breakfast while the detective grilled her, treating her like a common criminal. Jesus. After all, she was a renowned author, had won prizes, given keynote speeches. As she drove away, she cursed under her breath, chastising herself for getting into this situation.

She pulled into the parking lot at Clafoutis. It was one of the best French cafés and bakeries in Santa Fe. Even before the car door opened, the smell of freshly baked goods engulfed her. Harry looked over and smiled sweetly. He hadn't done that in a long time. Justine leaned over and squeezed his arm, thinking everything would be all right. The dreadful interview with the detective was over. Webster Madison was over. If she could finish the online dating article, everything would be over.

CHAPTER 20

Louise waited until Justine Dupont left the restaurant, then quickly walked the few blocks to the police station. Thomas Tucker, the train station attendant, stood at the top of the station steps. He fretted nervously as he held open the door for Louise. Susie clipped a visitor badge on the man's collar. As Tucker ran his fingers over the badge's surface, he squared his shoulders and stood up straighter. Police stations affected people differently—some became frightened, some belligerent, some proud. Thomas Tucker was honored to perform his civic duty. Louise led Tucker to the conference room where the sketch artist had set up a small easel with a thick piece of paper clipped to the top. Below was a row of drawing pencils in a variety of colors. Louise made introductions and left to get coffee. When she returned, the two men were sitting side by side, amicably chatting.

The artist stared at the blank sheet of paper, closed his eyes, and asked, "Mr. Tucker, tell me about the woman."

Tucker cleared his throat. Then, as if in a trance, he described the 911 caller. "She was young, in her thirties. Cute, freckles dotted her little turned-up nose. Don't see that much anymore." The attendant chuckled. "Catlike eyes, a strange blue-green with dark, curly lashes. Her lips painted red and full, like a model in a movie magazine. When she burst in the station out of breath, she had to bend down, hands on her thighs, to catch it. As she stood up her hair, a short golden bob that hung below her ears, swung back in place. Like magic. The girl could use a few pounds. She was tall and moved like a gazelle, graceful."

The artist opened his eyes and showed Tucker five different circular outlines for the shape of a woman's face. Tucker chose one of the ovals and the artist started fleshing out the details, turned-up nose spotted with freckles, cat eyes, plump lips, bobbed hair. Tucker guided the artist as he drew, adding details, making changes. It was a fascinating process. The artist seemed to be able to channel the old man's recollections. The hair was the most difficult. Tucker struggled to convey exactly how it looked. Witnesses sometimes mixed up images with their past recollections.

Louise glanced at her watch. "I know you aren't finished, but can I make a copy of what you have so far?"

The artist and Tucker both looked over at Louise, startled. Lost in the process, they had forgotten she was in the room. The artist unclipped the drawing and handed it to Louise to make a copy.

Louise returned the drawing. "Take as long as you need."

"I think we're about finished," the artist replied, checking with Tucker for consent.

Tucker nodded as he stared at the drawing.

"Mr. Tucker, I appreciate your help. Thank you. We'll be in touch." Louise intended for her comments to reassure Tucker, but he looked uncomfortable. "Do you need a ride?"

Tucker shook his head and Louise was relieved. She walked him out of the station and said goodbye. She headed for her cruiser and climbed in, but before starting the car, she pulled out her Ado List. The entire page was filled with tasks, making her spirits flag. Unless she turned the paper over, there was no room to add more items. She stuffed the list back in her purse and decided to pay Lautrec a visit. She needed to know what Lautrec and Madison had argued about, and she needed to convince Lautrec to identify Madison's body—get the medical examiner off her back.

Lautrec's complex wasn't far from downtown, but the roads were clogged with spring tourists looking for sunshine and warm weather. She briefly considered turning on her siren, sending cars skittering to the side of the road, clearing her path. She knew it was juvenile, not to mention against regulations. She pulled into the empty Zocalo parking lot, chose a spot near the entrance, and took the elevator to the second floor. Her plan for increasing her steps, getting into shape, taking control of her body, had lost its appeal, at least until this case was wrapped up. She rang the bell. Camille opened the door, phone to her ear, and squeezed her eyes shut as she mumbled into the receiver, "I'll have to call you back."

Louise gave her a sympathetic smile. It was genuine. She felt sorry for Camille even though the woman had everything—intelligence, beauty, wealth, talent. "I need to talk to you. Can I come in?"

Camille narrowed her eyes and pressed her plump, raspberry-colored lips together until they were barely a slit. She held the door open only wide enough for Louise to slip in sideways. It was a passive-aggressive move, but Louise couldn't blame her.

Camille stomped into the living room waving her arm, indicating where Louise should sit. It was the same chair she had been offered on her previous visit. Louise sat and looked around the room—immaculate, pristine, everything in order. *Who lives like this?* She scanned the room for any signs of life. Nothing. "I hate to ask you..."

"Well, then don't," proclaimed Camille.

Louise steeled herself. "The medical examiner needs someone to identify Webster Madison's body. There's no one else."

Camille's mouth dropped open but nothing came out. She looked as if Louise had demanded her to jump off the Rio Grande Gorge Bridge, which spanned six hundred feet above the river—infamous for suicides. Finally, Camille regained her composure and her eyes narrowed. For the first time they took on a meanness that caused Louise to lean away. "You aren't serious?" Camille snapped.

"Ms. Lautrec." Louise took in a breath and braced herself.

"Madison has no relatives. You are one of the few people who knew him. You saw him recently and would be able to identify his body."

"Then get one of the few other people." Camille stood up, indicating the conversation was over.

Louise stayed in her chair. "It's the law."

"The law?"

"Someone has to legally acknowledge that the body in the morgue is Webster Madison. It won't take long. I promise. In and out."

Camille slumped back into her chair. Her skin, which didn't look as if it had ever seen the New Mexico sun, paled to a pigmentless shade. "You promise? You promise?" Camille's voice rose with each question.

"Please," Louise pleaded.

"What about someone from his company, that British secretary?"

"British secretary?" Louise thought that maybe Camille knew more than she had said.

Camille glared across the room, daring Louise to ask.

Louise sighed, "I haven't been able to locate the secretary. The head of the company left the country Sunday night for Zurich."

Camille rolled her eyes. "Look harder. You're a detective. Now if you will excuse me, I have things to do."

Louise wondered what the woman had to do. Her house was immaculate. Maybe grocery shopping? But she knew she couldn't drag Camille to the morgue. The only other person that could identify Madison was Justine Dupont. There was no way in hell Louise would ask Justine Dupont to look at Webster Madison's dead body on a gurney.

As she climbed into the patrol car, Louise realized she had neglected to ask about the argument with Madison on his front porch. She wasn't about to ring Lautrec's door again. She scribbled it down on the back of her list, then cheered up as she took note that two things had been accomplished. There was a check beside *Dupont interview* and one beside *911 caller sketch*. After her interview with the Twisted Pines bartender this evening, there would be another check. On her way back to the station, she spied a taco food truck parked on the shoulder, and instantly her spirits buoyed.

Back in her office, she added the 911 caller drawing to the evidence wall while she ate all three carne adovada tacos. Once her hunger was sated, she felt groggy and listless. She needed to move and went to find Rupert. Hopefully he had found information about the cleaning service. She rounded the corner and groaned. His desk was tidied up, the computer turned off.

Louise found Susie in the break room, cleaning the coffee pot while humming a country and western song under her breath. Something about being ditched in a ditch full of cow pies. Louise didn't recognize the song and hoped it wasn't on her wake-up playlist.

"Any chance of a fresh pot?" Louise asked.

"Jesus, you scared the bejesus out of me." Susie clutched her chest. "Sure."

"Have you seen Rupert?"

"Had an emergency, something to do with his mother." Susie held the pot under the faucet. "Or was it his brother?"

Louise shrugged, not wanting to tax Susie's brain when she was making coffee. "Did he leave anything for me?"

Susie clicked on the pot before turning around. "Yeah."

Louise raised her eyebrows. She could almost see Susie's brain searching for the information among the other detritus.

"He's going to call you later this afternoon."

The coffee pot spurted, signaling that the last drops of water had processed through the grounds. Louise poured a cup and searched for some creamer in the fridge. She found a bowl of half-and-half containers most likely lifted from Dunkin'.

Susie scrunched her eyes tight. "Oh." Then she opened them wide. "The captain wants to talk to you. He's in his office."

Louise headed down the hall, coffee in hand. She took a large sip and gave a light tap on the door.

"Come in," the captain grumbled. She could hear the wheels of his chair moving around on the tiled floor.

"You wanted to see me, sir?"

"Have a seat." He motioned to the chair in front of his desk. "I heard from the court." He picked up a sheet of paper and slid it toward her. "You've been subpoenaed."

Louise looked at the paper.

"Ruiz's trial begins Monday. I tried to get it pushed back but..." The captain shrugged in defeat. "The DA wants to begin your deposition as soon as possible in case he needs more time. Doesn't want any surprises."

She couldn't suppress a groan.

"I'm sorry. Not what you had planned for this time in your life. I know you were putting in for retirement at the end of the fiscal year. This fiasco with Ruiz has thrown a wrench in it."

"Can't be helped, sir."

"How's the case going?"

Louise took another sip of her coffee, hoping the caffeine would get her little gray cells working. "I have a few leads. The sketch artist finished the portrait of the woman who reported the murder. She's my number one suspect. I'm circulating the drawing. There are still several things I need to follow up on. This deposition, not to mention the trial, is going to take up most of my time. I'm not sure how I'm going to manage both."

"My advice, get the deposition over as quickly as possible. Don't let it drag on. Here's the number. Get it arranged. Remember, answer the questions but don't give away anything—make them work for it."

Louise went back to her office and called the DA's office. She was told to report to the courthouse this afternoon. Her earlier positive mood quickly dissipated. Then she thought of her cousin Lisa and wondered why she hadn't responded to any of Louise's messages. She would give her the benefit of the doubt, give her one more call. She dialed the number, and the call went to voicemail. Louise left her condolences once again and said she needed to talk to her.

As she twisted her chair back and forth, something bugged her. She knew it had to do with Pascal. She felt responsible for bringing him in after the explosion, though he *had* stepped over the line. He had been a big help in her identifying Dupont, but she had paid him back by finding the articles on the thirty-nine boxes of missing pottery. Still, she hadn't given him an update about the Feds, much less helped with finding his father's missing lady friend. With the deposition this afternoon and Pascal's trial Monday, she knew she couldn't afford any record of their communication. She needed to talk to him, so she decided to call from her parents' landline. The call could still be traced, but it seemed like the safer option.

She knew her father would be at work and hoped her mother was out. When she pulled up to the house, she was relieved that her mother's car wasn't under the carport. She rang the doorbell, not wanting to startle Irene, the housekeeper.

A diminutive woman, barely five feet tall, opened the door and chuckled. "You lost your key again, *manita*?"

"Didn't want to scare your pants off," Louise said as she bent down and gave the woman a hug. Irene was part of the family, not an employee, but sometimes Louise suspected Irene would rather be the hired help. Irene's mother had come to work for Louise's parents when Irene was a baby. The two took up residence in the casita nestled under two cottonwood trees at the back of their property. When her mother's arthritis became debilitating, Irene took over the housekeeper job. Louise thought of Irene as a sister, but after high school each went their separate ways.

"Can't believe you're still working here," Louise said.

"Can't believe you're still a police officer."

This was their usual banter. Neither could understand why the other did what they did. Both had remained single over the years and had positions way below their potential.

"I need to make a call. Then maybe some coffee?"

"There's a fresh pot on the stove. I'm finishing up a berry pie."

Louise made her way to her father's study and sank into his weathered desk chair. The leather emitted a slight scent of tobacco, making her wonder if her father still snuck a puff on his pipe. Outside the window, a birdfeeder engulfed in finches swung in the spring breeze. She watched the birds maneuver for a spot before placing the call. The phone was a replica of an old-fashioned black rotary phone, a gift from her mother. Louise stuck her finger in a number, moved it clockwise around the dial, and let go. It made a satisfying whirl as it returned. She loved the rotary sound, even though it was only show. All phones were now connected to a touch-tone system.

"Ruiz."

"Hi. Got your message. Sorry, things have been crazy. I . . ."

Pascal jumped in. "Hey, no worries. I know you need to keep your distance. I was deposed yesterday. Figured you were too. I guess I'll be seeing you in court Monday. That is if they can complete the depositions. Not my worry though. That's not why I called."

Louise was relieved. She didn't want to talk about the deposition or the upcoming trial. "I wanted to let you know that, according to my mother, the Feds took over the missing pottery case. So maybe you should check it out with your little birdie."

Pascal laughed. "Yeah, maybe. Thanks, Louise. Appreciate it."

"What were you calling me about?" Louise asked.

"I came across some information on Albatross. Don't ask."

"Tweet tweet."

"Seems the company is involved in some questionable business practices. Looks like it's a shell company."

The English tongue twister, *she sells seashells by the seashore*, popped into Louise's head. "The company sells seashells?"

Pascal chuckled. "No. Might as well though. A shell company is one that exists only on paper, usually no office or employees. It might have a bank account, hold passive investments, or even own some assets, such as intellectual property."

"I don't get it. Why would someone have a company that doesn't exist or have anything to offer?"

"To move profits from a real company into the shell, maybe to launder money from selling illegal goods. The shell is a holding tank, but it can be used for tax evasion."

"But Albatross had employees, the head of the company, and a secretary. And the company contracted Madison."

"Have you checked out the company's office?"

"There isn't one. Justine Dupont saw Madison in the lobby of the Opulent Building. After he left, she checked the building directory, and there wasn't a listing for Albatross."

"Probably only a mail drop."

"And what about the secretary?"

"She could be a temp, maybe an out-of-work actress, works from home."

"What about Madison?"

"He's legit, or should I say *was*. Albatross contracted him to help fight an IRS case. The company is also under investigation by the Feds."

"Did Madison know that Albatross was a shell company?"

"Not sure how much he knew. After going through the company's finances, he must have suspected something wasn't above board. Madison signed a one-year lease with Albatross on the Santa Fe house. But Albatross doesn't own the property. Another entity, Laredo Enterprises, is the owner. It's a realty company and might be an asset of the shell company. When Roche hired Madison, he told him that the office building was being remodeled, suggested he work from home for a while."

"How do you know all this?"

"My source said it was on a phone transcript."

"Phone transcript? Isn't that illegal? Who's your source?"

"A little birdie."

"Hardy har."

"Guess who owns Katrin Simpson's house in Abiquiu?" Pascal asked.

Louise was tired of guessing games, and although she suspected what he was about to say, asked, "Who?"

"Laredo Enterprises."

"And where is Laredo Enterprises located?" Now Louise was playing the game.

"Rocky Mountain High. Denver, Colorado."

"Katrin Simpson is from Denver. Do you think she's involved?" Louise asked.

"Hope not. It could be a coincidence."

"Or it could be related. What are the chances?" *About 100 to 1, but still*, Louise thought. Pascal's involvement worried her. He was poking around and mixing things up. And his "little birdie" troubled her. She hoped Pascal didn't want payback, like on the witness stand. She owed him two favors now. She couldn't keep up with the man. "Have you made any progress in finding Katrin Simpson?"

"No, but I *am* a little worried that she rented a house that's connected to Albatross."

"The connection could have a perfectly rational explanation. Laredo Enterprises is in Denver and Katrin has a Denver address, but so do seven hundred thousand other residents."

"Yeah, señorita, but the plot thickens."

Louise needed to find information on Katrin Simpson. Though it seemed almost too convenient that Louise and Pascal's separate searches should meet at a crossroads, she didn't think it impossible that the woman could somehow be connected. After all, she rented a house owned by a subsidiary of Albatross, and now she was missing. As Pascal said, it could be a coincidence, but Louise knew coincidences to be a thing of the movies—this was real life.

"This is the second time you've helped me with the case. I wish I could do something in return."

"No worries, Louise. I crossed the line when I blew up the

warehouse door, and I'm not going to dodge the bullet. Your deposition is this afternoon. Sorry you got involved. And sorry you got stuck with my job, this murder, the shell company, the mess."

Louise didn't know what to say. "Yeah."

"Don't forget to keep me updated," Pascal said.

"Will do. Not sure where to go from here."

"Forward." The line went dead.

CHAPTER 21

A sense of contentment settled over Justine as she and Harry left the French bakery. At the next red light she glanced over at her husband. His eyes were already closed and his head had drifted to the right, resting against the window. She had noticed something different in Harry's eyes. A truce. Maybe she imagined it, but she wanted to believe she would be able to write again, and Harry would... who knows. As they had taken the last bite of crème brûlée, a peacefulness had clothed them like a warm blanket, smoothing out all the tension and worry. Maybe it was the French food, maybe the aroma of freshly baked goods, maybe the hugs and kindness from the café's owner.

As the light changed, Justine conceded she was never going to finish the online dating article—truth be told, she had barely begun. She had worked on an outline but when she started to write, the sentences didn't come. It was as if her block was back, locked in place. The research for the article had begun as a lovely dinner with Webster Madison and ended with her as a murder suspect.

She knew she wasn't to blame for Webster's death, but she felt culpable. It soured her stomach. For the first time she wondered who had killed the man, and why? What had Webster done to get himself murdered? She remembered how angry he had been at the Opulent Building, punching the wall. Was it something to do with his job, the company without an office?

She thought about the editor at the magazine and how furious he would be when she told him she wasn't going to write the article. She cringed at the thought and wondered if that could be a plausible cause for murder. She had put the editor off several times and tried to convince herself she didn't care, but when it came to writing, she always cared. She steeled herself and brushed away the thoughts. Then it occurred to her that she could do better, write an article that addressed women's need to find someone to share their life with. There had to be more options, even in this day and age, for meeting people. She thought of how she and Harry had met, how her sister and her friends met their spouses.

As she pulled into the driveway, she slammed on the brakes, causing Harry to bang his head. A light shone out of the living room window. She couldn't remember the last time she had been in that room and was sure she hadn't left the lamp on. The use of the house had shrunk to a few rooms—family room, bedroom, kitchen. She cut the engine, feeling silly even as her heart continued to pound in her chest. Her memory wasn't as good as it used to be. Maybe she had turned the lamp on days ago and this was the first time it was noticeable in the fading afternoon light. She reached over and unbuckled Harry. They made their way up the walk to the porch. As she fumbled for her keys, the front door flung open.

Justine screamed. "Jesus Christ, Leo. You scared the hell out of me. What the . . . what are you doing here?"

"Didn't you get my message?"

Before Justine could respond, Harry pitched forward and embraced Leo in a bear hug. His eyes dripped with tears. Justine, still shaken, was stunned at her husband's show of emotion.

"Dad. So good to see you, Pops." Leo patted Harry's back as he continued to mumble soothingly in his father's ear. "Missed you, Daddy-o. Gee whiz, you put on a few. Good for you, Papa Bear, need to keep up your strength."

Justine stood with her mouth slightly parted. Leo was here. He had come home.

Leo looked over Harry's shoulder. "Took a meeting in LA. I wired you, said I would stop in Santa Fe afterward." He gave Harry a squeeze. "Want to spend some time with Dad."

"Wired?" Louise asked.

"That's what they say in the UK—not Western Union—an email, sent it through your editor, Walter Barbscold?"

The mention of Walter Barbscold made Justine gasp, and a queasiness settled in her stomach. Her son hadn't been here for five minutes and he'd already upset her. "Why would you do that?"

"Do what?" Leo attempted to untangle himself from his father's hug.

Justine reached out and pulled her husband away. "Send it to Barbscold? Why didn't you pick up the *bloody*, as they say in the UK, phone?"

Leo frowned, his eyes not meeting hers. "It's costly, had some . . . setbacks lately." Then he reached over and gave Justine a quick hug and peck on the cheek.

Justine raised her eyes. "Let's go in. I need to put your father to bed and . . ."

"I'll do it, Mom."

Justine was taken aback. "Sure." She let Leo lead Harry down the hall. "Hope you're not hungry. We are stuffed, ate at the French bakery, had *crème* brûlée for dessert."

Leo called out, "Could you order me some Indian, vegetarian?"

Justine sighed, thinking, *Indian, vegetarian, good luck with that.* She pulled out the bottle of bourbon she kept under the sink behind the cleaning supplies, just in case, and made herself a drink. She googled Indian food and was surprised at the number of Indian restaurants in the area.

The food arrived as Leo came down the hall. "He's out like a light."

"Thanks, that was a treat." She smiled and meant it. "What do you want to drink?"

"Beer?"

"Sorry, no beer." She jiggled her glass. "Bourbon on the rocks?"

"When did you start drinking bourbon?"

"Don't ask."

It had been two years since Justine had seen her son. He had put on a few pounds himself but carried it well. His skin looked pale and his hair darker, but that was from living in the UK, where the sun rarely made it through the clouds. Otherwise Leo was the same. Obtuse. She wondered if he had sent an email to her editor, and if he had, why hadn't Walter forwarded it? Of course, they weren't talking these days, but still Walter could have forwarded the message to her.

She fixed Leo a drink and sat on the sofa next to him. "So, what are your plans?"

"As I said, I want to spend some time with Dad before, you know..."

"It might already be *before you know*," Justine said, not unkindly.

Leo's shoulders drooped as he took a sip of the bourbon.

"It's only Harry now. We rarely go out anymore. Not that anyone asks us. They all have learned to stand clear. The last time, a concert at the Lensic with the Ramseys, ended in a fiasco. Harry got lost in the crowd after the concert." Justine sighed heavily. "My fault, I was engrossed in a conversation, wasn't paying attention." She smiled at Leo. "Remember how your father loved to walk at night, after dark when things were quiet? He used to take you along. He loved how the shadows danced on the dark houses, sometimes there would be a window lighted, television on, movement inside. You two would make up stories about the people in the houses and tell me about them when you came home."

Leo nodded. He had cherished those times. He and his father in the dark.

"The night of the concert, somehow your father got to the Rail Runner station, boarded the last train south. Paid for his ticket with Monopoly money." Justine chuckled.

Leo shook his head. "He was always a prankster."

"The police couldn't find him in the crowd. I was frantic and put out a Silver Alert. The ticket man on the train saw the alert and his adventure was intercepted. The Ramseys had to drive me to pick him up at the Bernalillo police station." Justine produced a sardonic snort. "Haven't heard from the Ramseys since."

"Sorry. Didn't realize how things were." Leo looked over at the train set that circled around the television. "Does he still . . . work with the train?"

Justine smiled. "Yes. The damn thing is always jumping the tracks. Drives him crazy. I worry I'm going to fall over the tracks, break a hip." Justine prayed Leo wouldn't mention the play money, the Monopoly set. That would rub salt in her wounds.

"Well, we will *play* trains tomorrow. We can get some new accessories. Maybe a few buildings, farm animals, another train car?"

"That's the last thing we need." But secretly Justine was pleased. It was a relief to have someone else in charge, even if it was shopping for trains.

Leo got down on the floor, set the coal car back on the track, and connected the caboose. He straightened the little guy in the hatch who manned the back of the train, arm in the air. When he turned the switch, the engine lurched forward, sending all the cars off the track. A flash of déjà vu hit Justine, making her heart twinge.

"Let's leave it until the morning, Leo. I'm bushed and have an assignment that's way past deadline."

Leo raised his eyebrows. "Your novel?"

"I wish. I'm supposed to write an article for a senior magazine."

"A senior magazine?"

Justine was sorry she mentioned it. "Don't ask."

"I put my bag in my old bedroom."

Justine groaned. "I had the housekeeper strip the bed a few months ago, before she disappeared."

"Disappeared?"

Justine shrugged. She didn't have the strength to explain Sylvia and her disappearance right now.

Leo jumped up and gave his mother a peck on the cheek. "I know how to make a bed, Mother, I'm a grown man."

CHAPTER 22

At the station, Louise tried to tie up the loose ends that seemed to unravel as quickly as they were cinched. Rupert called and apologized for his absence. She gritted her teeth while politely inquiring about his family. He assured her everything was fine and said he had found a contact within the Babble online dating site. Before Louise could stop herself, she blurted out that it was a moot point. At least she had restrained herself from saying "a day late and dollar short" as her namesake, Grannie Lou, used to. She kept it under wraps that Pascal had been the one to identify Justine Dupont. She didn't want to rub it in his face, much less let it be known that she's in contact with Pascal.

"The woman in Madison's trash can is Justine Dupont. I interviewed her today."

There was silence on the line, and Louise wondered if Rupert had hung up in a huff. Then he asked, "What did you find out?"

Louise gave him a summary of the interview.

"Hmm—I'm working on Albatross."

"It's a shell company." Louise knew it was vindictive, but she couldn't help herself. He had left her stranded. She needed someone on board.

"How did you find out? Who's your source?"

She was not about to reveal her source. "A little birdie told me." She could tell, even over the phone, that Rupert was pissed off.

"I'll have a full report on Roche and his *shell* company by the end of the day," he said.

"Try and locate the secretary too." But unless Rupert had connections in high places, preferably with the FBI, he was out of his depth.

The afternoon dragged on. Louise stared at Ruiz's paperwork piled in the corner. If she didn't process it, it wouldn't get done, but it wasn't her job. She had bigger fish to fry—she had a murder to solve. She leaned back in her chair and as her eyes started to close, her phone rang.

"Hi, Dad. What's up"

"Did you get hold of your cousin?"

"I tried a couple times. I think Lisa is screening my calls. I've left messages."

"We decided to have a service for your uncle Saturday."

Louise was surprised. "Jesus. Saturday?"

"Sorry, it's the only time in the next month that was available."

"I'll ask the captain if I can take tomorrow off. He's a devout Catholic—he'll okay it. But I'm being deposed this afternoon. I don't know how long that's going to take but hope they can wrap it up today. They already have my statement of what went down. They're in a time crunch because Ruiz's trial begins Monday morning."

"You have to be at the service, honey. Your mother and I need your support. And please try Lisa again."

"I'll do my best. Is Uncle's body still in the morgue?" Louise shivered thinking of Webster Madison's body left in one of those drawers.

"Joseph wanted to be cremated. Apparently a blood relative has to identify the person before the state can cremate the body. It's a law. Have you heard of that?"

Louise thought, *oh yes, ad nauseum*, but only said, "It's to make sure the dead body is who the authorities think it is. It's for the corpse's protection."

"Hmm. Didn't know corpses needed protection. Anyway, the funeral home contacted me yesterday. I identified Joseph. I'm picking up his ashes later today."

Louise was relieved that she would get to say a proper goodbye to her uncle. "I'll try and call Lisa again, but don't hold your breath. Even if she wanted to come, it doesn't give her much time to get here." Louise sighed. "And what if Lisa doesn't want the trunk?"

"We'll cross that bridge when we come to it. I'm glad you decided to take the chest home. It will be easier for Lisa to pick it up, or more convenient if we have to send it to her. And don't forget you said you would help us go through the boxes from the ranch."

Louise suppressed a groan. She had forgotten about the boxes. "Where's the service?"

"Mora. St. Gertrude the Great Catholic Church. It's at 8 County Road A033. Nine a.m. Reception following at the ranch house."

"Oh, Lordy." Louise scribbled down the address.

"I know it's short notice, but let Lisa know about the service. Ask what we should do with the trunk. Might be best not to go into its contents unless she asks."

"I'll give it my best shot." She hung up and slumped in her office chair. Then made one last call to her cousin. While the phone rang, she composed a voicemail in her head.

"Why are you stalking me?" snapped a woman.

"Ah . . . Lisa?"

"Duh," she said sarcastically.

"This is your cousin Louise."

"Duh."

Louise didn't have patience for this. She was irritated. Were they back in junior high? What was wrong with this woman? But she knew what was wrong. Her mother had died and her father had abandoned her.

"As I said in the message I left, my father and I were clearing out the attic at the ranch house in Mora. We found a trunk belonging to your mother. The trunk has... various items. Family heirlooms. We thought you should have them."

"You thought?" Lisa almost spit the question.

Louise had never heard such vitriol from anyone, and she had heard a lot during late-night arrests. "Or you could let us know what to do with the trunk and the items."

"What's in the trunk?" Lisa asked.

"Uh," Louise cleared her throat, "some religious items."

"You've got to be kidding? According to my grandmother, my mother didn't have a religious bone in her body. She was a heathen."

"Well, they're things from the past. Maybe from your ancestors."

"Oh my God. The Holy Grail, perhaps?"

"Not exactly. May I be direct?"

"Jesus Christ."

Louise had had enough of this woman. "They're Jewish relics dating from the sixteenth century. Possibly from Spain during the time of the Inquisition." Louise was satisfied that she'd finally silenced her cousin.

"How do you know the trunk belonged to my mother?"

"The trunk has your mother's name, Simone, carved in the top. Apparently your grandmother sent it to her as a wedding present."

"My grandmother had one hell of a sense of humor. It may or may not be my mother's. As far back as I can tell the oldest daughter in each generation was named Simone... except me. That's where the buck stopped."

Louise thought about the significance of this. She imagined the trunk being passed down over the generations from one Simone to the next. "We also wanted to let you know that there's a memorial service for your father Saturday at nine. It'll be in Mora at St. Gertrude Catholic Church. I can text you the information. There's a reception following the service at the ranch house where his ashes will be spread. We were hoping you could attend. My parents would be glad to have you stay with them in Tesuque."

"That's not going to happen."

"Are you still living in Tucson?"

"No." Lisa hesitated. "After my grandmother passed, I moved to Patagonia, south of Tucson."

"I could arrange to have the trunk sent to you."

There was silence on the phone for longer than comfortable, and Louise wondered if Lisa had hung up.

"I'll let you know." The line went dead.

Louise glanced up at the clock above the whiteboard. Quarter to three. Time to meet the devil.

When she arrived at the courthouse, it stood large and foreboding in the late afternoon sun. Every time she entered the building, which thankfully wasn't often, thoughts of the infamous ghost sighting loomed. The brown stucco structure reeked of institution; the atmosphere was sterile, antiseptic, the least likely place for a ghost to take up residence. But in 2007 the image of a ghost had been captured on a video security camera. Someone uploaded the image to YouTube, and it quickly attracted attention as well as improbable suggestions as to its origin. A managing editor of the *Skeptical Inquirer* had investigated the sighting. There were several unsuccessful attempts to recreate the image using a moth and hundreds of ladybugs. The managing editor concluded that the ghost's origin was the result of a bug crawling across the camera lens. It wasn't the first time New Mexico had made the news with an outlandish sighting. Years earlier, a woman in northern New Mexico reported she saw Jesus's image in her tortilla.

Louise flashed her police ID, took off her coat, placed it along with her briefcase on the propeller belt, and walked through the security detector. Nothing beeped. She gathered her belongings and took the elevator to the fifth floor. As she entered the conference room, everyone looked up, their faces blank, keeping their cards close. She glanced at the clock on the wall and noted it was 2:55— she still had five minutes, she wasn't late. A sense of impatience radiated through the room. These people were eager to get to work and get it over.

The district attorney held out his hand and squeezed Louise's harder than necessary. She resented how he laid his other hand heavily on her shoulder, guiding her to a seat at the head of the table. The man reeked of intimidation and he knew it. It came with the territory, but she took an instant dislike to him. This was the DA's show. He was in charge. He pranced around the room, introducing the participants, then rubbed his hands together. "Let me go over the procedures."

Louise pushed her butt against the back of the chair, willing herself to sit up straight and not fidget. The DA's intense eyes glistened like dark pools, boring into her as he spelled out the rules. "First of all, you aren't on trial. Although"—he paused for effect—"you will be sworn in and under oath throughout the deposition." He swept his arm around the room. "We will assume that you understand the question presented if you answer it. So, if you don't understand a question, ask for clarification. There will be plenty of time to answer any questions you might have." The DA glanced at Ruiz's attorney before turning his attention back to Louise. "The law allows up to seven hours for a deposition. Since we are starting late in the day, we'll most likely have to finish in the morning."

Louise controlled a groan and nodded.

The DA pursed his lips. "Gestures can't be recorded, Detective. You will need to vocalize your answers."

"I understand." Louise felt like a schoolgirl caught chewing gum in class. Her body sagged at the thought of seven hours of questioning. The murder case would have to be pushed back more than a day. And who knew when she would ever have time to get back in the darkroom?

The court official swore her in. Even though there wasn't a judge present, Louise felt as if she was on the witness stand, culpable. The room's bare gray walls created a stark and chilly atmosphere. Louise wondered if the heat had already been turned down for the weekend. She was sorry she had taken off her coat. Despite the chill in the air, she felt sweat fleck her forehead. Maybe she should have obtained an attorney, but without a judge to rule on objections, there was little point for representation.

The DA tossed out a few questions that Louise suspected were either designed to put her at ease or catch her off guard, most likely the latter. Then he asked her to relate the events that occurred after receiving the call about the explosion at the film company's warehouse. While she recounted what happened that night, the DA continuously interrupted, asking for meaningless clarifications. It was annoying. Her responses were perfectly clear, the disruptions intrusive, and the entire process grueling. Retelling what happened that night should have taken half an hour max. But the DA's repeated requests for clarification after every other sentence made the process drag on and on. *No wonder court cases take forever*, she thought.

Finally, the DA, satisfied, passed the baton to Pascal's attorney. Patrice Fox-Elexor stood and leaned over to collect her papers, providing the DA with a view of her ample bosom, which blossomed out of her low-cut silk blouse. Papers in hand, she strutted over on her spiky heels with a slight sway of her hips and slithered into the chair across from Louise. She was young, probably mid-thirties, and immaculately dressed in a charcoal pantsuit—an attractive and confident woman. Once Fox-Elexor started her cross-examination, she was all business, no preamble.

Louise was asked to clarify every statement she had given to the DA, a strategy most likely used to lessen the damage. The attorney's performance was admirable. Her inquisition enraptured everyone in the room, even the DA. It was remarkable how she worded her questions, changed the direction of the preponderance of evidence, put doubt in the standard of proof. She probed whether Ruiz's actions were beyond a reasonable doubt. The DA was brutal, a pit bull, but Fox-Elexor was a border collie, clever and nuanced. Like a magician pulling rabbits out of a hat, the attorney seemed to pull mitigating factors out of thin air.

Louise nudged her sleeve back and glanced down at her watch. They had been going back and forth for over four hours without a break. She had to continually remind herself not to slouch, and she was sure she would lose control of her body at any minute, slip out of the chair in a puddle onto the floor. The image of her sprawled under the table between the participants' feet made her smile. No one else in the room seemed the least bit weary. She supposed they were used to hours of sitting, listening. At last Fox-Elexor asked the final question and nodded; she was satisfied with her cross-examination. Louise felt a rush of relief, thinking now it would be over. But the DA expressed an interest to redirect. Louise stifled a groan—her expression said it all.

Pascal's attorney and the DA had been notified that Louise would not be available Saturday, so if they didn't continue, they would have to finish on Sunday. Fox-Elexor piped up and voted to finish Sunday morning. The DA reluctantly agreed but wanted to have the last word—eight o'clock sharp. Louise knew the break would give both the attorneys a chance to go over what had been said and prepare further questions. On Sunday the DA would be given an opportunity to redirect and Pascal's lawyer would be offered to recross.

The DA laid out the procedures that would take place once the deposition was complete. "We're in a time crunch, people. He looked directly at Louise and scowled. The court reporter will prepare a transcript and copies will be sent to all parties involved for review. Any revisions need to be made in a timely fashion. I ask everyone to complete the task immediately. The commissioner has taken a hard line on this case and expects the trial to begin Monday morning."

CHAPTER 23

Louise gathered her belongings and left the conference room. She heard the elevator doors snap closed down the hallway. The muted lights emitted a peculiar greenish glow. Her footsteps clicked noisily on the tile floor. Although Louise wasn't one to believe in apparitions, she had to admit the courthouse reeked of ghostly phantoms. Maybe the spirits of past criminals lurked behind the walls. The building made her skin crawl. The elevator door opened. Empty. She hesitated and considered the stairs, but the deposition had sapped her energy.

As the elevator descended, she checked her phone—no messages. It was almost seven thirty. It was Friday, her workday over, but her weekend was shot. She might as well head to the Twisted Pines, hear the bartender's side of the story—see what he remembered from Sunday night. She was thirsty, in need of a glass of wine. When she exited the courthouse, the chilled night air hit her lungs, making her cough. She shivered as she wrapped her scarf tightly around her neck and pulled it up over her nose. Her wool coat hung open but when she tugged it closer around her body, she realized it was missing two buttons and a third dangled by a thread. She fiddled with the loose button. Jesus, she needed to clean up her act, get control of her life. At least have the dry cleaners sew a few buttons on her coat so she wouldn't freeze to death.

The Twisted Pines Pub was open, but it was early for the bar crowd. The place was empty except for a middle-aged couple having an intense conversation. They were huddled together, heads touching, nursing their drinks. The dim lights cast a yellow haze around the room. Louise was reluctant to touch anything as she made her way to the bar. The atmosphere was more sordid than she remembered. She wondered why the management didn't turn up the lights, blast some music, give the place a little life. She slid onto a stool and started to rest her hands on the bar but noticed something sticky and wet. She glanced toward a partially open door on the other side of the cash register and assumed the bartender was taking a leak or having a smoke.

The door to the back room swung open and a guy came in. He looked too young to be serving alcohol, but to Louise, who recently turned fifty, everyone looked young. The guy checked out his appearance in the mirrored wall behind the rows of glasses. He took out a comb and ran it through his shaggy mop. Louise grimaced. He didn't acknowledge her presence, but she was sure he had noticed her. What a prick. She was already pissed at the guy. The keeper of the drinks. She loathed men who acted like that but knew she would have to curb her annoyance.

Finally he picked up a dirty dish towel and sauntered over. The cigarette smoke wafted off his body like stale perfume. He ran the towel back and forth over the counter before he bothered to look up. "What will it be?" he said as he leaned around her, pretending to check on the couple across the room.

Louise wanted to pull out her badge, stuff it in his face, but this guy was cocky enough not to be intimidated.

"Cabernet. Not your house."

He raised his eyebrows but said nothing. The bartender took his time to select a bottle then brought it over for her inspection. Bogle, cabernet sauvignon. It was a middle-of-the-road cab, passable. She nodded and he filled a glass, pushed it in front of her, and turned to leave.

"I need some information. It involves a customer who was in here Sunday night. A man in his mid-fifties."

The bartender guffawed, exposing a missing incisor. "A lot of customers fit that description."

Louise took out her phone and held up a photo of Webster Madison, the one from the Babble dating site. The bartender grabbed the phone out of Louise's hand and studied the picture. He took his time, squinted, and tilted his head from side to side. "Can't say. Customer-bartender privilege." He grinned and winked as he handed the phone back.

Louise wanted to slap him but took out her badge and slid it across the bar.

He glanced at it and shot Louise an annoyed look. "Yeah, I remember him. Sundays are always slow. The guy sat in that corner." He pointed to a lone table near the restrooms. "Tried to take his order. The dude shooed me away, said he was waiting for someone. As I turned to go back to the bar the door flew open and this other dude rushed in all flustered, must have had his knickers in a twist." The bartender chortled, pleased with his antiquated analogy. "The first dude waved me back to the table flapping his arms, looked like a hysterical chicken." He laughed then leaned over the bar narrowing his eyes. "The two guys didn't shake hands, found that strange. They were business types. Business types always shake hands. Usually they can't help out-gripping each other. It's a power thing. But I could tell these two were pissed off with one another."

"What made you think that?"

"Well, they didn't raise their voices but they were jostling just the same."

"Jostling?"

"Yeah, you know, butting heads."

"Butting heads?"

He looked up at the ceiling, sighed, and shook his head. "Not physically. After they finished their drinks, the flustered dude, the second one, jumped up and knocked over his chair. He stomped out and slammed the door so hard it bounced open. Major asshole."

"What were the men drinking?"

"Bourbon. Maker's Mark."

Louise squared her shoulders then leaned forward. "Did either of the men ever leave the table, go to the restroom? Play the jukebox?"

"Jukebox? Nobody plays that old thing. We pipe in music. Spotify."

"What about the restroom?"

"Don't think so, could have."

"What happened after the second guy left?"

"Didn't notice; it started to get busy. The movie had let out."

Louise took out her notebook. "Could you describe the man, the one who came in all . . . flustered?" She could tell the bartender was beginning to enjoy his role, confidant to the police. What else did he have to do?

"Middle-aged, in his forties maybe."

Louise winced. If forties was middle-aged, what did that make her?

"The dude was well dressed. Expensive-looking clothes. He wore one of those wool overcoats, hung down to his knees, tweed. Don't see that much in Santa Fe. This dump mainly attracts dudes in ski jackets or those puffer coats."

"Anything else about his appearance?"

"Light-colored hair, almost white, cut short. Nazi-style. And weird-looking, icy blue eyes. Oh, and he had a nasty scar on his left cheek. I couldn't stop staring at it. Looked like he'd pissed someone off real bad, and that someone took a jagged knife to his face."

Louise was surprised the bartender was able to recall so many details. But in his line of work, he had a lot of time to study people. Before she could ask the next question, the middle-aged couple waved him over to settle their check. Louise sipped her drink and waited for him to return. She thought about the information and tried to piece it together like a jigsaw puzzle.

The bartender returned with the bottle of red in hand and shot her a loopy smile.

She signaled for him to pour another glass. "Did Madison leave the bar?"

"Madison?"

"The man you identified in the photo."

"The dude didn't leave right away. I lost track of him. Later I saw him standing next to this couple at the bar."

"Did you recognize the couple?"

"Yeah. She comes in from time to time. Always sits at the bar with her husband. He's sort of demented." He made a screwed-up face and circled his finger around his ear. "I was surprised the woman knew the dude, definitely detected a vibe between the two. I have radar. Being a bartender, you're sensitive to that kind of stuff. But still it was weird."

"Why was it weird?"

"The guy was a lot younger, a good-looking dude too. Not that I'm into men." He snorted, shaking his head. "The woman, she's a wreck and such a stuck-up bi . . . "

Louise cut him off. "Did the man order a drink?"

"Yeah, he said he'd have whatever the woman was drinking, which was funny cause that was the same drink he'd ordered with the Nazi dude. Bourbon, Maker's Mark."

"Thank you for the information. You've been helpful."

"Just want to do my part. Keep law and order."

Louise thought that was a crock, but she said nothing and gave him a close-lipped smile.

"Hey, what's this about?" he pressed.

"Can't say. If you think of anything else, please give me a call." She put a twenty on the bar along with her business card. "Keep the change."

The bartender gave a salute.

CHAPTER 24

Louise poured herself a glass of wine and settled on her sofa across from the adobe fireplace. It was late, after eleven, and she should be in bed, not drinking her third glass of wine. The memorial service was at nine in the morning. She would need to leave her condo by eight to get to the church on time. But at least she'd convinced her parents to let her drive herself, in case—not to jinx it—there was another crime she had to attend to.

She sipped her wine and promised herself she would go to bed soon. There had been no word back from Lisa about attending her father's memorial service. Louise couldn't blame the woman for keeping her distance. At the bequest of her uncle's new wife, he had sent his daughter away when she was only three years old. And her uncle rarely had any contact with the child after that. But Louise was disappointed; she wanted to meet her cousin, get to know her. Louise was an only child and didn't have many relatives, especially ones near her age.

The doorbell shattered the silence, startling Louise, who splashed cabernet on her white blouse. It was seldom she had visitors, and never unplanned. It was late at night, and her heart pounded in her chest. She worried it was bad news, an accident, or, God forbid, another death. The doorbell rang again. She jumped up, went to the door, and peered through the peephole. A middle-aged woman stood in the entrance, glaring back. Although there was no family resemblance, Louise knew right away: it was her cousin. She opened the door and started to speak, but Lisa breezed past, her heeled boots clicking on the tiles. She didn't look anything like what Louise had imagined. She was short, even shorter than Louise, maybe five feet at most. Her blacker-than-black hair with a few wisps of gray sprung in tight curls at every direction, out of control, like Medusa. The woman's eyes were dark pits, and her nose was nicely shaped but sharp. She couldn't have weighed more than a hundred pounds.

Louise followed Lisa into the living room where she had stopped, her eyes landing on the menorah that sat on the mantle. Louise's father had the trunk of religious relics brought to her condo. She had wanted to photograph the items again before shipping them to Lisa. It was important to document the contents, not only for her family, but for historical reasons. She had photographed each item and carefully packed everything back in the trunk. When she came to the menorah, she remembered how it could be converted to a cross to save someone's life during the Inquisition. A sadness settled over Louise. She didn't have much hope for the human race.

The sixteenth century candlestick had spent so many years hidden away, she couldn't bear to put it back in the trunk. So she placed the menorah on the fireplace mantle. It looked perfect.

"I'm so glad you decided to come to your father's memorial. It will be healing."

Lisa whipped around and looked at Louise as if she had lost her mind. She pressed her lips together and snapped, "I have no intention of attending the memorial service."

Louise was taken aback. She wondered why the woman was here. Why had she showed up at her door late at night, unannounced?

"I'm going to the cemetery, to see my mother's grave."

"Oh . . . where is she buried?"

"St. Gertrude Cemetery."

Louise nodded. She knew her uncle's ashes wouldn't be interned at St. Gertrude. They were to be spread at the ranch after the reception. It was too bad that her aunt and uncle's remains couldn't be put together. The couple reunited.

Lisa walked over to the mantle, stared at the menorah, and reached out toward it before letting her hand drop. "The church and the cemetery are named after St. Gertrude. The woman, Gertrude, was hailed as a mystic, practiced spirituality called 'nuptial mysticism.'"

"Gosh. I've never been to the cemetery, or the church for that matter. Once my—ah, our—grandparents passed, my family rarely visited Mora."

Lisa narrowed her eyes and continued her sermon. "Gertrude considered herself the bride of Christ."

"Oh?" Louise admonished herself, but the wine made her brain foggy, not to mention Lisa's visit itself.

"Well, of course not like a modern-day marriage. The bride of Christ refers to the *mystical* and spiritual union of the human soul with God. Rest assured, it's a celibate union."

"Thank God." Louise chuckled nervously as she stared longingly at her glass of wine sitting on the coffee table. There was an intensity and passion in her cousin that was unnerving.

"Gertrude was one of the great mystics of the thirteenth century. She was considered to be a prodigious theologian."

Louise asked, "Would you like something to drink?"

"Whiskey, rye whiskey if you have it."

A verse from a country and western song ran through Louise's head: *If I don't get rye whiskey, I surely will die.* But Louise didn't have any whiskey. "I have some brandy."

Lisa shrugged.

Louise picked up her wine, went to the kitchen, and downed what was left in the glass before refilling it. The situation called for more wine. She wondered how long her cousin planned to stay. Would she have to put her up for the night? She carried their drinks back to the living room.

Lisa was looking at a book of photographs by Dorothea Lange. She looked up at Louise. "You know what they say about photographers—they're artists that can't draw." She laughed as she shut the book and tossed it on the table.

Louise was incensed but let it slide. She wondered if Lisa knew she was a photographer.

Lisa took the brandy out of Louise's hand and settled in a wingback chair as if she was holding court. Louise began to regret encouraging her cousin to attend the memorial service. The thought of having a cousin was quickly losing its appeal. It was late, and the memorial service was early the next day.

"I want to visit my mother's grave before my father joins her. I plan to go to the cemetery tonight."

"Oh," was all Louise could think of to say. She considered reminding Lisa that her father's ashes would be spread at the ranch, but something held her back.

"I need you to come with me," Lisa said emphatically.

Louise was speechless. She had no intention of going anywhere with this woman, much less a cemetery in the middle of the night.

"I'll drive. Already looked up the directions." Lisa shot Louise an ominous smile. "Hey, you can bring your camera."

So she *did* know Louise was a photographer. The previous snide remark was intentional.

"It's late. I have the memorial service early tomorrow morning."

Lisa's shoulders slumped, and she pouted as a look of forlorn spread across her face. "It would mean a lot to me."

I bet, she thought. But she also felt responsible. After all, she had pleaded with Lisa to come to New Mexico, and here she was. Who knew, maybe visiting her mother's grave would be cathartic. And technically, Lisa's mother was her aunt, too.

"Okay, but I'm going to make some coffee."

"Fine." Lisa shrugged and downed the rest of her brandy.

Louise climbed into Lisa's late-model SUV, which had seen

better days. The seats were ripped, the windshield cracked, and the passenger seat belt didn't work. The car had a funny smell but Louise couldn't put her finger on it. She steeled herself for the ride as they headed onto the freeway and merged into thankfully light traffic. The moon, full and ominous, had made its way up from the horizon to the middle of the sky. The four glasses of wine had made her groggy. She sipped some coffee from the thermos but her stomach churned with queasiness. She tried not to look out the window. The moon's light bounced off the evergreen trees, creating disorienting shadows.

Louise couldn't believe she was speeding along on the freeway without a seat belt. Not to mention that her cousin had downed a healthy drink of brandy and refused coffee. And whether that was even her first drink of the evening, she couldn't be sure. The cemetery, although only thirty-nine miles away, would take several hours to drive to and from. It was almost midnight. She couldn't imagine what Lisa envisioned would take place at her mother's grave. Maybe a few prayers. She wondered if Jews said prayers. If so, she was sure they weren't to Jesus.

They drove in silence, which Louise was thankful for. Right past mile marker 468 on the highway, there was a *pop*. The car swerved to the left and then to the right. Louise gripped the broken seat belt, trying to steady herself. The wine made her weak and the coffee bilious. She willed herself not to get sick as she squeezed her eyes shut, hoping to transport herself out of the situation.

Lisa screeched, "Shit, motherfucking shit, shit, shit," as she eased the car over to the shoulder.

As they grinded to an abrupt stop on the shoulder, the swearing spurred Louise into action. She jumped out of the car to assess the damage. The bald tire was blown. Louise wondered how it had lasted this long. "Do you have a spare?"

"That is the spare," Lisa said defiantly.

Louise had dealt with similar situations over the years on the force. People stranded on the highway, out of gas, blown engines, etc.

You advised them to call AAA or another roadside service. Then you sat and waited, making sure they didn't get run over.

"Do you have roadside service?"

Lisa turned to Louise and with each word her voice rose louder and louder. "Do I look like someone who would have roadside service?"

Louise tried not to grimace as she dialed her service instead. She identified where they were and what the problem was. AAA assured her that someone from Las Vegas, New Mexico, would be there in fifteen, twenty minutes tops.

Louise, in her years as a duty cop, had encountered people hit by cars on the highway. "Let's wait in the car. It's safer."

Lisa rolled her eyes as she climbed into the driver's seat.

It took the tow truck forty-five minutes. He looked at the tire, shook his head, and dealt out the bad news. He would have to tow the car back to Las Vegas, and they would have to wait until morning to get a new tire.

Now it was Louise's turn to swear, saying all the words the nuns would wash her mouth out for, though she did it silently.

CHAPTER 25

Louise's parents were a bit surprised when she called them the next morning but were absolutely shocked at the news that she was stranded at Motel 6 in Las Vegas. She put them off, saying she would explain when they picked her up. But when they pulled up to the motel, Louise, dressed in jeans and blue pullover sweater, hopped into the back seat before they could protest.

"Please, don't ask. I need coffee first. There's a Dunkin' right before the freeway on-ramp."

For once her parents didn't say a word. They drove to Dunkin', ordered her a large, and continued on their way in silence. Louise saw her father glance over at her mother once, but she stared straight ahead, stone-faced. When they exited the highway at Mora, her mother, unable to contain herself any longer, turned around. "Well?" she snapped.

"Well what?" Louise asked.

Her mother shot her one of those looks that withered Louise.

"What do you want to know?"

"For starters, what were you doing in Las Vegas last night?" her mother asked, straining to stay composed.

Louise took in a deep breath and let it out slowly. "Lisa showed up at my condo late last night. She wanted to see her mother's grave. She asked me to go with her. We had a flat on the freeway and had to be towed to Las Vegas. We spent the night at the Motel 6."

Her mother was nonplussed. For once, she had no comment and turned around.

The three of them continued in silence to the church. Louise considered sharing Lisa's spiel about St. Gertrude being Jesus's wife but didn't think her parents would appreciate the humor. As they drove through a portico onto the church grounds, Louise looked up at the rustic, wooden carved sign that announced, *Santa Gertrudis.* A plaque above the entrance proclaimed the Archdiocese of Santa Fe established St. Gertrude in 1851. The church was modest, lacking embellishments, but was the center of Mora County, serving sixteen mission churches.

When they entered the church, several people were already seated on the wooden benches, mostly in the center. They all turned and stared at Louise. She felt their eyes on her as she followed her parents to the front. They looked to be ranchers and locals, and although they weren't dressed up fancy like her mother, they weren't wearing blue jeans they had slept in last night. Louise smoothed down the blue sweater she had grabbed before leaving her condo last night. If she had shown up for the service in her wine-stained white blouse, her mother would have blown a gasket for sure. This morning at the motel, she didn't even have a hairbrush with her, so she had to run her hands through her hair and pull it back with a rubber band she found at the bottom of her purse. It wasn't a great look, but . . .

The three took their seats in the first row as the room quickly filled up. Memorial services weren't that exciting, but they were something to do in a small town. Participation in the service was a requirement to attend the reception. A means to an end.

Louise fidgeted, wondering where the hell the priest was. She hoped he would appear soon and get on with it. She stared at the rustic altar made of large, rounded rocks set in concrete and covered with a simple holy cloth. On the left sat a statue of Mary, and on the right Joseph held baby Jesus. In the middle, a small crucifix with Jesus nailed to the cross hung forlornly. Louise began to regret that she had arranged for Lisa to meet her after the service. Her parents would be disappointed in her once again. They expected her to go with them to the ranch for the reception. Afterward they were going to spread Uncle's ashes. But her father had encouraged her to get Lisa to come, and she had promised Lisa she would go to the cemetery.

Finally, twenty minutes late, the priest swept into the church from a side door, appearing flustered. He offered no explanation or excuse. He grasped hold of the pulpit with both hands and steadied himself, taking several long, slow breaths. Then he began the service. It was the typical Catholic ashes-to-ashes funeral service: not short and not sweet. Louise's heart sank as she watched the priest begin to prepare communion. She, a lapsed Catholic, hadn't been to confession in years and had no right to take communion. And, with this crowd, the procedure would take forever. Her mother nudged her shoulder a little harder than necessary, and Louise had no option but to dutifully rise and lead the congregation to the altar. She knelt on the bare pew, glad to have jeans to protect her knees on the rough wood. Row by row the parishioners left their seats, slowly made their way to the altar, kneeled, and took communion—eating Jesus's body and drinking his blood. She found the sacrament primitive and a little disgusting, but she didn't share her thoughts with her parents.

Louise glanced at her watch as the priest concluded the service and made an announcement about the reception. Then he motioned for her parents to follow him to the entrance. They formed a reception line with the priest, shaking hands and mumbling their thanks to the congregation as they left the church. Louise looked around the courtyard for Lisa, but she wasn't there.

It was a little past eleven when they shook the last hand. Her parents thanked the priest and started toward their car. Louise was frantic. Where was Lisa? She pulled out her phone, but she had no messages. When she saw her parents getting into their car, she ran to catch up with them.

"Hey!"

Her mother turned with another one of those looks, narrowing her eyes. "Yes?"

"I told Lisa I would meet her after the service, go with her to her mother's grave site."

Her mother raised her eyebrows with a look of bewilderment. "Well, where is she?"

Louise shrugged.

"We can't leave you here in the middle of nowhere. What if she doesn't show up? Not to mention, you agreed to help with the reception. What about Uncle's ashes?"

Louise's phone rang and she answered without looking at the screen. "Lisa, where are you?"

There was a moment of silence before the captain spoke. "This isn't Lisa, Detective."

CHAPTER 26

Louise pulled back the covers and climbed out of bed. She wondered how things could have spiraled out of control the day before. She didn't want to think about her cousin Lisa, the Motel 6, and especially the call from the captain. Apparently, the manager of the Las Vegas Motel 6 had called the station and talked to him. He wanted clarification about an officer, Louise Sanchez, who had shown up at the motel with an unidentified woman in the middle of the night. Sanchez had secured the room using a Santa Fe Police Department American Express Corporate Card and left early in the morning. The other woman was still in the room, sound asleep after checkout time.

In the church parking lot, with her parents staring at her with crossed arms, Louise had tried to explain the situation to the captain, but even to her ears it sounded ludicrous. She had offered the excuse that it had been three in the morning when the tow truck driver dropped them off at the motel and she was shaken from the blow out on the freeway when she handed over the wrong credit card at the motel. She had conveniently left out that she was still groggy from four glasses of wine.

The captain had insisted she return to the station immediately, and her parents were beyond furious. They would have to deal with the reception and spreading of ashes on their own. They got in the car, slammed the door, and spun gravel out of the lot. She had tried calling Lisa, but she didn't pick up and Louise didn't leave a message. She had prayed there was an Uber in northern New Mexico that would take her to Santa Fe. By the time she got back, the captain had left for the day.

Though it was now Sunday, technically her day off, she had the deposition that morning. Again, she would have to forego a day in the darkroom. The darkroom, as well as everything else in her life, including Madison's murder, would have to wait. Her irritation and resentment needed an outlet. She chose Pascal. It was all his fault. If he hadn't blown up the warehouse door, she would still be a patrol cop, waiting out her last days until retirement. She would be spending Sundays in the darkroom. She wouldn't be deposed and have to attend a trial.

She picked up her cell phone and groaned. She had less than an hour to get to the courthouse, and she hoped the deposition wouldn't take all morning. She pulled on the same outfit she wore on Friday. This was a new low, but Jesus Christ, who cared?

She parked her car and spotted a coffee shop on the corner. She thought about what a fiasco the weekend had turned out to be. Friday night, she had wine at the Twisted Pines, then another glass at home. After Lisa showed up, she had another glass. She wondered, not for the first time, if her drinking was a problem.

As she entered the conference room, again everyone was seated and ready to go. She thought she detected looks of disapproval on their faces. The DA and Fox-Elexor vied for her favor, taking turns grasping her hand with such force it jarred her head and made her eyes water. She took her seat and downed half the coffee, wishing she had purchased a large. But she had heard that, during depositions, it was frowned upon to ask to use the bathroom. God knows what trouble one could get into on the toilet.

Fox-Elexor cross-examined Louise. The attorney had done her

homework. She interspersed new theories and honed her questions to draw out the answers she wanted. After she finished, the DA stepped forward to recross. Louise had a sense of déjà vu. Even though the man attempted to reword the questions, they were basically the same ones he asked two days ago on Friday. She wondered whether the DA was extremely self-assured or just plain lazy. Louise hoped it was the latter; that would be in Pascal's favor. She answered each question as she had on Friday, no reason to reword or embellish her answers. Her brain, too foggy from the wine and drama of the weekend, made it difficult for her to spice things up, slip in a different adjective or adverb. She repeated her answers, delivering the same response over and over like an automaton.

After two hours of the drill, everyone seemed satisfied. The DA waved his magic wand and declared the deposition over. But he warned that the process was far from finished. The proceedings would be typed and distributed that afternoon. The transcripts needed to be reviewed; any changes, additions, or subtractions were to be submitted to the clerk by the end of the day. Then Ruiz's attorney would have time to review them with her client. The trial would begin the next morning, eight sharp.

As they filed out of the conference room, everyone seemed relieved. Fox-Elexor left with the crowd this time and didn't stay behind to talk to the DA. Louise knew she had her work cut out for her. Pascal might dodge jail time for his role in blowing up the warehouse door, but his career as a detective would surely be in question. There was a hiring freeze in state government, and with Pascal's partner, Matt Padilla, still out of commission, the position would remain vacant indefinitely.

It wasn't even noon yet, but Louise felt that her Sunday was already ruined, nothing left to salvage. Between the fiasco with Lisa, her uncle's memorial service, and the deposition, she was drained, empty, worn out. Her creative juices depleted. Not good for working in the dark, developing pictures. She needed to get busy on the case, dedicate the rest of the day, buckle down, make progress. Monday morning, the trial would begin, and it could go on for days, weeks even. If she didn't make headway with the case this weekend, it would drag on forever. Clues would vanish, the trail would turn cold.

Parking her cruiser in the station lot, she headed toward the Santa Fe Plaza. It was considered the city center and had the ambience of a traditional Spanish plaza, a place to gather and meet, at least when the weather was pleasant. Across the street on the north side of the plaza, beneath the portal of the Palace of the Governors, native artisans laid out their blankets along the sidewalk and sold their wares. But this morning the artisans huddled up against the building in an attempt to avoid the wind. The plaza was uninhabited, the benches empty.

Louise brightened as she spotted a food truck parked across from the La Fonda hotel. She ordered a couple of fish tacos, a healthy choice. She had her pick of benches and chose the one partially sheltered by the gazebo. It was early April, but there was no spring in the air. Winter was far from over. She ate quickly as cold wisps of wind stung her cheeks and blew her hair in all directions. She looked up at the sky. Gloomy gray clouds choked out most of the cerulean-blue patches except for occasional snippets that forced their way through. All of a sudden a faint image of sun, dusted with debris, appeared. But it was gone as quickly as it appeared.

As she stuffed the last bite of taco in her mouth, she took care not to let the filling drip down her front. With her coat's buttons falling off, she didn't need anything else to add to her questionable appearance. The wind had pulled most of her hair from her ponytail. It flew around her head in a tangled mess. She crumbled up the taco wrapper and thought about the information the bartender had shared. Even though the guy was annoying and cocky, he had turned out to be surprisingly helpful. She wondered who the man was that joined Madison in the bar. Possibly Roche, the head of Albatross, the man behind the shell company. Was he the one who drugged Madison's bourbon? The bartender told her the men had argued.

Did the argument have anything to do with Madison's death? And where the hell was this guy Roche?

Louise pushed herself off the bench, tossed the wrapper in the trash, and left the plaza. A few tourists hurried along, heads down, not looking at the pottery or jewelry displayed on the multicolored woven blankets. They were in search of a warm place out of the wind, not souvenirs.

When she arrived, the station lobby was bright, the fluorescents turned on, meaning it was Susie's day off. Louise had to admit the lights were excruciatingly bright.

One of the new recruits had been coerced into manning the front desk. The officer was bent over his phone, swiping at the screen. He looked up, gave Louise a brief nod, and went back to his phone. The station was always open and staffed, but on weekends it took on an eerie emptiness.

The break room was dark. Louise flipped the switch and made a pot of coffee. It wasn't a Dunkin' brew, but it was hot and packed with caffeine. There were still a few half-and-half creamers in the fridge.

She carried the cup down to her office, once again reminding herself that it wasn't her office. It still belonged to Pascal Ruiz, at least until the trial was over. She pulled her chair up to the desk and stared across the room at Webster Madison's picture at the top of the whiteboard. She'd had Rupert download his profile picture from the Babble dating site. Underneath the photo she had written *Albatross*, and then in parentheses *(secretary and Roche)*. She scanned the images from the Babble and Able Bodies home pages. Along the bottom of the board were the pictures of three potential suspects: Justine Dupont, Camille Lautrec, and the unidentified 911 caller. But she couldn't imagine any of the three women spiking Madison's drink and plunging a knife in his heart.

For a murder, you need a motive, the opportunity, and the means. Dupont and Lautrec knew Madison and had both the means and the opportunity. They knew where he lived and didn't have alibis. She wondered if they had the physical fortitude to plunge a knife into the man's chest. Louise had read about women who exhibited amazing acts of strength when needed, like lifting a car to save their baby trapped underneath.

The 911 caller was a big question mark. She had a description, and the woman knew where Madison lived, but that's all Louise knew about her. Then there was Roche, who seemed a likely suspect, especially if he was the same man who argued with Madison Sunday night at the bar. The bartender told her the man had been upset. Maybe Madison discovered Albatross was money laundering and threatened to expose Roche, turn him in to the FBI. Louise slumped in her chair. All supposition. She needed proof, and she needed to locate Roche and the secretary.

She pushed herself out of the chair, grabbed a couple of markers, and drew black lines representing connections. Lines from Madison to Albatross, Babble, Able Bodies, Justine Dupont, Camille Lautrec, and the 911 caller. Then she drew lines from Babble to Dupont and Lautrec. She stepped back and sighed. She was getting nowhere.

CHAPTER 27

It was two in the morning. Louise couldn't shut her brain down—sleep escaped her. She tried to slow her breathing, counting to seven, holding it then exhaling to nine. Finally she attempted the Shakti mudra, guaranteed, according to Ayurvedic practices, to put you right to sleep. She joined her ring and little fingers of both hands, folding down the middle and index fingers until they curled over her thumbs. She lay on her side, slowed her breath, and ignored the ache in her hands. When she released the mudra, she felt more awake than ever, her eyes stuck open, lids propped by toothpicks.

Outside sporadic gusts of wind swept her window, rustling the debris below. A late spring snow had been predicted, but as often happened in the West, the wind took over and blew the moisture east. Spring weather in New Mexico was a crapshoot. She turned on her lamp and scanned the pile of books on her bedside table. She had the Little Free Library book-sharing movement to thank for the accumulation. They'd added a location one day at the end of her street. It wasn't your typical square birdhouse box; instead, someone had built a miniature replica of a Victorian mansion. The house was crowned with a red-shingled spire topped with a metal rooster weathervane. The first time she opened the tiny doors, she half expected to see diminutive, ornate period furnishings. But it only contained books and an old National Geographic. They were free for the taking, but the takers were encouraged to leave a book in exchange. Louise never remembered to bring a book and couldn't resist borrowing one. She had read only a few of her selections, mostly mysteries, which had an anesthetizing effect on her. Usually before she made it to the end of the first chapter, she was fast asleep.

As she leaned over, the stack tipped, scattering books across the floor. She reached down and picked up the closest one, adjusted her pillow, and sank back. The book was unfamiliar, and she had no memory of choosing it. The dust jacket showed a dystopian scene full of images reminiscent of Hieronymus Bosch's depictions of hell. That felt a little too close to home.

Reading about imagined societies full of great suffering or injustice wouldn't help her fall asleep. The only dystopian novel she had read was George Orwell's *1984*. It had been assigned in high school and at the time the supposition seemed preposterous. She had been amused at the thought of an autocrat infiltrating citizens' everyday lives. Posters that read *Big Brother Is Watching You* were amusing at the time. Now, with the state of the world, she wasn't sure—maybe Orwell had nailed it.

Hours later, Louise woke to her phone blasting ABBA's "Dancing Queen." She pried open her eyes, stuck tight with sleepers. The first two pages of the dystopian novel were spread open on her face. The book reeked of mold and mildew, and nausea gurgled in her stomach. Hopefully she hadn't contracted some disease from the acrid paper. She tossed the book on the floor and had to admit, it had done the trick, put her to sleep in less than five hundred words. She found her phone among the pile of books on the floor and put an end to the pop song. She groaned as she looked at the clock. She had slept only four hours and was due in court. It was the first day of Pascal's trial.

She pulled open the drapes, bathing the room in muted light. The trees stood absolutely still as if frozen in place; the wind had finally ceased. It was such a relief. The sun hadn't made it over the mountains yet, but the sky was cloudless, the stars and moon erased.

Louise stared at the drab offerings hanging in her closet, a sea of colorless clothes. She pulled out a pair of dark gray wool slacks and matched them with a light gray cashmere sweater. The outfit was tailored and well made, but when she looked in the mirror she was disheartened. Dowdy, dull, colorless. Pascal's attorney, a real-life fashion plate, made Louise look like a scullery maid. She rummaged around in her drawer and found a colorful scarf. It wasn't silk, but it had been handwoven by an artisan, or at least that's what her mother had said. She tried to tie the scarf in several different ways, gave up, and left it to hang loose down the front of her sweater. She pulled her hair back and attempted to contain it in a stylish chignon but settled for an unruly ponytail. After a cup of coffee and toast, she applied maroon lipstick, wiped it off, then applied it again.

As she drove to the courthouse her nerves took over. Even though it wasn't an actual trial with a jury, more a pretrial, there would be a judge, the district attorney, Pascal's lawyer, Pascal, and witnesses. She assumed she would be the star witness and wondered who else had been deposed or subpoenaed to testify. The captain? The district attorney had asked her to remain in the courtroom until the proceedings were over in case further questions arose. The deposition had been arduous, but the trial would be grueling.

CHAPTER 28

Pascal had insisted on driving to the courthouse. Gillian offered to drive so he could review his notes, but he didn't need to review. He knew what went down that night, and the only thing he was sorry about was dragging Gillian into the fiasco.

Pascal pulled into the courthouse garage and found a spot immediately. He hoped it was a good sign. They rode the elevator to the second floor in silence. When the doors opened, Gillian flashed him a smile and said she needed to pee. He started to say something, but she had already turned away.

As he made his way down the hall, he spotted his attorney leaning against the wall outside the courtroom, cell phone to her ear. He had to smile; the woman was decked to the nines and wearing red—fighting colors. Fox-Elexor was sexy, but all business. She caught sight of Pascal, ended her call, and came toward him, her high heels clicking vociferously on the tiled floor. She reached out her right hand to shake while her left one gave his arm a squeeze.

"Ready?" she purred.

He needed more coffee. More caffeine. Things weren't going to go his way. His career was down the tubes, over. The worst part was disappointing his father. His old man had gone out on a limb, asked an uncle for a favor, to put in a word, make the job happen for Pascal.

As they entered the courtroom, the DA glanced up, his eyes like poison daggers. Pascal could feel the man's hatred even across the room. He couldn't figure out why the DA was dead set on wreaking vengeance against him. Though the DA was known to be a dick and obsessed with winning, there was something else beneath his vendetta. Pascal knew the man wanted to disgrace and humiliate him, but he also wanted blood.

Pascal followed his attorney to the front of the courtroom. He saw Louise sitting in the first row out of his peripheral vision. He didn't glance at her and was thankful that she didn't make an effort to acknowledge him. The court was packed—everyone wanted to see the lawman go down, eat dirt. Several police officers lined the back wall. He couldn't believe this was how they wanted to spend their day off, but . . .

Once seated at the table, he sensed Gillian behind him but didn't turn. For some reason her presence made him nervous. She wasn't the one on trial, but when her time came to testify, if she wavered from her sworn statement, she could be.

The bailiff announced the judge in a booming voice that sent everyone in the room scrambling to their feet. The trial was a bench trial, without a jury. The judge would be the sole individual to determine Pascal's guilt and sentence. His attorney told him the burden of proof would rest on the state, but that didn't reassure him.

The prosecution was to present their case and all of their evidence first. The DA strutted around in front of the judge, as though to impress him. After he presented his opening arguments, he called Louise Sanchez to the stand.

Louise was asked to relate the events the night of the warehouse explosion. The DA fired several questions but could clearly see the judge getting antsy. He reluctantly forfeited the floor and Fox-Elexor asked several clarifying questions about Louise's testimony.

As the DA and defense continued to bat back and forth, Pascal noticed the judge becoming more and more exasperated. With each cross-examination and each objection, the judge grimaced. Finally, he raised his eyes to the ceiling before banging his gavel on the desk, so loudly that a voice from the back of the courtroom yelped. Then the judge rose and motioned to the DA and Fox-Elexor to follow him to his chambers. The bailiff announced a recess until the next morning. Pascal wondered if that was a good or bad sign.

CHAPTER 29

Louise was stunned; it took her a few minutes before she realized she was free to leave. She gathered her belongings and left the courtroom, stopping out in the hall to check her voicemail and smiling when she saw the medical examiner's name, Dr. Elena Maithe. But as she listened to the doctor's message, her smile faded.

"Detective, Dr. Maithe here. I realize you're tied up in court this morning, but I haven't heard from you regarding the identification of Madison's body. I need to get him out. Now. As much as I've enjoyed his company—the last of a long line of women, I'm sure—I can't keep him forever. He's not my type. I must insist you find someone to identify his body. I'm available this weekend if necessary. Waiting with bated breath for your response."

Louise played the message again. Insist? Not my type? Bated breath? Was the doctor trying to be funny? Her message seemed to include more than one double entendre. Maybe she couldn't control herself—too much time with dead bodies. Or maybe her intention was to send a subliminal message. Louise remembered the warmth of the doctor's hand on her shoulder, how the heat had traveled all the way down to her toes. But she knew about wishful thinking. And unless she found someone to identify Madison's body, she wouldn't get far with the good doctor. She needed to locate Albatross's secretary or Madison's boss. Otherwise, she would somehow have to convince Camille Lautrec to identify the body, and she didn't want to go there again.

She started to check her other messages but spotted the captain by the elevators having a heated discussion with the commissioner. She put her phone away, turned, and headed toward the stairwell. No way did she want to be part of that conversation, or any conversation with the captain. She walked down the three flights of steps to the lobby and wondered if walking *down* the stairs counted as exercise. She hoped so.

CHAPTER 30

The taco truck was still parked across from the La Fonda as Louise made her way toward the plaza. She willed herself not to stop. She needed to get her weight under control.

Susie was back at her command post when Louise arrived. "Hey, *señorita*? Did you bust out?"

"Got a reprieve until tomorrow morning."

Susie looked down at the counter, ripped off half a page of a yellow notepad, and handed it to Louise. "All for you, Ms. Personality."

Louise looked at the paper where Susie had scribbled three messages. One was totally unintelligible, and she could barely make out the phone number. "Hey, Suz, those pink message slips back-ordered again at Office Depot?"

Susie tilted her head with a lopsided smile.

Louise made her way to her office. Between the voicemails on her phone and Susie's messages, there were six calls to return. First on the list was Rupert. She punched in his number as she stared at the yellow sheet of paper, trying to decipher the other two messages.

"Montoya."

"Hey, Rupert. What did you find out about Albatross?"

"You were right about Roche. He established his company as a shell about five years ago under a fictitious name, Albatross." Rupert chuckled. "You can say what you want about the guy, but he does have a sense of humor."

"Possibly a deadly one. I vaguely remember reading about shell companies during the last recession. Run me through it again." She wasn't about to let on that Pascal had explained shell companies.

"Basically, a shell is an empty holding tank that skirts the legal lines, which is why it's hard to nail these guys. From what I found out, Roche is in partnership with his brother, who runs another company in Switzerland, Lucinda Liquid Gold. Lucinda is set up as a legitimate business. Roche bills Lucinda for fictitious goods and services and the money is deposited into Albatross. My source told me that funds from stolen goods are also being laundered through the company. They have only one bank account that stores the money, which, according to my source, is a considerable amount. Roche rents a mail drop address to collect the fruits of the fraud."

Louise already knew most of this information except for the detail about Lucinda Liquid Gold. *Stolen goods?* She couldn't help but wonder about the museum's missing Native American pottery. Pascal said there were a bunch of boxes in the studio next to Katrin Simpson's house in Abiquiu, which was owned by Laredo Enterprises.

She spoke up. "Justine DuPont saw Madison in the lobby of the Opulent Building, standing in front of a mail drop. It was Albatross's mail drop."

"The Feds have been investigating Albatross. They set up an internal auditor to complete a workup on the background of the company. They tried to make the audit appear as a routine vendor or purchasing review, collecting other vendors' records at the same time. Someone, maybe Roche or maybe his secretary, got suspicious. Madison was hired to run interception. They probably wanted to see what the Feds were up to. But it looks like someone from the inside tipped Roche off. The mole exposed the real purpose of the audit before the auditor had completed his forensic accounting analyses."

"So where is Roche?"

"Unfortunately, he left town Sunday night. Took a United flight from Santa Fe Regional to Denver and then on to Chicago. There he picked up an ITA flight to Zurich with a short layover in Frankfurt."

"What time was his flight to Denver?" Louise asked.

"Ten thirty."

"Are you positive?"

"Yes, I emailed you the documentation. Looks like Roche has an alibi for Madison's murder."

Louise usually did her best not to swear, but this news got the best of her. "Bloody hell."

"Along with the flight details, I also emailed you my report on the secretary, Celine Cheshire."

"You found the secretary?"

"Yeah. Interesting woman. Not only a secretary; she oversees the company's financial transactions from her home in Las Vegas—that's Las Vegas, Nevada, not New Mexico. She told me she loves to come to Santa Fe in the summer for Indian Market. Cheshire earned an MBA from Stanford in the nineties. She also works for a few other, what she refers to as, virtual companies. According to her, it's all up-and-up. She was adamant that she wasn't doing anything illegal or involved in any scams. She considers herself an illusionist. Before going to Stanford, she performed with a magician, Lance Burton, at the Monte Carlo in Vegas. I couldn't find anything to substantiate that. Her persona now is managing officer, competent secretary, or financial officer for virtual companies."

"Sounds like you two became bosom buds."

"She's way out of my league, not to mention too old, in her sixties, but I respect her diligence."

"Really?" Louise said with as much sarcasm as she could muster. "She's in the business of deception. The woman should be behind bars."

"Yeah, although she would have to get in a long line. If the Feds find her guilty, she'll probably plead a deal. Toss Roche and his brother under the wheel."

Louise was surprised Rupert had admiration for this bogus woman. She knew about his past involvement with an antiscamming hacker group that assisted elderly people. The group provided a humanitarian service; still, hacking was illegal. The FBI had investigated and curtailed the operation, shut it down. Rupert had been barred from police work because of his association with the group. The captain, never a champion of the Feds, hired him to spite the agency.

Louise had to ask. "I'm curious, Rupert, who's your source?"

"A little birdie."

His voice didn't have a bitter edge, but Louise couldn't blame him. She wondered if he was hinting that Ruiz was the source. It made her uncomfortable. If so, it would be the third time Ruiz had helped with the case. "Can't wait to read your report."

"Let me know if you need anything else, *boss*," he said sarcastically.

She could tell he was about to hang up and was hesitant to ask anything more of him. "Oh, almost forgot. Were you able to reach the manager at Able Bodies?"

He sighed. "I got his name and cell number. Going to set up a meeting this afternoon."

"We need to determine whether the 911 caller was an employee of the agency. We have a sketch of the woman. Susie has copies. Show it to the manager."

"I'm on it."

"And thanks, Rupert. Good work." She hoped some praise would alleviate his irritation at being given so much of her leftover work.

The news that Celine Cheshire lived in Las Vegas was disappointing. The woman probably never laid eyes on Madison, unless she murdered him. Louise would need to subpoena the woman in order to have her identify Madison's body, and Roche was in Zurich. She doubted he would willingly return to the US to identify the body either. And despite the US having an extradition treaty with Switzerland, the country often refused requests from the United States.

Louise's phone buzzed in her pocket. Without bothering to

check the screen, she wedged it between her ear and shoulder while pulling Rupert's report from the printer. "Detective Sanchez."

Dr. Maithe snapped, "Have you found someone to identify Madison's body?"

"Sorry, ah . . . I've been in court."

"I heard the judge recessed the trial midmorning."

Louise wondered how the doctor had obtained that information. Maybe she had a little birdie, too. There seemed to be no secrets in the world of crime and punishment.

"No, I haven't. Roche, the head of Albatross, and his secretary are both unavailable. Roche left for Zurich Sunday night and the secretary lives in Las Vegas, Nevada. She probably never met Madison in person."

"Probably?"

"Most likely," Louise stammered.

"Well?"

"I'll ask Camille Lautrec."

"When?"

"I'll see if I can arrange to bring her to the morgue in the morning."

"Please do." The line went dead.

Louise's body slumped in her chair. She had taken a fancy to Elena Maithe. Wondered if they might become friends, maybe something more—but the woman had a bitchy side to her. She was one of those people who demanded what they believed they were due. Louise knew that if she couldn't convince Lautrec to identify Madison, she wasn't going to make many points with the doctor. The medical examiner wasn't one to be put off, and probably not one to forgive.

Louise longed to be in her darkroom. Hide out in the blackness, the little red glow beaming warmth while she waited for the chemicals to make their magic—her pictures come to life.

She pushed herself out of her chair, pulled her shoulders back, and tucked in her chin. She needed to convince Lautrec to identify

Madison, and it was better to ask in person—at least Lautrec couldn't hang up on her.

Louise called Lautrec and told her she needed a signature on the typed statement. It wasn't a total lie, but it wasn't her real purpose either. When Louise arrived at Camille's condo, the woman opened the door quickly, like she'd been waiting anxiously. She wasn't outwardly hostile, but she didn't welcome Louise with open arms, either.

The condo, immaculate and orderly as usual, radiated that model-home vibe. Louise couldn't help but compare Camille's house with Justine's. Yin and Yang. The women's circumstances were not the same, but they were linked. Both had attracted Webster Madison's attention. There was a connection, some underlying factor between them, but Louise couldn't see it.

Lautrec led Louise into the living room and waved her toward a chair. The woman's face was neutral, her lips were pursed, and her body language reeked of annoyance. Louise took out the typed statement and handed it to Lautrec to sign. The woman barely glanced at it before she picked up a pen, scribbled her signature at the bottom of the page, and handed the document back to Louise. Then she started for the door.

"Camille?"

Lautrec, perhaps surprised to hear her name, turned with a startled expression.

"Camille," Louise pleaded.

"What?" the woman snapped, narrowing her eyes.

"The medical examiner is in a bind. She needs someone to identify Madison. It will only . . ."

Camille held out her hands to stop Louise from continuing. "I. Told. You. No. Have Roche or his secretary do it."

"They're both unavailable, out of the country, out of town."

Lautrec, exasperated, let out a noise somewhere between a grunt and a scream, shrieking and waving her hands as if to rid them of something.

Louise recoiled, worried the woman might strike her. She held her breath, inwardly praying Lautrec would run out of steam. "I'm sorry."

"Are you?"

"Yes," Louise whimpered.

"Then let's go." Camile went to the closet and took out her coat.

Louise fumbled with her phone, her fingers feeling detached and numb as she searched for the doctor's number. She hoped the medical examiner was still in the building, available. Lautrec might change her mind in the light of a new day.

"Yes?" The annoyance in the doctor's voice slithered over the line.

"Ms. Lautrec has agreed to identify the body. Are you available now?" Louise spoke the two sentences as fast as she could, worried the doctor would hang up.

"Now?"

Though it annoyed the doctor when others did it, here she was, repeating Louise. "Yes. Now," she said, gritting her teeth.

"Give me thirty minutes."

"How about twenty?"

There was silence; the line went dead. Elena Maithe definitely had an unpleasant side, and Louise didn't like that aspect of the woman. She also seemed to lack an appropriate sense of humor in professional settings. But for now she would chalk those things up to spending a lot of time down under with dead bodies. And, frankly, Louise knew she shared in these traits, too, at times.

Louise knew it was inappropriate to request to use the facilities in a civilian's house, but she needed to kill some time. It wouldn't take more than ten minutes to get to the medical examiner's office. "Could I use your powder room?"

Camille's disdain was obvious, but her breeding clearly didn't allow her to deny someone in need of a toilet, even a detective she despised. She pointed down the hall. Louise didn't have to pee, but she sat down anyway. The toilet was one of those fancy bidet brands equipped with a heated seat and offering a choice of water temperature for rinses. She was thankful it didn't play music. She flushed, washed her hands in the hammered-copper sink, and dried them on the pressed linen guest towel, which looked as if it had never been used. Her reflection in the mirror caused her to moan audibly. She tried to smooth back her hair, but it was useless.

As she turned to leave, she noticed a framed print on the wall. The colors as well as the composition made it easily recognizable. Gustav Baumann. It was a signed limited edition. Louise couldn't believe it had been sequestered to the john. *It must be worth thousands.* She glanced at her watch, still twenty-six minutes to kill. She didn't want Camille to think she was taking a dump, so she headed back to the living room.

Lautrec stood at the door, coat buttoned, purse on her arm, an annoyed look on her face. Louise followed her to the elevator. This woman didn't need to use the stairs—she didn't have an ounce of fat on her. They walked over to the cruiser and Louise blurted out, "I'm not allowed to have civilians ride in the front seat."

Lautrec glared as she tried to wrench open the back door. Louise unlocked the door and the woman slid into the car in one graceful move before Louise had a chance to guide her head in.

The traffic had picked up and slowed their progress across town. Louise heaved a sigh of relief; she didn't want to arrive early, didn't want Camille to have to wait more than five minutes in the building. The woman was short on patience, not that Louise could blame her.

Lautrec followed her into the lobby. They took the elevator up to the fourth floor and made their way down the hall to Dr. Maithe's windowless office. The door was closed. There was no way the doctor could be in the tiny room with the door closed, but Louise tried the doorknob anyway—locked. She took out her phone and punched in the doctor's number.

"Yes?" Dr. Maithe asked.

"We're here."

"We?"

Louise, exasperated, tried to collect herself. "Yes, we, Ms. Lautrec and I. She's here to identify Webster Madison's body?" Louise could easily strangle the woman.

"Where?"

Louise urged herself not to scream. "At your office." Even though the doctor spent her days with dead bodies, it was not an excuse for her obtuse behavior.

She heard the doctor exhale. She sounded more weary than annoyed, which was encouraging, a sign of civility that Louise needed at this point. "Go back to the lobby. I'll meet you there and take you down to the morgue."

Lautrec crossed her arms and glared at Louise, expecting an explanation.

"She'll meet us in the lobby."

Dr. Elena Maithe was waiting as the elevator doors opened. She reached out for Lautrec's hand and tenderly caressed it in both of hers, purring words of sympathy and encouragement.

Louise clamped her mouth shut and looked up at the ceiling. *Brother, what an act*, Louise thought. The woman was like a spider luring its prey into its web.

The three women descended to the basement in silence. As they exited the elevator, the acrid aroma of disinfectant engulfed them. Lautrec coughed and pulled her silk scarf over her nose. The doctor rested her hand on Lautrec's shoulder, guiding her into the morgue. A pang of jealousy shot through Louise's body before she could stop it. She knew it was ridiculous to feel jealous at a moment like this.

Once inside the room, the doctor resumed her medical examiner role. Webster Madison's gurney, thankfully, seemed to be the only one in the room. It was draped with a clean sheet. Louise was relieved the doctor had replaced the blood-splattered one from the autopsy, though it seemed obvious now that she would do so.

The doctor ushered Lautrec over to the side of the gurney. The woman's impeccable complexion had drained of color and taken on a greenish, reptilian hue. Louise hoped that Camille wouldn't faint.

"Ms. Lautrec, I need you to identify whether the body is Webster Madison or not. You don't have to speak, you can nod yes or no."

Lautrec's eyes flashed with fear, seeming to realize fully that she was indeed in a morgue next to a dead body, the body of her college boyfriend.

"Ms. Lautrec?" the doctor asked softly.

Lautrec opened her mouth but nothing came out.

"Are you ready?"

Lautrec bobbed her head, then swayed slightly as the doctor pulled down the sheet to Webster Madison's shoulders, careful not to reveal the wound to his chest. Louise couldn't imagine what it would be like to see a person you once loved dead on a gurney.

Finally, Camille's voice came out as a whisper. "Yes."

The doctor, with an audible sigh of relief, pulled the sheet back up over the dead man's head.

"I'll need you to pop upstairs and sign a form verifying the identification of the body." The doctor's tone was suddenly crisp, all business. She had gotten what she wanted and was ready to wrap things up. Wham, bam, thank you, ma'am.

"Shall we?" She swept her arm toward the door. "The papers are in my office. Only take a sec." As the two women followed the doctor through the door, Maithe mumbled something, but the group was concentrating on getting to higher ground and nobody asked for clarification. No one offered Lautrec soft words or a comforting touch to her shoulder, either—she was on her own now. As they climbed into the elevator, even Dr. Maithe seemed relieved to leave the basement, be back in the light of day, the light of the living.

Somehow the medical examiner had managed to cram two chairs into the closet-like space. Once they were seated, there was no room to close the office door, but the hallway was empty, giving them privacy.

The doctor squeezed behind her desk and sent a pile of papers to the floor. "Damn," she said, but made no attempt to pick up the papers. She reached across the desk and handed a form to Lautrec, instructing her to read and sign it.

Camille barely glanced at the paper before she scribbled her name at the bottom and handed it back to the doctor.

"Now"—the doctor folded her hands on top of the desk, tilted her head, and with a look of expectation asked—"what are the instructions for the body?"

Camille let out an audible gasp, then swallowed several times before she managed to stammer, "Instructions?"

"It seems Mr. Madison has no next of kin or any relatives, at least who can be located. Since you identified the body, you are legally in line to give directions for the arrangements."

"Legally? In line? Arrangements? I . . . I have no idea. Webster was an attorney. He must have left instructions, an executor, a will, his wishes?"

"You'd be surprised. A lot of people don't make arrangements for unexpected occurrences such as an early demise. Attorneys especially seem to think they're invincible."

It took all of Louise's resolve not to roll her eyes. Unexpected occurrences, early demise? That was an understatement. How about being stabbed in the heart? Murdered?

"Not that Webster Madison doesn't have the financial means to take care of a funeral and disposal of his body, but someone has to take responsibility, make decisions, provide instructions, make the arrangements."

Lautrec had reached her limit. The color in her face returned to its original glow. She obviously did not want to plan Webster's funeral. "I'm sorry, ladies. I'm done here." With that, she scooted her chair out into the hall, the legs screeching on the linoleum. As she rose, she shot a look of warning at the doctor and marched down the floor to the elevators.

Dr. Maithe didn't move, her lips parted in surprise. Then she squeezed out from behind the desk and started after Lautrec. She was too late. The elevator doors snapped closed. The woman was gone.

"You can't blame her," Louise said as she caught up with the doctor.

"Shit. Shit, shit, shit. Now what am I going to do?"

The doctor's use of profanity again surprised Louise. Her sympathies lay with Camille. The woman had fulfilled the doctor's request, identified the body. She hadn't signed on for planning her college boyfriend's funeral.

The doctor spun around and faced Louise. "What about that other woman?"

"What woman?" Louise was becoming wary of the doctor.

"Dupont."

"What about her?"

"Would she be willing to make the arrangements? I can have a funeral home pick up Madison. They can wait for her instructions. She could do it over the phone."

"Are you crazy?"

The doctor stared at Louise with an exasperated look. "If I don't get this off my plate, I will go crazy. I need this body out of my life. Now."

"What do you usually do with unclaimed bodies?"

"They're sent to storage, but Madison isn't unclaimed. Camille Lautrec identified and signed off on him. Legally she has seventy-two hours to arrange a funeral home to pick him up."

Louise realized that, as much as she was attracted to the medical examiner, she had spent way more time than necessary dealing with the woman. She needed to get back to work, solve Madison's murder. Tomorrow morning she would be stuck back in court again.

"Please, someone needs to arrange for his pickup."

Louise stared at the doctor's soft hazel eyes. The color made her knees go squishy, spongelike. Before she could stop herself, she said, "I'll talk to Dupont."

Dr. Maithe smiled, reached over, and gave Louise's forearms a squeeze. "Seventy-two hours." Then she turned and headed back to her office.

CHAPTER 31

Camille Lautrec stood on the sidewalk outside the building, but the morgue's stench still tickled her nose. The image of Webster's lifeless body on the gurney would be emblazoned in her memory forever. Thank God the medical examiner hadn't pulled the sheet down any further and exposed the stab wound—her knees would have buckled for sure. The thought of her body splayed across the icy linoleum, reeking of bleach and ammonia, made her stomach curdle.

Once in the elevator, she had arranged for an Uber to pick her up. There was no way she would get back in the police car with that detective. She was glad to be rid of both of those women. And what was the medical examiner thinking, asking her to plan Webster's funeral? The idea was ludicrous. A black Honda Accord pulled up to the curb. She glanced at her phone, checking to make sure it was the car she ordered. You couldn't be too careful these days. She had read about women picked up and assaulted by men impersonating Uber drivers.

She climbed in the back seat and sank into the leather, thankful for the dark tinted windows that shut out the insufferable New Mexico sun. Her eyes still burned from the morgue's disinfectant and her head throbbed. Santa Fe had seemed like the perfect move. She thought of it as downsizing, leaving LA behind where life had become unmanageable; traffic, smog, drought, fire, not to mention the possibility of earthquakes. And the loss of Renoir, her husband, made the city unbearable. Everywhere she went, she was reminded of him and the life they once had. The idea of working again in the opera, being useful, had been the clincher. She was offered a job, head of the Santa Fe Opera costume department. It was perfect, the season short, only producing five or six operas during the summer months. The pay wasn't much, nothing compared to Los Angeles, but she didn't need money. Renoir had left her comfortable. But his death had set her adrift, and she was desperate for something to anchor her.

She exited the Honda and tipped the Uber driver. As she opened her front door, she thought about Webster Madison, the man she had loved in college and, in her naivete, imagined she would forever. But after college, she had moved on and barely thought of Webster in the last twenty-five years. When she came across his profile on the online dating site, she was surprised he was living in Santa Fe. Middle age suited him—he had become even more handsome over the years. She hadn't bothered to read his profile and swiped left with a feeling of satisfaction. *Touché.*

She had no intention of reuniting with the man. Webster, she knew from past experience, was all about the conquest, pursuing and wooing. Once a woman dropped her guard and gave in, he was finished with her, no longer interested. They had gone their separate ways years ago, and in the words of a Thomas Wolfe novel, "You can't go home again." And who wants to? But that was before Isabelle knocked on her door.

CHAPTER 32

As soon as one fire was extinguished, another flared up. The case was beginning to feel like Southern California during the drought season. Louise marveled at the medical examiner's ability to manipulate and wondered if that was a technique taught in medical school. Lautrec had identified Madison's body, but now there was a seventy-two hour deadline to plan Madison's funeral. Louise considered making the arrangements herself. Have the guy cremated, say three Hail Marys, and spread his ashes along the acequia. Better than asking Justine Dupont.

Louise's head throbbed, desperate for caffeine. Like Hercule Poirot, she once again needed to get her little gray cells working. As she pulled into the Dunkin' parking lot, her car hit a large piece of dislodged asphalt. She winced but continued through the lot, dodging the potholes. She briefly considered exiting, not because she worried about the cruiser's undercarriage being ripped to shreds, but because doughnuts were hard to pass up. Her waistline couldn't stand any more calories.

Dunkin' was the hangout for patrol officers. Nobody she knew, in or out of uniform, would be caught dead waiting in line at Starbucks. The only time she had gone to Starbucks was with her mother after an exhibition at the Georgia O'Keeffe museum. While standing in line, Louise had stared at the menu: white chocolate, butterscotch,

Frappuccinos, something called the Pink Drink, cold brew, the list went on. All she had wanted was a bloody cup of coffee. At Dunkin,' things were simpler. The menu had gotten trendier over the years, sure, but she could still go in and ask for just a plain cup of coffee. And it tasted perfect.

She ordered a large coffee, averting her eyes from the selection of doughnuts under the glass counter and chose a table in the back corner. She kept an eye on the door—police routine. The only other customer was a teenager in a booth by the front window. The kid was hunched over his phone, giggling. Under the table his left foot rested on his skateboard, moving it back and forth.

As she pulled out her Ado List, a loud bang startled her. She looked up and saw two boys on the sidewalk making faces in the window. The teenager jumped up, grabbed his skateboard, and used his backside to push his way out the door. The three kids bumped fists then jumped on their boards and skated away. A pang of envy shot through Louise. Teenagers. The camaraderie. The carefree life. That is, if the boys didn't crack their skulls open.

She stared down at her list and realized there was nothing to check off. The calls she had returned got her nowhere and only resulted in more tasks. Lautrec had identified Madison's body, but that didn't get the medical examiner off her back. She was a detective. It wasn't her responsibility to find someone to plan a victim's funeral. Rupert's information on Albatross was interesting but not helpful. Maybe the cleaning company could identify the 911 caller. If she could find out who the woman was, what she was doing at Madison's Monday morning and why she said she was Camille Lautrec, she would have some answers.

She pulled out her phone. Somehow she had missed two calls and several messages from Gillian Jasper and Justine Dupont. With Ruiz's trial in the process, Gillian's call made her edgy. A record of their conversation could be misconstrued, but she was curious and returned the call.

Gillian answered out of breath. "Gillian Jasper."

"Detective Sanchez returning your call." Louise decided to keep the conversation professional.

"Hi. Sorry, just got back from a run; this altitude is a killer. Ah . . . I was calling you about something else, then this other thing came up and wanted your advice."

Louise detected Gillian's uneasiness. "Okay."

"I've been summoned."

"To appear in court?"

"Yes, tomorrow morning, at Pascal's trial."

Louise understood Gillian's anxiety. After the explosion at the warehouse, she had given a statement and signed it. If she changed anything, she could be charged with perjury, lying under oath. "Where's Pascal? Court was recessed earlier today."

"He's sequestered with his attorney, prepping for tomorrow."

"If you received a summons, it's only an invitation to appear in court, not an order. If you choose not to appear, the judge will decide the case without your testimony. Not that I recommend ignoring a summons. Are you sure it was a summons? They're usually issued for civil cases involving lawsuits."

"Hold on a sec—ugh, it says subpoena."

"You can't ignore a subpoena. It's an order to appear in court. If you ignore the order, the court will hold you in contempt. You could go to jail or face a fine. And if you lie under oath, it's perjury, which is a federal crime. That could result in probation, fines, or even a prison sentence."

"Oh, Lord," Gillian moaned. "But why would they subpoena me? They have my statement."

"Subpoenas are given to anyone who might have useful information about the case. It makes sense you received one. I can't believe they didn't do it sooner. You were at the scene of the crime, and the DA might want to question your side of the story. Grill you, try to poke holes in your testimony. In turn, Pascal's attorney might want to elaborate on your testimony to support his case. A written statement can't be argued or questioned."

"Jesus," Gillian lamented.

"Yeah, I hear you, sister. Also, keep in mind you signed a statement about the warehouse explosion. If you change your story now, you could be in trouble."

"What do you recommend?"

"If you're worried, you could ask a lawyer for advice. If you stick to your story, you shouldn't have a problem."

"Thanks, Detective."

"Do you know who initiated the subpoena?"

"No, but if it was Pascal's attorney, I think she would have told me."

"I'm a firm believer that it's always better to have your say, not let someone else decide what you said."

"I tell you, ever since I arrived in New Mexico, I've been mixed up with the law. I never even had a traffic ticket before coming here. Why is this happening to me?"

"Don't know," Louise said, but Pascal came to mind.

"Thanks again."

"What was the other thing you wanted to talk about?"

"Let's talk about it after the trial, that is, if I'm not serving time."

Louise worried that could be a possibility. "Sure." She hung up and considered adding Gillian, along with Camille and Justine, to the list of women she felt sorry for. The three had their lives upended by men. Maybe she better stick with women.

She dialed Justine Dupont before she'd thought about what she was going to say. Her stomach flipped and flopped with each ring. It was ridiculous to ask a woman to plan a funeral for a man she'd only met a few times. But maybe Justine had some suggestions. What did she think Madison would want? Was he the type to be buried, cremated, or composted? Religious service, wake, both, or neither? She started to hang up but then thought of the doctor and her promise—and Dr. Maithe wasn't one to be put off.

On the fifth ring the call went to voicemail and Louise tossed out a Hail Mary.

"This is Detective Sanchez . . ." Her tongue felt thick in her mouth. There was no way she could ask Dupont to plan Madison's funeral on voicemail. That would be chickenshit. "Could you return my call at your earliest convenience?"

Beads of sweat dotted her forehead as she downed the last dregs of her coffee and left Dunkin'. As she made her way across the parking lot, the sky, an iridescent blue without a hint of clouds, blinded Louise. She rummaged in her purse for her sunglasses. It was late afternoon, but the sun was intense. Before starting her car, she pulled out the message that Susie had scribbled on the crumpled piece of paper. She squinted, trying to discern the writing, and gave up. That call would have to wait.

St. Francis Drive was already clogged with cars heading toward the interstate. She edged her way into the traffic. The caffeine had perked her up but now she felt anxious. She was no closer to finding out who murdered Madison than the day she found him with a knife in his chest. At least he had been officially identified, not that it satisfied the medical examiner.

Her phone rang and she kicked herself for not connecting to Bluetooth. She didn't want to be seen driving a police car with a phone stuck to her ear. She glanced down at the screen but didn't recognize the number. The phone stopped ringing and a minute later she heard the voicemail notification. She hoped it was the person who'd left the indecipherable message. She cut off St. Francis to a secondary road and the traffic became lighter. Then she pulled into a parking space, killing the engine. She groaned as she listened to the voicemail—it was Justine Dupont returning her call. The coffee from Dunkin' churned in her stomach. She hadn't eaten lunch and now was sorry she hadn't grabbed a doughnut, waistline or not. She punched the return-call button before she lost her nerve.

"Hello."

"This is Detective Sanchez. Sorry I missed your call. Thanks for getting back to me."

There was silence on the other end of the line. Maybe Dupont was nodding her response.

"Ah . . . someone has identified Webster Madison's body. You're off the hook." There was silence on the line, so Louise continued. "Apparently not many people knew Madison. Well, besides you and a college girlfriend. Luckily the girlfriend agreed to identify him."

"Jesus," Justine muttered.

"It's a legal requirement."

"What about the people he worked for?" Justine asked.

"As you know, there isn't an office. Albatross is a shell company. The head of the company left Sunday night for Zurich, as in Switzerland, and the secretary lives in Las Vegas, as in Nevada."

"Okay . . . Detective?"

"There's another matter that needs to be resolved, Ms. Dupont."

"What other matter?"

"What to do about Madison."

Suddenly, Justine's voice raised. "What are you talking about? Haven't you pestered me enough?" Clearly, she didn't want to further discuss the matter.

Louise plunged ahead. How much worse could things get before Dupont hung up? "Only a few decisions. That's all. Cremation versus burial? Service versus wake?"

Justine had had enough. She ended the call.

Louise stared at her phone's dark screen. She wasn't surprised that Dupont had hung up on her—more so that it had taken as long as it did. The thought of a drink surfaced. She glanced at her watch. It wasn't five yet, but close enough. She could go over Madison's Sunday-night timeline with the bartender at the Twisted Pines again. Rupert had snagged Roche's photo from the internet. She hoped the bartender would identify Roche as the client Madison had met at the bar.

As Louise pulled into the Twisted Pines parking lot, it was only a quarter to five. She parked and scrolled through her email. All ads. Nobody emailed anymore, everyone texted. More immediate, harder to ignore. She scribbled down some questions to ask the bartender. Finally, five o'clock hit and she headed to the door. When she entered the bar, the change from the bright outdoors to the subdued interior blinded her. While her eyes adjusted, she scanned the room and was glad to find it empty. The bartender, busy drying and arranging glasses on the shelves, didn't bother to turn around as she approached the bar.

Louise pulled herself onto a barstool, the effort yet another wake-up call that she was out of shape. Again, she renewed her promise to do something about it, as soon as this case was solved.

The bartender spun around with eyes wide in mock surprise. "Starting a little early, Detective?"

Always the funny guy, Louise thought, contemplating a tug on his nose ring. It hung low, almost resting on his upper lip. Not a good look. "I'm hoping you can clarify a few things about Sunday night. You were very helpful last time. I appreciate it." Never hurt to compliment someone before pumping them for information.

"Clarify away," he said as he continued wiping a wine glass with a dingy rag.

Louise restrained a laugh. She couldn't figure out if he was trying to be funny or just plain dumb. He was the one who needed to clarify the information, not her.

"I want to go over the timeline for Madison and the guy he met, when each man arrived and left."

"Like I told you, Madison came in right before the movie crowd, around eight. The other guy came in about fifteen minutes later. They each ordered a bourbon, straight up." The bartender apathetically recited the details in a monotone as he replaced a glass on the shelf and picked up another one.

"And what else can you tell me?

"I told you, the guys, especially the second guy with the Nazi haircut, were a little steamed up, nothing physical, but definitely throwing spars. Around eight thirty, the friend stormed out. Madison stayed put, ordered another bourbon."

"And what about Ms. Dupont and her husband?"

"The Lone Ranger and Tonto?"

Louise nodded and forced herself to smile.

"They arrived a little before Madison, maybe quarter to eight.

"And?"

"The little lady ordered a bourbon too. Must be a connection there, don't you think, Detective? Partners in crime?"

If he only knew, Louise thought. "Could be a coincidence. About what time did Madison join Dupont at the bar?"

"It must have been around nine. He ordered another bourbon, his third. Both he and the little lady seemed a bit over their limit, but I let it slide. Madison left me a hefty tip."

"And Dupont? When did she leave?"

"Shortly after Madison, around nine thirty."

The front door banged open, filling the bar with sunlight, and they both turned. An enormous man, close to seven feet tall and carrying at least three hundred pounds, barged in. He slowly made his way to the far end of the bar and pulled his heft onto one of the stools.

"Gotta tend to this dude," the bartender said as he hooked his thumb toward the man.

"Glass of cabernet before you go," Louise asked as nicely as she could muster.

He poured her a glass of Ménage à Trois while raising his eyebrows up and down. Louise stifled a groan.

As she sipped her wine, the bartender made his way down to the end of the bar and got into an animated conversation with the big man. The bartender was a jerk, but at least he was someone to talk to. An overwhelming feeling of loneliness swept over her, realizing it was too early to be having a glass of wine alone in a mall bar. She decided to call Gillian.

"Hello."

"Hey, it's Louise Sanchez."

"Is everything okay, Detective?"

"As far as I know. I"—Louise wasn't sure how to broach the subject—"I wanted to ask you about something. It's nothing to do with the trial."

"Okay . . ." She seemed hesitant.

"How did you get started jogging?"

Gillian laughed, relief in her voice. "It's sort of a long story."

"I've got a little time."

Gillian took in a deep breath and let it out slowly. "When I was twelve my mother left. She took my baby sister and moved to Santa Fe. I stayed with my father in Bethesda outside of DC. Our house backed up onto Rock Creek Park. The day my mother left I walked into the woods and cried until there were no more tears. This pretty much became my daily routine. One afternoon I wandered into the woods and kept walking until the trees had blocked out the sun. I had to feel my way through the forest, tree by tree." Gillian paused.

Louise wasn't sure she wanted to hear the story and was about to interject when Gillian continued.

"Ahead I saw a small clearing that opened up and let the sun shine down through the trees. I saw something shiny on the ground, and as I reached down to see what it was, I heard the leaves rustle. It spooked me. I looked around frantically. At the edge of the clearing there was a shadow of a man. His arms hung down below his belly, and he was sort of gyrating. He was saying something, but my ears buzzed with fear. I knew enough not to talk to strangers. I felt vulnerable, alone in the woods. I turned to run and my legs moved in slow motion. It was like running through molasses. I had never been athletic, and I worried about my hands."

"Your hands?" Louise asked almost in a whisper.

"I'm a violinist. Your hands are your future. They're everything. Mess them up, you're finished. Done for."

"Well, at least you had an excuse not to exercise."

"Everything changed that day."

"What about the man?" Louise suspected where Gillian's story was heading and it made her uncomfortable. She was sorry she had asked and hoped Gillian's story ended well.

"I ran. I picked up speed but my legs wobbled. I thought I would crumble to the ground. My lungs ached as if any minute they would burst through my chest. Somehow adrenaline took over, pumped through my body, propelled me out of the woods. When I reached our back door, I felt euphoric. It was pure elation. My arms, legs, even my face were covered in scratches and blood. I was a mess. But my pain, both inside and out, vanished that day."

"Jesus," Louise muttered.

"Never cried again. Been running ever since."

Louise wanted that. She wanted euphoria. She wanted elation. "Would you be willing to help me get started jogging? That is, after the trial and this murder case is wrapped up?"

"Louise." Gillian's tone was stern, it reminded her of her mother. "If you put it off until you think you have time and everything in your life is in order, it will never happen. Running has to be your priority. Your commitment. You have to fit it in."

Priority and commitment were two things Louise often had trouble with. But as she took her last sip of wine, she thought maybe it was time to embrace Shia LeBeouf's hilarious motivational rant. *JUST DO IT!* "When can we start?"

"Tomorrow morning. Six sharp. Do you have shoes?"

"I have an old pair of sneakers."

"That'll do for now. We can shop for running shoes later."

"See you at six then." Louise needed to hang up. Excuses were popping into her head a mile a minute.

The bartender appeared and picked up her empty wine glass. "Another?"

"No, thanks. Think I'm done."

He raised his eyebrows and smirked.

Louise ignored his sarcasm. "One more thing." She picked up her phone, searched for Roche's photo, and held it out to the bartender. "Is this the man that joined Madison Sunday night?"

He snatched the phone out of her hand, using his thumb and finger to enlarge the picture while tilting his head side to side. Louise resisted the urge to grab the phone back.

"Yeah, that's him."

CHAPTER 33

Louise's phone rang on the coffee table, waking her. She had fallen asleep on the couch while watching a new TV series, which she would have to rewatch since she had no idea when she drifted off. She picked up her phone and groaned. It was her cousin Lisa. She considered letting the call go to voicemail, but then she'd probably get the voicemail when she called back anyway. She hadn't heard from her cousin since their ill-fated trip to Lisa's mother's grave

"Hey, Lisa."

"I need the menorah."

Louise, instantly perturbed, demanded, "Do you know what time it is?"

She could hear Lisa huffing into the receiver. "I have a watch," she snipped.

"Lisa . . . I'm sure you're aware that I'm in the middle of working on a murder case, not to mention I'm due in court in the morning. As soon as the case is wrapped up, I will be glad to ship your mother's trunk to you. But in the meantime, I hope you will consider that these are your family's heirlooms, your history. You should think twice before selling them off."

"Don't tell me what I should or shouldn't do," Lisa snapped. "I don't need the old trunk with that crap. Just need the menorah."

Louise was curious why all of a sudden Lisa had taken an interest in the menorah. "Oh?"

"I need money. I'm going to Spain, to find out the truth."

The truth. Louise had no idea what Lisa was talking about. "You're going to inherit the ranch in Mora. The sale will provide you with enough money for your travels or whatever else you want to do."

"Well, there's a problem. I talked to your father yesterday and that bitch, Julia, the one that threw me out, is claiming the ranch is hers. It's tied up in probate right now and nobody knows for how long."

Louise was surprised that her uncle's ex-wife thought she had claim to the ranch. They had divorced years ago. "I'm sure my father will get it straightened out. The ranch was left in your name."

"Are you listening to me, Louise? Because you don't seem to be. I need the money now. I'm turning sixty next month and time is running out. I need to find out who I am, where I came from."

What a crock, Louise thought. Lisa knew who she was. And anyway, her father had traced their family's line back to Spain without traipsing across the ocean. He used the internet and that ancestor website.

"Maybe you want to come with me? Find yourself, your roots?"

That was the last thing in the world Louise wanted to do. No way was she going anywhere with Lisa again. "I don't have time for a European trip right now. I have a murder case to solve and a June photography exhibition to prepare for."

"It's always about you, Louise," Lisa said sadly.

Louise was floored. What was this woman talking about?

"You know I'm the last of my mother's line, and she had to screw it up with your uncle. You aren't going to be having any babies at your age, so you're the last too. Maybe your side of the family are Cryptos. Ever thought of that?"

Louise had had about enough of this conversation. "I'll talk to my father in the morning and see what's going on. I'm sure there's a way to straighten this out, get the probate settled, the ranch sold, and get you your money."

"I'm texting you my address. Send the menorah." Lisa hung up without saying goodbye.

Louise turned off the TV. She had to get up in five hours and now was wide awake. She considered a glass of wine to settle her down but instead crawled into bed, feeling glad she was an only child when she finally drifted off.

It was pitch-black outside when her phone blasted a tune at exactly five a.m. She groaned and reconsidered jogging, especially if it was going to take place this early in the morning. Last night at the bar, Gillian's story had inspired her. Jogging was what she needed to turn her life around. And for the first time she had declined a second glass of wine. But mornings were always a challenge.

She remembered she was supposed to call her father about the ranch but she didn't have the time or energy right now. It would have to wait. She tugged on an old pair of sweats and dug through her closet for a pair of tennis shoes. They were iconic Chuck Taylor All Star sneakers, a far cry from running shoes. They had a replica of an All Star license plate on the heel. Converse had reissued the Chucks in conjunction with a big advertising campaign a few years ago. Both the high- and low-top sneakers had become all the rage. Louise had worn her red pair of low-tops whenever she was off duty. The sneakers were cushioned but didn't have much arch support, and the bottoms were virtually flat and slick. They would have to do for now.

Gillian had sent a text to meet at the Fort Marcy monument and reminded Louise to bring water. Louise didn't own a water bottle. She searched her kitchen for a container and ended up emptying a quart of milk into a wine carafe. The milk container, even after several rinses, still held a sour smell. After work she would purchase a real water bottle.

It had been a moonless night, and the sun wasn't expected up for another hour. As Louise drove to Fort Marcy, the sky looked like ink, only a few faint stars remaining. The monument, on the summit of a flat-topped hill, had been constructed in 1846 commemorating the Mexican–American War. The spot was perfect, commanding a view of the entire town.

The park was deserted this early in the morning. The streets were quiet, nobody up and about. Louise climbed out of her car and looked around for Gillian. She waited, her keys in hand, ready to defend herself if needed. She thought of her revolver, unavailable, locked securely in the glove compartment. Santa Fe wasn't a violent city, but the thought of Gillian's encounter back in Rock Creek Park made her jumpy. She wondered if Gillian had reported the man or shared the story with her father or a friend. That type of incident would be traumatic for a twelve-year-old, or for anybody, really. Louise was impressed that Gillian had found something positive in the experience. Something that stayed with her all these years. Maybe she, too, could find that.

"Hey!" Gillian called out as she jogged across the street.

"Hey." Louise waved, relieved that she wasn't alone anymore. It surprised her that the park had unnerved her. For some reason, she felt exposed and vulnerable.

"I wanted to meet here because the adjoining park has interval workout stations. Something you can do on your own between sprints."

Louise looked over at the park and couldn't imagine fitting one more thing into her schedule. How could she participate in the trial, solve the murder case, develop the film from Tent Rocks, and exercise? Too many balls to keep in the air. She put those thoughts aside and trailed after Gillian to the first station. Gillian demonstrated the workout routine, and Louise tried to duplicate it. They went from station to station until Louise's arms and legs ached with fatigue. She hated to disappoint Gillian, but there was no way she would be able to jog after working the stations.

"Let's start with a short, fifteen-minute jog along the canal—oops, I mean the Mother Ditch."

Louise chuckled as she climbed in her car. They drove to the path that lined the ditch and parked the cruiser alongside the bank.

"We already warmed up, but it never hurts to do a last-minute stretch of your quads and hamstrings." Gillian reached back for her left ankle and pulled it up to her butt, then did the same stretch on the right. Louise tried to locate her ankle, peering over her left shoulder. It was at least a foot away from her hand. "Don't get discouraged. You'll get more limber and flexible."

They started out at a slow jog. After only a few minutes, Louise's body protested, her legs throbbed, and her lungs burned. She wanted more than anything to stop, but she pushed her way through the pain. With Santa Fe's altitude at seven thousand feet, the air was thin and did little to inflate her lungs with oxygen. Gillian signaled when fifteen minutes were up, and Louise came to a stop. As she bent over, hands on her thighs for support, gasping for breath, she was sure she would crumble to the ground. There was no sense of elation, but she had jogged fifteen minutes. That was her reward. And the best part: it was over, at least for today.

"See you in court," Gillian said as she turned and headed home.

"Good luck. You'll be great," Louise replied. She hadn't brought it up during the workout, but she suspected Gillian was probably antsy about getting up on the stand.

Louise checked the time. She needed to hurry to squeeze in a shower before court, and she definitely needed a shower. She tugged off her Chucks and jumped on the scale, somewhat naively. Down two pounds. She felt proud of herself for skipping that glass of wine and going on the jog—though she knew the weight loss was probably just from sweating. She calculated how quickly she could reasonably lose the twenty extra pounds she'd been unable to shed as she perused the drab selection that hung listlessly in her closet. She promised herself she would buy at least two new outfits, maybe a size smaller for her new body.

Louise barely made it to the courtroom in time and scrambled to find a seat near the front. She glanced around, spotting Gillian, who looked worried. The courtroom door opened, and she spotted

Pascal with his attorney. Fox-Elexor wore another red suit, this one the color of blood. The skirt barely brushed her knees and fit so tight Louise was worried she wouldn't be able to sit down. Her high heels, black and white with open toes, revealed nails polished in cherry red. The four-inch heels put the attorney over six feet tall, which would be an advantage in the courtroom. Louise couldn't help but smile at the thought of the DA's short stature. As Pascal passed, she was thankful, once again, that he didn't acknowledge her presence. She hoped she wouldn't be the one to bring him down.

CHAPTER 34

Louise had found the trial even more tedious than the deposition. She sighed so often she worried the judge would cite her for contempt, and she wondered how anyone had the perseverance to sit through trials day after day. Besides Gillian's testimony, the rest was a rehash from the day before. Louise was pleased that Gillian had taken her advice, and her testimony never wavered from the one she gave the night of the warehouse explosion. But the DA attacked her doggedly, firing questions over and over while Pascal's attorney objected again and again. Louise was amazed how stoic Gillian was on the bench. She didn't flinch during the forty-five-minute barrage. Her face gave nothing away. Never once did she scratch her nose or push back her hair. Louise was impressed by Gillian's focus and wondered whether jogging had helped her to center. That would be something to strive for.

Then the bailiff, once again, announced a recess until the next morning. Louise slumped on the bench, worried that, at this rate, the trial would go on forever. Her days would be spent listening to the same argument and never solving Madison's murder. It was like that movie, *Groundhog Day*, that repeated the same scene over and over.

She dug in her purse for her phone and checked her messages. She wanted to give Gillian time to leave the courtroom. It would be awkward to run into her on the way out. No messages. Why didn't anyone call her back? She dialed forensics in the hopes they'd received the toxicology report on Madison's drink.

The secretary, the guardian of the office, answered. "Forensics."

"Detective Sanchez. I need to speak to one of the guys." Louise knew she was being childish asking for the guys but couldn't help it. The woman took her job way too seriously—she couldn't handle a conversation with her right now.

"Whom do you wish to speak with?" the woman quipped indignantly.

"Johnson or Wilson. They asked me to return their call." This wasn't exactly true, but Louise needed some clout.

"Which one, Johnson or Wilson?"

"Whoever is available."

"One moment . . . Detective."

Louise waited, phone to her ear, but wondered if the secretary had gone back to her files. While she waited, she thought about jogging and was surprised that she was looking forward to tomorrow's session with Gillian. Maybe she could lose another pound or two by next week. She tried not to think of the burrito she ate for lunch. It would cancel out any weight loss. Finally, she heard a click.

"Johnson."

"Hey, it's Sanchez. I was hoping to go over the report you sent yesterday."

"Just a sec." Johnson shuffled through some papers. "Here we go. These reports sometimes sound like a bunch of gobbledygook. I wanted to go over the results."

Louise suppressed a laugh. *Gobbledygook?* "Fire away."

"We got the report on the prints, fibers, toxicology. Unfortunately, the knife was clean as a whistle. Whoever plunged it into the stiff either wore gloves or wiped it afterward. Leads me to think the crime was calculated, premeditated, not a crime of passion. But you're the detective."

Louise squeezed her eyes closed and said nothing.

"Both wine glasses had a set of prints that weren't Madison's. We picked up four sets of prints from the front door, one being

Madison's. And three in the living room that weren't the victim's. If you got any suspects, we can see if they belong to any of them. We also lifted some prints from the phone at the train station. They're a little smudged, but if you find the little lady, we can see if they match."

Louise sighed. She didn't have any idea how to find the "little lady." She thought about Camille Lautrec and Justine Dupont. Her spirits sagged further at the idea of dragging the women into the station to be fingerprinted. "I'm kind of short on suspects right now."

"What about Madison's boss? I heard rumors the Feds were investigating him for some hanky-panky."

Hanky-panky? Louise chuckled under her breath. She wondered how Johnson knew about Roche. "Unless the Feds have his prints on file, we're out of luck."

"I doubt they have his prints. The alphabet boys were keeping a low profile. Didn't want to spook the guy while he was under investigation. We could dust his office, but . . . oh wait. Forgot he doesn't have one."

"Yeah." Louise remembered the company mailbox in the lobby of the Opulent Building. "Albatross has a mail drop in the Opulent Building off St. Francis. Could you dust that for prints?"

"I could dust the outside, will need a court order to get inside the box."

"Madison knew about the box, so his prints might be on it, but I bet Peter Roche's are too. The company has a secretary. She lives in Las Vegas, that's Nevada not New Mexico. Not sure how often she comes to Santa Fe, if ever. We have her contact info. I could subpoena her and check her prints for a match."

"I'll swing by the building this afternoon and dust the box."

"See if any match with what you have from the house. If you come up empty, let me know. I'll look into a court order to get inside," Louise said.

"Have you talked to Roche?"

"No. He left the country Sunday evening. Caught a flight to

Denver out of Santa Fe Regional around ten o'clock, then flew to Zurich the next morning."

"Hmm, doesn't seem like he's our man. The good doctor reports that Madison was stabbed early Monday morning, between one and three, and died instantly."

"How about the toxicology report?"

"The doc was right. It was the date-rape drug. Madison's levels were over the top. He probably couldn't have lifted a finger to protect himself."

"Fibers?"

"Yeah, we found some fibers on him but the house was clean. Again, we would need something to match them to."

"Anything else?" Louise had already read the forensic report, but she realized that all the prints, fibers, and drugs wouldn't help her solve the case. She needed a suspect. Roche was looking good for motive, if he found out Madison was planning to turn him in to the Feds. The two men had argued about something at the Twisted Pines Sunday night. But Roche had a solid alibi. She couldn't figure out a motive for Dupont or Lautrec. Neither had an alibi, and Dupont was at Madison's house Sunday night.

"Thanks, Johnson. Let me know if you get some prints from the mail-drop box." She needed to eliminate Dupont and Lautrec from the crime scene, and to do so, she needed their prints—and a big favor from Johnson. "Do you ever take people's prints in their homes?"

"Yeah, dead people."

Louise sighed. "Would you be willing to take the prints from two women who were acquainted with Madison at their home?"

"That's not exactly protocol, Detective," Johnson said, not unkindly.

"I know. But there are extenuating circumstances. I haven't determined any motive these two women might have, but neither has an alibi. I need to eliminate them as suspects, but it would be traumatic to drag them into the police station."

Johnson was silent.

"Justine Dupont's husband has dementia and . . ."

"Okay. No sob stories, please. Set it up and I'll see if I can accommodate."

"Thanks, Johnson. I won't forget it." As Louise hung up, she wondered why she said that. What was she thinking? Was she going to do him a favor sometime in return? That's how things spiral out of control. She should have learned that lesson after sitting in court for two days listening to Pascal's indiscretions. Maybe she and Pascal were cut from the same cloth. Sometimes the only way is to bend the rules.

Louise left the courtroom, and as the elevator descended to the lobby, she thought about Roche. Something about his foolproof alibi bothered her, but she couldn't put her finger on it. According to the bartender, Roche had arrived at the bar around eight fifteen Sunday night, drank a bourbon, argued with Madison, then left. He was booked on the ten thirty flight to Denver, but his connecting flight to Zurich via Chicago and Frankfurt didn't depart until quarter after eight the next morning. That left seven unaccounted-for hours. Louise wondered where Roche spent the night. Hotel room, the airport, or . . . ?

The cool afternoon air hit her as she left the courthouse. She inhaled a deep breath, clearing her lungs of the stale building air. She imagined another scenario where Roche somehow got back to Santa Fe that night. Maybe he took a late-night flight to Albuquerque, rented a car, drove back to Santa Fe, murdered Madison, then returned to Albuquerque and flew back to Denver in time to catch his flight to Chicago. She chuckled and shook her head, thinking she either needed more rest, caffeine, or a different job. This wasn't a movie; this was real life. As she made her way to her car, she came up with another possibility. Maybe Roche had an identical twin brother who agreed to switch passports and travel to Zurich in his place. Then once his brother was on his way, Roche went to Madison's house, slipped him the date-rape drug, and stabbed him to death. She definitely needed more caffeine.

She pulled into the station parking lot and realized that if she was to solve this case, she couldn't do it alone. She needed help. She needed a true partner, not someone to delegate tasks to or pass off assignments. She needed a teammate—she needed Rupert. He wouldn't be her first choice, but there wasn't anyone else. She needed someone to bat theories back and forth, like Inspector Morse and Sergeant Lewis. She fancied herself in Morse's role: educated, lifetime bachelor, sympathetic personality, though sometimes sullen with a snobbish temperament. Well, no one is perfect. Her indulgence in red wine was similar to his thirst for English ale. And Rupert fit the bill for Lewis: working class, devoted family man, easygoing, smart as a whip. Rupert would be her man. She only hoped she could convince him.

CHAPTER 35

Justine poured herself a large cup of steaming coffee and took a gulp, burning her tongue and making her eyes water. Leo had taken Harry on an outing, which provided her several hours of uninterrupted writing. But once alone, with no more obstacles, her chest tightened and her hands shook with trepidation. Before she opened her laptop, she put the thumb, index, and middle finger of her right hand together and brought them to her forehead, then swept them down to her heart and brushed them left to right, completing the sign of the cross as her grandfather had taught her. The ritual was meant to be a sanctification, not meant to bring luck, much less protect one from writer's block. She hoped God would overlook that and see it for what it was. A plea.

The hours flew by, and the words piled up on the page. As she finished the last paragraph, as if on cue, Harry and Leo burst through the door, packages in hand. She gave Harry a kiss on the cheek, and he smiled back with exhausted eyes. He needed a nap, and Leo needed a break.

"Thanks, Leo. I'll take it from here." She took Harry's arm and helped him into bed, lying beside him and closing her eyes.

It was dark outside when she woke. In the kitchen, she found a note from Leo. He had taken an Uber to meet some old friends for drinks downtown. Justine made a couple of sandwiches and she and Harry settled on the couch watching a nature show on public television. When Harry fell asleep, she turned off the television and edited her article.

It was close to midnight when Justine, bleary-eyed and woozy, finally finished. Harry snored peacefully on the couch, dressed in sweatpants, the ones he had worn to bed for the last two weeks. She made a mental note to do a load of laundry in the morning. At least she had taken off his shoes and covered him with a throw, his favorite faux fur. She smiled sadly, her heart heavy with melancholy. He looked peaceful. Erased were the wrinkles of worry on his forehead, and his closed lids hid the uneasiness in his eyes. His perplexed and confused expression, which was becoming more frequent, was extinguished by sleep. She longed to curl up next to him and nuzzle the back of his neck, inhaling his familiar scent.

She turned back to her laptop screen, and for the first time in a long time she felt accomplished. Her article was written, edited, and even though it was late, it was finished. Her assignment, although not the article she had been asked to write, was done. The editor, a gentle, benevolent man, had demonstrated incredible restraint as her deadline approached. He urged her to send an outline, then begged for a draft. The day before, when nothing showed up in his inbox by late afternoon, he broke ranks and texted a nasty message, expletives included. Gone were the kind, gentle words of encouragement, no more coaxing and cajoling. There were hints of legal action and overtones of indignation. *Unprofessional, unprincipled, undisciplined* were peppered throughout the message. The harsh words had done the trick, and with Leo taking Harry out for most of the day, Justine got to work.

The experience was cathartic. Not only had she written something, it was something practical and possibly useful for older women searching for someone with whom to share their life, or maybe just a movie and dinner. But more importantly, it had purged her curse. She no longer had writer's block. Her eyes stung and her vision blurred from too many hours staring at the computer screen, but she couldn't stop now. She could barely make her fingers work on the keyboard, and her hands cramped periodically, but she needed to redeem herself in the eyes of the magazine's editor, in her own eyes as well. She wrote a proposal for a self-help column and included a sample letter and response to showcase her vision. She wanted to call the column "Dear Mother" but didn't think that would go over well, so she settled for referring to herself as "Ms. M."

Justine typed an email to the editor, apologizing profusely for her tardiness. She didn't make excuses and hoped the article would impress the editor enough to overlook her brazenness. She attached the article as well as the self-help column proposal, then pushed send. Relief washed over her. She shut her laptop, leaned her head back, and closed her eyes. She wanted to bask in her accomplishment, but before she knew it, she was sound asleep.

She woke to the sound of the phone ringing and answered, not bothering to look at the screen. It was morning, the sky brightening outside. She must have slept there all night. "Hello?"

"Ms. Dupont, this is Detective Sanchez."

Justine couldn't suppress a groan. What did the detective want now? She tried to stand up, but her legs buckled and she grabbed the arm of the chair to steady herself. She looked over at the couch and found it empty. Where was Harry?

"What is it?" she snapped.

"Sorry. I need to have you fingerprinted."

"Fingerprinted?" Justine gasped.

"To eliminate you."

"Oh my God. Eliminate me from what?" Justine had the urge to throw the phone across the room as she caught sight of Harry in the doorway, stuffing a cookie in his mouth. He grinned at her and she almost laughed.

"Ms. Dupont, you were at Webster Madison's house Sunday night. We have prints from the door, the handle, and around the house. If we can eliminate yours, the other ones would most likely be the murderer's prints."

At the mention of Webster Madison, a picture of him, lying spread eagle on his living room carpet with a knife in his heart, flashed in her mind. He had been kind to her, praised her writing, made her feel like a woman. She was sorry she had answered the phone. Her mind raced. She thought about Leo. He knew nothing about any of this.

"We can do it at your house, at your convenience."

Justine lost her patience and snapped. "My convenience? That would be never."

Although Dupont had always tried to be pleasant and cooperative, this woman had crossed the line.

"When could we come take the prints, Ms. Dupont?"

Justine eyed Harry as he crossed the room and sank back onto the couch. He had the remote control in his hand. "This afternoon." She hung up as the television blasted at full volume.

CHAPTER 36

It was light outside when Pascal startled awake out of a deep sleep. He sat up, sitting on the edge of the bed, getting his bearings. He wondered, *What had I been thinking? Why had it been so important to get the costume? To win?* He rubbed his temples and sighed. The smell of coffee found its way to the bedroom. Gillian must have woken up before him. It was enough to spur him upright. He dressed quickly, trying not to think about the trial. It was Wednesday, the third day, and the weather didn't bode well.

The days had been slowly warming, giving New Mexicans false hope that winter was over. Most of the year, the high desert mornings were frigid until the sun went to work and warmed the air. It was too early for the sun to make it fully over the mountains, but Pascal could tell the day would be uncharacteristically gloomy for April. He stared out the window and saw that a layer of low clouds had settled in. Yesterday there had been talk of snow. Even in May, snow wasn't unheard of at Santa Fe's seven thousand feet.

He found Gillian in the kitchen making coffee and scrambling eggs. She was all about protein, the answer to everything. He gave her a peck on the cheek, and they ate the eggs in silence. There was nothing to say. The clouds were choking out any conversation.

After breakfast, they closed the front door and made their way to the car. Gillian shivered and pulled her coat tighter. Pascal reached an arm around her and squeezed. He could feel the moisture gathering in the low-slung clouds. He saw it as a presage, a change in the air. If it kept up, it would snow today.

The courthouse appeared surrounded in a gloomy haze. Once inside, the forced-air heat rattled in the halls but was slow to warm the cavernous building. If that was a reflection of the trial, it didn't bode well for a happy ending. People, burdened by heavy coats and hats, shuffled into the courtroom. Pascal spotted Louise near the front trying to wiggle out of her coat. Then Gillian let go of his hand to take her seat, and it was as if he was set adrift at sea. He watched as she seemed to fade away.

Pascal joined his attorney, who was dressed in baby blue. The bailiff asked the congregation to rise, and the judge stormed in, his lips pursed, face hiding nothing. The man wasn't pleased. He took his seat and stared at the papers spread out in front of him. Sensing the judge's black mood, the attendees sunk into the benches, absolutely silent. Nobody dared to slip off their coat, change their position, or even cough. Pascal had heard that the judge suffered from arthritis, and the damp weather probably exacerbated his condition.

Pascal tried not to fidget as the judge looked up and scanned the courtroom. "I have considered the evidence, testimonies, and depositions from the witnesses, as well as the arguments from both sides of the bench." He gave a curt nod to the DA and Fox-Elexor. "I have pondered this case and concluded that it isn't cut and dry." The judge let his eyes drift around the courtroom, daring anyone to object. "On one hand, it's a simple case of breaking and entering, and if found guilty, punishable by law." The judge turned and stared directly at Ruiz. He was somehow able to meet the judge's gaze without flinching.

"But on the other hand, the case demonstrates how desperation to solve a crime can tempt one to commit a crime." The judge looked down at the papers resting on the bench before looking up. "Odysseus, in Homer's *Odyssey*, was presented with two choices, whether to go near Scylla or Charybdis. He choose Scylla as the lesser of two evils. He lost six of his companions, but if he had gone near Charybdis, all would have been doomed. This proverb comes to mind as I am faced with the selection of two immoral decisions." The judge, quite uncharacteristically, chuckled before continuing. "Like Odysseus, I have two choices, both which are bad, but one which is the lesser of two evils. In other words, my choice is between the devil and the deep-blue sea, or between a rock and a hard place." The judge gave a nod to the deputy.

The deputy stood up and announced in a deep baritone voice, "The court calls Pascal Ruiz."

Pascal rose and approached the bench.

The judge seemed to weigh his options as he studied the man standing before him. Everyone knew he had made up his mind long before entering the courtroom. Finally, he delivered his verdict in a subdued tenor. "Pascal Ruiz, I find you guilty of breaking and entering."

Murmurs spread through the courtroom, and someone let out a low gasp, likely Gillian. The judge rapped his gavel on the bench, and the room silenced. "The misdemeanor usually carries a jail sentence of less than a year. The breaking and entering involved damage, blowing up the warehouse door, although nothing was stolen. But I suspect if Officer Sanchez"—the judge gave a quick nod toward Louise—"hadn't intervened, Ruiz would have taken the costume. Regardless, it's your first, and I hope last, offense. I am waiving the jail sentence."

Relief poured over Pascal as he steadied his knees, which began to wobble.

The judge shot a warning look at the DA, daring him to object before turning back to Pascal. "Pascal Ruiz, you are sentenced to two-year's probation. Your probation term began when you were put on administrative leave from the police department. Your position as detective with the Santa Fe police is immediately terminated. You are free to go." The judge rose, and the crowd scrambled to their feet.

The DA dashed after the judge, but he brushed the man off with a wave of his arm.

Gillian pushed herself through the crowd and threw her arms around Pascal. The captain gave him a curt nod as he left the courtroom. Pascal took it as a sign that the captain was relieved with the verdict. And he, personally, was relieved it was over.

CHAPTER 37

Louise couldn't believe the trial was over, just like that. She sank back down on the bench and considered what it meant for her. In terminating Pascal's position, it left her stuck in a temporary role, possibly indefinitely, at least until Matt Padilla was back. She couldn't make up her mind whether she was pleased or not. She thought about the proverb the judge had shared and realized she, too, was between a rock and hard place.

She gathered her belongings and left the courthouse. She had an hour to kill before meeting Johnson, who had agreed to take Dupont and Lautrec's fingerprints at their homes. She had time to drive back to the station and check in with Rupert. With the trial over, she had no more excuses—she needed to wrap up this case, solve Madison's murder.

As she climbed into her car she remembered she had told Lisa that she would check with her father about the probate. She connected to her car's Bluetooth and dialed her father.

"Hi, sweetie."

"Hi, Dad. I had a call from Lisa. She told me about the problem with selling the ranch."

"It's stuck in probate but I'm sure it will be resolved soon. I'm trying to prevent having to negotiate with that woman's family."

"Lisa wants me to send her the menorah. She's going to sell it so she can go to Spain and 'find herself.'"

Louise heard her father sighing. "It's hers, Louise. Send it to her. What claim do we have on it?"

Louise didn't want to hear those words. She loved the menorah. She knew her father was right and she knew it was irrational to want to keep it, but she didn't want it sold.

"Let me know what happens with the probate."

"Will do. How's the case coming?"

"Not solved yet."

Louise didn't want to talk to Lisa again, or ever. Tomorrow she would box up the menorah and mail it. She didn't know what to do with the chest, but for now it could wait.

Back at the station she stopped by Rupert's desk, hoping that meeting him on his own turf would put him more at ease. She needed him on her side. Rupert's eyes were glued to his computer screen, and he didn't bother to look up. "What's up?"

"I wondered if you would be my partner on this case. Equals. Work it together. I could use your help, your expertise."

Rupert sat up a little straighter in his chair and a slight smile escaped from his lips. Louise could tell that he was pleased. She didn't dare share her Morse and Lewis analogy. She the top-dog investigator, he a mere sergeant.

"I would need the captain's approval," he said in a low voice.

Louise had run the idea by the captain and he had been skeptical at first, but gave the okay as long as Rupert didn't neglect his other duties—computer searches and equipment repairs. As far as Louise was concerned, that stuff could wait. There was a murder to solve. "He already gave the okay. Can you come to my office? I don't have long but want to go over the case."

Rupert nodded and picked up his iPad. He wasn't the type of officer to carry a little notebook and pencil. He typed away on the device as she brought him up to date on the case. Then she took him on a tour of her wall of photos and copied documents, explaining each person's connection to Madison.

"I have two theories about how Roche committed the murder with his rock-solid alibi."

Rupert raised his eyebrows.

"One, Roche has a twin brother who took his flight to Denver while Roche stayed behind to murder Madison."

Rupert tilted his head and gave her a skeptical look. "And the other theory?"

"Roche took the flight to Denver Sunday night and somehow got back to Santa Fe, murdered Madison, and returned to Denver for his morning flight to Chicago."

"I'll check with the Santa Fe airport, any flights from Denver after midnight, and if Roche was a passenger." As Rupert turned to leave, he added sarcastically, "Oh yeah, and I'll see if Roche has a twin brother."

Louise was relieved that Rupert had agreed to be her partner, but she could do without the sarcasm.

It was midafternoon when Louise drove to the Dupont-Pearlman residence. The wind had ceased, but the sun still hadn't made an appearance, and the clouds continued to sink lower. She was the first to arrive and as she opened her car door, she caught a glimpse of the neighbor across the street, hiding behind the curtain in her front window. Poor woman must not have much of a life. Louise hoped she hadn't caught wind of Dupont's involvement in Madison's murder. That would be tantalizing gossip to spread around the neighborhood.

Johnson pulled up behind her in a black SUV with *FORENSICS* plastered on the side in large green letters. Louise groaned—more fodder for the neighbor. He opened the back of his vehicle and hauled out a gray metal case. *DACTYLOSCOPY* was written in red block letters across the box. Hopefully the neighbor couldn't read it from across the street. They made their way to the front porch and Louise gave the whale knocker a couple of raps.

"Nice," Johnson said as he took in the residence.

"Yeah. Amazing what money can buy. But . . ."

The door swung open, and Justine Dupont appeared, dressed in flaxen linen trousers matched with a light blue cashmere sweater. A string of pearls hung around her neck. She had taken pains to pin her hair in a neat chignon and even put on lipstick. Louise was astounded. Her appearance was like night and day, and she had to admit, cleaned up, the woman made a striking figure for her age. You couldn't mistake Dupont's demeanor as friendly, but she gave them a courteous nod.

Louise tilted her head slightly toward Johnson. "Mr. Johnson, from forensics."

Johnson smiled and held out his hand.

Justine gave it a quick squeeze, then waved them into the house and directly into the living room.

As Louise looked around the room, she was astounded. The room had been transformed; furniture polished, floors vacuumed, laundry vanished. Justine must have worked like a dog to get the place in order.

"It's probably best to do this in the kitchen. It can get a little messy," Johnson suggested as he looked around the immaculate room.

Louise caught a flash of fear in Justine's eyes and wondered if the cleanliness and order didn't go beyond the living room. She imagined the mounds of laundry and detritus stuffed in the kitchen.

"My husband is having his lunch in the kitchen. I don't want to disturb him. Let's do it here on the table." She led them over to the gorgeous tigereye dining table. Louise took in the La Mer place mats imported from Italy. They had the dreamy look of the Mediterranean, cool ocean breezes and sunlight. Justine shoved them aside and pulled out a chair.

Johnson asked, "Do you have some newspaper we could put down? Don't want to get ink on the woodwork."

Justine pursed her lips, found a stack of newspapers, and dumped them on the table. "I appreciate you coming to the house. My husband . . . I can't leave him alone." She shot Johnson a sweet smile.

Johnson nodded as he spread a section of the paper onto the table. Then he pulled out his equipment: a large ink pad, a stack of prepared cards, a cotton cloth, and a bottle of some kind of liquid. "The technique of fingerprinting is known as dactyloscopy. You know dactyl, Greek for finger." Johnson wiggled his finger at Justine and grinned. "Copy your finger."

Justine raised her eyebrows and, not without sarcasm, said, "Oh?"

"I will do a set of rolled and flat prints, each on a separate card."

Justine nodded and pressed her lips in a grimace.

Louise was sure the woman could do without the explanations. She wanted Johnson to get to work, get it over with.

"I will manipulate your finger by rolling it in the ink then rolling it onto the prepared card. I need to make sure the entire print makes an impression."

Louise made an effort not to raise her eyebrows or say something sarcastic. She, too, wished he would get on with it. If Harry was indeed having lunch in the kitchen, any minute he might wander in, disrupt the entire process, blast the TV.

Johnson methodically took hold of one of Justine's fingers. Louise noticed her nails had been manicured and wondered how she had time to do them. Johnson picked up one of Justine's fingers and rolled it in the ink, made the impression, and wiped her digit clean with a cloth dipped in what reeked of alcohol. Then he repeated the process twenty times. It only took fifteen minutes, but it seemed like forever.

While Johnson was packing up his gear, Louise took out the artist sketch of the 911 caller. "Do you recognize this woman?"

Justine's face was blank as she studied the picture, then shook her head.

"She's the person who found Webster Madison Monday morning and called in the murder."

Justine seemed to pale at this. She gripped the back of the chair with both hands.

Louise switched gears. "As I mentioned on the phone, we're

trying to locate someone who can make arrangements for Webster Madison's body."

The color in Justine's face drained as if someone had pulled the plug, letting out the blood.

"Funeral arrangements," Louise added.

Justine shook her head, scrunched her forehead, and curled her lips as if she had taken a bite of something sour.

"The medical examiner needs instructions about Madison's body. If nobody comes forward and makes some decisions, his body will be turned over to the state. You wouldn't want that."

Justine seemed to get control of herself. Color eked back into her face. "How can you possibly think I should be the one to do that? I hardly knew the man."

Louise shrugged. She knew Justine was right.

Justine marched to the door and swung it open. Gone was the cordial woman. They barely made it out before the door slammed shut.

Johnson chuckled. "Plan the man's funeral?"

"If you never ask, you'll never know."

"Yeah, I guess you know now."

As Louise fastened her seat belt, she glanced across the street. The neighbor, no longer hiding behind the curtain, stood in plain sight, hands on her hips.

CHAPTER 38

Louise returned to the station from Dupont's house. She found Rupert's desk empty and hoped he hadn't had another family emergency. His boys were of that age where broken bones and cracked skulls happened on a regular basis. She needed him on board now that they were partners. There wasn't much to do sitting around the office. She hadn't heard back from Lautrec and decided to swing by her condo.

Lautrec's condo parking lot was empty except for two sedans parked at the other end of the lot under a tree. As she made her way up the stairs, there was little sign of life in the building. The silence in the hall was unsettling. As she rang the doorbell, she couldn't shake the thought that the place felt like a tomb—cold, vacuous, impersonal.

Louise didn't hear any movement behind the door. She was disappointed that Lautrec wasn't at home and turned to leave as the door opened. There Camille stood, immaculately dressed and coiffed. She made no attempt to be civil as she scowled at Louise. "What do you want now?"

"I left you a message but hadn't heard back from you. I was in the neighborhood, decided to stop. I was worried your phone might be out of service." Louise admonished herself for telling a lie.

"My phone is working fine." Camille started to close the door, but Louise reached out and stopped it.

"I'm sorry." Louise couldn't believe she was apologizing again. "I need to have you fingerprinted. For elimination."

"Elimination?"

"Forensics found some sets of prints at Madison's house and on the front door. We need to determine if any of those are yours. Any other prints might be the person responsible for his murder."

"When?"

"When?" Louise was taken aback, shocked at the woman's change of heart.

"When do you want to take my prints?" Camille spit out each word, causing Louise to lean away.

"I can call forensics and make arrangements. They're willing to come to your house."

Camille pursed her lips in irritation as she swung the door open. Louise followed behind while digging in her purse for Johnson's card. Thank God he had given her his private cell number. The last thing she wanted to do right now was finesse his secretary. She silently said a Hail Mary as she dialed his number. Johnson answered on the first ring.

"Detective Sanchez. I'm with Camille Lautrec, one of the women we need to fingerprint. I want to see when we can arrange a time."

"I could do it now. Do you want to come to my office?"

Camille stood with her arms crossed, a defiant look on her face.

"He's available to do it now. Do you want him to come here or go to forensics?"

"Forensics? The building, the morgue, where I had to identify Webster's dead body?" Camille was becoming unglued.

Louise made her decision quickly. "He can come here. It will only take a few minutes."

Camille nodded, closing her eyes.

She gave Johnson the address and wanted to ask him to hurry but didn't have the nerve. He was doing her a favor and not for the first time. The list of favors was piling up and it would take her forever to pay them all back.

"Will this ever end?" Camille mumbled as she slumped onto the sofa.

Louise didn't reply. She was doing her best not to lie, and she knew that this probably wouldn't be the end. She took the chair across from Camille and tried not to fidget. She remembered the sketch artist's drawing and pulled it out of her satchel. She leaned forward, holding it out to Camille. "Do you recognize this woman?"

Camille squeezed her eyes shut again, clearly not wanting to engage with the detective. As she opened her eyes, a gasp escaped her lips. She snatched the drawing out of Louise's hand as the color drained from her face. It was the same reaction Camille had when Louise told her about Madison's death. Louise was thankful that Camille was sitting down. At least she wouldn't have to help her off the floor again.

A cloud drifted in front of the sun, casting the room momentarily in shadow. Louise shivered. Camille's hand shook as she held the sketch. It was as if the drawing had dropped from the sky. Coming to haunt her. A mysterious omen.

"Ms. Lautrec?" Louise coaxed softly. "Do you recognize the woman?"

The resolve that seemed ever-present in Camille's eyes washed away fully. She gave a slight nod, not taking her eyes from the drawing.

Louise needed Camille to talk, tell her story. Once Johnson arrived and started his rambling explanation of the fingerprinting process, Camille would come unhinged, all would be lost. Camille would never open her door again. This was her last chance.

"Who is she, Camille?" Louise used Lautrec's first name, more personal, as if they were friends.

"My . . . my daughter."

With that statement all the air in the room was sucked out. Louise felt her throat constrict, and the implications zinged through her head. She took in a deep breath to steady herself. "What was your daughter doing at Webster Madison's house Monday morning?"

Camille looked up, startled, as if Louise had appeared out of nowhere. "What?"

"The woman in the drawing is the one who found Madison Monday morning. She was the one who called 911."

"Oh no. Isabelle?" Camille wailed.

"Is that the woman's name?"

Camille nodded as her eyes drifted back to the sketch. "She's lovely, isn't she? Don't know about the blond hair. But it's a good cut, becoming stylish." Her voice sounded wispy, far away.

"I think it would be best if you started from the beginning. We need to sort this out before Johnson arrives."

Camille stared at Louise with a glint of fear in her eyes. "Johnson?"

"To take your fingerprints."

"Oh." Camille let out a sigh filled with despair.

"Tell me about Isabelle," Louise coached.

Camille's eyes hardened. "She knocked on my door a few weeks ago, tracked me down like an animal. Had hired one of those birth mother detectives. It wasn't right. It was supposed to be a closed adoption. No contact. *Finito.*"

Louise scrambled to make sense of what Camille was saying. Isabelle, birth mother, adoption. She made a quick calculation of Camille and Isabelle's ages, figuring Camille must have gotten pregnant in college. Most likely with her boyfriend, Webster Madison.

"Is Madison Isabelle's father?"

Camille gave one simple nod. "I made it clear to Isabelle that I wasn't interested in being her mother, having a relationship." Camille let out a callous laugh. "She told me she wasn't either. She wanted to know who her father was. She wanted to meet him."

Camille paused, looking down at her hands, then continued. "A week before we graduated from college, I found out I was pregnant, but we had already grown apart." She shook her head in exasperation. "He spent two years pursuing me relentlessly, and then when I finally slept with him, he lost interest. Tale as old as time." She scoffed, clearly still annoyed at the memory.

Men—for them it was about the conquest, the subjugation, the power. Once again, she was glad she preferred women.

"Anyway, I had no intention of keeping the baby. I never told Webster. We both had plans. We went our separate ways."

"You didn't have an abortion?" The question popped out before Louise could stop herself. With what little she knew about this woman, she couldn't imagine Camille sacrificing nine months of her life for a baby she wasn't going to keep.

"I considered it. Kept putting it off until it was too late and . . ." Camille sighed as if all her secrets were slipping out, exposed, no longer safely tucked away, hidden. "The baby was part of me, part of Webster. I wanted that part to live, but not with me. If Webster had been a different person . . ." Camille looked back at the drawing and a single tear ran down her cheek.

The doorbell buzzed, startling both women. Louise jumped up and answered the door. Johnson blundered in, carrying his gray case with the bright red letters. He followed Louise into the living room, shook Camille's hand, and asked, "Kitchen? This can be a little messy."

Camille set the drawing on the coffee table face down and led the two of them to the kitchen. It was ultramodern, all stainless-steel, top-of-the-line appliances and cherrywood cabinets with glass doors. The kitchen looked as if it had never been used. Spotless, orderly. Johnson arranged his equipment on the granite island. Camille, looking dazed, pulled up a stool and sat next to him. Johnson started in on the same spiel he had given Dupont. His voice seemed to calm and subdue Lautrec. When he had finished, he loaded up his equipment and headed toward the door.

"Thanks, Johnson," Louise said, and she meant it. She was careful not to add, *I owe you one.*

Johnson smiled, tipped an imaginary hat, and left.

Louise made her way back to the living room. The interview was over, at least for now. Lautrec had been through enough for one day. She needed Isabelle's contact information and then she would leave the woman in peace.

Camille hesitated in the entrance to the living room. For the first time, she seemed unsure of herself, stuck in limbo, unable to decide whether to go in or out.

"I need Isabelle's last name and where I can find her."

"I have no idea," Camille said, still standing in the doorway.

Louise was surprised. "You don't know her last name?"

"I'm not sure that Isabelle is her first name. I named her that before she was born and put it on her birth certificate. But her adoptive family could have changed it. They have the right to do that."

"Do you know where she was staying in Santa Fe?"

"No."

"What did you tell her about her father?"

"I told her that her father didn't know about her. I would need to speak to him first. Get his permission. If he agreed to see her, I would give her his information. That's why I went to see Webster a few weeks ago. I came clean, told him everything, about the baby, the adoption, and about his daughter wanting to meet him."

"What happened?"

A sad laugh escaped from Camille. "Typical Webster. Never one to draw things out or prolong his agony. In less than half an hour, he sped through the stages of grief for his love child. First he was shocked, then he refused to believe he was her father, and then his anger took over and he attacked me, not physically. He tried to bargain but was unsuccessful for once. Finally he seemed to accept it. I think his curiosity got the better of him. He agreed to meet Isabelle."

"If you didn't know where she was staying, how were you going to arrange a meeting?"

"The meeting was prearranged. We were to meet in the plaza the next morning."

"And?"

"We met." Camille shrugged. "I told her that her father had agreed to meet her. I gave her Webster's name, address, and phone number. That was the last I heard from her."

Louise took out her notebook and held her pen expectantly. "I'll need some information about Isabelle—date of birth, hospital, adoption agency."

Camille stared at Louise, weighing her options. "I don't have that information at my fingertips."

"Could you get it, please?"

Camille didn't look like a woman with much fight left in her. "Have a seat. It'll take me a few minutes."

Louise lowered herself into the chair, the one she had been assigned the first time she came to the condo. She knew the only exit was the front door. She was sure Camille wouldn't attempt to squeeze through a second-story bathroom window.

After several minutes, Camille returned carrying a pink box tied with a white silk ribbon. She sank into the couch and stared at the box on her lap before opening it. Even from across the room Louise could see the look of anguish on her face. Camille appeared to hold her breath as she untied the ribbon. With a tenderness Louise hadn't seen before, the woman opened the box and took out a small photograph. She stared at it before setting it down next to her on the couch. Then she shuffled through the contents, finally locating Isabelle's birth certificate. She exhaled and, in a monotone voice, reported the information. "Baby Isabelle, born July 4, 1994 at 6:52 a.m. Holy Ghost Hospital, Los Angeles, California."

Louise scribbled down the information, then raised her eyebrows. "Adoption agency?"

"Anglicans for Life."

CHAPTER 39

Camille Lautrec's confession had stunned Louise. It was the last thing she expected out of the woman. She sat in her car trying to digest the information. Rupert had left a text that he was on his way to Santa Fe Regional Airport to check the Denver flight log for Sunday night. Since the World Trade Center bombings, passenger information couldn't be released over the phone; even the police had to obtain the information in person. September 11 had changed everything. It was all about security now, and everyone had to follow the proper channels.

The United supervisor would be able to confirm whether Roche was on the plane. Then Rupert would need to go to the Albuquerque airport and check the flights and passenger lists to and from Denver. She realized he wouldn't make it back to the station until the next morning, but she expected him to text her if he found out anything.

Louise felt hopeful about the case for the first time. She sensed they were getting closer to finding out who killed Madison, but she hoped it wasn't Camille's daughter, Isabelle. She opened her web browser and searched for the adoption agency, Anglicans for Life. Nothing came up. Maybe the agency was no longer needed now that there was acceptance of single motherhood, accessible birth control, and availability for abortions. She placed a call to the Episcopal Diocese of Los Angeles.

A woman answered in a singsong voice. "Episcopal Diocese of Los Angeles."

"Good afternoon. This is Detective Louise Sanchez from Santa Fe, New Mexico. I am looking for information on an Episcopal adoption agency that was in operation in the 1990s. Anglicans for Life."

There was silence on the line. Then the woman responded curtly, "You will need to speak to Bishop Black."

"Can you connect me to the bishop?"

Again, there was a long pause before the woman answered. "No."

Louise was taken aback but waited for clarification.

The woman went on. "He's . . . not here, been called away."

"Is there someone else I could speak with?"

"No."

"This is a police matter. It involves a murder case. I need to find out information on a woman who was adopted from that agency."

"One moment."

There was a click, and ethereal music drifted into the phone. While Louise waited, she thought about Isabelle. She wondered how the woman was able to track down her birth mother—a closed adoption, even with the help of an adoption detective, would be difficult. She knew that these detectives had become popular with adoptees seeking their birth parents, especially before open adoptions were available. She assumed it was similar to solving a crime: research connections between individuals, search public and private records or historical documents, and conduct interviews with persons of interest.

She didn't know if Isabelle hired an adoption detective, but it was irrelevant anyway. If she did, that information would have to come from Isabelle, and Isabelle was the person Louise needed to find. Louise was still holding the phone when the music stopped and she was left with silence. She glanced at her screen. Call failed. She groaned. LA was an hour earlier, and if the diocese kept regular business hours, they must still be there. She dialed the number again and an automated voice answered, directing her to enter the extension of the party she wished to talk to. Louise disconnected. *That wasn't very Christian.*

It had been a long day and she was starving. There was nothing to do but wait and see what Rupert found at the airports. She headed to Trader Joe's for something easy and appealing to make for dinner. None of the prepared food looked appetizing, so she made her way over to the meat display and chose a marinated chicken breast. She could bake it, make a salad, sip some wine while the sunset turned the Sangre de Cristo's blood red. But if the weather report was right, she didn't have long. Soon the mountains would be dusted with snow.

Her phone dinged as she set the bag of groceries in the back seat of the cruiser. It was a text message from Rupert. He confirmed Roche was on the passenger list for the ten thirty flight Sunday from Santa Fe to Denver. The disappointment hit Louise like a punch in the stomach. A minute ago, she was optimistic about the case. She tried to convince herself that Roche's flight to Denver was only a bump in the road. If Rupert could find evidence that Roche, after arriving in Denver Sunday night, flew back to New Mexico, their theory could still pan out. It sounded so implausible now—she tried her best not to dwell on it.

CHAPTER 40

Rupert walked out of the Santa Fe Regional Airport and immediately noticed the change in the weather. A light dusting of snow was falling from heavy clouds. The sky gave no indication that it would let up and with the temperature rapidly dropping, the roads would soon become icy. He climbed into his cruiser and pulled his laptop out of his backpack to check on flights between Denver and Albuquerque. Three airlines offered direct flights—Frontier, United, Southwest.

He closed his laptop and steeled himself for the drive to Albuquerque. It wasn't dark yet but as he descended La Bajada Hill, the cloud-covered sky enveloped the interstate in a gloomy haze. The juniper-studded grasslands that bordered the freeway were still visible. As he reached the bottom of the hill, the light snow turned to drizzle. In the distance the Jemez Mountains faded into the dusk. The Sandias' treeless facade cast in gray-black was more daunting than usual. He preferred the Sangre de Cristo range, with its verdant evergreen trees.

Rupert parked in the covered structure across from the Albuquerque airport terminal. As he entered the airport, only a few attendants manned the ticket counters. Most people were accustomed to printing their boarding passes at home or using the kiosks. He waited in line for the United Airlines attendant. He showed his identification and asked for information on flights from Denver

Sunday night and back to Denver early Monday. The last flight to Albuquerque left Denver at 7:50 p.m., but there was a flight to Denver Monday morning at 5:25 a.m. He asked to see the passenger list on the morning flight and was told it would require a supervisor's approval. The attendant made a call, and Rupert moved out of line while he waited. Roche wasn't on the United flight Monday morning.

Then he made his way to the Southwest Airlines counter. No one was waiting in line. The two attendants behind the counter were giggling. When he pulled out his identification, both women raised their hands in surrender, then burst out laughing.

The taller woman told him the last flight to Albuquerque Sunday night left at 6:30 p.m., but there was an early flight Monday morning at 7:20 a.m. Neither flight fit Roche's schedule, but he asked to see the passenger list anyway. He wasn't there.

Finally he made his way over to the Frontier Airlines desk, which was tucked at the end of the corridor, unmanned. As he waited for an attendant, he started to doubt Louise's theory. It didn't seem like Roche could have flown to Albuquerque, driven to Santa Fe, murdered Madison, and gotten back to Denver in time. Even though Roche had ten unaccounted-for hours after he arrived in Denver Sunday night, the man still had an alibi. The entire idea was beginning to feel like a waste of time.

A young man in a uniform bearing the Frontier logo hurried over and squeezed behind the counter. Rupert again showed his identification and asked for the same information. There were no late-night flights to Albuquerque from Denver on Frontier either. The airline had an early-morning flight that departed at 5:50, but again Roche wasn't on the passenger list.

Rupert climbed back in his cruiser. The temperature had dropped, causing the misty rain to turn to wet snow. He knew that if La Bajada hadn't already iced up, it soon would. He needed to get back to Santa Fe. As he pulled onto the airport exit road, he spotted the sign for car rentals. It seemed implausible that Roche had rented a car since he hadn't been on any of the flights, unless he flew in by private plane. He might as well cross the car rental off his list. He didn't want to make the trip again.

Luckily, there was only one central building that housed all the car rental companies. The only customer in the building was finishing his transaction with Thrifty Rental. Rupert walked up to the Avis counter, where a young man sat on a stool looking bored. He perked up when Rupert pulled out his identification and asked to speak to the manager or supervisor. The man led him to an office tucked at the end of the hall, across from the restrooms. He opened the door without knocking. A middle-aged woman looked up, annoyed as the attendant blurted, "Police!" and quickly left.

The manager shook her head. "Sorry, it's a boring job for young people. Tedious for the old. What can I do for you, Officer?"

"I need to know if a Mr. Roche rented a car after eleven two Sunday nights ago, and if so, when and where he returned it." He gave her the specific date details. "He could have rented the car round trip or one way."

"This is going to take some time. We have five rental companies." The woman sighed. "Better have a seat." She nodded toward a chair in the corner stacked with papers. "Put the pile on the floor." She turned back to her monitor and searched the rental contracts. "The good news is we don't rent many cars in the middle of the night since there are few flights arriving after ten."

Rupert tried to make himself comfortable on the hard plastic chair. Once again he thought Louise's idea was ludicrous. If Roche had rented a car at the airport, how did he get from Denver to Albuquerque?

After several minutes the woman removed her glasses and wiped them with a cloth, then put them back on before meeting Rupert's gaze. "There wasn't a car rented in Roche's name. There was only one rental around 1:30 a.m. Sunday, which was a little unusual since there weren't any flights arriving around that time."

Rupert sat up straighter in his chair. Maybe Roche took a private plane to Albuquerque and someone with him rented the car. "Which rental company?"

"Avis. And you're in luck. The young man that brought you to my office was on duty that night. Do you have a picture of this Roche guy?"

Rupert could kick himself; he should have asked Sanchez for a photo. "No. I'll have one texted to me. I'll need a copy of the rental agreement," he said to the manager.

She pushed herself out of her chair and stretched before making her way across the room to the printer. When the agreement had printed, she handed it to Rupert.

"Thanks for all your help. Appreciate it. I'll check with the guy at the Avis counter." He took out a card and handed it to the woman. "If you think of anything else, don't hesitate to call."

The woman studied the card. "What's this about, Officer?"

"It's a murder investigation."

She nodded but said nothing. Rupert made his way back to the Avis counter.

"You want to rent a car, Officer?" The man gave him a quirky smile.

"You rented a car to Ms. Cheryl Simpson on Monday morning around one." He set the contract on the counter.

"Yeah. I remember her. Couldn't forget that lady. She was a looker, or should I say hooker?" He giggled, pleased with his rhyme.

Rupert thought working nights must be getting to this guy. Sleep deprivation. "Hooker?"

"Yeah, she sauntered in on four-inch heels, wearing this sparkly miniskirt that barely covered her tush." He guffawed.

Rupert rolled his eyes. "Was she alone?"

"Yeah, but . . ." He paused, opening his eyes wide. "After she filled out the rental agreement, I started to escort her to the car. We usually hand over the keys and tell them the number of the parking space, but if it's a single woman late at night, we have to walk them to the car. You know, so they don't get attacked or raped or anything."

Rupert wondered what the "anything" might be, but didn't ask. "You walked her to the car?"

"No, I started to and . . ."

"And?" Rupert found the interview excruciating. This kid was a pain in the ass. He was losing his patience as he glanced out the window and noticed the snow coming down heavier.

"There was a dude standing in the lot. She practically grabbed the keys out of my hand, said thanks, and sauntered off. She didn't scream or nothing, so I figured he was probably a John."

"A John?"

"You know, a client."

"Could you describe the man?"

"Hey"—the kid scrunched up his face and bobbed his head—"it was dark, man."

Rupert held up his phone with Roche's photo. "Could this be the guy?"

The kid grabbed the phone out of Rupert's hand. He pursed his lips while he studied the photo and nodded his head in unison with each statement. "Same build, same age, same hair, not that he had much." He handed the phone back and grinned. "But couldn't say for sure. Wouldn't want to swear on a Bible or nothing."

Rupert pulled out his card. "If you think of anything else, let me know. And thanks."

"No *problema*, man."

At least the punk didn't add *señor*. This was exactly why he preferred online research, and the reason he was the computer geek at the station. Computers weren't sassy, they didn't talk back or diss you. He wondered how he'd let Sanchez partner him up, send him on this wild goose chase.

He brushed the snow off his windshield with his coat sleeve and climbed into the cruiser. The temperature had dropped at least fifteen degrees in the last hour. He cranked up the engine and turned on the defroster full blast as he studied the rental agreement—Cheryl Simpson, Colorado license, Denver address. The woman paid for the rental with an American Express Corporate Card from Laredo Enterprises. If she was a hooker, she was a high-class one. The Colorado connection intrigued him. Then again, it could be a coincidence. He considered doing a preliminary search for the woman while his windshield defrosted, but the snow was accumulating fast, and he realized he better get going before the roads became impassable. The cruiser was equipped with four-wheel drive, but that wouldn't help on black ice. Climbing two thousand feet up La Bajada would be a challenge in light snow, much less this storm. He knew Sanchez had asked him to keep her updated, but she would have to wait.

CHAPTER 41

The day Isabelle showed up at her condo, Camille had been in the kitchen making a tuna salad. She had squeezed lemon on her fingers to dislodge the fishy smell before drying them on a tea towel. When she had opened the door, a young woman stood unsteadily on three-inch high heels and stared menacingly. Her pale, freckled face quivered with cold, her upturned nose moist around the nostrils. Camille had never set eyes on the woman, but somehow she knew exactly who she was. She could feel it in her core. Without thinking, Camille tried to slam the door shut, but the young woman held out her arms and braced them against the door.

Camille had carried the baby for nine months. After the birth, she had refused to see or hold the infant. The next morning, she packed her small bag and left the clinic before being discharged. The arrangements, the adoption, and the stipulations had all been previously made. There was no room for hesitation—she would crumble, and there was no room in her life for crumbling.

Camille knew she hadn't been honest with the detective about her pregnancy, telling her that she wanted to keep something of her and Webster's relationship, but that was a lie. She didn't want anything of Webster, only a piece of her to exist in another person. Camille realized she would never truly *know* that person, but she would know she existed, that she was out there somewhere. It was selfish. Her pregnancy wasn't intentional, it wasn't a conscious decision, but carrying the baby was.

Now Isabelle stood in her doorway again, no longer defiant, a look of anguish spread across her freckled face, no longer any trace of hostility. Camille realized she never should have told Isabelle who her father was, should have said she didn't know, never should have given her Webster's number. But it was too late, pointless to linger on it. Camille let out a long breath. "I'm . . . sorry."

Isabelle narrowed her eyes but said nothing, just stood, arms hanging useless at her side.

Camille, never having much patience for martyrdom, suddenly barked, "Oh, for God's sake, come inside."

Isabelle hesitated, started to turn away, but then stopped, defeated, and followed Camille into the condo. "My parents won't take my calls. They're furious. I'm out of money." She met Camille's eyes. "They never told me."

"Told you?"

"That I was adopted. I swear they even convinced themselves they were my birth parents." Isabelle threw up her hands. "How crazy is that? Totally nuts."

"How did you find out?"

"I was going to Spain, to find my roots, get in touch with my heritage." Isabelle let out a sardonic chortle. "I needed my birth certificate to apply for a passport and looked in my father's filing cabinet. I came across a folder with my name on it." Isabelle held out her arms and exclaimed. "Ta-da!"

"Take off your coat and have a seat." Camille started to point to the straight-backed chair allotted to strangers, the one she had made the detective sit in, but instead waved her arm toward the couch. "Tea, coffee?"

"Tea," Isabelle said as she sunk into the soft down of the sofa.

Camille returned with a Tiffany teapot on a silver tray, along with a pitcher of warmed cream, cups with saucers, and shortbread biscuits. She poured Isabelle's tea. "Cream?"

Isabelle nodded.

Camille placed a biscuit on the saucer. As she handed the cup to Isabelle, she tried to push away the feelings that welled up inside her. "Your parents never told you that you were adopted?"

"My father is Spanish, from Barcelona, my mother Canadian. Obviously, I look nothing like either with my blond hair and light skin, not to mention my height. My brother is five-six and looks Aztec, nothing like me or my parents, but I never thought about it. I guess my mom and dad weren't the only ones in denial." Isabelle opened her backpack, took out a photograph, and held it out to Camille.

It was one of those tacky family Christmas photos you order from the drugstore and send to all your friends and relatives hoping they will put it on the refrigerator. It was taken outside in front of an enormous blue spruce sprayed gold and hung with red, white, and blue balls. Gaudy. Her parents made a handsome couple, the father smiling adoringly down at his petite wife. The two children stood on either side of them, staring expressionless into the camera lens.

Camille shook her head. "What were your parents thinking? Why would they hide your adoption? I had stipulated that it wasn't an open adoption. They had nothing to fear. I wasn't going to swoop in and take you away."

Isabelle's face faltered at this statement, then resumed its cold expression..

"I take it your brother was adopted?" Camille asked.

Isabelle shrugged. "We never thought about it or questioned our relationship as brother and sister, but what do you think?" She raised her eyebrows and nodded her chin toward the photo still in Camille's hand.

Camille found it strange that Isabelle and her brother never wondered why they looked so different from each other, much less their parents. "Were your parents Episcopalian?"

Isabelle looked at Camille with surprise. "They were both raised Catholic. The story they fed us, if you can believe anything they say, was that they began to have doubts about the Church. It was around the time when the abuse accusations and cover-ups hit the fan. When the convictions began, they left and joined an Episcopal diocese. I think they were relieved the priests were allowed to marry, less likely to bugger little boys."

"I guess that's where they connected with the adoption agency. Anglicans for Life."

Isabelle shrugged.

Camille wondered what to do with Isabelle. Her first thought was to give her money and send her back to California, encourage her to mend things with her parents and be done with the situation. But Isabelle might have to testify at Webster's trial. She was the one who found him and reported it. Again, Camille chastised herself for telling Isabelle that Webster was her father. The man was trouble even dead.

Camille sipped her tea, lost in thought. She didn't need this complication in her life. She needed to focus on her new position at the opera. There were five operas in the upcoming season for which to design costumes. Four of the operas she was familiar with and had made preliminary sketches. But she had barely skimmed the libretto for the fifth one. It was a modern opera, Jake Heggie's *Dead Man Walking*, based on true events regarding a Catholic nun who fights for the life of a man on death row. She had never cared for modern operas; costuming was challenging and this one would be dreary

CHAPTER 42

Louise pulled back the curtains and looked out the window. The snow was coming down harder now, the enormous flakes billowing like puffs of cotton. It would soon be a blizzard. The mountains had long since disappeared and the steel-gray clouds continued to sink lower and lower, making Louise feel claustrophobic, blocked in, trapped. Late-spring snows in the high desert weren't uncommon, but they were always a surprise. At the first sign of warm weather, people shed their parkas and dug into their gardens. They were done with winter, but as often happened, winter wasn't done with them.

She heard the sound of muffled chimes from somewhere across the room. She hoped the call was Rupert with some good news. If Roche's alibi held up, he couldn't have murdered Madison, and it seemed unlikely Camille's daughter stabbed her father. If Isabelle was going to kill anyone, it would be Camille, right? After all, she was the one responsible for depriving Isabelle of her birth parents.

Louise crossed the room and searched in her purse for her phone. She answered the call on the last ring. "Hello?"

"It's Gillian."

"Hey. How's Pascal holding up?"

"He's relieved he didn't go to jail." Gillian sighed. "He knew he would lose his job but . . . I don't think he considered how he would feel. It still hasn't sunk in. He's sort of at a loss right now. Not sure what to do."

"Yeah, I get it. I wasn't expecting to be a detective forever either." Louise wished they could change the subject.

"Well, he might go private. He's been hired to find his father's missing lady friend and he's looking into some old pottery that's gone missing."

"That should keep him busy," Louise said.

"I guess. I try not to get involved—have my own fish to fry."

"From the looks of the weather, I guess we won't be jogging in the morning."

"At least not on the streets. If it doesn't clear up in a day or two we could try the mall."

Louise wasn't sure she wanted to jog her fat butt around the shopping mall.

"That's not why I was calling," Gillian continued.

"Oh."

"Remember when I called you the other day? I told you I had two things to talk to you about but one could wait until after the trial?"

"Yeah."

"Well now that the trial is over, I have a proposition for you."

Louise thought it had to do with jogging. "Okay."

"I inherited my mother's art gallery, La Mariposa Dorada. It's a few blocks south of the plaza. I've decided to take it over and have been working on a plan for a reopening."

Louise knew the gallery, The Golden Butterfly. She had attended a few openings over the years, even submitted some photos once for a group show. The art was eclectic, not your typical Southwest landscapes, but high end and geared toward wealthy collectors. "That's . . . a lot to take on," Louise said, trying to figure out where the conversation was going.

Gillian laughed. "You can say that again, but I'm excited. Not to mention, I need a job."

"What about the Santa Fe Orchestra? Pascal told me you auditioned."

"I was offered a position as an alternate. It's part-time, but it'll encourage me to practice. Not my strong suit. My violin has been collecting dust, and there's a lot of it in this town."

"The gallery sounds great, but that's a big endeavor."

"Pascal's been supportive, helped me sort through the gallery storeroom. I'm shooting for a grand opening the first of July. It will be the perfect timing. The tourists will flock back to town for the opera season, Spanish Market, Indian Market, and International Folk Art Festival."

"Send me an invite. What's your opening show going to be?" Louise asked more out of politeness than interest. She still couldn't figure out why Gillian was telling her all this. They weren't exactly close friends or confidants.

"Your photographs."

Louise was stunned. It was as if the breath had been knocked out of her. She reached over to steady herself on the table. "My photographs? You can't be serious."

"I am serious. And it's time you take yourself seriously, as an artist."

Louise was taken aback. Gillian had been nicer to her than anyone had in a long time. Nicer than she deserved. She helped her start jogging, sure, but to give her a solo show too?

"I came across two of your photographs in the storeroom. They were the epitome of New Mexico, the land, the space, the culture, your love for the Southwest. I have to say, the black-and-whites are my favorite. They remind me of Ansel Adams or Dorothea Lange. Through your lens you captured the spirit of this place. I believe they would be extremely marketable."

Seldom had anyone talked about her photographs, much less compared her work to Ansel Adams, one of the greatest landscape photographers in the West, or Dorothea Lange, one of Louise's personal favorites. Her parents had hung several pieces of her work in their house and often pointed them out to their guests. She knew they were proud of her, but after she dropped out of college and joined the police force, they stopped talking about them.

"I don't know what to say," Louise whispered.

"Well, yes would be appropriate. It's going to be a tight timeline though. Hopefully you have a body of work ready to go, but if not, you need to get busy. I'll need the work by June, framed and ready to hang. My mother used Artisans for framing. They're a little pricey, but they're the best. I think simple, black-wood frames with double white mats would complement your work. But I welcome suggestions."

Louise's head spun, making it difficult to think clearly. "I'm honored, but I'm not a recognized photographer. I don't have a reputation in this town or anywhere else for that matter. You're taking a big gamble opening the gallery with an unknown."

"After the opening you won't be an unknown. Besides, my intention is to represent artists who have been overlooked, haven't received a fair representation in this town. And I'm in a fortunate position to do so. Money isn't an object, at least for the time being."

"I don't know what to say."

"Like I said, yes would do."

"Okay, okay," Louise said, trying to convince herself she could pull it off.

"Let's meet soon and work out the details. When's your day off?"

Louise wanted to laugh. She didn't have any days off until the murder was solved. "Sunday morning."

They wrapped up their conversation, and as Louise hung up the phone, she suppressed any thoughts of Webster Madison's murder. She wanted to bask in the prospect of an upcoming exhibition. But her heart raced as she thought of what an exhibition entailed. She hadn't been in the darkroom for weeks, and the film shot out at Tent Rocks was still undeveloped.

She rummaged through her wine rack for the bottle of Möet & Chandon Impérial champagne her parents had given her for her fiftieth birthday. She had saved it to share with someone, but someone had never happened. She held the bottle and laughed as she read the label, which boasted its undertones and "nuances" of apple, fresh nuts, and gooseberry. "Well, we shall see about that tonight."

CHAPTER 43

It took Rupert more than two hours to get back to Santa Fe. The roads were icy and the heavy snowfall made visibility zilch. He crawled along the interstate, keeping as much distance as possible from the few other cars that had ventured out. By the time he pulled into his driveway, his arms ached with fatigue. His wife flung open the front door and stood with hands on her hips as the snow wisped around her body. Her lips were pursed with annoyance, but he could see the worry in her eyes. Although Sanchez was overdue for an update, she would have to wait.

The next morning, as he sipped his coffee, he searched the Denver database for a Cheryl Simpson. Attached to the rental car agreement was a photocopy of the woman's Colorado driver's license. The picture was blurry, which was suspect. The license listed her age and description—thirty-four, 105 pounds, five foot two, blue eyes, blond hair. It made him think of the old Dean Martin song "Five Foot Two," which his great-auntie sang while dancing him around the kitchen.

The computer listed several Simpsons. A few Cheryls and a few with the initial C, but none of which matched the address on the license. He would need to check the Colorado DMV, but that would have to be done at the station. He poured himself a second cup of coffee and called Sanchez.

Louise picked up on the first ring. "Hey, thought you were going to give me an update? Did you get lost in a snowdrift last night?" He could tell she was trying to sound worried, but her concern came out flat.

"Long night. Slow getting back from Albuquerque. The weather," Rupert mumbled.

"What did you find out?"

"None of the airlines had flights leaving late Sunday night from Denver. Roche wasn't listed on any of the flights going back to Denver early Monday morning."

"It had been a long shot." There was disappointment in her voice. "Sorry for sending you on a wild goose chase . . . and in a snowstorm."

"I stopped by the airport car rental. A woman rented a car late Sunday night when there were no flights arriving. Found that a little suspect."

"Yeah. But maybe she was just dropped off after a meeting or something."

"Maybe. I have a copy of the rental agreement and her Colorado driver's license."

Louise perked up. "Colorado?"

Rupert smiled. He knew that would get her attention. "Denver address. The rental agent saw a man in the parking lot get in her car. I showed him the photo you texted me of Roche. The agent said the guy fit the description, but it was dark, couldn't swear to it."

"Holy moly," Louise exclaimed. "This fish stinks. Definitely smelly."

Rupert couldn't help himself and burst out laughing. "Fish, smelly?"

"We need to track this lady down. Meet me at the station. We can check the Colorado DMV. Maybe put out a POI on her."

Rupert was hesitant. *Whoa, one step at a time.* Sanchez, like Ruiz, could be a loose cannon. He needed to keep her under control, but he agreed. "See you in half an hour."

"Good work, Montoya."

When Rupert walked up the steps of the station, several officers were making their way out to start their shift. He nodded to the group of men as they jostled each other. Harold Butler was a few steps behind them. "Hey, Rupert. Too bad about your buddy Ruiz."

"Been out of town. Haven't heard."

"He got the axe, lost his job. He squirmed his way out of a jail sentence, but at least they gave him two-year probation." Butler shook his head in disgust. "Blowing up a warehouse." He turned and made his way down the steps. Rupert knew there was no love lost for Ruiz around the station. Most of the officers thought Pascal was a dilettante, and they weren't far off.

Rupert pulled open the door and nodded to Susie, who was leaning on the counter flipping through a magazine. He made his way to the breakroom where Louise was staring at an empty box of doughnuts.

"Sometimes it doesn't pay to come to work," she said as she closed the lid.

"I hear you."

She led the way to her office and Rupert pulled up a chair next to hers. They waited in silence while the computer warmed up. Louise pulled up the Colorado DMV. "What's the woman's name?"

"Cheryl Simpson. I checked the general database. No Cheryl Simpson listed at the address on her license," Rupert said.

"Simpson?" Her interest seemed piqued at this.

"What else do you have?"

"Besides her driver's license, an American Express Corporate Card, Laredo Enterprises."

"Let's start with the Colorado DMV. See if her license is legit."

Rupert logged in to the restricted portal that allowed law enforcement agencies to peruse data from other states.

"Simpson's name didn't come up in the Denver database," he said. "Neither did the address on her license. It has to be a fake."

Louise tapped at her phone, then held up Google Maps to Rupert. "The numbers on that side of the street stop at 5285. There doesn't seem to be a 5287."

"Could be a new dwelling. Hasn't been entered into Google Maps yet."

"When we're done here, check with the Denver police. See if they can send someone out to confirm whether there is or isn't a residence at that number."

"That still doesn't explain why there's no record of the address or the woman's name in the system."

"True. But let's see what Denver has to say. We need all the pieces of this puzzle."

"Okay. As soon as I find anything out I'll let you know." Rupert gave her a sheepish look. "Promise."

"Check out the American Express account. See if they have a different address for this Ms. Simpson."

CHAPTER 44

Louise longed to go home, sequester herself in her darkroom, spend the day in the comfort of the little red light. But she was a detective and had a murder to solve. The sooner the case was resolved, the sooner she could get back into the darkroom.

She needed to find Camille Lautrec's daughter, Isabelle. Lautrec had said Isabelle was staying somewhere downtown but didn't know where. The last thing Louise wanted to do was traipse around Santa Fe inquiring with hotels, but Isabelle was the missing link. Louise had been unsuccessful in contacting Bishop Black at the LA Episcopal Diocese, and the diocese wasn't answering the phone.

As she made her way down the station steps, her phone rang. She looked at the screen and groaned—the medical examiner. She wasn't in the mood to listen to any complaints about Madison's funeral arrangements. But if she didn't answer, the woman would leave a message and she would have to return the call. "Sanchez."

"No preamble with you, Detective."

"No time for chitchat. I'm working a murder." She couldn't hide the petulance.

"I realize that." The doctor sounded unusually empathetic.

"I'm still trying to locate the 911 caller, but you'll be happy to hear the woman is Madison's daughter. And if I can find her, she might be the perfect candidate to plan his funeral."

"Thank God. I was getting ready to plan it myself. Thinking of starting with a viewing. I bet all the ladies in town would attend." The doctor chuckled.

Again, Louise was caught off guard by the joke. It seemed unprofessional, even to herself. She couldn't figure out the woman—sometimes she seemed a little off. "Yeah, sounds good."

"Anyway, that wasn't what I called about."

Louise got a funny feeling in her stomach. For once the doctor didn't want to talk about Madison's funeral arrangements.

"I was wondering . . . would you care to have dinner sometime? I haven't been in Santa Fe long and don't know many people. I thought maybe we could get to know each other, you know, as friends."

Friends, Louise thought. She felt unsteady on her feet and looked down at the steps. She cautioned herself not to read too much into the offer. "Sure," she chirped, trying to sound natural.

"Oh goodie. How about tomorrow night? Where do you like to eat?"

"Tomorrow night?"

"Or the next."

"No, tomorrow is fine. How about the Terracotta Wine Bistro? It's good if you haven't been."

"Perfect. I'll make a reservation for eight. See you then. Ta-ta!"

Louise stared at the phone. *Oh goodie, ta-ta.* She shook her head and skipped down the remainder of the steps. She crossed the plaza and started humming happily to herself. First an opportunity for an art exhibition, and now a date. Well, maybe not a date, but at least it would be a night out with a new friend.

CHAPTER 45

Louise couldn't believe all that had happened in less than two weeks—Madison's murder, the deposition, Pascal's trial, her uncle's memorial, and then a snowstorm, which left slush and mud today. With a cloudless sky, the temperature had warmed to the high forties, and the forecast for the next day was even more promising: fifty-five degrees and sunny.

Louise needed to find Isabelle and began to canvass the hotels around the plaza. She worked her way out in concentric circles, distributing the sketch artist's drawing along with her card. So far, no one had recognized the woman. The process was tedious and as the afternoon wore on, she became crankier and crankier. The city was full of hotels, not to mention vacation rentals and bed and breakfasts. She realized this was another wild goose chase.

There was one more hotel on her list, the St. Francis, named for the patron saint of Santa Fe. As she pulled open the lobby door, she resisted the urge to make the sign of the cross—it would be self-serving. The hotel's interior was bathed in a palette of natural colors and furnished with handcrafted wood furniture by local artisans—the epitome of Santa Fe. It was listed on the National Register of Historic Places.

A young man tapped away on a keyboard behind the registration desk. As Louise approached, he looked up, flashing a warm smile. "Welcome to the St. Francis. How may I assist you?"

Louise took out her identification and held it out. "Detective Sanchez, Santa Fe Police Department."

A startled look brushed past his face, but he quickly recovered. "How may I help you, Detective?"

"We're looking for a young woman." Louise took out the drawing and handed it to the man.

"Ah—yes. It's a good likeness. Isabelle Seville. She stayed with us for a few weeks. I hope she's not in any trouble."

Either her adoptive parents had kept her name or Isabelle changed it when she turned twenty-one. The clerk's use of the past tense didn't register with Louise. "No. She isn't in trouble. I need to talk to her."

"Oh, I'm sorry." The clerk gave her a sincere look, and Louise wondered if it was genuine or part of his training. "Ms. Seville checked out yesterday."

Louise stifled a groan, gritting her teeth. Missed her by a day. "I will need any information you have on her. Name, address, phone. Anything else you can think of that would be helpful."

"I have to call my supervisor. Confidentiality. You understand." The clerk flashed her an apologetic smile as he picked up the phone.

"Of course," she said, trying not to sound petulant.

The clerk set the phone back in its cradle when he'd finished speaking with his supervisor.

"Did Ms. Seville happen to mention where she was going after she checked out, back home or to continue her travels, perhaps?"

"I asked her if she enjoyed her stay in Santa Fe. I always ask clients that; it's expected. She had the oddest reaction. The color drained from her face, and I was worried she was going to faint or be sick. I asked if she was all right, but she recovered quickly. She said Santa Fe was an unusual place, the city different from what they say."

Louise knew the reason for Isabelle's reaction. She felt sorry for the woman. She had come so close to finding her father and possibly having a relationship with him. Though she didn't know much about Madison—maybe it was for the best.

The clerk stood up. "Oh, she asked about the train to Albuquerque. I gave her the schedule." The clerk made his way around the counter. "If you'll follow me, my supervisor will get you the information you requested."

She wondered about the train as she followed the clerk down the hall to the supervisor's office. Why take a train to Albuquerque? There wasn't much between there and Santa Fe that would attract a tourist. And there were much easier ways to get to the airport.

The clerk opened the door to the office and left. The supervisor had already written down Isabelle's contact information and handed it to her. Louise glanced at the paper and thanked the man, then promptly left the hotel, thinking about Camille and Isabelle living so close to one another in California all those years. She still couldn't fathom Camille being willing to carry her daughter for nine months. But then Louise remembered Camille's remark about keeping a piece of her and Webster Madison.

A weariness overshadowed Louise as she walked back to the station. She hadn't expected to spend the afternoon walking the streets, and now a nasty blister had festered on her right heel. It was three o'clock and she hadn't had lunch. Her stomach rumbled as she limped down the street. She wanted nothing more than to call it a day, pick up a Lotaburger with seasoned fries, and head home. Then soak in a hot tub with a glass of cabernet. But she had a murder to solve.

Carl Nuthers was finishing a meatball sub as she came into the station breakroom. The aroma made her weak. She nodded to Carl and turned away. Her blood sugar was dropping, making it hard for her to concentrate. She opened the fridge and found a peach yogurt, ignoring the expired expiration date. What did it matter—what was yogurt but fermented bacteria?

She pulled open the door to her office and hesitated. It was hers now. *Actually* hers, not Pascal's. She found a spoon in the desk drawer, wiped it on a tissue, and ate the yogurt, trying not to think about bacteria.

Church bells rang and she dug in her purse to find her phone. "Sanchez."

"Hey, how do you like your new office?"

She sighed. "I'm sorry, Pascal. I mean it."

"No worries. Need to turn a new leaf; thinking of going private."

"That's what I heard."

"I can't stop thinking about that missing pottery. It's gotten under my skin. Maybe, now that the trial is over, I can work on it. You haven't heard anything or gotten an update, have you?"

"Well, forensics said the Feds took over before they could get out of the car at the scene. You might want to check with your little birdie."

"Yeah, might do that."

"By the way, have you found Katrin Simpson?"

"No. My father's been bugging me about driving up to Denver. Check out her home address, the one we got from the Ghost Ranch registration form. I finally caved and we're leaving in the morning."

"It'll be a bonding experience," Louise said, trying to sound sincere.

"Yeah, sure."

"We're looking into a Cheryl Simpson who owns Laredo Enterprises. She may be involved in Madison's murder. Let's hope there isn't any connection between the two Simpsons, Katrin and Cheryl."

"Laredo Enterprises owns the Abiquiu house. Could be a coincidence, but . . ."

"Yeah, yeah, I know what they say. There are no coincidences. How's the case coming?"

"It's a clusterfuck for sure." She gave Pascal the short version.

"Well, good luck with that."

"Yeah. We all have our crosses to bear."

"Tell me about it."

"Safe travels," Louise said. "If you find Katrin, I'd appreciate any information on the house she rented in Abiquiu, or Albatross, or if she happens to know Cheryl Simpson."

"Okey dokey, Detective."

She hung up and placed a call to Rupert, which went directly to voicemail. Hopefully he was still at the station. She scraped out the last spoonful of yogurt and tossed the container in the trash, suffering a twinge of guilt for not recycling. She found Rupert at his desk, phone to his ear, but when he looked up, he quickly ended the call. "Do you want the good news or bad news?"

"I'll take any news at this point." Louise pulled up a chair.

"The Denver police were accommodating—you need to send them a thank you note, maybe chocolates." Rupert chuckled. He was in rare form after spending the afternoon doing his favorite thing: sitting in front of his computer. He didn't have to drive to Albuquerque in a snowstorm, or beat the streets in high heels getting blisters as she had. "They sent an officer to check out the address. It exists, but it's under construction. Nobody's living there now. Only a shell."

"Shell" made Louise think of Albatross. She couldn't tell whether that was Rupert's good or bad news, but she didn't ask. "What else?"

"The officer tried to talk to the men working on the house. They either didn't speak English or pretended not to. The foreman had left for the day. But the construction company—get this, you're going to love it . . ." Rupert paused for dramatic effect. "Mile High Construction, a subsidiary of Albatross."

It took a few seconds for the implication to sink in. "Have you looked into the company?"

"Preliminary search. The officer gave me the information from the sign posted at the site. Mile High is a national company. Its main branch is in Denver, and the CEO is a Mr. Alger Roche."

"Alger Roche? Is he related to Peter Roche?"

"Still looking into it. But if that's the case, the Roche boys are extremely industrious. Remember the brother in Switzerland who owns that company, Lucinda Liquid Gold?"

Louise nodded.

"Albatross probably bills Lucinda for fictitious goods or services, and it's likely the company does the same with Mile High Construction, and maybe Laredo Enterprises, the realty company. The money from the companies is funneled through Albatross and comes out squeaky clean, tax free."

Louise thought about the house in Abiquiu that Katrin Simpson rented. She needed to tell Rupert, lay out all the information. "I just found out that Laredo Enterprises owns the Santa Fe house Madison was leasing. And that's not all." She went on to explain the Abiquiu house and Katrin Simpson. "Alger and Peter have to be brothers, but we need to confirm it."

Rupert narrowed his eyes and stared at Louise.

Louise ignored his stare. "Since Cheryl Simpson's Colorado license had the construction site address on it, she must be involved with the company also. She could be a business partner, maybe Alger Roche's wife or relative. See if you can find a picture of Roche's wife. We could run it by the Avis agent."

Rupert started to say something, but Louise interrupted. "Don't worry. I'm not going to ask you to go to the Albuquerque airport again. We can text the agent the picture."

"Not sure the department would be thrilled to find out you've been working with Ruiz. But since we're partners now, I'll keep quiet." He gave her a sly smile. "I'll work on getting a photo of Roche's wife, and I'll check out the website for Laredo Enterprises. See if Cheryl Simpson is listed."

"Okay," Louise said. She needed to slow down, sort out the information on the Roche brothers and their companies. She sensed Madison's murder slipping away between her fingers; it was becoming a tangled web of possible illegal activities. Madison worked for Albatross, whom the Feds were investigating. And possibly the companies owned by Peter Roche's brothers as well.

She returned to her office and thought about the overly secured studio on the Abiquiu property. Pascal was right; it didn't sit well.

The studio had to store something of worth: stolen antiquities, illegal contraband—or maybe valuable pottery? She hadn't considered it seriously until now. And Mile High Construction was building a house for Cheryl Simpson, maybe his wife? Hans Roche owns the Swiss company, Lucinda Liquid Gold, which could be another entity that launders money through Albatross. She wondered what other assets or companies Albatross owned. This was beyond her pay grade.

Louise believed she was close to solving Madison's murder, her first case as a detective, but she realized she might not get a chance if the Feds decided to take over. It wouldn't be the first time. If the Feds moved in, all her work would be for naught.

She slumped in her office chair and stared at the whiteboard. She realized she had spent too much time focusing on the wrong people. Justine DuPont and Celeste Lautrec. The women had no motive and little opportunity. On the other hand, according to Pascal, Webster was feeding information to the Feds about Albatross. If Roche found out, he had motive and means, but also the perfect alibi. If only she could discredit Roche's alibi, then she could subpoena him for questioning, but it was pointless. Roche was in Switzerland.

Louise's phone buzzed. Rupert had found a photo of Alger Roche's wife, in addition to one of Cheryl Simpson from Laredo's website. The wife was older, heavyset, didn't fit the rental agent's description. She called the Albuquerque airport car rental, hoping the Avis agent would be on duty. The agent wasn't available, so she asked to speak to the manager.

"This is Detective Sanchez, with the Santa Fe police."

"One of your officers was here yesterday. It took forever to go through all those contacts. Is this related?" the manager said wearily.

"Sorry. I need to talk to the Avis rental agent whom the officer spoke with yesterday. The one who was on duty Sunday night."

"Nathan Tyler. He's not in today."

"I'll need his phone number."

Louise heard a drawer being pulled open, then the shuffling of papers. "Nathan's cell is 505-639-2588. Anything else, Detective?"

"The officer said you thought it was strange that the woman rented a car Sunday night because there weren't any flights arriving around that time. I was wondering if the car had been returned, and where?"

The supervisor groaned, not hiding her annoyance. Louise waited while the woman pulled up Simpson's contract on the computer. "The car was rented one way, returned to the Santa Fe airport at quarter to five, Monday morning."

Louise was jubilant. "Thank you, thank you."

The supervisor didn't reply.

Louise thought it was no coincidence that Simpson had returned the car to Santa Fe Regional early Monday morning. Maybe she was flying to Denver, and Roche was with her.

She dialed Nathan Tyler's number, but it went directly to voicemail. "Waz-up dude? Leave your worries."

Louise shook her head and left a message for him to return her call as soon as possible. She imagined he was the type of guy that never bothered checking his voicemail, but a few minutes later her phone rang. "Detective Sanchez."

"You rang?" Nathan Tyler said, giggling.

Louise raised her eyes to the car's headliner. "An officer talked to you yesterday about a woman, Cheryl Simpson, who rented a car late Sunday night from Avis."

"Yeah, that slutty one."

Louise bristled and took in a deep breath, thinking of the old adage, *you get more flies with honey than vinegar*. "Okay. I was wondering, Nathan, do you think you could identify the woman from a photograph?" She was familiar with Nathan's type. He could most likely be lured by a challenge.

"Maybe..." Nathan said hesitantly.

Louise lowered the ante, knowing he was also the kind of guy who didn't like to lose. "Give it your best shot. That's all I ask."

"I'm sort of in the middle of something right now. Text it to me. I'll get back to you."

Louise suppressed her annoyance and forced herself to sweet-talk him. "I'm texting two photos. I need to know right away, Nathan. It's super important. I would appreciate it."

"Yeah, sure," he said distractedly.

Louise uploaded the photos of Alger Roche's wife and Cheryl Simpson in the message app, entered Nathan's cell number, and pushed send. She supposed Nathan relished keeping people waiting. It was a power thing. It probably was all he had going. She would give him ten minutes before calling him back.

Her phone dinged. "Not the fat broad. The second pic. That's the hoe."

Louise was appalled and knew she should thank him, but her fingers froze. She would regret it later if she had to have Nathan Tyler deposed or testify in court. His thank you would have to wait. She was elated with the news even though it meant more complications. She needed to find out who Cheryl Simpson was along with her relationship to Peter Roche. She thought about Pascal's case. How the stolen costume from the opera grounds began as a simple burglary then evolved into a fiasco, resulting in his downfall. She wondered about Katrin Simpson, the lady friend of Pascal's father. Was Katrin related to Cheryl Simpson? And where the hell was Katrin?

The thought of a bottle of Sangiovese chilling in her fridge mollified her. It wasn't the smoothest red, but she preferred its earthy and rustic taste. She got a kick out of the grape variety—the blood of Jupiter—from the Latin *sanguis Jovis*. She had half a chicken piccata left over from the previous night that would go perfect with the wine.

CHAPTER 46

Louise felt exhilarated after her early-morning run. The temperature was barely above freezing, but the day held a promise of spring-like weather. The cloudless sky let the sun get busy and do its work. Her fifteen-minute jog seemed effortless. Gillian had suggested they might pump it up to twenty for their next session. As Louise climbed into her car, she thought it was finally time to purchase running shoes.

She drove back to the station feeling elated and practically skipped inside. Her phone rang as she entered the dark lobby. The lights were out and Susie was nowhere in sight.

"Hey, Dad. Hope you have some good news."

"I'm meeting with the probate judge this afternoon. It turned into a fiasco. Julia is in a nursing home. She has dementia and her relatives are trying to get money for her care. I don't think they have a leg to stand on, but we'll see. It will be over one way or another tomorrow."

"That's sad about Julia. Let me know how things turn out."

Louise was relieved her father hadn't asked about the menorah, which was still sitting on her mantle. As she rounded the corner, Rupert was at his desk, hunched over his computer clicking away.

"How's the research?" Louise asked.

When he looked up, his expression told her things hadn't gone well. He either hadn't found anything, or what he had found was bad news. He pursed his lips together then exhaled through his nose. "We got a call from the Feds."

That was the last thing she expected. Her heart hit an irregular beat as she tried to ward off her worst fear. She wanted to swear, say all the words the nuns would have washed her mouth out for saying, but instead asked, "Yeah?"

"Somehow, somebody tipped them off. They know that we know about the Roche brothers and that Peter Roche is good for Madison's murder. I smell the stench of a mole tunneling into the station. Don't know how else they could have found out what we know."

Louise groaned. They had been on a roll, so close. "What did they say?"

"They want everything we have. They're going to talk to the captain."

"Tough shit. The murder is ours. They can have the Roche brothers and all their bloody companies, but no way are they taking over Madison's murder." Louise could feel her voice rising with her frustration. "No way."

Rupert shook his head and smiled sadly. "They're sending someone over this morning."

Louise was indignant. She stormed down the hall to the captain's office and banged on the door.

Susie poked her head around the corner and mouthed, "He's in a meeting."

"With . . . ?"

Susie cupped her hands on either side of her mouth and in a stage whisper said, "F-B-I. Two of them. Black suits with those silly skinny ties. Mirrored sunglasses." She cringed. "Gives me the creeps."

Louise squeezed her eyes shut, wishing she could go back an hour earlier. Before the Feds, before she knew. She went back to Rupert's desk and tilted her head toward the lobby. Rupert rose and followed her out of the station. They crossed the street and made their way to the plaza. The morning sun hadn't warmed enough to make the place inviting. They had their choice of empty benches.

"I suspect, if not a mole, a bug." Louise spit out the words.

Rupert wrinkled his forehead, not understanding.

"Bugged the station. They're ruthless sons of bitches, too lazy to get their own information. Have to ride on our coattails." Louise inhaled and let her breath out in a growl.

Rupert nodded his head.

"What did you find out about the Roches?" Louise asked.

"There are three brothers, Peter, Alger, and Hans. They have a sister too, lives in Amsterdam, married to a college professor. I don't think she's involved. Oh, by the way, your twin theory doesn't pan out. The three brothers don't look enough alike to pass through TSA. Different heights, body types, hair color, ages."

Louise laughed. "I was grasping at straws. What else did you find out about the brothers?"

"All three brothers are shareholders of Albatross, and each one owns a subsidiary, which are mostly legit businesses. Typically shell companies operate on the periphery, billing a legitimate business for supplies, equipment, and other expenses. That's how they can launder or pass money through the shell company tax free."

Louise shivered and pulled her coat tighter around her. "Let's get some coffee."

"Sure."

They crossed the street to the Plaza Cafe and took a seat near the front window. After their coffee was served, Louise said, "I texted photos of Alger Roche's wife and Cheryl Simpson to the Avis agent yesterday. He confirmed Cheryl was the person who rented the car Sunday night, though he used a few, let's say, *special* choice words."

Rupert gave her a questioning look.

"Don't ask." She shook her head and continued. "The rental was one way, and Simpson dropped the car off at Santa Fe Regional Airport early Monday morning."

Rupert sat up and nearly knocked over his coffee cup. "Wow. Okay. So, Peter Roche flies to Denver Sunday night and then he and Cheryl Simpson maybe hire a private plane to Albuquerque. Then Simpson rents a car at the airport and the two of them drive back to Santa Fe."

"Yeah, but why complicate things? Why not hire a plane to Santa Fe?"

"Because it makes it harder to follow the trail," Rupert offered.

"Okay, so Roche goes to Madison's house, drugs and stabs him before catching a plane in the morning back to Denver, then continues his itinerary to Zurich."

Rupert was quiet for a moment. "One thing bothers me. The bartender said Madison and Roche had a heated argument at the Twisted Pines Sunday night. Madison knew Roche was supposed to be on his way to Zurich, so if Roche knocks on Madison's door in the middle of the night, wouldn't Madison be suspicious?"

"You have a point," Louise agreed. Roche wouldn't be able to slip the drugs to Madison without a fight, and there wasn't any sign of a fight.

"Maybe Cheryl Simpson slipped him the drugs. Let's say she calls Madison, says she's in town, asks to stop by for a nightcap. Maybe she implies she has some information on the company. They have a drink, and she slips him the drug. Then Peter Roche comes in and finishes him off. They drive to the airport, return the rental car, and hop on a plane back to Denver. Roche is able to make his connection to Chicago then jets off to Zurich, securing his airtight alibi. Cheryl Simpson goes home."

"It's all plausible. I get Peter Roche's motive, but what's Cheryl Simpson's? Why is she willing to go to all this trouble to help Peter Roche murder Madison. What's in it for her?"

"Good point. Usually people are driven to crime for either love or money. Maybe she and Peter are having an affair, or Peter offered her a bundle of money, or both."

"I'm betting on love. Cheryl already has money. We need to confirm Roche and Simpson are on the passenger list and the flight log for an early-morning flight to Denver last Monday at Santa Fe Regional. It would be great if we could also confirm the private plane to Albuquerque. Bonus if we find something to show Cheryl and Peter were having an affair."

Rupert typed some notes on his iPad. "Anything else, boss?"

"It's best if we don't go back to the station right away. Maybe don't answer our phones either. Don't want the Feds cornering us until we have all our ducks in a row."

Rupert raised his eyebrows but didn't say anything. Louise knew he couldn't afford another run-in with the Feds.

Louise went on. "If we can confirm our supposition, we could issue warrants. With Peter Roche in Zurich, without extradition, we can only rattle the man's cage. Maybe get a hold of Cheryl Simpson. Twist her wrist. Offer a plea bargain to rat out Roche."

"So, if Simpson's motive is love, what's Roche's for killing Madison?" Rupert asked.

"According to the bartender, Madison and Roche had a heated argument at the bar. Maybe Madison threatened to go to the Feds, turn in Roche. If we could bust Roche's alibi, then the man had the opportunity, motive, and means."

"I hate to say it, but it's all speculation at this point. Do you have anything else that would put Roche at Madison's house?"

Louise could kick herself. She had forgotten about the fingerprints on the Albatross mail drop. "No, but forensics was supposed to get prints from Albatross's mailbox at the Opulent Building. I'll stop by their office, see what they found out. If we can match those prints with ones at the murder scene, we have more than a hypothesis."

Rupert pursed his lips. "You realize they're going to win? They always do. The Feds trump every time."

Louise smiled and winked. "But they will have to catch us first. It's a cat-and-mouse chase. Let's give them a run for their money."

Rupert shook his head. "You're the boss."

Louise thought, *Yes, I am the boss*. She liked the ring of that.

Forensics wasn't far from the café, and the walk would give Louise time to mull over the scenario they had concocted. Rupert had turned out to be an excellent Sergeant Lewis to her Inspector Morse. As she entered the building, she half hoped to run into the medical examiner and half hoped not to. She wouldn't mind seeing the woman but didn't want to confess she hadn't found Isabelle yet. Plus, she was in no mood to listen to complaints about funeral arrangements. She called Johnson from the lobby, hoping to dodge the dreadful secretary. He assured her he would meet her in the reception area.

"I thought you would be pestering me for the prints," Johnson said when he arrived.

"Things have been a little hectic. Were you able to eliminate Dupont and Lautrec's prints from the murder scene?"

"Yes, eventually. Lautrec's prints didn't come out clear enough. My ink was at the end of its life. I would have changed it out, but when you called you sounded a little stressed."

Louise groaned. If she had to ask Camille for her prints again, the woman was apt to come unglued. "Please tell me you were able to salvage her prints?"

"No, but I was nearby and swung by her condo." Johnson tried to flash her a seductive grin, but it came off slightly deranged. "Her daughter answered the door and let me in before Lautrec could protest. She wasn't happy about it, but she acquiesced. I guess it's my charm." Johnson shrugged.

"Her daughter?" Louise stammered.

"Except for the eyes there isn't much resemblance, not that they aren't both good lookers."

Good lookers? Johnson was definitely stuck in the fifties, maybe the forties. "Did she mention the daughter's name?"

"Isabelle I think."

Louise's mouth dropped open. "I've been combing the city and getting blisters looking for that woman. She's the 911 caller, the one who reported Madison's murder."

"Gee whiz. No kidding?"

Louise stared at Johnson. *Duh*, she thought but didn't say. She was afraid to ask but did anyway. "Please tell me you were able to get some prints from the Albatross mailbox. And some of those prints were found in Madison's house."

"Yes."

"And?"

"Yes. I was able to lift several prints from the mailbox. Some were a little smudgy, overlapped with others, but I got at least one good one. It was a match with a print from the inside doorknob. The murderer must have panicked after the stabbing and forgot to wipe it clean."

"Unless the mailman killed Madison, I presume the prints are Roche's," said Louise.

"Unfortunately, I can't say for sure unless you can get Roche's prints for comparison. But you'll be happy to know the girls are in the clear. Their prints weren't found inside the house."

"Girls?" Louise asked, tilting her head.

"Women," Johnson sputtered.

Louise raised her eyes to the ceiling. "It's okay, Johnson. Old habits die hard. I appreciate all you've done. Gone beyond the call of duty. Thanks."

Louise called Lautrec as she exited the forensics building.

"Ms. Lautrec?" Louise asked.

"Yes?"

"This is Detective Sanchez."

She almost growled into the receiver. "What do you want?"

"Mr. Johnson at forensics informed me that Isabelle is at your house. As you know, I have been searching all over the city for her."

"Isabelle knocked on my door; she was out of money. What could I do?"

"That was..." Louise thought of several appropriate responses—decent, civilized, the right thing. But instead she offered, "Well, you could have let me know."

"What do you want?" Camille said, exasperated.

"Since Isabelle found Madison and reported his murder, she is a material witness. The only fingerprints forensics found at Madison's house, other than his, were a woman's. That adds Isabelle to the suspect list."

"You can't really believe that Isabelle killed her father, plunged a knife in his heart the first time she saw him?"

"I need to take her statement." After the Dupont interview mess, Louise would conduct Isabelle's by the book. "I'll arrange for forensics to take her fingerprints at the same time." She thought of adding, *kill two birds with one stone*, but thought better of it.

"I'll let her know."

Louise steeled herself. "Have Isabelle at the station at two this afternoon."

There was silence on the line.

"Ms. Lautrec, if there's a trial, Isabelle will be put on the stand." Louise knew there wasn't much chance of that if she couldn't produce a plausible suspect.

"I'll see she gets to the station this afternoon." Camille was clearly done with this conversation.

"And . . ." Louise hesitated, knowing full well she was pushing Camille's limit. "As you know, the medical examiner needs someone to give instructions regarding Mr. Madison's funeral arrangements. It seems Isabelle would be the appropriate person. He was her father after all. The process might be healing for her."

"Healing?" There was cynicism in her voice. "The first and last time Isabelle saw her birth father he was dead, a butcher knife in his chest."

"Talk to Isabelle. I'll text you the medical examiner's number." Louise didn't want to plead, but someone needed to step up and do the right thing for Webster Madison, even if he was a womanizer. Everyone deserved to be put to rest. "Please."

The line went dead.

CHAPTER 47

Johnson crossed the street with his forensic bag of goodies in hand as Camille's silver Mercedes-Benz Coupe pulled up in front of the police station. When the passenger door opened, Louise, watching from the lobby, could feel Camille's contempt permeate out of the car. Isabelle stretched her long legs out the open door, one at a time, and attempted to pull herself to her feet. Johnson rushed over and took her arm. He ushered her up the steps and into the lobby. He turned to Louise and lowered his voice. "The plot thickens."

Louise raised her eyes to the ceiling. Then she nodded at Isabelle, before escorting the two down the hall. She had chosen the least offensive interview room, but it was still dismal with its institutional gray-green walls bedecked with splotches of dirty plaster covering holes that had been punched or kicked. The room reeked of sweat and tears.

Johnson and Isabelle took seats side by side at the oblong metal table. Louise pulled out a chair across from them. Johnson got to work unpacking his equipment. Each time he set down an item, the table wobbled annoyingly. Finally, he folded a piece of paper and stuck it under one of the legs, then looked at Isabelle with a sorry smile. "You know the drill."

Isabelle obediently held out her pale hand. Her skin looked as if it had never seen the sun, much less washed a dish or cleaned a toilet. Tiny blue veins pumped blood underneath her almost-transparent skin. Johnson tenderly applied the lightest of pressure as he took each print, then with utmost care dabbed away the ink with a tissue soaked in solution.

Louise watched silently, incapable of small talk. She was glad no one spoke, giving her time to rehearse the interview, home in on what she wanted to know from Isabelle.

When Johnson finished the prints, he packed up his equipment and beamed at Isabelle.

"Thanks, Johnson." Louise meant it. He had more than once helped her out.

As Johnson left, she pulled out her recorder and was relieved Isabelle didn't protest. Isabelle was a witness; she had reported the murder and Louise needed to hear her version of the morning she found Madison's body. She reached over to turn on the recorder but stopped. "Before you give your statement, I'd like some background information, some context, why you came to Santa Fe."

There was a pained expression on Isabelle's face as she picked at her cashmere sweater.

"Your mother told me about the adoption, you inquiring about your birth father and wanting to meet him. I'd like to hear your side of the story, in your own words. I don't need to record it, but if anything you say is pertinent to the case"—Louise softened her voice—"your father's murder, it will need to be included in your statement."

Isabelle stared, wide-eyed. Louise suspected the young woman was trying to figure out what to say, what she was willing to share.

"I recently found out I was adopted. My parents never told me. I never suspected." Even the short version brought tears to Isabelle's eyes. She pressed her lips together, trying to hold back the tears. Louise pulled out a plastic bottle of water from her bag and handed it to Isabelle. After several swallows, Isabelle continued in a shallow voice. "I contacted this agency; they track down birth parents. They found my birth mother, Camille Lautrec, and gave me her contact information. I came to Santa Fe, knocked on her door." Isabelle took another sip of water and wiped her nose. "I assured her I wasn't interested in a relationship. I wanted to know about my father. She told me who my father was. She contacted him and he agreed to talk to me."

Louise wondered why Isabelle didn't want a relationship with her mother but wanted one with her father. But this wasn't the time to sort that out, and it wasn't any of her business.

"I called Webster to arrange a meeting. He said he could see me at his house at eight Monday morning, the Monday . . ." Isabelle squeezed her eyes shut.

"Okay. Take a minute." Louise reached over and patted the young woman's hand. It trembled under her touch and was cold as ice. "Isabelle, let's stop here. I need to record your official statement about that Monday morning." Louise leaned forward and switched on the recorder. "Interview with Isabelle Seville." She added the purpose, date, and time. "Ms. Seville, you arranged to meet Webster Madison at his house Monday morning, the twenty-second of April at eight a.m. Is that correct?"

"Yes."

"Why so early in the morning?"

"He said he had a meeting scheduled later that morning."

"Did he mention whom the meeting was with?"

"No"—Isabelle picked at her sweater again—"but he said he was sorry, said the meeting was important, couldn't be rescheduled."

Louise made a note to follow up on the important meeting. Who could it have been? Not Roche, since he had left for Zurich early Monday morning. The Feds? Maybe Pascal could check with his little birdie. "Why didn't you arrange to meet later that day?"

"I had already been in Santa Fe for two weeks. I planned to leave later that day. I was getting short of money."

Louise thought that was plausible but still, eight o'clock in the morning to meet your birth father for the first time? "How did you get to Madison's house?"

"Uber."

Louise made note to check with the Uber driver. Clarify what time Isabelle arrived at Madison's and whether she was alone. "So the Uber dropped you off at eight o'clock at Madison's house?"

"Yes." Isabelle stared at Louise, a look of trepidation spread across her face. "I . . . I started to ring the bell but noticed the door was slightly ajar. I thought maybe my . . . father had left it open for me. I pushed the door open and called out, but nobody answered. I made my way to the living room and—" Isabelle let out a guttural sob, pressing her face against the sleeve of her sweater.

Louise pulled out the last tissue from a crumpled box on the table and handed it to Isabelle. She couldn't stand the thought of the baby-blue cashmere becoming crusted with snot. She gave Isabelle a minute to collect herself. "Try and think back. When you came into the living room, what do you remember?"

Isabelle closed her eyes and took in a deep breath, letting it out slowly. "The room was cold, empty, with terrible artwork. I saw him lying on the carpet. His feet were bare and I wanted to cover them up. They were blue and looked cold. I stood there and didn't even scream, cry, or anything. It was like I was stuck in one of those nightmares where you can't move. I walked closer. I needed to see him, my father. His eyes were open, blue like mine, and for a second I wondered if he was playing a joke. His shirt was open at the neck, showing an Aries pendant with these piercing green eyes. I'm an Aries too." Isabelle brightened for a moment, but then her face scrunched up again. "When I saw the knife in his chest, I screamed and ran out of the house." Isabelle slumped in the metal chair and covered her eyes with her hands.

Louise gave her a minute. "Did you have a cell phone on you?"

Isabelle nodded.

Louise raised her chin toward the recorder. "You need to vocalize your answers."

"Yes."

"Then why did you run all the way to the train station to report the murder?"

"I . . ." Isabelle picked at her sweater again. "I was going to leave town. Take the train to Albuquerque, fly back to LA. Go home. Forget about my birth parents."

"But?" Louise prodded.

"I couldn't wipe the memory away. I knew I needed to report it."

"Why did you identify yourself as Camille Lautrec, say you were the housekeeper?"

Isabelle's face hardened. "I don't know about the housekeeper part, that just popped out of my head. But I wanted her, Camille, to suffer. I wanted her to experience what it's like to have people think of you as someone you aren't."

Louise exhaled. She felt sorry for Isabelle, though she suspected the woman, like her birth mother, could be quite unpleasant. Temperamental, snooty. *Why can't people accept what life deals them, and if it's good, just be happy?*

"After you spoke to the emergency operator at the train station, what did you do?

"Wandered around. Ate breakfast. Went back to my hotel and slept."

Louise raised her eyebrows but wondered what she would have done in a similar situation. Probably buy a bottle of red wine. "Anything else you would like to tell me?"

Isabelle met Louise's eyes and started to speak, but shook her head.

Louise sighed. "You need to vocalize your response."

"No."

Louise leaned forward and switched off the recorder. "Since you found Webster Madison and reported the crime, you are a witness. Once we find who murdered your father, the case will go to trial. You will need to testify. So, I'm sorry Isabelle, but you can't leave town until the investigation is over and the case closed."

"What am I supposed to do?" she wailed.

Louise shrugged.

Isabelle narrowed her eyes. "You need to vocalize your answer, Detective."

Louise suppressed a smile. *Touché.* "Stay in town."

Isabelle pushed her chair back and rose. She hesitated at the door and placed her palm over a bit of plaster, which was clearly covering a hole made by an angry fist. Louise wondered whether Isabelle was angry, sad, or just plain confused—and she pitied her. Isabelle would never know her birth father.

Louise went back to her office. She realized the interview hadn't shed any light on Madison's murder, but she was sure Isabelle was in the clear. She swiveled her desk chair around and stared out the window at the cracked adobe wall in need of a fresh coat of stucco. Only a sliver of sky, so blue it looked purple, was visible in the far-right corner of the window. The view depressed her, made her think of the case. She needed to get busy, follow up on the Uber driver, make sure Isabelle was alone that morning. And find out what meeting Madison had scheduled the Monday he was murdered—the meeting he never had, and, possibly, the meeting someone didn't want him to have. But right now, diet be damned, she needed a couple of carne adovada tacos. On her way out, she stopped by Rupert's desk and asked him to check out Isabelle's Uber ride. Delegate.

CHAPTER 48

As Louise rummaged in her purse for her front door key, her phone rang. She hoped it was Rupert with good news, or any news really. But it was Pascal. She stifled her irritation; the man was like a bad penny, always showing up. She needed some distance from him. He was a distraction, and her focus needed to be on the case. "Hey, Pascal. Just a sec." She unlocked her door and sunk into her couch. "What's up?"

"I'm still in Denver with my dad. I wanted to let you know that we found my father's lady friend, Katrin Simpson."

"That's good news, I hope. What's her story for skipping town?"

"She has cancer. It had been in remission when she signed up for the Ghost Ranch retreat, but a few weeks ago she started having symptoms again. My father had told her about my mother's illness and death. She said she couldn't put my father through that again, packed up, and went home to Denver. She's under treatment, chemo. Don't know what the prognosis is but my father wants to stay, help take care of her. I'm heading back to Santa Fe tomorrow. I'll see if he changes his mind in the morning. Katrin seems nice."

"I'm sorry to hear about Katrin's cancer. Did you ask her about Cheryl Simpson and the house in Abiquiu?"

"Yeah. It's not a coincidence they have the same last name. Turns out Cheryl Simpson is related to Katrin, but not by blood."

After her interview with Isabelle Seville, Louise thought that blood had little to do with the truth. "What's the relation?"

"Cheryl Simpson is Katrin's niece, by marriage. Katrin's second husband was George Simpson. George's brother was Bernard Simpson. Bernard had a son, Nelson Simpson, who married Cheryl. So, Cheryl is Katrin's niece-in-law, I think. Cheryl divorced Nelson years ago but never changed her name."

"Convoluted. Not sure I follow all that."

"Yeah, took me a while to unravel. There's more. Cheryl's father-in-law, Bernard Simpson, was the CEO of Laredo Enterprises, the realty company. Cheryl had worked her way up in the agency over the years. When Bernard died seven years ago, she took over as CEO."

"The plot thickens. But how did Katrin come to rent the house in Abiquiu?"

"Katrin lost track of that side of the family long before George passed away. When she decided to attend the retreat in Abiquiu, she started searching for somewhere to rent. She saw the house listed on a vacation rentals site and Cheryl Simpson was listed as the agent. Katrin recognized her picture. Turned out Cheryl was only interested in renting the house long term, but Katrin fell in love with the place and signed a year's lease. She had been excited about the studio, but Cheryl said it was off-limits. The company was using it for storage."

"Yeah, probably stolen goods," Louise said.

"Most likely pottery. I swear the two pots I saw through the windows were either Maria Martinez's or good copies."

Louise's head ached from all the crazy coincidences.

"Oh, I have more news."

She hoped it was something useful; she needed to get back to her work. "Yeah?"

"I asked a friend of mine who lives out near the Ojo Caliente mineral springs to run by the studio in Abiquiu, see if the boxes were still there. And guess what?"

"They're gone?"

"Yeah, but that's not all," Pascal said excitedly. "When my friend turned off the highway, a Mercedes utility van came barreling down. There was hardly enough room to pull over and the van slowed down to a crawl to maneuver past him. Guess what was written on the side of the van?"

"Gourmet to Go?"

"Hardy har. Mile High Construction. And I'd bet you the bank the van was loaded with boxes from the studio. And that the boxes contained the archive's missing Native American pottery. I suspect the pottery is on its way to Zurich via Denver right now. You might want to pass the information along to your little Fed friends. Have them check it out."

"Sure, that would be the right thing to do. But at this moment, they're on my shit list. They want us to back off the case, not blow their cover. It's the pits."

"You know where I stand on the Feds."

"Maybe your little birdie could check it out?"

"She, um, my little birdie knew about the missing pottery, was keeping an eye on it. But I'll pass on the info about the Mile High Construction truck."

"She?" Louise laughed.

Pascal sighed into the phone.

"Thanks for the update. I'm glad Katrin isn't mixed up with Roche, the stolen pottery, or any of the shell companies."

"Me too. My dad told me he saw an old Native American pot in a box of Katrin's. I was worried it was connected to the missing pottery."

"What was the story?"

"Her first husband was a graduate student in archaeology at UNM. He found that piece of pottery on his first dig at the Coronado Historic Site near Bernalillo. Later, he was killed in a freak accident during an excavation at another site in southern New Mexico. After his death, Maxwell Museum presented the bowl to Katrin. She always keeps it with her and brought it to Abiquiu."

"Geez, she lost two husbands. Hope she's not a black widow. Your dad better watch out." Pascal laughed. "Miss Gloom and Doom."

Louise's phone buzzed and she saw the call was from Rupert. "Sorry. Got to take this call."

"Over and out."

"Tell me you have good news?" Louise said on the other line.

"Busted." Rupert chuckled. "Always wanted to say that. I checked with the Santa Fe airport and both Peter Roche and Cheryl Simpson were booked on the five forty-five flight Monday morning to Denver on Frontier Airlines."

Louise was speechless. She couldn't believe they had blown Roche's alibi. If he hadn't intended to kill Madison, what was he doing back in Santa Fe after leaving the night before for Zurich?

"Sanchez? You still with me?"

Louise struggled to wrap her mind around the information. "Did you get a copy of the flight log?"

"Yeah. But now what?"

"We have to talk to the captain. I don't want to lose control of the case. We're close enough I can taste it. If the Feds get ahold of this, it'll be like a stray dog going after a steak bone."

Rupert laughed. "Should I go back to the station?"

"Yeah. Rupert, no matter what happens, I want you to know that I couldn't have done it without you. Your brain, your skills, your . . ."

"Okay, okay," he said, chuckling. "Thanks. Appreciate the appreciation."

Louise still hadn't heard back from her father about the probate of the ranch. He was supposed to meet with the judge early this afternoon. She pulled herself off the couch and headed for the kitchen. She eyed the wine bottle on the kitchen counter, feeling tempted, but she opened the fridge instead. She took out a bottle of water. It was almost four o'clock and she needed to be alert. She needed to wrap up this case. Not to mention, she had a date that night.

CHAPTER 49

As Louise leaned against the counter sipping the bottled water, her phone rang, startling her. She looked at the screen. It was her father. "I hope you have good news."

"It's been settled, it's over. Lisa gets the ranch."

Louise could hear the exhaustion in his voice and knew the meeting must have been emotionally draining.

"I called Lisa and left a message. The realtor informed me that someone already put in a bid on the ranch. If Lisa agrees to the amount, we can be done with it."

"Thanks, Dad. I appreciate you letting Lisa know. Wasn't looking forward to talking to her again."

"Did you send her menorah?"

"I . . . not yet." Her father's sigh of disappointment wrenched her heart. She hated to disappoint him. "I'll pack it up in the morning. Promise. Sorry, but I need to call the captain."

"Bye, sweetie."

Louise put in a call to the station. Susie put her on hold for over five minutes. Finally the captain barked into the phone. "Where have you been, Sanchez?"

"Solving a murder, sir." She knew her quip wouldn't go over well, but it had popped out of her mouth before she could stop herself. There was silence on the line.

"I hope you're good for it," the captain said with a touch of annoyance.

"Montoya and I had a theory. It panned out. We're pretty sure Peter Roche murdered Webster Madison."

"I thought he had an airtight alibi."

"Well, it was all a ruse, sir. We busted his alibi wide open."

Louise took the captain through the scenario.

"That's one for the books. I guess you heard the Feds were here this morning. They had been investigating Albatross, but someone from the inside tipped off Roche. Probably why he took off for Zurich. The IRS has been looking into the company's finances. Roche hired Madison to go over the books, make sure everything would appear on the up and up. Then the Feds, in turn, enlisted Madison to help with their investigation. A mole tipped off Roche about the FBI's interest and possibly Madison's involvement. The Feds suspected Roche had found out about Madison's involvement and was behind his murder, but since Roche had a solid alibi, they thought he hired someone else to do it."

"Yeah, well, they didn't spend any time or effort in debunking his alibi."

"Murder is small potatoes to the Feds."

"Anyway, it's a moot point." Louise sighed heavily into the phone. "Peter Roche is in Zurich and the Swiss don't usually extradite people, especially citizens. Roche has dual citizenship with Switzerland."

"I'm sorry, Sanchez. The Feds want to take over. I told them the murder is still ours, and they're giving us twenty-four hours to wrap everything up. Then we have to give them all we got. They're going to try to extradite Peter Roche, but . . ." The captain chuckled.

"What about the accomplice, Cheryl Simpson? She lives in Denver. She helped Roche get to Santa Fe and most likely slipped Madison the drug. Can't we at least have her arrested and charged?"

"From what you told me, it's only a theory. There's no evidence that proves Cheryl Simpson was involved in his murder. Even if she had flown with Roche to Albuquerque, rented a car, and drove him to Santa Fe, there's nothing that puts her at Madison's house Sunday night. Or anything to put Roche there either. It's all conjecture."

"I'm positive she was at the scene. Monday morning, she dropped the car at the Santa Fe airport. Both she and Roche took a flight back to Denver. What was Roche doing back in Santa Fe that night? The night Madison was murdered. If we could question her, maybe get her fingerprints..."

"I think we're done, Sanchez. Time to throw in the towel." He paused. "I'm sorry."

"What if I can get information on the private plane that flew them to Albuquerque?"

"Like I said, time to bring in the Feds. If Cheryl Simpson is onto us, she's likely to leave the country. The Feds won't take kindly to us interfering. This has been a lengthy ongoing case involving multiple companies, and there will be hell to pay if we mess it up."

"But what about the Feds messing up our case?" Louise whined. Rupert was right, the Feds always trump.

"Nothing we can do. By the way, where are you?"

"Home. Hiding out."

The captain chuckled. She had rarely heard him laugh before and somehow it made her feel better. "I think we need to do this sooner rather than later. I don't like it any better than you do, but let's not give the Feds a chance to accuse us of interfering with their case."

"Their case?"

The captain ignored her question. "I'll call Agent Sandler. See if he can meet us this afternoon."

Louise couldn't stifle the groan. The last thing she wanted to do this afternoon was talk to the Feds. She planned on soaking in fragrant bath water in preparation for her dinner date with the good doctor. "I'm on my way."

Agent Sandler was late. While Louise waited, she stared at the paperwork on her desk and had a sudden urge to knock everything onto the floor, scatter papers everywhere, kick them around. It was childish. She called Rupert, telling him the bad news, and was thankful he didn't say, "I told you so." She wanted him to be in on the interview with the Feds. She didn't trust herself and needed backup.

It was after six when Agent Sandler sauntered into the station. Rupert and Louise were called to the conference room. Sandler and two other agents, who were not introduced, sat at the end of the table, reeking of impatience. Sandler, all business, announced that the bureau was taking over the case but was willing to hear the detective's theory on how Roche pulled off the murder.

Louise grimaced at the "theory" remark. She presented what they had discovered as Rupert handed over supporting documents. The agents listened with blank faces, revealing nothing. She was grateful that Sandler didn't interrupt, though she could tell Rupert was annoyed that he'd barely glanced at the documents.

"The Federal Bureau of Investigation appreciates your cooperation." Agent Sandler nodded to the captain, Louise, and Rupert, then he started to get up.

Louise couldn't stop herself. "That's it?"

"We'll take it from here." He pressed his lips together and gave one nod as emphasis.

"Madison's murder? Will Peter Roche and Cheryl Simpson be arrested and charged?"

The agent smiled, but it wasn't a sweet smile. "Detective Sanchez, we are in the middle of an ongoing investigation into the Roche brothers and their companies. The murder is inconsequential. We can't let it interfere with our investigation."

"Inconsequential? Someone was murdered and that someone had been helping you with your case, not to mention that's probably the reason he was killed in the first place." The captain shot Louise a warning look. She ignored it and doubled down. "That makes you as culpable as Roche for Madison's murder."

The captain rose to his feet. "Sanchez, Montoya. In my office. Now."

Sandler stood and shook the captain's hand. "We'll let you know if we need anything else." He gave Louise a hard look and nodded at Rupert. The other two federal agents filed out behind Sandler like little penguins.

Louise and Rupert followed the captain to his office. They didn't sit, but stood arms crossed like petulant children.

"Listen, I dislike this as much as you do, maybe even more. It's the second case in the last couple of months pulled out from under our feet. I know someone with the Denver police. They don't take a fancy to the Feds interfering either. This guy owes me a favor. I'll give him a call, see if he can pick up Cheryl Simpson."

Louise's mouth dropped. "You would do that? On what grounds?"

The captain winked at her. Another first. "Nothing to do with our case. Some minor infraction, traffic violation, maybe something to do with the rental car. Bring her into the station, get her prints. It won't help with our case, but it will make the Feds mad as a hatter."

Rupert and Louise broke out in laughter.

The captain smiled. "Sometimes revenge is all that's left at the end of the day."

The captain promised to give them a report in the morning, which was fine with Louise. She had enough for one day. All their work on Madison's murder had been for naught. The Feds had ripped the case out of their hands and warned them to back off.

She was glad she had forgotten to tell the FBI about the Mile High Construction van that was most likely packed with boxes of stolen pottery. Let them do their own work for a change. She thought of mentioning it to the captain, but there was no way to explain the situation without involving Pascal. And that was out of the question. But an anonymous tip to the New Mexico Museum Foundation President (her mother), might get some balls rolling.

She tried to look on the bright side. With the Feds taking over the case or sweeping it under the rug, she now had time to get back in the darkroom, work on developing the photos for her upcoming show. She looked at her watch and groaned for the umpteenth time. Only forty-five minutes to get ready for her dinner date. There was no time for a luxurious soak, only a quick shower, touch of lipstick, and splash of perfume. She hoped the restaurant had muted light.

ACKNOWLEDGMENTS

I owe a ton of gratitude to Patti DePalma Slesinski for creating the northern New Mexico map featured in the beginning of the book. Her map design was adapted for the book cover also.

Thanks go to my sister, Julie Harrison, who willingly read, edited, and offered sage advice while encouraging me to keep writing.

I would like to acknowledge Jeanne Whitehouse (1939–2024), who read-critiqued-reread while advising me to write-rewrite-write. I will miss her friendship and input.

And thanks to my beta readers, Linnea Hendrickson and Marlys Harrison, who offered both praise and editorial suggestions for *Death in the Land of Enchantment*.

Last but not least, I want to thank my family and friends who have always been there for me.

IT TAKES A VILLAGE

www.ingramcontent.com/pod-product-compliance
Lightning Source LLC
LaVergne TN
LVHW041748060526
838201LV00046B/946